"Intricate and marvelous . . . addictively dazzling . . . Akunin's agile leaps of time, tone, and narrative style are matched by a frisky erudition: The book itself is a luxury literary cruise."   —*Entertainment Weekly*

"Fiendishly witty . . . a ravishing jewel box of a mystery . . . [Akunin] knows his Arthur Conan Doyle, and his Fandorin likes to indulge in showy displays of Holmesian observations."   —*Time*

"[A] charmingly crafted story . . . with its fast pace, hairpin turns, and cunning protagonist . . . The novel moves briskly yet doesn't spare us a rich trove of historical details that are both fun to read and illuminating. Not since the filming of *Titanic* has this much attention been lavished on describing a ship."   —*Los Angeles Times*

"Pays homage to Dame Agatha Christie's Hercule Poirot mysteries, and is a delightful spoof of them as well. A perfect summer read."
—*The Dallas Morning News*

"Akunin's witty, retro detective novels . . . are enormously popular. . . . Amusing . . . gripping."   —*Newsday*

"Akunin writes like a hybrid of Caleb Carr, Agatha Christie, and Elizabeth Peters. . . . The atmospheric historical detail gives depth to the twisting plot."   —*Publishers Weekly*

"Fandorin, star of *The Winter Queen*, Akunin's scintillating English-language debut, has returned in good form. This is another intelligent and deftly plotted work . . . full of surprises and incisive in its characterization and psychological depth. Essential for mystery collections."
—*Library Journal*

BORIS AKUNIN is the pen name of Grigory Chkhartishvili, who was born in the republic of Georgia in 1956. A philologist, critic, essayist, and translator of Japanese, Akunin published his first detective stories in 1998 and has already become one of the most widely read authors in Russia. He has written eleven Erast Fandorin novels to date, and is the author of two other series as well. He lives in Moscow.

—

ANDREW BROMFIELD was born in Hull in Yorkshire, England, and is the acclaimed translator of the stories and novels of Victor Pelevin. He also translated into English Boris Akunin's debut Erast Fandorin mystery, *The Winter Queen*.

ALSO BY BORIS AKUNIN

The Winter Queen

Murder on the Leviathan

BORIS AKUNIN

Translated by Andrew Bromfield

Random House Trade Paperbacks

New York

MURDER ON THE
LEVIATHAN

A Novel

2005 Random House Trade Paperback Edition

Translation copyright © 2004 by Random House, Inc.
Reader's Guide copyright © 2005 by Random House, Inc.

This work was originally published in Russian in 1998.
Copyright © 1998 by Boris Akunin. This English language
translation was originally published in 2004 in hardcover by Random House,
an imprint of The Random House Publishing Group,
a division of Random House, Inc.

Library of Congress Cataloging-in-Publication Data
Akunin, B. (Boris)
[Leviafan. English]
Murder on the Leviathan: a novel / Boris Akunin; translated by Andrew Bromfield.
p.   cm.
ISBN 0-8129-6879-4
I. Bromfield, Andrew. II. Title.
PG3478.K78 L4813 2004
891.73'5—dc22   2003070379

Random House website address: www.atrandom.com
Printed in the United States of America
4 6 8 9 7 5 3

Murder on the Leviathan

*Record of an examination of the scene of the crime
carried out on the evening of March 15, 1878,
in the mansion of Lord Littleby on the Rue de Grenelle
(Seventh Arrondissement of the city of Paris)*

[*A brief extract*]

. . . For reasons unknown, the household staff were gathered in the pantry, which is located on the ground floor of the mansion to the left of the entrance hall (room 3 on diagram 1). The precise locations of the bodies are indicated on diagram 4, where:

No. 1—the body of the butler, Étienne Delarue, age 48,

No. 2—the body of the housekeeper, Laura Bernard, age 54,

No. 3—the body of the master's manservant, Marcel Prout, age 28,

No. 4—the body of the butler's son, Luc Delarue, age 11,

No. 5—the body of the maid, Arlette Foche, age 19,

No. 6—the body of the housekeeper's granddaughter, Anne-Marie Bernard, age 6,

No. 7—the position of the security guard Jean Lesage, age 42 years, who died in the Saint-Lazare hospital on the morning of March 16 without regaining consciousness,

No. 8—the body of the security guard Patrick Trois-Bras, age 29,
No. 9—the body of the porter, Jean Carpentier, age 40.

The bodies shown as Nos. 1–6 are in sitting positions around the large kitchen table. Nos. 1–3 have frozen with their heads lowered on their crossed arms; No. 4's cheek is lying on his hands; No. 5 is reclining against the back of her chair; No. 6 is in a kneeling position beside No. 2. The faces of Nos. 1–6 are calm, without any indication whatever of fear or suffering. On the other hand, Nos. 7–9, as the diagram shows, are lying at a distance from the table, and No. 7 is holding a whistle in his hand. However, none of the neighbors heard the sound of a whistle yesterday evening. The faces of Nos. 8 and 9 are set in expressions of horror, or at the very least of extreme astonishment (photographs will be provided tomorrow morning). There are no signs of a struggle. A rapid examination also failed to reveal any sign of injury to the bodies. The cause of death cannot be determined without a postmortem. From the degree of rigor mortis, the forensic medical specialist, Maître Bernhem, determined that death occurred at various times between ten o'clock in the evening (No. 6) and six o'clock in the morning, while No. 7, as stated above, died later in the hospital. Anticipating the results of the medical examination, I venture to surmise that all the victims were exposed to a potent and fast-acting poison inducing a narcotic effect, and the time at which their hearts stopped beating depended either on the dose of poison received or the physical strength of each victim.

The front door of the mansion was closed but not locked. However, the window of the conservatory (item 8 on diagram 1) bears clear indications of a forced entry: The glass is broken and in the narrow strip of loose cultivated soil below it is the indistinct imprint of a man's shoe with a sole 26 centimeters in length, a pointed toe, and a steel-shod heel (photographs will be provided). The felon probably gained entry to the house via the garden only after the servants had been poisoned and sank into slumber; otherwise they would certainly have heard the sound of breaking glass. It remains unclear, however, why, after the servants had been rendered harmless, the perpetrator found it necessary to enter the house through the garden when he could quite easily have walked through into the house from the pantry. In any event, the perpetrator made his way from the conservatory up to the second floor, where Lord Littleby's personal apartments are located (see diagram 2). As the diagram shows, the left-hand section of the second floor consists of only two rooms: a hall housing a collection of Indian curios and the master's bedroom, which communicates directly with the hall. Lord Littleby's body is indicated on diagram 2 as No. 10 (see also the outline drawing). His lordship was dressed in a smoking jacket and woollen pantaloons and his right foot was heavily bandaged. An initial examination of the body indicates that death occurred as a result of an extraordinarily powerful blow to the parietal region of the skull with a heavy oblong-shaped object. The blow was inflicted from the front. The carpet is spattered with blood and brain tissue to a distance of several meters from the body. Likewise spattered with blood is a broken glass display case that, according to its nameplate, previously contained a statuette of the Indian god Shiva (the inscription on the nameplate reads: "Bangalore, 2nd. half XVIII century, gold"). The missing sculpture was displayed against a background of painted Indian shawls, one of which is also missing.

FROM THE REPORT BY DR. BERNHEM ON THE RESULTS
OF PATHOLOGICAL AND ANATOMICAL EXAMINATION
OF THE BODIES REMOVED FROM THE RUE DE GRENELLE

. . . However, whereas the cause of Lord Littleby's death (body No. 10) is clear, the only aspect that may be regarded as unusual being the force of the blow, which shattered the cranium into seven fragments, in the case of Nos. 1–9 the picture was less obvious, requiring not only a postmortem, but also chemical analyses and laboratory investigation. The task was simplified to some extent by the fact that J. Lesage (No. 7) was still alive when he was initially examined. Certain typical indications (pinhole pupils, suppressed breathing, cold, clammy skin, rubefaction of the lips and earlobes) indicated a presumptive diagnosis of morphine poisoning. Unfortunately, during the initial examination at the scene of the crime we had proceeded on the apparently obvious assumption that the poison had been ingested perorally, and therefore only the victims' oral cavities and glottises were subjected to detailed scrutiny. Since no pathological indications were discovered, the forensic examination was unable to provide any conclusive answers. It was only during examination in the morgue that each of the nine deceased was discovered to possess a barely visible injection puncture on the inner flexion of the left elbow. Although it lies outside my sphere of competence, I can venture with reasonable certainty the hypothesis that the injections were administered by a person with considerable experience in such procedures: 1) the injections were administered with great skill and precision, and not one of the subjects bore any visible signs of hematoma; 2) since the normal interval before narcotic coma ensues is three minutes, all nine injections must have been administered within that period of time. Either there were several operatives involved (which is unlikely), or the single operative possessed truly remarkable skill—even if we are to assume he had prepared a loaded syringe for each victim in advance. Indeed, it is hard to imagine that a person in full possession of his faculties would offer his arm for an injection if he had just witnessed someone else lose consciousness as a result of the procedure. Admittedly, my assistant, Maître Jolie, believes that all these people could have been in a state of hypnotic trance, but in my many years in this line of work I have never encountered anything of the sort. Let me also draw the commissioner's attention to the fact that Nos. 7–9 were lying on the floor in poses clearly expressive of panic. I assume that these three were the last to receive the injection (or that they offered greater resistance to the narcotic) and that before they lost consciousness they realized something suspicious was happening to their companions. Laboratory analysis has demonstrated that each of the victims received a dose of morphine approximately three times in excess of the lethal threshold. Judging from the condition of the body of the little girl (No. 6), who must have been the first to die, the injections were administered between nine and ten o'clock on the evening of March 15.

TEN LIVES FOR A GOLDEN IDOL!

NIGHTMARE CRIME IN FASHIONABLE DISTRICT

Today, March 16, all Paris is talking of nothing but the spine-chilling crime that has shattered the decorous tranquillity of the aristocratic Rue de Grenelle. The Revue Parisienne's *correspondent was quick to arrive at the scene of the crime and is prepared to satisfy the legitimate curiosity of our readers.*

And so, as usual, shortly after seven o'clock this morning, postman Jacques le Chien rang the doorbell of the elegant two-story mansion belonging to the well-known British collector, Lord Littleby. M. Le Chien was surprised when the porter, Carpentier, who always took in the post for his lordship in person, failed to open up, and, noticing that the entrance door was slightly ajar, he stepped into the hallway. A few moments later the seventy-year-old veteran of the postal service ran back out into the street, howling wildly. Upon being summoned to the house, the police discovered a scene from the kingdom of Hades—seven servants and two children (the eleven-year-old son of the butler and the six-year-old granddaughter of the housekeeper) lay in the embrace of eternal slumber. The police ascended the stairs to the second floor, and there they discovered the master of the house, Lord Littleby, lying in a pool of blood, murdered in the very repository that housed his celebrated collection of oriental rarities. The fifty-five-year-old Englishman was well known in the highest social circles of our capital. Despite his reputation as an eccentric and unsociable individual, archeological scholars and orientalists respected Lord Littleby as a genuine connoisseur of Indian history and culture. Repeated attempts by the directors of the Louvre to purchase items from the lord's diverse collection had been disdainfully rejected. The deceased prized especially highly a golden statuette of Shiva, the value of which is estimated by competent experts to be at least half a million francs. A deeply mistrustful man, Lord Littleby was very much afraid of thieves, and two armed guards were on duty in the repository day and night.

It is not clear why the guards left their post and went down to the ground floor. Nor is it clear what mysterious power the malefactor was able to employ in order to subjugate all the inhabitants of the house to his will without the slightest resistance (the police suspect that use was made of some rapidly acting poison). It is clear, however, that he did not expect to find the master of the house himself at home, and his fiendish calculations were evidently thwarted. No doubt we should see in this the explanation for the bestial ferocity with which the venerable collector was slain. The murderer apparently fled the scene of the crime in panic, taking only the statuette and one of the painted shawls displayed in the same case. The shawl was evidently required to wrap the golden Shiva—otherwise the bright luster of the sculpture might have attracted the attention of some late-night passerby. Other valuables (of which the collection contains a goodly number) remained untouched. Your correspondent has ascertained that Lord Littleby was at home yesterday by chance, through a fatal confluence of circumstances. He had been due to depart that evening in order to take the waters, but a sudden attack of gout resulted in his trip being postponed—and condemned him to death.

The immense blasphemy and cynicism of the murders in the Rue de Grenelle defy the imagination. What contempt for human life! What monstrous cruelty! And for what? For a golden idol that it is now impossible to sell! If melted down, the Shiva will be transformed into an ordinary two-kilogram ingot of gold. A mere two hundred grams of yellow metal—such is the value placed by the criminal on each one of the ten souls who have perished. Well may we exclaim after Cicero: O tempora, o mores!

There is, however, reason to believe that this supremely heinous crime will not go unpunished. That most experienced of detectives at the Paris prefecture, M. Gustave Gauche, to whom the investigation has been entrusted, has confidentially informed your correspondent that the police are in possession of a certain important piece of evidence. The commissioner is absolutely certain that retribution will be swift. When asked whether the crime was committed by a member of the professional fraternity of thieves, M. Gauche smiled slyly into his gray mustache and enigmatically replied: "Oh, no, young man, the thread here leads into good society." Your humble servant was unable to extract so much as another word from him.

J. DU ROI

WHAT A CATCH!
THE GOLDEN SHIVA IS FOUND!
WAS THE "CRIME OF THE CENTURY"
IN THE RUE DE GRENELLE
THE WORK OF A MADMAN?

Yesterday, March 17, between five o'clock and six o'clock in the afternoon, thirteen-year-old Pierre B. was fishing by the Pont des Invalides when his hook became snagged so firmly at the bottom of the river that he was obliged to wade into the cold water. ("I'm not so stupid as to just throw away a genuine English hook!" the young fisherman told our reporter.) Pierre's valor was richly rewarded: The hook had not caught on some common tree root but on a weighty object half buried in the silt. Once extracted from the water, the object shone with an unearthly splendor, blinding the eyes of the astonished fisherman. Pierre's father, a retired army sergeant and veteran of the Battle of Sedan, guessed that it must be the famous golden Shiva for which ten people had been killed only two days earlier, and he handed in the find at the prefecture.

What are we to make of this? For some reason a criminal who did not baulk at the cold-blooded and deliberate murder of so many people has chosen not to profit from the spoils of his monstrous initiative! Police investigators and the public alike have been left guessing in the dark. The public appears inclined to believe that belated pangs of conscience must have led the murderer, aghast at the horror of his awful deed, to cast the golden idol into the river. Many go so far as to surmise that the miserable wretch also drowned himself somewhere nearby. The police, however, are less romantically inclined and discern clear indications of insanity in the inconsistency of the criminal's actions.

Shall we ever learn the true story behind this nightmarish and unfathomable case?

A BEVY
OF PARISIAN
BEAUTIES

A series of twenty photocards forwarded cash on delivery for a price of 3 fr. 99 cent., including the cost of postage. A unique offer! Hurry—this is a limited edition! Paris, Rue Cuypel, Patoux et Fils printing house.

PART ONE

PORT SAID
TO ADEN

Commissioner Gauche

AT PORT SAID another passenger boarded the *Leviathan*, occupying stateroom number eighteen, the last first-class cabin still vacant, and Gustave Gauche's mood immediately improved. The newcomer looked highly promising: that self-assured and unhurried way of carrying himself, that inscrutable expression on the handsome face. At first glance he seemed quite young, but when he removed his bowler hat, the hair on his temples was unexpectedly gray. A curious specimen, the commissioner decided. It was clear straight off that he had character and what they call "a past." All in all, definitely a client for papa Gauche.

The passenger walked up the gangway, swinging his shoulder bag, while the porters sweated as they struggled under the weight of his ample baggage: expensive suitcases that squeaked, high-quality pigskin traveling bags, huge bundles of books, and even a folding tricycle (one large wheel, two small ones, and an array of gleaming metal tubes). Bringing up the rear came two poor devils lugging an imposing set of gymnastic weights.

Gauche's heart, the heart of an old sleuth (as the commissioner himself was fond of testifying), had thrilled to the lure of the hunt when the newcomer proved to have no golden badge—neither on the silk lapel of his dandified summer coat, nor on his jacket, nor on his watch chain. Warmer now, very warm, thought Gauche, vigilantly scrutinizing the fop from beneath his bushy brows and puffing on his favorite clay pipe. But of course, why had he, old fool that he was, assumed the murderer would board the steamship at Southampton? The crime was committed on the fifteenth of March, and today was already the first of April. It would have been perfectly easy to reach Port Said while the *Leviathan* was rounding the western rim of Europe. And there you had it, everything fitted: the right kind of character for a client, plus a first-class ticket, plus the most important thing—no golden whale.

For some time Gauche's dreams had been haunted by that accursed badge with the abbreviated title of the Jasper-Artaud Partnership steamship company, and without exception his dreams had been uncommonly bad. Take the latest, for instance.

The commissioner was out boating with Mme. Gauche in the Bois de Boulogne. The sun was shining high in the sky and the birds were twittering in the trees. Suddenly a gigantic golden face with inanely goggling eyes loomed up over the treetops, opened cavernous jaws that could have accommodated the Arc de Triomphe with ease, and began sucking in the pond. Gauche broke into a sweat and laid on the oars. Meanwhile it transpired that events were not taking place in the park at all, but in the middle of a boundless ocean. The oars buckled like straws, Mme. Gauche was jabbing him painfully in the back with her umbrella, and an immense gleaming carcass blotted out the entire horizon. When it spouted a fountain that eclipsed half the sky, the commissioner woke up and began fumbling around on his bedside table with trembling fingers—where were his pipe and those matches?

Gauche had first laid eyes on the golden whale at the Rue de Grenelle, when he was examining Lord Littleby's earthly remains. The Englishman lay there with his mouth open in a soundless scream—his false teeth had come halfway out and his forehead was a bloody soufflé. Gauche squatted down: He thought he had caught a glimpse of gold glinting between the corpse's fingers. Taking a closer look, he chortled in delight. Here was a stroke of uncommonly good luck, the kind that occurred only in crime novels. The helpful corpse had literally handed the investigation an important clue—and not even on a plate, but in the palm of its hand. There you are, Gustave, take it. And may you die of shame if you dare let the person who smashed my head open get away, you old numskull.

The golden emblem (at first, of course, Gauche had not known that it was an emblem; he had thought it was a bracelet charm or a monogrammed hairpin) could only have belonged to the murderer. Naturally, just to be sure, the commissioner had shown the whale to the junior manservant (what a lucky lad—the fifteenth of March was his day off, and that had saved his life!), but the manservant had never seen his lordship with the trinket before.

After that the entire ponderous mechanism of the police system had whirred into action, flywheels twirling and pinions spinning, as the minister and the prefect threw their very finest forces into solving "the crime of the century." By the evening of the following day Gauche already knew that the three letters on the golden whale were not the initials of some prodigal hopelessly mired in debt, but the insignia of a newly established Franco-British shipping consortium. The whale proved to be the emblem of the miracle ship *Leviathan*, newly off the slipway at Bristol and currently being readied for its maiden voyage to India.

The newspapers had been trumpeting the praises of the gigantic steamship for more than a month. Now it transpired that on the eve of the *Leviathan*'s first sailing the London Mint had produced gold and silver commemorative badges: gold for the first-class passengers and senior officers of the ship, silver for second-class passengers and subalterns. Aboard this luxurious vessel, where the achievements of modern science were combined with an unprecedented degree of comfort, no provision at all was made for third class. The company guaranteed travelers a comprehensive service, making it unnecessary to take servants along on the voyage. "The shipping line's attentive valets and tactful maids are on hand to ensure that you feel entirely at home on the *Leviathan*," promised the advertisement printed in newspapers right across Europe. Those fortunate individuals who had booked a cabin for the first cruise from Southampton to Calcutta received a gold or silver whale with their ticket, according to their class—and a ticket could be booked in any major European port, from London to Constantinople.

Very well, then, having the emblem of the *Leviathan* was less useful than having the initials of its owner, but this only complicated matters slightly, the commissioner had reasoned. There was a strictly limited number of gold badges. All he had to do was to wait until the nineteenth of March (that was the day appointed for the triumphant first sailing), go to Southampton, board the steamer, and see which of the first-class passengers was missing a golden whale. Or else (this was more likely), which of the passengers who had laid out the money for a ticket failed to turn up for boarding. That would be papa Gauche's client. Simple as potato soup.

Gauche thoroughly disliked traveling, but this time he couldn't resist. He badly wanted to solve the Crime of the Century himself. Who could tell, they might just make him a superintendent at long last. He had only three years left to retirement. A third-class pension was one thing; a second-class pension was different altogether. The difference was one and a half thousand francs a year, and that kind of money didn't grow on trees.

So he had taken the job on. He thought he would just nip across to Southampton and then, at worst, sail as far as Le Havre (the first stop), where there would be gendarmes and reporters lined up on the quayside. A big headline in the *Revue Parisienne:* "Crime of the Century Solved: Our Police Rise to the Occasion." Or better yet: "Old Sleuth Gauche Pulls It Off!"

But ha! The first unpleasant surprise had been waiting for the commissioner at the shipping line office in Southampton, where he discovered that the infernally huge steamship had a hundred first-class cabins and ten senior officers. All the tickets had been sold: all hundred and thirty-two of them. And a gold badge had been issued with each one. Yes—a total of a hundred and forty-two suspects. But then, only one of them would have no badge, Gauche had reassured himself.

On the morning of the nineteenth of March, the commissioner, wrapped up against the damp wind in a warm woollen muffler, had been standing close to the gangway beside the captain, Mr. Josiah Cliff, and the first lieutenant, M. Charles Renier. They were greeting the passengers. The brass band played English and French marching tunes in turn, the crowd on the pier generated an excited buzz, and Gauche puffed away in a rising fury, biting down hard on his wholly blameless pipe. For, alas, due to the cold weather all the passengers were wearing raincoats, overcoats, greatcoats, or capotes. Just try figuring out who has a badge and who doesn't! That was unpleasant surprise number two.

Everyone due to board the steamship in Southampton had arrived, indicating that the criminal must have shown up for the sailing despite the loss of the badge. Evidently he must think policemen were total idiots. Or was he hoping to lose himself in the immense crowd? Or perhaps he simply had no other choice?

In any case, one thing was clear: Gauche would have to go as far as Le Havre. He had been allocated the cabin reserved for honored guests of the shipping line.

Immediately after the ship had sailed a banquet was held in the first-class grand salon, an event the commissioner had especially high hopes for, since the invitations bore the instruction "Admission on presentation of a gold badge or first-class ticket." Why would anyone bother to carry a ticket around when it was so much simpler to pin on your little gold leviathan?

At the banquet Gauche let his imagination run wild as he mentally frisked everyone present. He was even obliged to stick his nose into some ladies' décolletés to check whether they had anything dangling in there on a gold chain, perhaps a whale, perhaps simply a pendant. How could he not check?

Everyone was drinking champagne, nibbling on various savory delicacies from silver trays, and dancing, but Gauche was hard at work, eliminating from his list those who had their badge in place. The men caused him the biggest problems. Many of the swine had attached the whale to their watch chains or even stuck it in their waistcoat pockets, and the commissioner was obliged to inquire after the exact time on eleven occasions.

Surprise number three was that all the officers had their badges in place, but no less than four passengers were wearing no emblem, including two of the female sex! The blow that had cracked open Lord Littleby's skull like a nutshell was so powerful it could surely have been struck only by a man, and a man of exceptional strength at that. On the other hand, as a highly experienced specialist in criminal matters, the commissioner was well aware that in a fit of passion or hysterical excitement even the weakest of ladies was capable of performing genuine miracles. He had no need to look far for examples. Why, only last year a milliner from Neuilly, a frail little chit of a thing, had thrown her unfaithful lover out a fourth-floor window—and he had been a well-nourished rentier twice as fat and half as tall again as herself. So it would not do at all to eliminate women who happened to have no badge from the list of suspects. Although who had ever heard of a woman, especially a woman of good society, mastering the knack of administering injections like that?

With one thing and another, the investigation on board the *Leviathan* threatened to drag on, and so the commissioner had set about dealing with things in his customary thorough fashion. Captain Josiah Cliff was the only officer of the steamship who had been made privy to the secret investigation, and he had instructions from the management of the shipping company to afford the French guardian of the law every possible assistance. Gauche exploited this privilege quite unceremoniously by demanding that all individuals of interest to him be assigned to the same salon.

It should be explained at this point that, out of considerations of privacy and comfort (after all, the ship's advertisement had claimed: "On board, you will discover the atmosphere of a fine old English country estate"), those individuals traveling first-class were not expected to take their meals in the vast dining hall along with the six hundred bearers of democratic silver whales, but were assigned to their own comfortable "salons," each of which bore its own aristocratic title and looked like a high-class hotel: crystal chandeliers, stained oak and mahogany, velvet-upholstered chairs, gleaming silver tableware, prim waiters, and officious stewards. For his own purposes Commissioner Gauche had singled out the Windsor Salon, located on the upper deck in the very bow of the ship: Its three walls of continuous window afforded a magnificent view, so that even on overcast days there was no need to switch on the lamps. The velvet upholstery here was a fine shade of golden brown and the linen table napkins were adorned with the Windsor coat of arms.

Set around the oval table with its legs bolted to the floor (a precaution against any likelihood of severe pitching and rolling) were ten chairs with their tall backs carved in designs incorporating a motley assortment of gothic decorative flourishes. The commissioner liked the idea of everyone sitting around the same table, and he had ordered the steward not to set out the nameplates at random, but with strategic intent: He had seated the four passengers without badges directly opposite himself so that he could keep a close eye on those particular birds. It had not proved possible to seat the captain himself at the head of the table, as Gauche had planned. Mr. Josiah

Cliff did not wish (as he himself had expressed it) "to have any part in this charade," and had chosen to base himself in the York Salon, where the new viceroy of India was taking his meals with his wife and two generals of the Indian army. York was located in the prestigious stern, as far removed as possible from plague-stricken Windsor, where the head of the table was taken by first mate Charles Renier. The commissioner had taken an instant dislike to Renier, with that face bronzed by the sun and the wind, that honeyed way of speaking, that head of dark hair gleaming with brilliantine, that dyed mustache with its two spruce little curls. He was a buffoon, not a sailor.

In the course of the twelve days that elapsed since they had sailed, the commissioner had subjected his salon mates to close scrutiny, absorbed the rudiments of society manners (that is, he had learned not to smoke during a meal and not to mop up his gravy with a crust of bread), more or less mastered the complex geography of this floating city, and grown accustomed to the ship's pitching, but he had still made no progress toward his goal.

The situation was now as follows:

Initially his list of suspects had been headed by Sir Reginald Milford-Stokes, an emaciated ginger-haired gentleman with unkempt sideburns. He looked about twenty-eight or thirty years old and behaved oddly, either gazing aimlessly into the distance with those wide green eyes of his and not responding to questions, or suddenly becoming animated and prattling on about the island of Tahiti, coral reefs, emerald lagoons, and huts with roofs made of palm leaves. Clearly some kind of mental case. Why else would a baronet, the scion of a wealthy family, go traveling to some godforsaken Oceania? What did he think he would find there? And note, too, that twice the damned aristocrat had ignored a question about his missing badge. He either stared straight through the commissioner or, when he did happen to glance at him, he seemed to be scrutinizing some insignificant insect. A rotten snob. Back in Le Havre (where they had stood for four hours) Gauche had made a dash to the telegraph office and sent off an inquiry about Milford-Stokes to Scotland Yard: Who was he, did he have any record of violent behavior, had he ever dabbled in the study of medicine? The reply that had arrived just before they sailed contained nothing of great interest, but it had explained the strange mannerisms. Even so, the ginger gentleman did not have a golden whale, which meant it was still too early for Gauche to remove him from his list of potential clients.

The second suspect was M. Gintaro Aono, a "Japanese nobleman" (or so it said in the passenger register). He was a typical oriental, short and skinny. With that thin mustache and those narrow, piercing eyes, he could be almost any age. He remained silent most of the time at table. When asked what he did, he mumbled, embarrassed: "An officer in the Imperial Army." When asked about his badge, he became even more embarrassed, cast a glance of searing hatred at the commissioner, excused himself, and left the room without even finishing his soup. Decidedly suspicious! An absolute savage. He fanned himself in the salon with a bright-colored paper contraption, like some pederast from one of those dens of dubious delight behind the Rue de Rivoli, and he strolled about the deck in his wooden slippers and cotton robe without any pants at all. Of course, Gustave Gauche was all in favor of liberty, equality, and fraternity, but a popinjay like that really ought not to have been allowed into first class.

And then there were the women.

Mme. Renate Kleber. Young, barely twenty perhaps. The wife of an employee of a Swiss bank, traveling to join her husband in Calcutta. She could hardly be described as a beauty, with that pointed nose, but she was lively and talkative. She informed him she was pregnant the very moment they were introduced. All her thoughts and feelings were governed by this single circumstance. A sweet and ingenuous woman, but absolutely unbearable. In twelve days she had succeeded in boring the commissioner to death by chattering about her precious health, embroidering nightcaps, and other such nonsense. Nothing but a belly on legs, although she was not very far along yet and the belly was only just beginning to show. Gauche, naturally, had chosen his moment and asked where her emblem was. The Swiss lady had blinked her bright little eyes and complained that she was always losing things. Which seemed very likely to be true. For Renate Kleber the commissioner felt a mixture of irritation and protectiveness, but he did not take her seriously as a client.

When it came to the second lady, Mlle. Clarissa Stamp, the worldly-wise detective felt a far keener interest. There was something about her that seemed not quite right. She appeared to be a typical Englishwoman, nothing out of the ordinary. No longer young, with dull, colorless hair and rather sedate manners, but just occasionally those watery eyes would give a flash of devilment. He'd seen her type before. What was it the English said about still waters? There were a few other small details worthy of note—mere trifles really, no one else would have paid any attention to that kind of thing, but nothing escaped Gauche, the old dog. Miss Stamp's dresses and her wardrobe in general were expensive and brand-new, everything in the latest Parisian style. Her handbag was genuine tortoiseshell (he'd seen one like it in a shop window on the Champs Elysées—three hundred fifty francs), but the notebook she took out of it was old and cheaply made. On one occasion she had sat on the deck wearing a shawl (it was windy at the time), and it was exactly like one that Mme. Gauche had, made of dog's hair. Warm, but not at all the thing for an English lady. And it was curious that absolutely all of Clarissa Stamp's new things were expensive, while her older ones were shoddy and of the very lowest quality. This was a clear discrepancy. One day just before five o'clock tea Gauche had asked her: "Why is it, my dear lady, that you never put on your golden whale? Do you not like it? It seems to me a very stylish trinket." And what was her response? She had blushed an even deeper color than the "Japanese nobleman" and said she had worn it already but he simply hadn't noticed. That was a lie. Gauche would have noticed all right. The commissioner had a certain subtle ploy in mind, but he would have to choose exactly the right psychological moment. Then he would see how she would react, this Clarissa.

Since there were ten places at the table and only four passengers without emblems, Gauche had decided to make up the complement with other specimens who were also noteworthy in their own way, even though they possessed badges. It would widen his field of inquiry: In any case, the places were there.

First of all he had demanded that the captain assign the ship's chief physician, M. Truffo, to Windsor. Josiah Cliff had muttered a little but eventually gave way. The reason for Gauche's interest in the physician was clear enough—skilled in the art of administering injections, he was the only medic on board the *Leviathan* whose status entitled him to a golden whale. The doctor turned out to be a rather short, plump Italian with an olive complexion, a high forehead, and a bald patch with a few sparse strands of hair combed backward across it. It was simply impossible to imagine this comical specimen in the role of a ruthless killer. In addition to the doctor, another place had to be allocated to his wife. Having married only two weeks previously, the physician had decided to combine duty and pleasure by making this voyage his honeymoon. The chair occupied by the new Mme. Truffo was completely wasted. The dreary, unsmiling English-woman who had found favor with the shipboard Aesculapius appeared twice as old as her twenty years and inspired in Gauche a deadly ennui—as, indeed, did the majority of her female compatriots. He immediately dubbed her "the sheep" because of her white eyelashes and bleating voice. As it happened, she rarely opened her mouth, since she did not know French and for the most part conversations in the salon were, thank God, conducted in that most noble of tongues. Mme. Truffo had no badge of any kind, but that was only natural, since she was neither an officer nor a paying passenger.

The commissioner had also spotted in the register of passengers a certain specialist in Indian archeology, one Anthony F. Sweetchild, and decided that an Indologist might just come in handy. After all, the deceased Lord Littleby had also been something of the kind. Mr. Sweetchild, a lanky beanpole with round-rimmed spectacles and a goatee, had himself struck up a conversation about India at the very first dinner. After the meal Gauche had taken the professor aside and cautiously steered the conversation around to the subject of Lord Littleby's collection. The Indian specialist had contemptuously dismissed his late lordship as a dilettante and his collection as a "cabinet of curiosities" assembled without the benefit of scholarship. He claimed that the only item of genuine value in it was the golden Shiva and said it was a good thing the Shiva had turned up on its own, because everybody knew the French police were good for nothing but taking bribes. This grossly unjust remark set Gauche coughing furiously, but Sweetchild merely advised him to smoke less. The scholar went on to remark condescendingly that Littleby had, admittedly, acquired a fairly decent collection of decorative fabrics and shawls, which happened to include some extremely curious items, but their significance lay in the area of Indian arts and crafts. The sixteenth-century sandalwood chest from Lahore with carvings on a theme from the *Mahabharata* was not too bad, either—and then he had launched into a diatribe that soon had the commissioner nodding off.

Gauche had selected his final salon mate by eye, as they say. Quite literally so. The commissioner had only recently finished reading a most diverting volume translated from the Italian. One Cesare Lombroso, a professor of forensic medicine in the Italian city of Turin, had developed an entire theory of criminalistics, according to which congenital criminals were not responsible for their antisocial behavior. In accordance with Dr. Darwin's theory of evolution, mankind passed through a series of distinct stages in its development, gradually approaching perfection. But a criminal was an evolutionary reject, a random throwback to a previous stage. It was therefore a very simple matter to identify the potential robber and murderer: He resembled the monkey from whom we are all descended. The commissioner had pondered long and hard about what he had read. On the one hand, by no means had every one of the varied crew of thieves and murderers with whom he had dealt in the course of thirty years of police work resembled gorillas; some of them had been such sweet angels that a single glance at them brought a tender tear to one's eye. On the other hand, there had been plenty of anthropoid types, too. As a convinced anticlerical, old Gauche did not believe in Adam and Eve. Darwin's theory appeared rather more sound to him. And then he had come across a certain individual among the first-class passengers, a type who might have sat for a picture entitled "The Typical Killer": low forehead, prominent ridges above small eyes, flat nose, and crooked chin. And so the commissioner had requested that this Etienne Boileau, a tea trader, be assigned to the Windsor Salon. He had turned out to be an absolutely charming fellow—ready wit, father of eleven children, and confirmed philanthropist.

It had looked as though papa Gauche's voyage was unlikely to terminate even in Port Said, the next stop after Le Havre. The investigation was dragging on. Moreover, the keen intuition developed by the commissioner over the years was already hinting to him that he had drawn a blank, that there was no serious candidate among the company he had assembled. He was beginning to discern the sickening prospect of cruising the entire confounded length of the route to Port Said and Aden and Bombay and

Calcutta—and then hanging himself from the first palm tree he saw in Calcutta. He couldn't go running back to Paris with his tail between his legs! His colleagues would make him a laughingstock; his superiors would carp about the small matter of a first-class voyage at the treasury's expense. They might even kick him out on early retirement.

At Port Said, since the voyage was turning out to be a long one, with an aching heart Gauche bankrupted himself buying some more shirts, stocked up on Egyptian tobacco, and, for lack of anything else to fill his time, spent two francs on a cab ride along the famous waterfront. In fact, there was nothing exceptional about it. An enormous lighthouse; a couple of piers as long as your arm. The town itself made a strange impression, neither Asia nor Europe. A glance at the residence of the governor-general of the Suez Canal, and it seemed like Europe. The streets in the city center were crowded with European faces; there were ladies strolling about with white parasols and wealthy gentlemen in panama hats and straw boaters plodding along, large paunches to the fore. But once the carriage turned into the native quarter, a fetid stench filled the air and everywhere there were flies, rotting refuse, and grubby little Arab urchins pestering people for small change. Why did these rich idlers bother to go traveling? It was the same everywhere: Some grew fat from gorging on delicacies while others' bellies were swollen by hunger.

Exhausted by these pessimistic observations and the heat, the commissioner returned to the ship feeling dejected. But then it happened: He had a new client. And he looked like a promising one.

THE COMMISSIONER PAID the captain a visit and made some inquiries. It turned out that his name was Erast P. Fandorin and he was a Russian subject. For some reason this Russian subject had not given his age. A diplomat by profession, he had arrived from Constantinople, was traveling to Calcutta, and from there going on to Japan to take up his post. From Constantinople? Aha! He must have been involved in the peace negotiations that had concluded the recent Russo-Turkish War. Gauche punctiliously copied all the details on a sheet of paper and stowed it away in the special calico-bound file in which he kept all the materials having to do with the case; he never let it out of his sight. He leafed through it and reread the reports and newspaper clippings, and in pensive moments he drew little fishes and houses in the margins of the papers. It was the secret dream of his heart breaking through to the surface: the dream of how he would become a divisional commissioner, earn a decent pension, buy a nice little house somewhere in Normandy, and live out his days there with Mme. Gauche. The retired Paris *flic* would go fishing and press his own cider. What was wrong with that? But if only he had a little bit of capital to add to his pension—he needed twenty thousand at least . . .

He was obliged to make another visit to the port—luckily the ship was delayed waiting for its turn to enter the Suez Canal—and dash off a brief telegram to the prefecture, asking whether the Russian diplomat Erast P. Fandorin was known in Paris and whether he had entered the territory of the Republic of France at any time in the recent past.

The reply arrived quickly, after only two and a half hours. It turned out that the fellow had crossed into French territory not once, but twice. The first time in the summer of 1876 (all right, we can let that go) and the second time in December 1877, just three months earlier. His arrival from London had been recorded at the passport and customs control point in Pas-de-Calais. It was not known how much time he had spent in France. He could quite possibly still have been in Paris on the fifteenth of March. He could even have dropped round to the Rue de Grenelle with a syringe in his hand—stranger things had happened.

It now seemed that one of the places at the table would have to be freed up. The best thing, of course, would be to get rid of the doctor's wife, but he could hardly encroach on the sacred institution of marriage. After some thought, Gauche decided to pack the tea trader off to a different salon, since the theoretical hopes he had inspired had proved to be unfounded and he was the least promising of all the candidates. The steward could reassign him, tell him there was a place with more important gentlemen or prettier ladies. After all, stewards were there to arrange such things.

The appearance of a new personality in the salon caused a minor sensation. In the course of the journey they had all become thoroughly bored with one another, and now here was a fresh gentleman, and such a superior individual at that. Nobody bothered to inquire after poor M. Boileau, that representative of a previous stage of evolution. The commissioner noted that the person who evinced the liveliest reaction was Miss Clarissa Stamp, the old maid, who started babbling about artists, the theater, and literature. Gauche himself was fond of passing his leisure hours in an armchair with a good book, preferring Victor Hugo to all other authors. Hugo was at once so true to life, so high-minded, that he could always bring a tear to the eye. Besides, he was marvelous for dozing off over. But of course Gauche had never even heard of these Russian writers with those hissing sibilants in their names, so he was unable to join in the conversation. Anyway, the old English trout was wasting her time; "M. Fandorine" was far too young for her.

Renate Kleber was not slow off the mark, either. She made an attempt to press the new arrival into service as one of her minions, whom she bullied mercilessly into bringing her shawl or her parasol or a glass of water. Five minutes after dinner began, Mme. Kleber had already initiated the Russian into the detailed history of her delicate condition, complained of a migraine, and asked him to fetch Dr. Truffo, who for some reason was late that day. However, the diplomat seemed to have realized immediately who he was dealing with and politely objected that he did not know the doctor by sight. The ever-obliging Lieutenant Renier, the pregnant banker's wife's most devoted nursemaid, volunteered and went racing off to perform the errand.

The initial impression made by Erast Fandorin was that he was taciturn, reserved, and polite. But he was a bit too neat and polished for Gauche's taste: the starched collar sticking up like alabaster, the jeweled pin in the necktie, the red carnation (how very suave) in the buttonhole, the perfectly parted hair with not a strand out of place, the carefully manicured nails, the thin black mustache that seemed to have been drawn on with charcoal.

It was possible to tell a great deal about a man from his mustache. If it was like Gauche's, a walrus drooping at the corners of the mouth, it meant the man was a down-to-earth fellow who knew his own worth, not some gull easily to be taken in. If it was curled up at the ends, especially into points, he was a lady's man and bon vivant. If it merged into his sideburns, he was a man of ambition with dreams of becoming a general, statesman, or banker. And when it was like "M. Fandorine's," it meant he entertained romantic notions about himself.

What else could he say about the Russian? He spoke decent enough French, even though he stammered. There was no sign of his badge. The diplomat showed most interest in the Japanese, asking him all sorts of tiresome questions about his country, but the samurai answered guardedly, as if anticipating some kind of trick. The point was that the new passenger had not explained to the company where he was going and why; he had simply given his name and said that he was Russian. The commissioner, though, could understand the Russian's inquisitiveness, since he knew he was going to live in Japan. Gauche pictured to himself a country in which every single person was the same as M. Aono; everybody lived in doll's houses with bowed roofs and disemboweled themselves at the drop of a hat. No, the Russian was not to be envied.

After dinner, when Fandorin took a seat to one side in order to smoke a cigar, the commissioner settled into an armchair beside him and began puffing away at his pipe. Gauche had previously introduced himself to his new acquaintance as a Parisian rentier who was making the journey east out of curiosity (that was the cover he was using). But now he turned the conversation to the matter at hand, approaching it obliquely and with due caution. Fiddling with the golden whale on his lapel (the very same one retrieved from the Rue de Grenelle), he said casually, as though he were simply striking up a conversation, "A beautiful little bauble. Don't you agree?"

The Russian glanced sideways at his lapel but said nothing.

"Pure gold. So stylish!" said Gauche admiringly.

Another pregnant silence followed, but a perfectly civil one. The man was simply waiting for what would come next. His blue eyes were alert. The diplomat had clear skin, as smooth as a peach, with a bloom on his cheeks like a young girl's. But he was no mama's boy; that much was obvious immediately.

The commissioner decided to try a different tack.

"Do you travel much?"

A noncommittal shrug.

"I believe you're in the diplomatic line?"

Fandorin inclined his head politely in assent, extracted a long cigar from his pocket, and cut off the tip with a little silver knife.

"And have you ever been in France?"

Again an affirmative nod of the head. *Monsieur le Russe is no great conversationalist*, thought Gauche, but he had no intention of backing down.

"More than anything I love Paris in the early spring, in March," the detective mused out loud. "The very best time of the year!"

He cast a keen glance at the other man, wondering what he would say.

Fandorin nodded twice, though it wasn't clear if he was simply acknowledging the remark or agreeing with it. Beginning to feel irritated, Gauche furrowed his brows in an antagonistic scowl.

"So you don't like your badge, then?"

His pipe sputtered and went out.

The Russian gave a short sigh, put his hand into his waistcoat pocket, extracted a golden whale from it with his finger and thumb, and finally condescended to open his mouth: "I observe, monsieur, that you are interested in my b-badge. Here it is, if you please. I do not wear it because I do not wish to resemble a janitor with a name tag, not even a golden one. That is one. You do not much resemble a rentier, M. Gauche—your eyes are too probing. And why would a Parisian rentier lug a civil-service file around with him? That is two. Since you are aware of my professional orientation, you would appear to have access to the ship's documents. I assume therefore that you are a detective. That is three. Which brings us to number four. If there is something you want to find out from me, please do not beat about the bush. Ask directly."

You try having a conversation with someone like that.

Gauche had to think quickly. He whispered confidentially to the excessively perspicacious diplomat that he was the ship's house detective, whose job it was to see to the passengers' safety, but secretly and with the greatest possible delicacy, in order not to avoid offending the refined sensibilities of his public. It was not clear whether Fandorin believed him, but at least he did not ask any questions.

Every cloud has a silver lining. The commissioner now had, if not an intellectual ally, then at least an interlocutor, and someone who possessed remarkable powers of observation and quite exceptional knowledge on matters of criminology.

They often sat together on the deck, glancing now and then at the gently sloping bank of the canal as they smoked (Gauche his pipe, the Russian his cigar), and discussed various intriguing subjects—for instance, the very latest methods for the identification and conviction of criminals.

"The Paris police conducts its work in accordance with the very latest advances in scientific method," Gauche once boasted. "The prefecture there has a special identification unit headed by a young genius, Alphonse Bertillon. He has developed a complete system for classifying and recording criminal elements."

"I met with Dr. Bertillon during my last visit to Paris," Fandorin said unexpectedly. "He told me about his anthropometric method. Bertillonage is a clever theory, very clever. Have you already begun to apply it in practise? What have the results been?"

"There haven't been any yet," the commissioner said with a shrug. "First, one has to apply bertillonage to all the recidivists, and that will take years. It's bedlam in Alphonse's department: They bring in the prisoners in shackles, measure them up from every angle like horses at a fair, and jot down the data on little cards. But then pretty soon it will make police work as easy as falling off a log. Let's say you find the print of a left hand at the scene of a burglary. You measure it and go to the card index. Aha, middle finger eighty-nine millimeters long, look in section number three. And there you find records of seventeen burglars with a finger of the right length. After that, the whole thing is as easy as pie: Check where each of them was on the day of the robbery and nab the one who has no alibi."

"You mean criminals are divided up into categories according to the length of the middle finger?" the Russian asked with lively interest.

Gauche chuckled condescendingly into his mustache.

"There is a whole system involved, my young friend. Bertillon divides all people into three groups according to the length of the skull. Each of *those* three groups is divided into three subgroups according to the width of the skull. That makes nine subgroups in all. Each subgroup is in turn divided into three sections according to the size of the middle finger of the left hand. Twenty-seven sections. But that's not all. There are three divisions in each section according to the size of the right ear. So how many divisions does that make? That's right, eighty-one. Subsequent classification takes into account the height, the length of the arms, the height when seated, the size of the foot, and the length of the elbow joint. A total of 18,683 categories! A criminal who has undergone full bertillonage and been included in our card index will never be able to escape justice again. They used to have it so easy—just give a false name when you're arrested and you could avoid any responsibility for anything you did before."

"That is remarkable," the diplomat mused. "However, bertillonage does not offer much help with the solution of a particular crime if an individual has not previously been arrested."

Gauche spread his arms helplessly.

"Well, that is a problem science cannot solve. As long as there are criminals, people will not be able to manage without us professional sleuths."

"Have you ever heard of fingerprints?" Fandorin asked, presenting to the commissioner a narrow but extremely firm hand with polished nails and a diamond ring.

Glancing enviously at the ring (a commissioner's annual salary at the very least), Gauche laughed.

"Some kind of gypsy palmistry?"

"Not at all. It has been known since ancient times that the raised pattern of papillary lines on the tips of the fingers is unique to every individual. In China, coolies seal their contracts of hire with the imprint of their thumb dipped in ink."

"Well now, if only every murderer were so obliging as to dip his thumb into ink and leave an imprint at the scene of the crime." The commissioner laughed good-naturedly.

The diplomat, however, was not in the mood for joking.

"Monsieur ship's detective, allow me to inform you that modern science has established with certainty that an imprint is left when a finger comes into contact with any dry, firm surface. If a criminal has so much as touched a door in passing, or the murder weapon, or a windowpane, he has left a trace that allows the p-perpetrator to be identified and unmasked."

Gauche was about to retort ironically that there were twenty thousand criminals in France, that between them they had two hundred thousand fingers and thumbs and you would go blind staring at all of them through your magnifying glass, but he hesitated, recalling the shattered display case in the mansion on the Rue de Grenelle. There had been fingerprints left all over the broken glass. But it had never entered anyone's head to copy them, and the shards had been thrown out with the garbage.

My, what an amazing thing progress was! Just think what it meant. All crimes were committed with hands, were they not? And now it seemed that hands could inform every bit as well as paid informants! Just imagine—if you were to copy the fingers of every bandit and petty thief, they wouldn't dare turn their filthy hands to any more dirty work! It would be the end of crime itself.

The very prospect was enough to set a man's head spinning.

Reginald Milford-Stokes

---

2 April 1878
18 hours, 34½ minutes, Greenwich Mean Time

My precious Emily,

Today we entered the Suez Canal. In yesterday's letter I described the history and topography of Port Said to you in detail, and now I simply cannot resist the temptation of relating to you certain curious and instructive facts concerning the Great Canal, this truly colossal monument to human endeavor, which next year celebrates its tenth anniversary. Are you aware, my adorable little wife, that the present canal is actually the fourth to have existed and that the first was excavated as long ago as the fourteenth century before Christ, during the reign of the great Pharaoh Rameses? When Egypt fell into decline, the desert winds choked up the channel with sand, but under the Persian king Darius, five hundred years before Christ, slaves dug out another canal at the cost of 120,000 human lives. Herodotus tells us that the voyage along it took four days and that two triremes traveling in opposite directions could easily pass each other without their oars touching. Several ships from Cleopatra's shattered fleet fled to the Red Sea by this route and so escaped the fearful wrath of the vengeful Octavian.

Following the fall of the Roman Empire, time again separated the Atlantic and Indian Oceans with a barrier of shifting sand a hundred miles wide, but no sooner was a powerful state established in these barren lands by the followers of the prophet Mohammed than people took up their mattocks and pickaxes once again. As I sail through these dead salt meadows and endless sand dunes, I marvel unceasingly at the stubborn courage and antlike diligence of humankind in waging its never-ending struggle, doomed to inevitable defeat, against all-powerful Chronos. Vessels laden with grain plied the Arabian canal for two hundred years, and then the earth erased this pitiful wrinkle from its forehead and the desert was plunged into sleep for a thousand years.

Regrettably the father of the new Suez was not a Briton, but the Frenchman Lesseps, a representative of a nation which, my darling Emily, I quite justifiably hold in the most profound contempt. This crafty diplomat persuaded the Egyptian governor to issue a *firman* for the establishment of "The Universal Company of the Suez Maritime Canal." The company was granted a ninety-nine-year lease on the future waterway, and the Egyptian government was allotted only fifteen percent of the net revenue! And these villainous French dare to label us British pillagers of the backward peoples! At least we win our privileges with the sword, not by striking grubby bargains with greedy local bureaucrats.

Every day one thousand six hundred camels delivered drinking water to the workers digging the Great Canal, but still the poor devils died in the thousands from thirst, intense heat, and infectious diseases. Our *Leviathan* is sailing over corpses, and I seem to see the yellow teeth of fleshless, eyeless skulls grinning out at me from beneath the sand. It took ten years and fifteen million pounds sterling to complete this gargantuan construction job. But now a ship can sail from England to India in almost half the time it used to take. A mere twenty-five days or so and you arrive in Bombay. It is quite incredible! And the scale of it! The canal is more than a hundred feet deep, so that even our gigantic ark can sail fearlessly here, with no risk of running aground.

Today at lunch I was overcome by a quite irresistible fit of laughter; I choked on a crust of bread, began coughing, and simply could not calm myself. The pathetic coxcomb Renier (I wrote to you about him, he is the *Leviathan*'s first lieutenant) inquired with feigned interest what was the cause of my merriment, and I was seized by an even stronger paroxysm, for I certainly could not tell him about the thought that had set me laughing: that the French had built the canal, but the fruits had fallen to us, the English. Three years ago Her Majesty's government bought a controlling block of shares from the Egyptian khedive, and now we British are the masters of Suez. And incidentally, a single share in the canal, which was once sold for fifteen pounds, is now worth three thousand! How's that! How could I help but laugh?

But I fear I must have wearied you with these boring details. Do not blame me, my dear Emily, for I have no other recreation apart from writing long letters. While I am scraping my pen across the vellum paper, it is as though you are here beside me and I am making leisurely conversation with you. You know, thanks to the hot climate here I am feeling very much better. I can no longer recall the terrible dreams that haunt me in the night. But they have not gone away. In the morning when I wake up, the pillow-case is still soaked with tears and sometimes gnawed to shreds.

But that is all nonsense. Every new day and every mile of the journey bring me closer to a new life. There, under the soothing sun of the equator, this dreadful separation that is tearing my very soul apart will finally come to an end. How I wish it could be sooner! How impatient I am to see your tender, radiant glance once again, my dear friend.

What else can I entertain you with? Perhaps at least with a description of our *Leviathan*, a more than worthy theme. In my earlier letters I have written too much about my own feelings and dreams and I have still not presented you with a full picture of this great triumph of British engineering.

The *Leviathan* is the largest passenger ship in the history of the world, with the single exception of the colossal *Great Eastern*, which has been fur-rowing the waters of the Atlantic Ocean for the last twenty years. When Jules Verne described the *Great Eastern* in his book *The Floating City*, he had not seen our *Leviathan*—otherwise he would have renamed the old *G.E.* "The Floating Village." That vessel now does nothing but lay tele-graph cables on the ocean floor, but *Leviathan* can transport a thousand people and ten thousand tons of cargo in addition. This fire-breathing monster is more than six hundred feet long and eighty feet across at its widest. Do you know, my dear Emily, how a ship is built? First they "lay it out in the molding loft," that is to say, they make a full-scale drawing of the vessel directly on the smoothly planed floor of a special building. The drawing of the *Leviathan* was so huge that they had to build a shed the size of Buckingham Palace!

This miracle of a ship has two steam engines, two powerful paddle wheels on its sides, and in addition a gigantic propeller on its stern. Its six masts, fitted with a full set of rigging, tower up to the very sky and with a fair wind and engines running full ahead the ship can make a speed of sixteen knots! All the very latest advances in shipbuilding have been used in her. These include a double metal hull, which ensures the vessel's safety even if it should strike a rock; special side keels to reduce pitching and rolling; electric lighting throughout; waterproof compartments; immense coolers for the spent steam—it is impossible to list everything. The entire experience of centuries of effort by the indefatigably inventive human mind has been concentrated in this proud vessel cleaving fearlessly through the ocean waves. Yesterday, following my old habit, I opened the Holy Scriptures at the first page that came to hand and I was astonished when my eyes fell upon the lines about Leviathan, the fearsome monster of the deep from the Book of Job. I began trembling at the sudden realization that this was no description of a sea serpent, as the ancients believed it to be, nor of a sperm whale, as our modern-day rationalists claim—no, the biblical text clearly refers to the very same Leviathan that has undertaken to deliver me out of darkness and terror into happiness and light. Judge for yourself: "He maketh the deep to boil like a pot: he maketh the sea like a pot of ointment. He maketh a path to shine after him: one would think the deep to be hoary. Upon earth there is not his like, who is made without fear. He beholdeth all high things: he is king over the children of pride."

The pot—that is the steam boiler; the pot of ointment—that is the fuel oil; the shining path—that is the wake at the stern. It is all so obvious!

And I felt afraid, my darling Emily. For these lines contain a terrible warning, either to me personally or to the passengers on the *Leviathan,* or to the whole of mankind. From the biblical point of view, pride is surely a bad thing? And if Man with his technological playthings "beholdeth all high things," is this not fraught with some catastrophic consequences? Have we not become too proud of the keenness of our intellect and the skill of our hands? Where is this king of pride taking us? What lies in store for us?

And so I opened my prayerbook to pray—the first time for a long, long time. And there I read: "It is in their thoughts that their houses are eternal and their dwellings are from generation to generation, and they call their lands after their own names. But man shall not abide in honor; he shall be likened unto the beasts who die. This path of theirs is their folly, though those that come after them do commend their opinion."

But when, in a paroxysm of mystical feeling, I opened the Book once again with a trembling hand, my feverish gaze fell on the boring passage in Numbers where the sacrifices made by the tribes of the Israelites are itemized with a bookkeeper's tedious precision. And I calmed down, rang my silver bell, and told the steward to bring me some hot chocolate.

The level of comfort prevailing in the section of the ship assigned to the respectable public is absolutely staggering. In this respect the *Leviathan* is truly without equal. The times are gone when people traveling to India or China were cooped up in dark, cramped little cubbyholes and piled one on top of another. You know, my dearest wife, how keenly I suffer from claustrophobia, but on board the *Leviathan* I feel as though I were in the wide open spaces of the Thames embankment. Here there is everything required to combat boredom: a dance hall, a musical salon for concerts of classical music, even a rather decent library. The decor in a first-class cabin is in no way inferior to a room in the finest London hotel, and the ship has a hundred such cabins. In addition, there are two hundred and fifty second-class cabins with six hundred berths (I have not looked into them—I cannot endure the sight of squalor) and they say there are also capacious cargo holds. The *Leviathan*'s service personnel alone, not counting sailors and officers, numbers more than two hundred—stewards, chefs, valets, musicians, chambermaids. Just imagine—I do not regret in the least not bringing Jeremy with me. The idle loafer was always sticking his nose into matters that did not concern him, and here at precisely eleven o'clock the maid comes and cleans the room and carries out any other errands I may have for her. This is both rational and convenient. If I wish I can ring for a valet and have him help me dress, but I regard that as excessive—I dress and undress myself. It is most strictly forbidden for any servant to enter the cabin in my absence, and on leaving it I set a hair across the crack of the door. I am afraid of spies. Believe me, my sweet Emily, this is not a ship, but a veritable city, and it has its share of riffraff.

For the most part my information concerning the ship has been garnered from the explanations of Lieutenant Renier, who is a great patriot of his own vessel. He is, however, not a very likeable individual and the object of serious suspicion on my part. He tries his hardest to play the gentleman, but I am not so easily duped. I have a keen nose for low breeding. Wishing to produce a good impression, this fellow invited me to visit his cabin. I did call, but less out of curiosity than from a desire to assess the seriousness of the threat that might be posed by this swarthy gentleman (concerning his appearance, see my letter of the twentieth of March). The meagerness of the decor was rendered even more glaringly obvious by his tasteless attempts at *bon ton* (Chinese vases, Indian incense burners, a dreadful seascape on the wall, and so forth). Standing on the table among the maps and navigational instruments was a large photographic portrait of a woman dressed in black, with an inscription in French: "Seven feet under the keel, my darling! Françoise B." I inquired whether it was his wife. It turned out to be his mother. Touching, but it does not allay my suspicions. I am as determined as ever to take independent readings of our course every three hours, even though it means that I have to get up twice during the night. Of course, while we are sailing through the Suez Canal this might seem a little excessive, but I do not wish to lose my proficiency in handling a sextant.

I have more than enough time at my disposal and apart from the writing of letters my leisure hours are filled by observing the Vanity Fair that surrounds me on all sides. Among this gallery of human types there are some who are most amusing. I have already written to you about the others, but yesterday a new face appeared in our salon. He is Russian—can you imagine that? His name is Erast Fandorin. You are aware, Emily, of my feelings regarding Russia, that misshapen excrescence that has extended over half of Europe and a third of Asia. Russia seeks to disseminate its own parody of the Christian religion and its own barbarous customs throughout the entire world, and Albion stands as the only barrier in the path of these new Huns. If not for the resolute position adopted by Her Majesty's government in the current eastern crisis, Tsar Alexander would have raked in the Balkans with his bear's claws, and . . .

But I have already written to you about that and I do not wish to repeat myself. And in any case, thinking about politics has rather a bad effect on my nerves. It is now four minutes to eight. As I have already informed you, life on the *Leviathan* is conducted according to British time as far as Aden, so that it is already dark here at eight o'clock. I shall go and take readings of the longitude and latitude, then have dinner and continue with my letter.

Sixteen minutes after ten—

I see that I did not finish writing about Mr. Fandorin. I do believe I like him, despite his nationality. Good manners, reticent, knows how to listen. He must be a member of that estate referred to in Russia by the Italian word *intelligenzia,* which I believe denotes the educated European class. You must admit, dear Emily, that a society in which the European class is separated into a distinct stratum of the population and also referred to by a foreign word can hardly be ranked among the civilized nations. I can imagine what a gulf separates a civilized human being like Mr. Fandorin from some bearded *kossack* or *muzhik,* who make up ninety percent of the population of that Tartarian-Byzantine empire. On the other hand, a distance of such magnitude must elevate and ennoble an educated and thinking man to an exceptional degree, a point that I shall have to ponder at greater length.

I liked the elegant way in which Mr. Fandorin (by the way, it seems he is a diplomat, which explains a great deal) put down that intolerable yokel Gauche, who claims to be a rentier, although it is clear from a mile away that the fellow is involved in some grubby little business or other. I should not be surprised if he is on his way to the East to purchase opium and exotic dancers for Parisian dens of vice. [The last phrase has been scratched out.] I know, my darling Emily, that you are a real lady and will not attempt to read what has been crossed out here. I got a little carried away and wrote something unworthy for your chaste eyes to read.

And so, back to today's dinner. The French bourgeois, who just recently has grown bold and become quite terribly talkative, began discoursing with a self-satisfied air on the advantages of age over youth. "I am older than anyone else here," he said condescendingly, à la Socrates. "Gray-haired, bloated, and decidedly not good-looking, but you needn't go thinking, ladies and gentlemen, that papa Gauche would agree to change places with you. When I see the arrogance of youth, flaunting its beauty and strength, its health, in the face of age, I do not feel envious in the least. Why, I think, that is no great trick; I was like that myself once. But you, my fine fellow, still do not know if you will live to my sixty-two years. I am twice as happy as you are at thirty, because I have been fortunate enough to live in this world for twice as long." And he sipped at his wine, very proud of the originality of his thought and his seemingly unimpeachable logic. Then Mr. Fandorin, who had so far not said a word, suddenly remarked with a very serious air, "That is undoubtedly the case, M. Gauche, if one takes the oriental viewpoint on life, as existence at a single point of reality in an eternal present. But there is also another way of reasoning that regards a man's life as a unified work that can only be judged when its final page has been read. Moreover, this work may be as long as a tetralogy or as short as a novella. And yet who would undertake to assert that a fat, vulgar novel is necessarily of greater value than a short, beautiful poem?" The funniest thing of all was that our rentier, who is indeed both fat and vulgar, did not even understand the reference to himself. Even when Miss Stamp (by no means stupid, but a strange creature) giggled and I gave a rather loud snort, the Frenchie failed to catch on and stuck with his own opinion, and all credit to him for that.

It is true, however, that in the conversation that followed over dessert, Mr. Gauche demonstrated a degree of common sense that quite amazed me. There are, after all, certain advantages in not having a regular education: A mind unfettered by authorities is sometimes capable of making interesting and accurate observations.

Judge for yourself. The amoeba-like Mrs. Truffo, the wife of our muttonhead of a doctor, started up again with her mindless prattle about the joy and delight Mme. Kleber will bring to her banker with her "tiny tot" and "little angel." Since Mrs. Truffo does not speak French, the task of translating her sickly sentiments on the subject of family happiness being inconceivable without "baby babble" fell to her unfortunate husband. Gauche huffed and puffed and then suddenly declared: "I cannot agree with you, madam. A genuinely happy married couple has no need whatsoever of children, since husband and wife are perfectly sufficient for each other. Man and woman are like two uneven surfaces, each with bumps and indentations. If the surfaces do not fit tightly against each other, then glue is required, otherwise the structure—in other words, the family—cannot be preserved. Children are that selfsame glue. If, however, the surfaces form a perfect fit, bump to indentation, then no glue is required. Take me and my Blanche, if you like. Thirty-three years we've lived in perfect harmony. Why would we want children? Life is splendid without them." I am sure you can imagine, dear Emily, the tidal wave of righteous indignation that came crashing down on the head of this subverter of eternal values. The most zealous accuser of all was Mme. Kleber, who is carrying the little Swiss in her womb. The sight of her neat little belly so carefully exhibited at every opportunity sets me writhing. I can just see the miniature banker nestled inside with his curly mustache and puffy little cheeks. In time the Klebers will no doubt produce an entire battalion of Swiss Guards.

I must confess to you, my tenderly adored Emily, that the sight of pregnant women makes me feel sick. They are repulsive! That inane bovine smile, that disgusting manner of constantly listening to their own entrails. I try to keep as far away from Mme. Kleber as possible. Swear to me, my darling, that we shall never have children. The fat bourgeois is right a thousand times over! Why do we need children when we are already boundlessly happy without them? All we need to do is survive this forced separation.

But it is already two minutes to eleven. Time to take a reading.

Damnation! I have turned the whole cabin upside down. My sextant has disappeared. This is no delusion! It was lying in the trunk together with the chronometer and the compass, and now it is not there! I am afraid, Emily! Oh, I had a premonition of this. My worst suspicions have been confirmed!

Why? What have I done? They are prepared to commit any vileness in order to prevent our reunion! How can I check now that the ship is following the right course? It is that Renier, I know! I caught the expression in his eyes when he saw me handling the sextant on deck last night! The scoundrel!

I shall go to the captain and demand retribution. But what if they are in it together? My God, my God, have pity on me!

I had to pause for a while. I was so agitated that I was obliged to take the drops prescribed for me by Dr. Jenkinson. And I did as he told me, and started thinking of pleasant things. Of how you and I will sit on a white veranda and gaze into the distance, trying to guess where the sea ends and the sky begins. You will smile and say: "Darling Reggie, here we are together at last." Then we will get into a cabriolet and go for a drive along the seashore.

Lord, what nonsense is this! What cabriolet?

I am a monster, and there can be no forgiveness for me.

Renate Kleber

⚮

SHE WOKE UP in an excellent mood, smiled affably at the spot of sunlight that had crept onto her round cheek where it was creased by the pillow, and listened to her belly. The baby was quiet, but she felt terribly hungry. There was still an entire fifty minutes until breakfast, but Renate had no lack of patience, and she simply did not know the meaning of boredom. In the morning, sleep released her as swiftly as it embraced her at night, when she simply sandwiched her hands together and laid her head on them, and a second later she was immersed in sweet dreams.

As Renate performed her morning toilet, she purred a frivolous little song about poor Georgette who fell in love with a chimney sweep. She wiped her fresh little face with an infusion of lavender and then styled her hair quickly and deftly, fluffing up the bangs over her forehead, drawing her thick chestnut tresses into a smooth bun, and arranging two long ringlets over her temples. The effect was precisely what was required—demure and sweet. She glanced out the porthole. Still the same view: the regular border of the canal, the yellow sand, the white mud-daub houses of some wretched little hamlet. It was going to be hot. That meant the white lace dress, the straw hat with the red ribbon, and she mustn't forget her parasol—a stroll after breakfast was de rigueur. Only she couldn't be bothered to drag her parasol around with her. Never mind; someone would fetch it.

Renate twirled in front of the mirror with evident satisfaction, stood sideways, and pulled her dress taut over her belly. Although, to tell the truth, there was not much to look at as yet.

Renate asserted her rights as a pregnant woman by arriving ahead of time for breakfast, when the waiters were still laying the table. She immediately ordered them to bring her orange juice, tea, croissants with butter, and everything else. By the time the first of her tablemates arrived—it was the fat M. Gauche, another early bird—the mother-to-be had already dealt with three croissants and was preparing to set about a mushroom omelette. The breakfast served on the *Leviathan* was not some trifling continental affair, but the genuine full English variety: with roast beef, exquisite egg dishes, blood pudding, and porridge. The French part of the consortium provided nothing but the croissants. At lunch and dinner, however, the menu was dominated by French cuisine. Well, one could hardly serve kidneys and beans in the Windsor salon!

The first mate appeared, as always at precisely nine o'clock. He inquired solicitously as to how Mme. Kleber was feeling. Renate lied and said she had slept badly and felt absolutely shattered, and it was all because the porthole didn't open properly and it was too stuffy in the cabin. Alarmed, Lieutenant Renier promised he would make enquiries in person and have the fault rectified. He did not eat eggs or roast beef—he was a devotee of some peculiar diet, sustaining himself largely on fresh greens. Renate pitied him for that.

Gradually the others also appeared. The conversation over breakfast was usually listless—the older passengers had not yet recovered from a wretched night, while the younger were still not fully awake. It was rather amusing to observe the repulsive Clarissa Stamp attempting to coax a response out of the stammering Russian diplomat. Renate shook her head in disbelief: How could she make such a fool of herself? After all, dearie, he could be your son, despite those impressive streaks of gray. Surely the handsome boy was too tough a morsel for this aging, insipid creature?

The very last to arrive was the Ginger Lunatic (Renate's private name for the English baronet). Tousled hair sticking out in all directions, red eyes, a twitch at the corner of his mouth—he was a terrible mess. But Mme. Kleber was not in the least bit afraid of him, and, given the chance, she never missed the opportunity to have a bit of fun at his expense. This time she passed the milk jug to the Lunatic with a warm, guileless smile. As she had anticipated, Milford-Stokes (what a silly name!) squeamishly set his cup to one side. Renate knew from experience that now he would not even touch the milk jug, and would drink his coffee black.

"Why do you draw back like that, sir?" she babbled in a quavering voice. "Don't be afraid; pregnancy is not infectious." Then she concluded, no longer quavering: "At least not for men."

The Lunatic cast her a glance of withering scorn that broke against the serenely radiant glance opposed to it. Lieutenant Renier concealed a smile behind his hand; the rentier chuckled. Even the Japanese half smiled at Renate's prank. Of course, this M. Aono was always smiling, even when there was absolutely no reason for it. Perhaps for the Japanese a smile was not an expression of merriment at all; perhaps it indicated something quite different—boredom, perhaps, or repugnance.

When he had finished smiling, M. Aono disgusted his neighbors at table by playing his usual trick: He took a paper napkin out of his pocket, blew his nose into it loudly, crumpled it up, and deposited it neatly on the edge of his dirty plate. A fine ikebana arrangement for them to contemplate. Renate had read about ikebana in one of Pierre Loti's novels, and now recalled the mellifluous-sounding word. It was an interesting idea—composing bouquets of flowers not simply to look nice, but with a philosophical meaning. She would have to try it sometime.

"What are your favorite flowers?" she asked Dr. Truffo.

He translated the question for his horse-faced Englishwoman, then replied:

"Pansies."

Then he translated his reply into English as well.

"I just adore flowers!" exclaimed Miss Stamp (what an impossible ingénue). "But only live ones. I love to walk across a flowering meadow! My heart simply breaks when I see poor cut flowers wither and drop their petals! That's why I never allow anyone to give me bouquets." And she cast a languid glance at the handsome young Russian.

What a shame, otherwise absolutely everyone would be tossing bouquets at you, thought Renate, but aloud she said: "I believe that flowers are the crowning glories of God's creation and I think trampling a meadow in bloom is a crime."

"In the parks of Paris it is indeed considered a crime," M. Gauche pronounced solemnly. "The penalty is ten francs. And if the ladies will permit an old boor to light up his pipe, I will tell you an amusing little story on the subject."

"Oh, ladies, pray do indulge us!" cried the owlish Indologist Sweetchild, wagging his beard à la Disraeli. "M. Gauche is such a wonderful raconteur!"

Everyone turned to look at the pregnant Renate, on whom the decision depended, and she rubbed her temple as a hint. Of course, she did not have the slightest trace of a headache—she was simply savoring the sweetness of the moment. However, she too was curious to hear this "little story," and so she nodded her head with a pained expression and said: "Very well, smoke. But then someone must fan me."

Since repulsive Clarissa, the owner of a luxurious ostrich-feather fan, pretended this remark did not apply to her, the Japanese had to fill the breach. Gintaro Aono seated himself beside Renate and set to work, flapping his bright fan with the butterfly design in front of the long-suffering woman's nose so zealously that the bright kaleidoscope rapidly made her feel genuinely dizzy. The Japanese received a reprimand for his excessive fervor.

Meanwhile the rentier drew on his pipe with relish, puffed out a cloud of aromatic smoke, and embarked on his tale.

"Believe it or not as you wish, but this is a true story. There was once a gardener who worked in the Luxembourg Gardens—little papa Picard. For forty years he had watered the flowers and pruned the shrubs, and now he had only three years to go until he retired and drew his pension. Then, one morning, when little papa Picard went out with his watering can, he saw a swell dolled up in a white shirt and tails sprawled in the tulip bed. He was stretched out full-length, basking in the morning sunshine, obviously recovering from his nocturnal revels—after carousing until dawn, he had fallen asleep on his way home." Gauche screwed up his eyes and surveyed his audience with a sly glance. "Picard, of course, was furious—his tulips were crushed—and he said: 'Get up, monsieur, in our park lying in the flower beds is not allowed! We fine people for it, ten francs.' The reveler opened one eye and took a gold coin out of his pocket. 'There you are, old man,' he said, 'now leave me be. I haven't had such a wonderful rest in

ages.' Well, the gardener took the coin but did not go away. 'You have paid the fine, but I have no right to leave you here, monsieur. Be so good as to rise.' At this the gentleman in the tails opened both eyes, but he seemed in no haste to rise. 'How much do I have to pay you to get out of my sun? I'll pay any amount you like if you'll just stop pestering me and let me doze for an hour.' Old papa Picard scratched his head and moved his lips while figuring something out. 'Well then, sir,' he said eventually, 'if you wish to purchase an hour's rest lying in a flower bed in the Luxembourg Gardens, it will cost you eighty-four thousand francs and not a single sou less.' "
Gauche chuckled merrily into his gray mustache and shook his head, as if in admiration of the gardener's impudence. " 'And not a single sou less,' he said, so there! And let me tell you that this tipsy gentleman was no ordinary man, but the banker Laffite himself, the richest man in the whole of Paris. Laffitte was not in the habit of making idle promises; he had said 'any amount,' and now he was stuck with it. It would have been shameful for him to back down and break his word as a banker. Of course, he wasn't happy about simply giving away that kind of money to the first rascal he met. But what could he do about it?" Gauche shrugged, mimicking a state of total perplexity. "Then suddenly Laffitte ups and says: 'Right, you old scoundrel, you'll get your eighty-four thousand, but only on one condition: You have to prove to me that lying for an hour in your rotten flower bed is really worth the money. If you can't prove it, I'll get up this very moment and give you a good drubbing with my cane, and that bit of mischief will cost me a forty-franc administrative fine.' " Crazy Milford-Stokes laughed loudly and ruffled up his ginger mane in approval, but Gauche raised a yellow-stained finger as if to say: Don't be so hasty with your laughter; it's not the end yet. "And what do you think, ladies and gentlemen? Old papa Picard, not batting an eye, began adding up the balance: 'In half an hour, at precisely eight o'clock, monsieur the park director will arrive, see you in the flower bed, and start yelling at me to get you out of there. I shall not be able to do that, because you will have paid for a full hour, not half an hour. I shall get into an argument with monsieur the director, and he will kick me out of my job with no pension and no severance pay. I still have three years to go before I retire and take the pension due to

me, which is set at one thousand two hundred francs a year. I intend to live at my ease for twenty years, so altogether that makes twenty-four thousand francs already. Now for the matter of accommodation. They will throw me and my wife out of our municipal apartment. And then the question is— where are we going to live? We shall have to buy a house. Any modest little house somewhere in the Loire region will run to twenty thousand at least. Now, sir, consider my reputation. Forty years I've slaved away loyally in this park, and anyone will tell you that old papa Picard is an honest man. Then suddenly an incident like this brings shame on my old gray head. This is bribery, this is graft! I think a thousand francs for each year of irreproachable service would hardly be too much by way of moral compensation. So altogether it comes to exactly eighty-four thousand.' Laffitte laughed, stretched himself out a bit more comfortably in the flower bed, and closed his eyes again. 'Come back in an hour, you old rogue,' he said, 'and you'll be paid.' And that is my wonderful little story, ladies and gentlemen."

"So a year of faultless conduct went for a thousand f-francs?" the Russian diplomat said with a laugh. "Not so very expensive. Evidently with a discount for wholesale."

The company began a lively discussion of the story, expressing the most contradictory opinions, but Renate Kleber gazed curiously at M. Gauche as he opened his black file with a self-satisfied air and began rummaging through his papers. He was an intriguing specimen, this old grandpa, no doubt about it. And what secrets was he keeping in there? Why was he shielding the file with his elbow?

That question had been nagging at Renate for a long time. Once or twice she had tried to exploit her position as a mother-to-be by glancing over Gauche's shoulder as he conjured with that precious file of his, but the mustachioed boor had impudently slammed the file shut in the lady's face and even wagged his finger at her, as much as to say: Now that's not allowed.

Today, however, something remarkable happened. When M. Gauche, as usual, rose from the table ahead of the others, a sheet of paper slid silently out of his mysterious file and floated to the floor. Engrossed in some gloomy thoughts of his own, the rentier failed to notice it and left the salon. The door had scarcely closed behind him before Renate adroitly raised her body with its slightly thickened waist out of her chair. But she was not the only one to have been so observant. The well-brought-up Miss Stamp (such a nimble creature!) was the first to reach the scrap of paper.

"Ah, I think M. Gauche has dropped something!" she exclaimed, deftly grabbing up the scrap and fastening her beady eyes upon it. "I'll catch up to him and return it."

But Mme. Kleber was already clutching the edge of the paper in her tenacious fingers and had no intention of letting go.

"What is it?" she asked. "A newspaper clipping? How interesting!"

The next moment everyone in the room had gathered around the two ladies, except for the Japanese blockhead, who was still pumping the air with his fan, and Mrs. Truffo, who observed this flagrant invasion of privacy with a reproachful expression on her face.

The clipping read as follows:

"THE CRIME OF THE CENTURY": A NEW ANGLE?

The fiendish murder of ten people that took place the day before yesterday in the Rue de Grenelle continues to exercise the imagination of Parisians. Of the possible explanations proposed thus far, the two most prevalent are a maniacal doctor and a fanatical sect of bloodthirsty Hindu devotees of the god Shiva. However, in the course of conducting our own independent investigation, we at *Le Soir* have uncovered a circumstance that could possibly open up a new angle on the case. It would appear that in recent weeks the late Lord Littleby was seen at least twice in the company of the international adventuress Marie Sanfon, well known to the police forces of many countries. The Baron de M., a close friend of the murdered man, has informed us that his lordship was infatuated with a certain lady, and on the evening of the fifteenth of March had intended to set out for Spa for some kind of romantic rendezvous. Could this rendezvous, which was prevented by the most untimely attack of gout suffered by the unfortunate collector, possibly have been arranged with Mlle. Sanfon? The editors would not make so bold as to propose our own version of events, but we regard it as our duty to draw the attention of Commissioner Gauche to this noteworthy circumstance. You may expect further reports from us on this subject.

CHOLERA EPIDEMIC ON THE WANE

The municipal health authorities inform us that the foci of the cholera infection they have been combating energetically since the summer have finally been isolated. The vigorous prophylactic measures taken by the physicians of Paris have yielded positive results, and we may now hope that the epidemic of this dangerous disease, which began in July, is beg—

"What could that be about?" Renate asked, wrinkling up her brow in puzzlement. "Something about a murder, and cholera or something of the kind."

"Well, the cholera obviously has nothing to do with the matter," said Professor Sweetchild. "It's simply the way the page has been cut. The important thing, of course, is the murder in the Rue de Grenelle. Surely you must have heard about it? A sensational case—the newspapers were all full of it."

"I do not read the newspapers," Mme. Kleber replied with dignity. "In my condition it places too much strain on the nerves. And in any case I have no desire to learn about all sorts of unpleasant goings-on."

"Commissioner Gauche?" said Lieutenant Renier, peering at the clipping and running his eyes over the article once again. "Could that be our own M. Gauche?"

Miss Stamp gasped: "Oh, it couldn't be!"

At this point even the doctor's wife joined them. This was a genuine sensation and everyone started talking at once.

"The police, the French police, are involved in this!" Sir Reginald exclaimed excitedly.

Renier muttered: "So that's why the captain keeps asking me about the Windsor salon . . ."

M. Truffo translated as usual for his spouse, while the Russian took possession of the clipping and scrutinized it closely.

"That bit about the Indian fanatics is absolute nonsense," declared Sweetchild. "I made my opinion on that clear from the very beginning. In the first place, there is no bloodthirsty sect of followers of Shiva. And in the second place, everyone knows the statuette was recovered. Would a religious fanatic be likely to throw it into the Seine?"

"Yes, the business of the golden Shiva is a genuine riddle," said Miss Stamp with a nod. "They wrote that it was the jewel of Lord Littleby's collection. Is that correct, professor?"

The Indologist shrugged condescendingly.

"What can I say, madam? Lord Littleby only started collecting relatively recently, about twenty years ago. In such a short period, it is difficult to assemble a truly outstanding collection. They do say that the deceased did rather well out of the suppression of the Sepoy Mutiny of 1857. The notorious Shiva, for instance, was presented to the lord by a certain maharajah who was threatened with court-martial for intriguing with the insurgents. Littleby served for many years in the Indian military prosecutor's office, you know. Undoubtedly his collection includes quite a few valuable items, but the selection is rather chaotic."

"But do tell me, at least, why this lord of yours was killed," Renate demanded. "Look, M. Aono doesn't know anything about it, either, do you?" she asked, appealing for support to the Japanese, who was standing slightly apart from the others.

The Japanese smiled, moving only his lips, and bowed, and the Russian mock-applauded.

"Bravo, Mme. Kleber. You have quite c-correctly identified the most important question here. I have been following this case in the press. And in my opinion the reason behind the c-crime is more vital than anything else. That is where the key to the riddle lies. Precisely in the question of why. For what purpose were ten people killed?"

"Ah, but that is very simple!" said Miss Stamp, shrugging. "The plan was to steal everything that was most valuable from the collection. But the thief lost his head when he came face-to-face with the owner. After all, it had been assumed his lordship was not at home. It must be one thing to inject someone with a syringe, but quite another to smash a man's head open. Then again, I wouldn't know; I have never tried it." She twitched her shoulders. "The villain's nerves gave out and he left the job half finished. But as for the abandoned Shiva . . ." Miss Stamp pondered. "Perhaps *that* is the heavy object with which poor Littleby's brains were beaten out. It is quite possible that a criminal also has normal human feelings, and he found it repugnant or even simply frightening to hold the bloody murder weapon in his hand. So he walked as far as the embankment and threw it in the Seine."

"Concerning the murder weapon, that seems very probable," the diplomat agreed. "I th-think the same."

The old maid flushed brightly with pleasure and was clearly embarrassed when she caught Renate's mocking glance.

"You are saying quite outrageous things," the doctor's wife rebuked Clarissa Stamp. "Shouldn't we find a more suitable subject for table talk?"

But the colorless creature's appeal fell on deaf ears.

"In my opinion, the greatest mystery here is the death of the servants," said the lanky Indologist, keen to contribute to the analysis of the crime. "How did they come to allow themselves to be injected with such abominable muck? Not at pistol point, surely! After all, two of them were guards, and they were both carrying revolvers in holsters on their belts. That's where the mystery lies!"

"I have a hypothesis of my own," Renier announced with a solemn expression. "And I am prepared to defend it against any objections. The crime in the Rue de Grenelle was committed by a person who possesses exceptional mesmeric powers. The servants were in a state of mesmeric trance—that is the only possible explanation! Animal magnetism is a terrifying force. An experienced manipulator can do whatever he chooses with you. Yes, yes, madam," the lieutenant said, turning toward Mrs. Truffo, who had twisted her face into a doubtful grimace, "absolutely anything at all."

"Not if he is dealing with a lady," she replied primly.

Tired of playing the role of interpreter, Dr. Truffo wiped the sweat from his gleaming forehead with his handkerchief and rushed to the defense of the scientific worldview.

"I am afraid I must disagree with you," he started jabbering in his strongly accented French. "Mr. Mesmer's teaching has been exposed as having no scientific basis. The power of mesmerism or, as it is now known, hypnotism, has been greatly exaggerated. The honorable Mr. James Braid has proved conclusively that only psychologically suggestible individuals are subject to hypnotic influence, and then only if they have complete trust in the hypnotist and have agreed to allow themselves to be hypnotized."

"It is quite obvious, my dear doctor, that you have not traveled in the East!" said Renier, flashing his white teeth in a smile. "At any Indian bazaar, a fakir will show you miracles of mesmeric art that would make the most hardened skeptic gape in wonder. But those are merely tricks for showing off! Once in Kandahar I observed the public punishment of a thief. Under Muslim law, theft is punished by the amputation of the right hand, a procedure so intensely painful that those subjected to it frequently die from the shock. On this occasion the accused was a mere child, but since he had been caught for the second time, there was nothing else the judge could do; he had to sentence the thief to the penalty prescribed under Shariah law. The judge, however, was a merciful man. He sent for a dervish who was well known for his miraculous powers. The dervish took the convicted prisoner's head in his hands, looked into his eyes, and whispered something—and the boy became calm and stopped trembling. A strange smile appeared on his face, and did not leave it even when the executioner's ax severed his arm up to the very elbow! And I saw all this with my own eyes, I swear to you."

Renate grew angry. "Ugh—how horrible! You and your Orient, Charles. I am beginning to feel faint!"

"Forgive me, Mme. Kleber," said the lieutenant, taking fright. "I only wished to demonstrate that in comparison with that a few injections are child's play."

"Once again, I am afraid that I cannot agree with you—" The stubborn doctor was preparing to defend his point of view, but just at that moment the door of the salon swung open and in came either a rentier or a policeman—in short, M. Gauche.

Everybody turned toward him in consternation, as if they had been engaged in some action that was not entirely decent.

Gauche ran a keen gaze over their faces and spotted the ill-starred clipping in the hands of the diplomat. His face darkened.

"So that's where it is . . . I was afraid of that."

Renate went over to this old man with the gray mustache, looked his massive figure over mistrustfully up and down, and blurted out: "M. Gauche, are you really a policeman?"

"The same c-commissioner Gauche who was leading the investigation into the Crime of the Century?" asked Fandorin. (Yes, that was the Russian diplomat's name, Renate recalled.) "In that case, how are we to account for your masquerade, and in general for your p-presence on board?"

Gauche breathed hard for a few moments, raised his eyebrows, lowered them again, and reached for his pipe. He was obviously racking his brains in an effort to decide what to do.

"Please, sit down, ladies and gentlemen," said Gauche in an unfamiliar, imposing bass, and turned the key to lock the door behind him. "Since this is the way things have turned out, I shall have to be frank with you. Be seated, be seated, or else somebody's legs might just give way under them."

"What kind of joke is this, M. Gauche?" the lieutenant asked, annoyed. "By what right do you presume to command here, and in the presence of the captain's first mate?"

"That, my young man, is something the captain himself will explain to you," Gauche replied with a hostile sideways glance at Renier. "He knows what is going on here."

Renier dropped the matter and, following the others' example, took his place at the table.

The talkative, good-humored grumbler for whom Renate had taken the Parisian rentier was behaving differently now. A certain dignity had appeared in the broad set of his shoulders, his gestures had become imperious, his eyes had acquired a new, harder gleam. The mere fact that he could maintain a prolonged pause with such calm confidence said a great deal. The strange rentier's piercing gaze paused in turn on each person present in the room, and Renate saw some of them flinch under its weight. To be honest, even she was a little disturbed by it, but then she immediately felt ashamed of herself and tossed her head nonchalantly. He may be a police commissioner, but what of that? He was still an obese, short-winded old duffer and nothing more.

"Please do not keep us guessing any longer, M. Gauche," she said sarcastically. "Excitement is dangerous for me."

"There is probably only one person here who has cause for excitement," Gauche replied mysteriously. "But I shall come back to that. First, allow me to introduce myself to the honorable company once again. Yes, my name is Gustave Gauche, but I am not a rentier—alas, I have no investments from which to draw income. I am, ladies and gentlemen, a commissioner in the criminal police of the city of Paris, and I work in the department that deals with particularly serious and complicated crimes. The post I hold is entitled Investigator for Especially Important Cases." The commissioner pronounced the title with distinct emphasis.

The deadly silence in the salon was broken only by the hasty whispering of Dr. Truffo.

"What a scandal!" squeaked the doctor's wife.

"I was obliged to embark on this voyage, and to travel incognito because . . ." Gauche began puffing his cheeks in and out energetically in an effort to revive his half-extinguished pipe. ". . . because the Paris police have strong grounds for believing that the person who committed the crime in the Rue de Grenelle is on board the *Leviathan*."

"Ah!" The sigh rustled quietly round the salon.

"I presume you have already discussed the case, which is a mysterious one in many respects." The commissioner jerked his double chin in the direction of the newspaper clipping, which was still in Fandorin's hands. "And that is not all, mesdames et messieurs. I know for a fact that the murderer is traveling first-class . . ." (another collective sigh) ". . . and moreover, happens to be present in this salon at this very moment," Gauche concluded. He then seated himself in a satin-upholstered armchair by the window and folded his arms expectantly just below his silver watch chain.

"Impossible!" cried Renate, clutching involuntarily at her belly.

Lieutenant Renier leapt to his feet.

The ginger baronet began chortling and applauding demonstratively.

Professor Sweetchild gulped convulsively and removed his glasses.

Clarissa Stamp froze with her fingers pressed against the agate brooch on her soft collar.

Not a single muscle twitched in the face of the Japanese, but the polite smile instantly disappeared.

The doctor grabbed his wife by the elbow, forgetting to translate the most important thing of all, but to judge by the frightened expression in her staring eyes, Mrs. Truffo had guessed it for herself.

The Russian diplomat asked quietly, "What reasons do you have?"

"My presence here," the commissioner replied imperturbably, "is explanation enough. There are other considerations, but there is no need for you to know about them . . . Well, then"—there was a clear note of disappointment in the policeman's voice—"I see no one is about to swoon and cry out: 'Arrest me, I killed them!' But, of course, I was not really counting on that. So listen to me." He raised a stubby finger in warning. "None of the other passengers must be told about this. And it is not in your interests to tell them—the rumor would spread instantly, and people would start treating you like lepers. Do not attempt to transfer to a different salon—that will merely increase my suspicion. And you would not be able to do it; I have an arrangement with the captain."

Renate began babbling in a trembling voice.

"Dear M. Gauche, can you not at least spare me this nightmare? I am afraid to sit at the same table as a murderer. What if he sprinkles poison in my food? I shan't be able to swallow a single morsel now. You know, it's dangerous for me to be worried. I won't tell anyone, anyone at all, honestly!"

"My regrets, Mme. Kleber," the sleuth replied coolly, "but there can be no exceptions. I have grounds to suspect every person here, and not least of all you."

Renate threw herself against the back of her chair with a weak moan and Lieutenant Renier stamped his foot angrily: "You take too many liberties, monsieur . . . Investigator for Especially Important Cases! I shall report everything to Captain Cliff immediately."

"Go right ahead," said Gauche indifferently. "But not just at this moment; a bit later. I haven't quite finished my little speech yet. So as yet I do not know for certain which of you is my client, but I am close, very close, to my goal."

Renate expected these words to be followed by an eloquent glance, and she strained her entire body forward in anticipation. But no—the policeman was looking at his stupid pipe. He was probably lying and didn't have his eye on anyone in particular.

"You suspect a woman, it's obvious!" exclaimed Miss Stamp with a nervous flutter of her hands. "Otherwise why would you be carrying around a newspaper article about some Marie Sanfon? Who is this Marie Sanfon? And anyway, it doesn't matter who she is. It's plain stupid to suspect a woman! How could a woman ever be capable of such brutality?"

Mrs. Truffo rose abruptly to her feet, ready to rally to the banner of female solidarity.

"We shall speak of Mlle. Sanfon on some other occasion," the detective replied, giving Clarissa Stamp a mysterious look. "I have plenty of these little articles, and each of them contains its own version of events." He opened his file and rustled the newspaper clippings; there must have been several dozen of them. "Very well, mesdames et messieurs, I ask you please not to interrupt me anymore!" The policeman's voice had turned to iron. "Yes, there is a dangerous criminal among us. Possibly a psychopath." (Renate noticed the professor quietly shift his chair away from Sir Reginald.) "Therefore, I ask you all to be careful. If you notice something out of the ordinary, even the very slightest thing, come to me immediately. And it would be best, of course, if the murderer were to make a full and frank confession; there is no escape from here in any case. That is all I have to say."

Mrs. Truffo put her hand up like a pupil in school: "In fact I *did* see something extraordinary, only yesterday! A charcoal black face, definitely not human, looked in at me from outside while I was in our cabin! I was so scared!" She turned to her other half and jabbed him with her elbow: "I told you, but you paid no attention!"

"Oh," said Renate with a start, "and yesterday a mirror in a genuine tortoiseshell frame disappeared from my toiletry set."

Monsieur the Lunatic apparently also had something to report, but before he had a chance the commissioner slammed his file shut.

"Do not try to make a fool of me! I am an old bloodhound! You won't throw Gustave Gauche off the scent! If necessary, I shall have every one of you put ashore and we will deal with each of you separately! Ten people have been killed; this is not a joke. Think, mesdames et messieurs, think!"

He left the salon, slamming the door loudly behind him.

"Gentlemen, I am not feeling well," Renate declared in a weak voice. "I shall go to my cabin."

"I shall accompany you, Mme. Kleber," said Charles Renier, immediately leaping to her side. "This is simply intolerable! Such incredible insolence!"

Renate pushed him away.

"No thank you. I shall manage quite well on my own."

She walked unsteadily across the room and leaned against the wall by the door for a moment. In the corridor, which was empty, her stride quickened. Renate opened her cabin and went inside, took a travel bag out from under the bed, and thrust a trembling hand in under its silk lining. Her face was pale but determined. In an instant her fingers had located a small metal box.

Inside the box, glittering with cold glass and steel, lay a syringe.

Clarissa Stamp

THINGS HAD BEGUN to go wrong first thing in the morning, when Clarissa quite distinctly spotted two new wrinkles in the mirror—two fine, barely visible lines running from the corners of her eyes toward her temples. It was all the sun's fault. It was so bright here that no parasol or hat could save you. Clarissa spent a long time inspecting herself in that pitiless polished surface and stretching her skin with her fingers, hoping it might be the way she'd slept and that the wrinkles would smooth out. Just as she finished her inspection, she turned her neck and spotted a gray hair behind her ear. That really made her feel glum. Might it perhaps be the sun's fault too? Did hairs fade? Oh no, Miss Stamp, no point in deceiving yourself. As the poet said:

> *November's chill breath trimmed her braids with silver,*
> *Whispering that youth and love were lost forever.*

She took greater pains than usual with her appearance. The gray hair was mercilessly plucked out. It was stupid, of course. Wasn't it John Donne who said the secret of female happiness was knowing when to make the transition from one age to the next, and there were three ages of woman: daughter, wife, and mother? But how could she progress from the second state to the third when she had never been married?

The best cure for thoughts like that was a walk in the fresh air, and Clarissa set out to take a turn round the deck. Huge as *Leviathan* was, it had long since been measured out by her leisurely, even paces—at least the upper deck, which was intended for the first-class passengers. The distance round the perimeter was three hundred fifty-five paces. Seven and a half minutes, if she didn't pause to admire the sea or chat with casual acquaintances.

At this early hour none of her acquaintances were on deck, and Clarissa completed her promenade along the starboard side of the ship unhindered all the way to the stern. The ship was ploughing a smooth path through the brownish surface of the Red Sea and a lazy gray furrow extended from its powerful propeller right out to the horizon. Oh, but it was hot!

Clarissa looked enviously at the sailors polishing the copper fittings one level below. Lucky beasts, in nothing but their linen trousers—no bodice, no bloomers, no stockings with tight garters, no long dress. You couldn't help envying that outrageous Mr. Aono, swanning about the ship in his Japanese dressing gown, and no one in the least bit surprised, because he was an oriental.

She imagined herself lying in a canvas deck chair with absolutely nothing on. No, she could be in a light tunic, like a woman in ancient Greece. And it was perfectly normal. In a hundred years or so, when the human race finally rid itself of prejudice, it would be absolutely natural.

There was Mr. Fandorin riding toward her, the rubber tires on his American tricycle squeaking. They did say that kind of exercise was excellent for developing the elasticity of the muscles and strengthening the heart. The diplomat was dressed in a light sporting outfit: checked pantaloons, gutta-percha shoes with gaiters, a short jacket, and a white shirt with its collar unbuttoned. His bronzed face lit up in a friendly smile of greeting. Mr. Fandorin politely raised his cork helmet and went rustling by. He did not stop.

Clarissa sighed. The idea of a stroll had been a failure; all she had succeeded in doing was soak her underclothes with perspiration. She had to go back to her cabin and change.

Breakfast had been spoiled for Clarissa by that *poseuse* Mme. Kleber. What an incredible ability to transform her own weakness into a means of exploiting others! At the precise moment when the coffee in Clarissa's cup had cooled to the required temperature, that unbearable Swiss woman had complained that she felt stifled and asked for someone to loosen her bodice. Clarissa usually pretended not to hear Renate Kleber's whining and some male volunteer was always found for her, but a man was clearly not suitable for such a delicate task, and as luck would have it Mrs. Truffo was not there—she was helping her husband attend to some lady who had fallen ill. Apparently the tedious creature had previously worked as a nurse. What remarkable social climbing—straight up to the wife of the senior doctor and dining in first-class! And she tried to act like a real British lady, but somewhat overdid it.

Anyway, Clarissa had been forced to fuss with Mme. Kleber's laces, and in the meantime her coffee had gone completely cold. It was a trivial matter, of course, but it was that Kleber woman through and through.

After breakfast she went out for a walk, did ten circuits, and began feeling tired. Taking advantage of the fact that there was no one nearby, she peeped carefully in at the window of cabin number eighteen. Mr. Fandorin was sitting at the secretary, wearing a white shirt with red, white, and blue suspenders, a cigar clenched in the corner of his mouth. He was tapping noisily with his fingers on a bizarre black apparatus made of iron, with a round roller and a large number of keys. Clarissa was so intrigued that she let her guard down and was caught red-handed. The diplomat jumped to his feet, bowed, threw on his jacket, and came across to the open window.

"It's a Remington t-typewriter," he explained. "The very latest model, only just on sale. A most c-convenient device, Miss Stamp, and quite light. Two porters can carry it without any difficulty. Quite indispensable on a journey. You see, I am p-practising my stenography by copying out a piece of Hobbes."

Still red with embarrassment, Clarissa nodded slightly and walked away, then sat down under a striped awning close by. There was a fresh breeze blowing. She opened *The Charterhouse of Parma* and began reading about the selfless love of the beautiful but aging Duchess Sanseverina for the youthful Fabrice del Dongo. Moved to shed a sentimental tear, she wiped it away with her handkerchief, and, as if by design at that moment, Mr. Fandorin emerged on the deck, wearing a white suit with a broad-brimmed panama hat and carrying a cane. And looking exceptionally handsome.

Clarissa called to him. He approached, bowed, and sat down beside her. Glancing at the cover of her book, he said: "I am willing to b-bet that you skipped the description of the Battle of Waterloo. A pity—it is the finest passage in the whole of Stendhal. I have never read a more accurate description of war."

Strangely enough, Clarissa was indeed reading *The Charterhouse of Parma* for the second time, and both times she had simply leafed through the battle scene.

"How could you tell?" she asked curiously. "Are you a mind reader?"

"Women always skip battle scenes," said Fandorin with a shrug. "At least women of your temperament."

"And just what is my temperament?" Clarissa asked in a wheedling voice, feeling she cut a poor figure playing the coquette.

"An inclination to view yourself skeptically and the world around you romantically." He looked at her, his head inclined slightly to one side. "And specifically concerning yourself, I can say that recently there has been some kind of sudden change for the b-better in your life and that you have suffered some k-kind of shock."

Clarissa started and glanced at her companion with frank alarm.

"Don't be frightened," the astonishing diplomat reassured her. "I know absolutely nothing about you. It is simply that I have developed my powers of observation and analysis with the help of special exercises. Usually a single insignificant detail is enough for me to recreate the entire p-picture. Show me a charming button like that"—he pointed delicately to a large ornamental pink button on her jacket—"and I will tell you immediately who lost it—a very big pig or a very small elephant."

Clarissa smiled and asked: "And can you see right through absolutely everybody?"

"Not right through, but I do see a lot. For instance, what can you tell me about that gentleman over there?"

Fandorin pointed to a thickset man with a large mustache observing the shoreline through a pair of binoculars.

"That's Mr. Babble, he's—"

"Stop!" said Fandorin, interrupting her. "I'll try to guess myself."

He looked at Mr. Babble for about thirty seconds, then said: "He is traveling to the east for the first time. He married recently. A factory owner. Business is not going well; there is a whiff of imminent bankruptcy about the gentleman. He spends almost all his time in the billiard room, but he plays badly."

Clarissa had always prided herself on being observant, and she began inspecting Mr. Babble, the Manchester industrialist, more closely.

A factory owner? Well, that was possible to guess. If he was traveling first-class, he must be rich. It was clear from his face that he was no aristocrat. And he didn't look like a businessman, either, in that baggy frock coat, and his features lacked animation. All right, then.

Recently married? Well, that was simple enough—the ring on his third finger gleamed so brightly that it was obviously brand new.

Plays billiards a lot? Why was that? Aha, his jacket was smeared with chalk.

"What makes you think Mr. Babble is traveling to the East for the first time?" she asked. "Why is there a whiff of bankruptcy about him? And what is the basis for your assertion that he is a poor billiards player? Perhaps you have been there and seen him play?"

"No, I have not been in the b-billiard room, because I cannot stand pastimes that involve gambling, and I have never laid eyes on this gentleman before," Fandorin replied. "It is evident that he is traveling this way for the first time from the stubborn persistence with which he is studying the empty shoreline. Otherwise Mr. Babble would be aware that he will not see anything of interest on that side until we reach the Strait of Mandeb. That is one. This gentleman's business affairs must be going very badly, otherwise he would never have embarked on such a long journey, especially so soon after his wedding. A badger like that might leave his set if the end of the world is nigh, but certainly not before. That is two."

"What if he is taking a honeymoon voyage together with his wife?" asked Clarissa, knowing that Mr. Babble was traveling alone.

"And lingering forlornly on the deck like that, and loitering in the billiard room? And he plays quite incredibly badly—his jacket is all white at the front. Only absolutely hopeless players scrape their bellies along the edge of the table like that. That is three."

"Oh, all right, but what will you say about that lady over there?"

Clarissa, now completely engrossed in the game, pointed to Mrs. Blackpool, who was proceeding majestically along the deck, arm-in-arm with her female companion.

Fandorin scanned the estimable lady in question with a disinterested glance.

"With that one everything is written on the face. She is on her way back from England to join her husband. She has been to visit their grown-up children. Her husband is a military man. A colonel."

Mr. Blackpool was indeed a colonel in command of a garrison in some city or other in northern India. This was simply too much.

"Explain!" Clarissa demanded.

"Ladies of that kind do not travel to India on their own b-business, only to the places where their husbands are serving. She is not of the age to have embarked on a journey like this for the first time—so she must be returning. Why could she have traveled to England? Only in order to see her children. I am assuming her parents have already passed away. It is clear from her determined and domineering expression that she is a woman used to command. That is the look of the first lady of a garrison or a regiment. They are usually regarded as a level of command senior to the commanding officer himself. Perhaps you would like to know why she must be a colonel's wife? Well, because if she were a general's wife, she would be traveling first-class, and this lady, as you can see, has a silver badge. But let us not waste any more time on trifles." Fandorin leaned closer and whispered: "Let me tell you about that orangutan over there. A curious specimen."

The monkey-like gentleman who had halted beside Mr. Babble was M. Boileau, the former Windsor habitué who had forsaken the ill-fated salon in time and so slipped through Commissioner Gauche's net.

Speaking in a low voice directly into Clarissa's ear, the diplomat told her: "The man you see there is a criminal and a villain. Most probably a dealer in opium. He lives in Hong Kong and is married to a Chinese woman."

Clarissa burst into laughter.

"Well, you're really wide off the mark this time! That is M. Boileau from Lyon, a philanthropist and the father of eleven entirely French children. And he deals in tea, not opium."

"I rather think not," Fandorin replied calmly. "Look closely. His cuff is bent up and you can see the blue circle of a tattoo on his wrist. I have seen one like that before in a book about China. It is the mark of one of the Hong Kong triads, secret criminal societies. Any European who becomes a member of a triad must be a master criminal operating on a truly grand scale. And of course, he has to marry a Chinese woman. A single look at the face of this 'philanthropist' should make everything clear to you."

Clarissa didn't know whether to believe him or not, but Fandorin continued with a serious expression: "And that is by no means all, Miss Stamp. I can tell a lot about a person even if I am b-blindfolded—from the sounds that he makes and his smell. Why not test me for yourself?"

And, so saying, he untied his white satin necktie and handed it to Clarissa.

She fingered the fabric—it was dense and opaque—and then blindfolded the diplomat with it. As though by accident, she touched his cheek—it was smooth and hot.

The ideal candidate soon put in an appearance from the direction of the stern—the well-known suffragette Lady Campbell, making her way to India in order to collect signatures for her petition for married women to be given the vote. Mannish and massive, with cropped hair, she lumbered along the deck like a cart horse. He would never guess it was a lady and not a boatswain.

"Right, who is this coming our way?" Clarissa asked, choking in anticipatory laughter.

Alas, her merriment was short-lived.

Fandorin wrinkled up his brow and began tossing out staccato phrases.

"A skirt hem rustling. A woman. A heavy stride. A strong c-character. Elderly. Plain. Smokes tobacco. Short-cropped hair."

"Why does she have short-cropped hair?" Clarissa squealed, covering her eyes and listening carefully to the suffragette's elephantine footfall. How, how did he do it?

"If a woman smokes, she must have bobbed hair and be progressive in her views," Fandorin declared in a firm voice. "And this one also despises fashion and wears a kind of shapeless robe, bright green with a scarlet belt."

Clarissa was dumbstruck. It was absolutely incredible! She took her hands away from her eyes in superstitious terror and saw that Fandorin had already removed the necktie and even retied it in an elegant knot. The diplomat's blue eyes were sparkling merrily.

It was all very pleasant, but then the conversation ended badly. When she stopped laughing, Clarissa very delicately broached the subject of the Crimean War and what a tragedy it had been both for Europe and Russia. She cautiously recalled her own memories of the time, remembering them as somewhat more infantile than they were in reality. She was anticipating reciprocal confidences, and hoping to learn exactly how old Fandorin really was. Her worst fears were confirmed.

"I was not b-born yet then," he confessed, artlessly clipping Clarissa's wings.

After that everything went from bad to worse. Clarissa had tried to turn the conversation to painting, but she got everything so mixed up that she couldn't even explain properly why the pre-Raphaelites had called themselves pre-Raphaelites. He must have thought her an absolute idiot. Ah, but what difference did it make now?

AS SHE WAS making her way back to her cabin, feeling sad, something terrifying happened.

She saw a gigantic black shadow quivering in a dark corner of the corridor. Clutching at her heart, Clarissa let out an immodest squeal and made a dash for her own door. Once she was in her cabin, it was a long time before she could calm her wildly beating heart. What was that thing? Neither man nor beast. Some concretion of evil, destructive energy. Her guilty conscience. The phantom of her Paris nightmare.

No more, she told herself, she had put all that behind her. It was nothing. It was delirium, a delusion, nothing more. She had sworn she would not torment herself with remorse. This was a new life, bright and happy—"And may your mansion be illumined by the lamp of bliss."

To soothe her nerves, she put on her most expensive day dress, the one she had not even tried on yet (white Chinese silk with a pale green bow at the back of the waist) and put her emerald necklace around her neck. She admired the gleam of the stones.

Very well, so she wasn't young. Or beautiful, either. But she was far from stupid, and she had money. And that was much better than being an ugly, aging fool without a penny to her name.

Clarissa entered the salon at precisely two o'clock, but the entire company was already assembled. Strangely enough, rather than fragmenting the Windsor contingent, the commissioner's astounding announcement of the previous day had brought them all closer together. A common secret that cannot be shared with anyone else binds people to one another more tightly than a common cause or a common interest. Clarissa noticed that her fellow diners now gathered around the table in advance of the times set for breakfast, lunch, five o'clock tea, and dinner, and lingered on afterward, something that had hardly ever happened before. Even the captain's first mate, who was only indirectly involved in the whole affair, spent a lot of time sitting on in the Windsor salon with the others rather than hurrying off about his official business (but then, of course, the lieutenant might possibly be acting on the captain's orders). It was as though the Windsorites had joined some elite club that was closed to the uninitiated. Several times Clarissa caught swift, stealthy glances being cast in her direction. Glances that could mean one of two things: "Are you the murderer?" or "Have you guessed I am the murderer?" Every time it happened, she felt a sweet trembling sensation welling up from somewhere deep inside, from the very depths of her, a pungent cocktail of fear and excitement. The image of the Rue de Grenelle rose up clearly before her eyes, the way it looked in the evening: beguilingly quiet and deserted, with the bare branches of the black chestnut trees swaying against the sky. God forbid the commissioner should somehow find out about the Ambassador Hotel. The very thought of it terrified Clarissa, and she cast a furtive glance in the policeman's direction.

Gauche presided at the table like the high priest of a secret sect. They were all constantly aware of his presence and followed the expression on his face out of the corner of their eyes, but Gauche appeared not to notice that at all. He assumed the role of a genial philosopher happy to relate his "little stories" while the others listened tensely.

By unspoken agreement, *that* was discussed only in the salon, and only in the commissioner's presence. If two Windsorites chanced to meet somewhere in neutral territory—in the music salon, on the deck, in the reading hall—they did not discuss *that* under any circumstances. And not even in the salon did they return to the tantalizing subject on every occasion. It usually happened spontaneously, following some entirely chance remark.

Today at breakfast, for instance, a general conversation had completely failed to materialize, but now as Clarissa took her seat the discussion was in full swing. She began studying the menu with a bored expression on her face, as though she had forgotten what she had ordered for lunch, but she could already feel that familiar tingle of excitement.

"The thing that bothers me about the crime," Dr. Truffo was saying, "is the complete pointlessness of it. Apparently all those people were killed for absolutely nothing. The golden Shiva ended up in the Seine, and the killer was left empty-handed."

Fandorin rarely participated in these discussions, preferring to remain silent most of the time, but for once even he felt compelled to express an opinion.

"That is not quite true. The p-perpetrator was left with the shawl."

"What shawl?" asked the doctor, confused.

"The painted Indian shawl. In which, if we are to believe the newspapers, the killer wrapped the stolen Shiva."

This joke was greeted with rather nervous laughter.

The doctor gestured expressively.

"But a mere shawl . . ."

Sweetchild gave a sudden start and raised his spectacles from his nose, a gesture of his that indicated intense agitation.

"No, don't laugh! I made enquiries as to exactly which shawl was stolen. And it is, gentlemen, an extremely unusual piece of material with a story of its own. Have you ever heard of the Emerald Rajah?"

"Wasn't he some kind of legendary Indian nabob?" asked Clarissa.

"Not legendary, but quite real, madam. It was the name given to Bagdassar, the ruler of the principality of Brahmapur. The principality is located in a large, fertile valley, surrounded on all sides by mountains. The rajahs trace their line of descent from the great Babur and are adherents of Islam, but that did not prevent them from reigning in peace for three hundred years over a little country in which the majority of the population are Hindus. Despite the difference in religion between the ruling caste and their subjects, the principality never suffered a single rebellion or feud. The rajahs prospered and grew rich, and by Bagdassar's time the house of Brahmapur was regarded as the wealthiest in the whole of India after the nizams of Hyderabad, whose wealth, as you are no doubt aware, eclipses that of every monarch in the world, including Queen Victoria and the Russian emperor Alexander."

"The greatness of our queen does not consist in the extent of her personal fortune, but in the prosperity of her subjects," Clarissa remarked primly, stung by the professor's remark.

"Undoubtedly," agreed Sweetchild, who was already in full swing and not to be halted. "However, the wealth of the rajahs of Brahmapur was of a very special kind. They did not hoard gold; they did not stuff trunks to overflowing with silver; they did not build palaces of pink marble. No, for three hundred years these rulers knew only one passion—precious stones. Do you know what the Brahmapur Standard is?"

"Isn't it a style of faceting diamonds?" Dr. Truffo asked uncertainly.

"The Brahmapur Standard is a jewelers' term referring to a diamond, sapphire, ruby, or emerald that is faceted in a particular manner and is the size of a walnut, which corresponds to one hundred and sixty *tandool*s; in other words, it is eighty carats in weight."

"But that is very large," Renier exclaimed in amazement. "Stones as large as that are very rare. If my memory does not deceive me, even the Regent diamond, the glory of the French state jewels, is not very much larger."

"No, lieutenant, the Pitt diamond, also known as the Regent, is almost twice as large," the professor corrected him with an air of authority, "but eighty carats is still a considerable size, especially if one is dealing with stones of the first water. But can you believe, ladies and gentlemen, that Bagdasssar had five hundred and twelve such stones, and all of absolutely irreproachable quality!"

"That's impossible!" exclaimed Sir Reginald.

Fandorin asked: "Why exactly five hundred and t-twelve?"

"Because of the sacred number eight," Sweetchild gladly explained. "Five hundred and twelve is eight times eight times eight, that is, eight to the power of three or eight cubed, the so called 'ideal number.' There is here, undoubtedly, some influence from Buddhism, in which the number eight is regarded with particular reverence. In the northeastern part of India, where Brahmapur lies, religions are intertwined in the most bizarre fashion imaginable. But the most interesting thing of all is where this treasure was kept, and how."

"And where was it kept?" Renate Kleber inquired curiously.

"In a simple clay casket without any adornment whatever. In 1852 I visited Brahmapur as a young archeologist and met the rajah Bagdassar. An ancient temple had been discovered in the jungle within the principality, and the rajah invited me to assess the significance of the find. I carried out the necessary research, and what do you think I discovered? The temple turned out to have been built in the time of King Chandragupta, when—"

"Stop, stop, stop!" the commissioner interrupted. "You can tell us about archeology some other time. Let's get back to the rajah."

"Ah, yes indeed," said the professor, fluttering his eyelashes. "That really would be best. Well then, the rajah was pleased with me and as a token of his favor he showed me his legendary casket. Oh, I shall never forget the sight!" Sweetchild narrowed his eyes as he continued: "Imagine a dark dungeon with only a single torch burning in a bronze bracket beside the door. The rajah and I were alone; his retainers remained outside the massive door, which was protected by a dozen guards. I got no clear impression of the interior of this treasure house, since my eyes had no time to adjust to the semidarkness. I only heard the locks clanging as his highness opened them. Then Bagdassar turned to me and in his hands I saw a cube that was the color of earth and appeared to be very heavy. It was the size of . . ." Sweetchild opened his eyes and looked around. Everyone was sitting and listening with bated breath, and Renate Kleber had even parted her lips like a child. "Oh, I don't know. I suppose about the size of Miss Stamp's hat, if one were to place that piece of headgear in a square box." As though on command, everyone turned and began staring curiously at the diminutive Tyrolean hat decorated with a pheasant feather. Clarissa endured this public scrutiny with a dignified smile, in the manner she had been taught as a child. "This cube resembled most closely one of the ordinary clay bricks they use for building in those parts. His highness later explained to me that the coarse, dull uniformity of the clay surface made a far better foil than gold or ivory for the magnificent glimmering light of the stones. Indeed, I was able to see that for myself when Bagdassar slowly raised a hand studded with rings to the lid of the casket, then opened it with a rapid movement and . . . I was blinded, ladies and gentlemen!" The professor's voice quavered. "It . . . it is impossible to express it in words! Picture to yourselves a mysterious, multicolored, lambent radiance spilling out of that dark cube and painting the gloomy vaults of that dungeon with shimmering patches of rainbow-colored light! The round stones were arranged in eight layers, and in each layer were sixty-four faceted sources of quite unbearable brilliance! And the effect was certainly enhanced by the flickering flame of the solitary torch. I can still see Rajah Bagdassar's face bathed from below in that magical light . . ."

The professor closed his eyes again and fell silent.

"And how much, for instance, are these glass baubles worth?" the commissioner's rasping voice inquired.

"Yes, indeed, how much?" Mme. Kleber repeated enthusiastically. "Say, in your English pounds?"

Clarissa heard Mrs. Truffo whisper rather loudly to her husband: "She's so vulgar!" But even so she pushed her mousy curls back off her ear in order not to miss a single word.

"You know," Sweetchild said with a genial smile, "I've often wondered about that. It's not an easy question to answer, since the value of precious stones fluctuates according to the market, but as things stand today—"

"Yes, please, as things stand today, not in the time of King Chandragupta," Gauche put in gruffly.

"Hmm . . . I don't know exactly how many diamonds, how many sapphires, and how many rubies the rajah had. But I do know that he valued emeralds most of all, which was how he acquired his popular name. In the course of his reign seven emeralds were acquired from Brazil and four from the Urals, and for each of them Bagdassar gave one diamond and some additional payment. You see, each of his ancestors had a favorite type of stone he preferred to all others and tried to acquire in greater numbers. The magical number of five hundred and twelve stones had already been reached in the time of Bagdassar's grandfather, and since then the ruler's primary goal had not been to increase the number of stones, but to improve their quality. Stones that fell even slightly short of perfection or that the current ruler did not favor for some reason, were sold—hence the fame of the Brahmapur Standard, which gradually spread around the world. Their place in the casket was taken by other, more valuable stones. Bagdassar's ancestors carried their obsession with the Brahmapur Standard to quite insane lengths. One of them purchased a yellow sapphire weighing three hundred *tandool*s from the Persian shah Abbas the Great, paying ten caravans of ivory for this marvel, but the stone was larger than the standard size and the rajah had his jewelers cut away all the excess!"

"That is terrible, of course," said the commissioner, "but let us get back to the question of the stones' value."

This time, however, it proved less easy to direct the flow of the Indologist's speech into the required channel.

"The question of value can wait for a moment!" he said, peremptorily dismissing the detective's request. "Is it really so important? When one considers a noble stone of such size and quality, the first thing that comes to mind is not money but the magical properties that have been attributed to it since ancient times. The diamond, for instance, is considered a symbol of purity. Our ancestors used to test their wives' fidelity by placing a diamond under their sleeping spouse's pillow. If she was faithful, she would immediately, without waking, turn to her husband and embrace him. If she was unfaithful, she would toss and turn and attempt to throw the diamond to the floor. And the diamond is also reputed to guarantee its owner's invincibility. The ancient Arabs used to believe that in battle the general who owned the larger diamond would be victorious."

"Ancient Arab mistaken," said Gintaro Aono, interrupting the inspired speaker in full flow.

Everyone stared in astonishment at the Japanese, who very rarely joined in the general conversation and never interrupted anyone. The oriental continued hastily in that odd accent of his.

"In the Academy of St. Cyr we were taught that the duke of Burgundy Charles the Bold speciarry took the huge Sancy diamond with him into battle against the Swiss, but it did not save him from defeat."

Clarissa felt sorry for the poor devil—making a rare attempt to show off his knowledge at such an inopportune moment.

The Japanese gentleman's remark was greeted with deadly silence, and Aono blushed in painful embarrassment.

"Yes, indeed, Charles the Bold," the professor said with a sharp nod of dissatisfaction, and he concluded without his former ardor. "The sapphire symbolizes devotion and constancy; the emerald confers improved sharpness of vision and foresight; the ruby protects against illness and the evil eye . . . But you were asking about the value of Bagdassar's treasures?"

"I realize it must be an incredibly large sum, but could you at least give us an approximate idea of how many zeros, at least?" Mme. Kleber enunciated clearly, as if she were addressing a dull-witted pupil, demonstrating yet again that once a banker's wife, always a banker's wife.

Clarissa would have enjoyed listening to more on the subject of the magical properties of precious stones and would have preferred to avoid talk of money. Apart from anything else, it was so vulgar.

"Very well, then, let me just add it up." Sweetchild took a pencil out of his pocket and poised himself to write on a paper napkin. "Formerly the diamond was considered the most expensive stone, but since the discovery of the South African fields it has fallen significantly in value. Large sapphires are found more often than other precious stones, and so on average they are only worth a quarter as much as diamonds, but that does not apply to yellow and star sapphires, and they made up the majority of Bagdassar's collection. Pure rubies and emeralds of great size are also rare and have a higher value than diamonds of the same weight . . . Very well, for simplicity's sake, let us assume all five hundred and twelve stones are diamonds, and all of the same value. Each of them, as I have already said, weighs eighty carats. According to Tavernier's formula, which is used by jewelers all over the world, the value of a single stone is calculated by taking the market value of a one-carat diamond and multiplying it by the square of the number of carats in the stone concerned. That would give us . . . a one-carat diamond costs about fifteen pounds on the Antwerp exchange. Eighty squared is six thousand four hundred. Multiply by fifteen . . . mmm . . . ninety-six thousand pounds sterling—so that is the value of an average stone from the Brahmapur casket. Multiply by five hundred and twelve . . . about fifty million pounds sterling. And in actual fact even more, because, as I have already explained, colored stones of such a great size are more valuable than diamonds," Sweetchild concluded triumphantly.

"Fifty million pounds? As much as that?" Renier asked in a voice suddenly hoarse. "But that's a billion and a half francs!"

Clarissa caught her breath, all thoughts of the romantic properties of precious stones driven out of her head by astonishment at this astronomical figure.

"Fifty million! But that's half the annual budget of the entire British Empire!" she gasped.

"That's three Suez Canals!" mumbled the redheaded Milford-Stokes. "Or even more!"

The commissioner also took a napkin and became absorbed in some calculations of his own.

"It is my salary for three hundred thousand years," he announced in dismay. "Are you not exaggerating, Professor? The idea of some petty native princeling possessing such immense wealth!"

Sweetchild replied as proudly as if all the treasure of India belonged to him personally.

"Why, that's nothing! The jewels of the nizam of Hyderabad are estimated to be worth three hundred million, but of course you couldn't get them all into one little casket. In terms of compactness, certainly, Bagdassar's treasure had no equal."

Fandorin touched the Indologist's sleeve discreetly.

"Nonetheless, I p-presume this sum is rather abstract in nature. Surely no one would be able to sell such a huge number of gigantic p-precious stones all at once? It would bring down the market price."

"You are mistaken to think so, monsieur diplomat," the scholar replied with animation. "The prestige of the Brahmapur Standard is so great that there would be no shortage of buyers. I am certain that at least half the stones would not even leave India—they would be bought by the local princes, in the first instance by the nizam, whom I have already mentioned. The remaining stones would be fought over by the banking houses of Europe and America, and the monarchs of Europe would not let slip the chance to add the masterpieces of Brahmapur to their treasuries. Oho, if he had wished, Bagdassar could have sold the contents of his casket in a matter of weeks."

"You keep referring to this man in the p-past tense," remarked Fandorin. "Is he dead? And, if so, what happened to the casket?"

"Alas, that is something nobody knows. Bagdassar's own end was tragic. During the Sepoy Mutiny the rajah was incautious enough to enter into secret dealings with the rebels, and the vice-regent declared Brahmapur enemy territory. There was malicious talk of Britannia simply wishing to get its hands on Bagdassar's treasure, but of course it was untrue. That is not the way we English go about things."

"Oh, yes," nodded Renier with a dark smile, exchanging glances with the commissioner.

Clarissa stole a cautious glance at Fandorin—surely he could not also be infected with the bacillus of Anglophobia? The Russian diplomat, however, sat there with an air of absolute equanimity.

"A squadron of dragoons was dispatched to Bagdassar's palace. The rajah attempted to escape by fleeing to Afghanistan, but the cavalry overtook him at the Ganges crossing. Bagdassar considered it beneath his dignity to submit to arrest and he took poison. The casket was not found on him; in fact, he had with him nothing but a small bundle containing a note in English. In the note, which was addressed to the British authorities, the rajah swore that he was innocent and requested them to forward the bundle to his only son. The boy was studying in a boarding school somewhere in Europe—it's the thing among Indian grandees of the new breed. I should mention that Bagdassar was no stranger to the spirit of civilization; he visited London and Paris several times. He even married a Frenchwoman."

"Oh, how unusual!" Clarissa exclaimed. "To be an Indian rajah's wife! What became of her?"

"Never mind the damned wife, tell us about the bundle," the commissioner said impatiently. "What was in it?"

"Absolutely nothing of any interest," said the professor with a regretful shrug of his shoulders. "A volume of the Koran. But the casket disappeared without a trace, although it was looked for everywhere."

"And was it a perfectly ordinary Koran?" asked Fandorin.

"It could hardly have been more ordinary: printed by a press in Bombay, with devout comments in the deceased's own hand in the margins. The squadron commander decided that the Koran could be forwarded as requested, and for himself he took only the shawl in which it was wrapped as a souvenir of the expedition. The shawl was later acquired by Lord Littleby for his collection of Indian paintings on silk."

To clarify the point, the commissioner asked: "So that is the same shawl in which the murderer wrapped the Shiva?"

"The very same. It is genuinely unusual. Made of the very finest silk, almost weightless. The painting is rather trivial—an image of the bird of paradise, the sweet-voiced Kalavinka. But it possesses two unique features that I have never encountered in any other Indian shawl. First, where Kalavinka's eye should be is a hole, the edges of which have been sewn up very carefully with brocade thread. Second, the shawl itself is an interesting shape—not rectangular, but tapering. A sort of irregular triangle, with two crooked sides and one absolutely straight."

"Is the shawl of any g-great value?" asked Fandorin.

"All this talk about the shawl is boring," complained Mme. Kleber, sticking out her lower lip capriciously. "Tell us more about the jewels! They ought to have searched a bit more thoroughly."

Sweetchild laughed.

"Oh, madam, you cannot even imagine how thoroughly the new rajah searched for them. He was one of the local *zamindar*s who had rendered us invaluable service during the Sepoy Mutiny and received the throne of Brahmapur as a reward. But greed unhinged the poor man's mind. Some wit whispered to him that Bagdassar had hidden the casket in the wall of one of the buildings. And since in size and appearance the casket looked exactly like an ordinary clay brick, the new rajah ordered all buildings constructed of that material to be taken apart. The houses were demolished one after another and each brick was smashed under the personal supervision of the new ruler. Bearing in mind that in Brahmapur ninety percent of all structures are built of clay bricks, in a few months a flourishing city was transformed into a heap of ruins. The insane rajah was poisoned by his own retainers, who feared a popular revolt even more fierce than the Sepoy Mutiny."

"Serve him right, the Judas," Renier declared with feeling. "Nothing is more abominable than treachery."

Fandorin patiently repeated his question: "But nonetheless, Professor, is the shawl of any g-great value?"

"I think not. It is more of a rarity, a curiosity."

"But why are things always b-being wrapped in it—first the Koran, and then the Shiva? Could this piece of silk perhaps have some ritual significance?"

"I've never heard of anything of the sort. It is simply a coincidence."

Commissioner Gauche got to his feet with a grunt and straightened his numbed shoulders.

"Mm, yes, an entertaining story, but unfortunately it has nothing to contribute to our investigation. The murderer is unlikely to be keeping this piece of cloth as a sentimental souvenir. It would be handy if he was, though," he mused. "One of you, my dear suspects, simply takes out a silk shawl with a picture of the bird of paradise—out of sheer absent-mindedness—and blows his nose into it. Old papa Gauche would know what to do then, all right."

The detective laughed, clearly in the belief that his joke was very witty. Clarissa gave the vulgar lout a disapproving look.

Catching her glance, the commissioner narrowed his eyes.

"By the way, Mademoiselle Stamp, about your wonderful hat. A very stylish item, the latest Parisian chic. Is it long since your last visit to Paris?"

Clarissa braced herself and replied in an icy tone, "The hat was bought in London, commissioner. And I have never been to Paris."

What was Mr. Fandorin staring at so intensely? Clarissa followed the line of his gaze and turned pale.

The diplomat was studying her ostrich-feather fan, and the words inscribed in gold on its ivory handle: *"Meilleurs souvenirs! Hotel AMBASSADEUR. Rue de Grenelle, Paris."*

What an appalling blunder!

Gintaro Aono

The fifth day of the fourth month,
in sight of the Eritrean coast

Below—the green stripe of the sea,
Between—the yellow stripe of sand,
Above—the blue stripe of the sky.
Such are the colors
Of Africa's flag.

This trivial pentastich is the fruit of my hour-and-a-half-long efforts to attain a state of inner harmony—the confounded harmony that has stubbornly refused to be restored.

I have been sitting alone on the stern, watching the dreary coastline of Africa and feeling my infinite isolation more acutely than ever. I can at least be thankful that the noble habit of keeping a diary was instilled in me from childhood. Seven years ago, as I set out to study in the remote country of Furansu, I dreamed in secret that one day the diary of my travels would be published as a book and bring fame to me and the entire clan of Aono. But alas, my intellect is too imperfect and my feelings are far too ordinary for these pitiful pages ever to rival the great diaristic literature of former times.

And yet if not for these daily entries I should certainly have gone insane long ago.

Even here, on board a ship traveling to East Asia, there are only two representatives of the yellow race—myself and a Chinese eunuch, a court official of the eleventh rank who has visited Paris to obtain the latest perfumes and cosmetics products for the Empress Dowager Tz'u Hsi. For the sake of economy he is traveling second-class, of which he is greatly ashamed, and our conversation was broken off the moment it emerged that I am traveling first-class. What a disgrace for China! In the court official's place I should certainly have died of humiliation, for on this European vessel each of us is the representative of a great Asian power. I understand courtier Chan's state of mind, but it is nonetheless a pity that he feels too ashamed even to leave his cramped cabin—there are things we could have talked about. That is, although we could not talk about them, we could communicate with the aid of ink, brush, and paper, for while we speak different languages, we use the same hieroglyphs.

Never mind, I tell myself, hold on. The difficulties remaining are mere trifles. In a month or so you will see the lights of Nagasaki, and from there it is a mere stone's throw to your hometown of Kagoshima. And what do I care that my return promises me only humiliation and disgrace, that I shall be the laughingstock of all my friends? For I shall be home once again, and, after all, no one will dare to express his contempt for me openly, since everyone knows that I was carrying out my father's will, and that orders are not a matter for discussion. I have done what I had to do, what my duty obliged me to do. My life may be ruined, but if that is what the welfare of Japan requires . . . But enough, no more of that!

And yet who could have imagined that returning to my homeland, the final stage of my seven-year ordeal, would prove so hard? In France at least I could take my food alone, I could delight in solitary walks and communing with nature. But here on the ship I feel like a grain of rice that has fallen by accident into a bowl of noodles. Seven years of life among the red-haired barbarians have failed to inure me to some of their disgusting habits. When I see the fastidious Kleber-san cut a bloody beefsteak with her knife and then lick her red-stained lips with her pink tongue, it turns my stomach. And these English washbasins in which you have to plug the drain and wash your face in contaminated water! And those appalling clothes, the invention of some perverted mind! They make you feel like a carp wrapped in greased paper, being roasted over hot coals. Most of all I hate the starched collars that leave a red rash on your chin and the leather shoes, a genuine instrument of torture. Exploiting my position as an "oriental savage," I take the liberty of strolling around the deck in a light *yukata*, while my unfortunate dining companions stew in their clothes from morning till night. My sensitive nostrils suffer greatly from the smell of European sweat, so harsh, greasy, and fleshy. Equally terrible is the round-eyes' habit of blowing their noses into handkerchiefs and then putting them back into their pockets, together with the mucus, then taking them out and blowing heir noses into them again. They will simply not believe it at home; they will think I have made it all up. But then, seven years is a long time. Perhaps by now our ladies are also wearing those ridiculous bustles on their hindquarters and tottering along on high heels. It would be interesting to see how Kyoko-san would look in a costume like that. After all, she is quite grown up now—thirteen years old already. In another year or two they will marry us. Or perhaps it will happen even sooner. Oh, to be home soon!

Today I found it especially difficult to attain inner harmony because:

1. I discovered that my finest instrument, capable of easily cutting through the very thickest muscle, has been stolen from my travel bag. What does this strange theft mean?

2. At lunch I once again found myself in a position of humiliation—far worse than the incident with Charles the Bold (see my entry for yesterday). Fandorin-san, who continues as before to be very curious concerning Japan, began questioning me about Bushido and samurai traditions. The conversation moved on to my family and my ancestors. Since I had introduced myself as an officer, the Russian began to question me about the weapons, uniforms, and service regulations of the Imperial Army. It was terrible! When it emerged that I had never even heard of the Berdan rifle, Fandorin-san looked at me very strangely. He must have thought the Japanese army is staffed with absolute ignoramuses. In my shame I completely forgot my manners and ran out of the salon, which of course only rendered the incident even more embarrassing.

It was a long time before I was able to settle my nerves. First I went up onto the boat deck, which is deserted because the sun is at its fiercest there. I stripped to my loincloth and for half an hour practiced the kicking technique of *mawashi-geri*. When I had reached the right condition and the sun began to look pink, I seated myself in the *ʒa-ʒen* pose and attempted to meditate for forty minutes. And only after that did I dress myself and go to the stern to compose a *tanka*.

All of these exercises were helpful. Now I know how to save face. At dinner I shall tell Fandorin-san that we are forbidden to talk to strangers about the Imperial Army and that I ran out of the salon in such haste because I am suffering from terrible diarrhea. I think that will sound convincing and in the eyes of my neighbors at table I shall not appear to be an ill-mannered savage.

The evening of the same day

So much for harmony! Something quite catastrophic has happened. My hands are trembling in shame, but I must immediately note down all the details. It will help me to concentrate and make the correct decision. To begin with, only the facts; conclusions later.

And so.

Dinner in the Windsor salon began as usual at eight o'clock. Although during the afternoon I had ordered red-beet salad, the waiter brought me bloody, half-raw beef. Apparently he thought I had said "red beef." I prodded the slaughtered animal's flesh, still oozing blood, and observed with secret envy the captain's first mate, who was eating a most appetizing vegetable stew with lean chicken.

What else happened?

Nothing out of the ordinary. Kleber-san, as always, was complaining of a migraine but eating with a voracious appetite. She looks the very picture of health, a classic example of an easy pregnancy. I am sure that when her time comes the child will pop out of her like a cork out of sparkling French wine.

There was talk of the heat, of tomorrow's arrival in Aden, of precious stones. Fandorin-san and I discussed the relative advantages of Japanese and English gymnastics. I found myself in a position to be condescending, since in this sphere the superiority of the East over the West is self-evident. The difference, of course, is that for them physical exercise is sport, a game, but for us it is the path to spiritual self-improvement. It is spiritual improvement that is important—physical perfection is of no importance, it is automatically dragged along behind, as carriages follow a steam locomotive. I should mention that the Russian is very interested in sport and has even heard something of the martial-arts schools of Japan and China. This morning I was meditating on the boat deck earlier than usual and I saw Fandorin-san there. We merely bowed to each other and did not enter into conversation, because each of us was occupied with his own business: I was bathing my soul in the light of the new day, while he, dressed in gymnast's tights, was performing squats and push-ups with each arm in turn and lifting weights that appeared to be very heavy.

Our common interest in gymnastics rendered our evening conversation unforced, and I felt more relaxed than usual. I told the Russian about jujitsu. He listened with unflagging interest.

At about half past eight (I did not notice the precise time), Kleber-san, having drunk her tea and eaten two cakes, complained of feeling dizzy. I told her that this happens to pregnant women when they eat too much. For some reason she evidently took offence at my words and I realized that I had spoken out of turn. How many times have I sworn not to do so? After all, I was taught by wise teachers: When you find yourself in strange company, sit, listen, smile pleasantly, and from time to time nod your head— you will acquire the reputation of being a well-bred individual, and at the very least you will not say anything stupid. It is not the place of an "officer" to be giving medical advice!

Renier-san immediately leapt to his feet and volunteered to accompany the lady to her cabin. He is in general a most considerate man, and especially with Kleber-san. He is the only one who is not yet sick of her interminable caprices. He stands up for the honor of his uniform; I applaud him.

When they left, the men moved to the armchairs and began smoking. The ship's Italian doctor and his English wife went to visit a patient and I attempted to impress upon the waiter that they should not put either bacon or ham in my omelette for breakfast. After so many days, they should have grown used to the idea by now.

Perhaps about two minutes later we suddenly heard a woman's high-pitched scream.

First, I did not immediately realize it was Kleber-san screaming. Second, I did not understand that her bloodcurdling scream of "Oscure! Oscure!" meant *"Au secours! Au secours!"* But that does not excuse my behavior. I acted disgracefully, quite disgracefully. I am unworthy of the title of samurai!

But everything in order.

The first to reach the door was Fandorin-san, followed by the commissioner of police, then Milford-Stokes-san and Sweetchild-sensei, and I was still glued to the spot. They have all decided, of course, that the Japanese army is staffed by pitiful cowards. In actual fact, I simply did not understand immediately what was happening.

When I did understand, it was too late—I was the last to come running up to the scene of the incident. I was even behind Stamp-san.

Kleber-san's cabin is very close to the salon, the fifth door on the right along the corridor. Peering over the shoulders of those who had reached the spot before me, I saw a quite incredible sight. The door of the cabin was wide open. Kleber-san was lying on the floor and moaning pitifully, with some immense, heavy, shiny black mass slumped across her. I did not immediately realize that it was a Negro of immense stature. He was wearing white canvas trousers. The handle of a sailor's dirk was protruding from the back of his neck. From the position of his body, I knew immediately that the Negro was dead. A blow like that, struck to the base of the skull, requires great strength and precision, but it kills instantly and surely.

Kleber-san was floundering in a vain effort to wriggle out from under the heavy carcass that was pinning her down. Lieutenant Renier was bustling about beside her. His face was whiter than the collar of his shirt. The scabbard hanging at his side was empty. The lieutenant was completely flustered, torn between dragging this unsavory deadweight off the pregnant woman and turning to us and launching into an incoherent explanation of what had happened to the commissioner.

Fandorin-san was the only one who remained calm and composed. Without any visible effort, he lifted up the heavy corpse and dragged it off to one side (I remembered his exercises with the weights), then helped Kleber-san into an armchair and gave her some water. I came to my senses and checked quickly to make sure she was not wounded or bruised. She did not seem to be. Whether there is any internal damage will become clear later. Everyone was so agitated that they were not surprised when I examined her. White people are convinced that all orientals are part shaman and know the art of healing. Kleber-san's pulse was ninety-five, which is perfectly understandable.

Interrupting each other as they spoke, Renier-san and Kleber-san told us the following story.

The lieutenant:

He saw Kleber-san to her cabin, wished her a pleasant evening, and took his leave. However, he had scarcely taken two steps away from her door when he heard her desperate scream.

Kleber-san:

She went into her cabin, switched on the electric light, and saw a gigantic black man standing by her dressing table with her coral beads in his hands (I actually saw these beads on the floor afterward). The Negro threw himself on her without speaking, tossed her to the floor, and grabbed hold of her throat with his massive hands. She screamed.

The lieutenant:

He burst into the cabin, saw the appalling (he said "fantastic") scene, and for a moment was at a loss. He grabbed the Negro by the shoulders, but was unable to shift the giant by even an inch. Then he kicked him in the head, but again without the slightest effect. It was only then, fearing for the life of Kleber-san and her child, that he grabbed his dirk out of its sheath and struck a single blow.

It occurred to me that the lieutenant must have spent a turbulent youth in taverns and bordellos, where skill in handling a knife determines who will sober up the following morning and who will be carried off to the cemetery.

Captain Cliff and Dr. Truffo ran in. The cabin became crowded. No one could understand how the African had come to be on board the *Leviathan*. Fandorin-san carefully inspected a tattoo covering the dead man's chest and said he had seen one like it before. Apparently during the recent Balkan conflict he was held prisoner by the Turks, and there he saw black slaves with precisely the same zigzag lines in concentric circles around the nipples. They are the ritual markings of the Ndanga tribe, recently discovered by Arab slave traders in the very heart of equatorial Africa. Ndanga men are in great demand at markets throughout the East.

It seemed to me that Fandorin-san said all this with a rather strange expression on his face, as though he were puzzled by something. However, I could be mistaken, since the facial expressions of Europeans are freakish and do not correspond at all to ours.

Commissioner Gauche listened to the diplomat carefully. He said there were two questions that interested him as a representative of the law: How the Negro had managed to get on the ship and why he had attacked Mme. Kleber.

Then it emerged that things had begun disappearing in a mysterious fashion from the cabins of several of the people present. I remembered the item that had disappeared from my cabin, but naturally I said nothing. It was also established that people had seen a massive black shadow (Miss Stamp) or a black face peeping in at their window (Mrs. Truffo). It is clear now that these were not hallucinations and not the fruit of morbid imaginings.

Everyone turned on the captain. Apparently the passengers had been in mortal danger all the time they had been on board and the ship's command had not even been aware of it. Cliff-san was scarlet with shame. And it must be admitted that a terrible blow has been struck to his prestige. I tactfully turned away so that he would suffer less from his loss of face.

Then the captain asked the witnesses to the incident to move into the Windsor salon and addressed us with a speech of great power and dignity. Above all he apologized for what had happened. He asked us not to tell anyone about this "regrettable occurrence," since it might cause mass psychosis on board the ship. He promised that his sailors would immediately comb all the holds, the 'tween-decks, the wine cellar, the storerooms, and even the coal bins. He gave us his guarantee that there would not be any more black burglars on board his ship.

The captain is a good man, a genuine old sea dog. He speaks awkwardly, in short, clipped phrases, but it is clear that he is strong in spirit and he performs his job with sober diligence. I once heard Truffo-sensei telling the commissioner that Captain Cliff is a widower and dotes on his only daughter, who is being educated in a boarding school somewhere. I find that very touching.

Now I seem to be gradually recovering my composure. The lines of writing are more even and my hand is no longer shaking. I can go on to the most unpalatable moment of all.

During my superficial examination of Kleber-san, I noticed that she was not bruised. There were also several other observations that ought to be shared with the captain and the commissioner. But I wished above all to reassure a pregnant woman who was struggling to recover her wits after a shock—who seemed intent, in fact, on plunging into hysterics.

I said to her in a most soothing tone of voice: "Perhaps this black man had no intention of killing you, madam. You entered so unexpectedly and switched on the light and he was simply frightened. After all, he—"

Kleber-san interrupted before I could finish.

"He was frightened?" she hissed with sudden venom. "Or perhaps it was you who were frightened, my dear Asian monsieur? Do you think I didn't notice your nasty little yellow face peeping out from behind other people's backs?"

No one has ever insulted me so outrageously. The worst thing of all was that I could not pretend these were the foolish words of an hysterical woman and shield myself from them with a smile of disdain. Kleber-san's thrust had found my most vulnerable spot!

There was nothing I could say in reply; I was badly hurt, and the grimace on her tear-stained face when she looked at me was humiliating. If at that moment I could have fallen through the floor into the famous Christian hell, I would certainly have pressed the lever of the trapdoor myself. Worst of all, my sight was veiled by the red mist of rage, and that is the condition I fear most. It is in this state of frenzy that a samurai commits those deeds that are disastrous for his karma. Then afterward he must spend the rest of his life seeking to expiate the guilt of that single moment of lost self-control. He can do things for which even *seppuku* will not be sufficient atonement.

I left the salon, afraid I would not be able to restrain myself and do something terrible to a pregnant woman. I am not sure that I could have controlled myself if a man had said something like that to me.

I locked myself in my cabin and took out the sack of Egyptian gourds I bought at the bazaar in Port Said. They are small, about the size of a human head, and very hard. I bought fifty of them.

In order to disperse the scarlet mist in front of my eyes, I set about improving my straight chop with the edge of the hand. Because of my extreme agitation, I delivered the blow poorly: Instead of two equal halves, the gourds split into seven or eight pieces.

It is hard.

PART TWO

———— ✺ ————

ADEN TO
BOMBAY

Gintaro Aono

The seventh day of the fourth month, in Aden

The Russian diplomat is a man of profound, almost Japanese intellect. Fandorin-san possesses the most un-European ability to see a phenomenon in all its fullness, without losing his way in the maze of petty details and technicalities. The Europeans are unsurpassed masters of everything that concerns *doing;* they have superlative understanding of *how.* But true wisdom belongs to us orientals, since we understand *why.* For the hairy ones, the fact of movement is more important than the final goal, but we never lower our gaze from the guiding star twinkling in the distance, and therefore we often neglect to pay due attention to what lies closer to hand. This is why time and again the white peoples are the victors in petty skirmishes, but the yellow race maintains its unshakable equanimity, in the certain knowledge that such trivial matters are unworthy of serious attention. In all that is truly important, in the genuinely essential matters, victory will be ours.

Our emperor has embarked on a great experiment: to combine the wisdom of the East with the intellect of the West. Yet while we Japanese strive meekly to master the European lesson of routine daily conquest, we do not lose sight of the ultimate end of human life—death and the higher form of existence that follows it. The red-hairs are too individualistic, their precious ego obscures their vision, distorting their picture of the world around them and making it impossible for them to see a problem from different points of view. The soul of the European is fastened tightly to his body with rivets of steel; it cannot soar aloft.

But if Fandorin-san is capable of illumination, he owes it to the semi-Asiatic character of his homeland. In many ways Russia is like Japan: the same reaching out by the East for the West. Except that, unlike us, the Russians forget about the star by which the ship maintains its heading and spend too much time gazing idly around them. To emphasize one's individual "I" or to dissolve it in the might of the collective "we"—therein lies the antithesis between Europe and Asia. I believe the chances are good that Russia will turn off the first road on to the second.

However, I have become carried away by my philosophizing. I must move on to Fandorin-san and the clarity of mind he has demonstrated. I shall describe events as they happened.

The *Leviathan* arrived in Aden before dawn. Concerning this port, my guidebook says the following: "The port of Aden, this Gibraltar of the Orient, serves England as her link with the East Indies. Here steamships take on coal and replenish their reserves of fresh water. Aden's importance has increased immeasurably since the opening of the Suez Canal. The town itself, however, is not large. It has extensive dockside warehouses and shipyards, and a number of trading stations, shipping offices, and hotels. The streets are laid out in a distinctively regular pattern. The dryness of the local soil is compensated by thirty ancient reservoirs that collect the rainwater that runs down from the mountains. Aden has a population of 34,000, consisting primarily of Indian Moslems." For the time being I must be content with this scanty description, since the gangway has not been lowered and no one is being allowed ashore. The alleged reason is quarantine for medical reasons, but we vassals of the principality of Windsor know the true reason for the turmoil and confusion: Sailors and police from ashore are combing the gigantic vessel from stem to stern in search of Negroes.

After breakfast we stayed on in the salon to wait for the results of the manhunt. It was then that an important conversation took place between the commissioner and the Russian diplomat in the presence of our entire company (even for me it has already become "ours").

At first people spoke about the death of the Negro, then as usual the conversation turned to the murders in Paris. Although I took no part in the discussion on that topic, I listened very attentively, and at first it seemed to me that they were trying yet again to catch a green monkey in a thicket of bamboo or a black cat in a dark room.

Stamp-san said: "So we have nothing but riddles. We don't know how the black man managed to get on board, and we don't know why he wanted to kill Mme. Kleber. It's just like the Rue de Grenelle. More mystery."

But then Fandorin-san said: "There is no mystery there at all. It is true that we still haven't cleared up the business with the Negro, but I think we have a fairly clear picture of what happened in the Rue de Grenelle."

Everyone stared at him in bewilderment, and the commissioner smiled scornfully and said: "Is that so? Well, then, out with it; this should be interesting."

Fandorin-san: "I think what happened was this. That evening someone arrived at the door of the mansion on the Rue de Grenelle . . ."

The commissioner (in mock admiration): "Oh, bravo! A brilliant deduction!"

Someone laughed, but most of us continued listening attentively, for the diplomat is not a man to indulge in idle talk.

Fandorin-san (continuing imperturbably): ". . . someone whose appearance completely failed to arouse the servants' suspicions. It was a physician, possibly wearing a white coat and certainly carrying a doctor's bag. This unexpected visitor requested everyone in the house to gather immediately in one room, because the municipal authorities had instructed that all Parisians were to receive a prophylactic vaccination."

The commissioner (starting to get angry): "What idiotic fantasy is this? What vaccination? Why should the servants take the word of a total stranger?"

Fandorin-san (sharply): "If you do not take care, M. Gauche, you may find yourself demoted from Investigator for Especially Important Cases to Investigator for Rather Unimportant Cases. You do not pay sufficient attention to studying your own materials, and that is unforgivable. Take another look at the article from *Le Soir* that mentions Lord Littleby's connection with the international adventuress Marie Sanfon."

The detective rummaged in his black file, took out the article in question, and glanced over it.

The commissioner (with a shrug): "Well, what of it?"

Fandorin-san (pointing): "Down here, at the bottom. Do you see the headline of the next article—CHOLERA EPIDEMIC ON THE WANE? And what it says about 'the vigorous prophylactic measures taken by the physicians of Paris'?"

Truffo-sensei: "Why, yes indeed, gentlemen, Paris has been plagued by outbreaks of cholera all winter. They even set up a medical checkpoint in the Louvre for the boats arriving from Calais."

Fandorin-san: "That is why the sudden appearance of a physician did not make the servants suspicious. No doubt their visitor acted confidently and spoke very convincingly. He could have told them it was late and that he still had several more houses to visit, or something of the kind. The servants evidently decided not to bother the master of the house, since he was suffering from an attack of gout, but of course they called the security guards down from the second floor. And it only takes a moment to give an injection."

I was delighted by the diplomat's perspicacity and the ease with which he had solved this difficult riddle. His words even set Commissioner Gauche thinking.

"Very well, then," the latter said reluctantly. "But how do you explain the fact that after poisoning the servants this medico of yours didn't simply walk up the stairs to the second floor, but went outside, climbed over the fence, and broke into the house through a window in the conservatory?"

Fandorin-san: "I've thought about that. Did it not occur to you that two culprits might have been involved? That one dealt with the servants while the other broke in through the window?"

The commissioner (triumphantly): "It did occur to me, my dear brainy monsieur, indeed it did. That is precisely the assumption that the murderer wanted us to make. It's perfectly obvious he was simply trying to confuse the trail! After he poisoned the servants, he left the pantry and went upstairs, where he ran into the master of the house. Very probably the thief simply smashed in the glass of the display case because he thought there was no one else in the house. When his lordship came out of his bedroom to see what all the noise was about, he was murdered. Following this unexpected encounter, the culprit beat a hasty retreat, not through the door, but through the window of the conservatory. Why? In order to pull the wool over our eyes and make it seem as though there were two of them. You fell for his little trick hook, line, and sinker. But old papa Gauche is not so easily taken in."

The commissioner's words were greeted with general approval. Renier-san even said: "Damn it, Commissioner, but you're a dangerous man!" (This is a common turn of speech in various European languages. It should not be taken literally. The lieutenant meant to say that Gauche-san is a very clever and experienced detective.)

Fandorin-san waited for a while and asked: "Then you made a thorough study of the footprints and came to the conclusion that this person jumped down from the window and did not climb up onto the windowsill?"

The commissioner did not answer that, but he gave the Russian a rather angry look.

At this point Stamp-san made a comment that turned the conversation in a new direction.

"One culprit, two culprits—but I still don't understand the most important thing: What was it all done for?" she said. "Clearly not for the Shiva. But what, then? And not for the sake of the scarf, either, no matter how remarkable and legendary it may be!"

Fandorin-san replied to this in a matter-of-fact voice, as if he were saying something perfectly obvious: "But of course, it was precisely for the sake of the scarf, mademoiselle. The Shiva was only taken in order to divert attention. It was then thrown into the Seine from the nearest bridge because it was no longer needed."

The commissioner observed: "For Russian *boyar*s (I have forgotten what this word means; I shall have to look it up in the dictionary), half a million francs may perhaps be a mere trifle, but most people think differently. Two kilograms of pure gold was 'no longer needed'! You really are getting carried away, monsieur diplomat."

Fandorin-san: "Oh, come now, Commissioner, what is half a million francs compared to the treasure of Bagdassar?"

"Gentlemen, enough of this quarreling!" the odious Mme. Kleber exclaimed capriciously. "I was almost killed, and here you are, still harping on the same old tune. Commissioner, while you were so busy tinkering with an old crime, you very nearly had a new one on your hands!"

That woman simply cannot bear it when she is not the center of attention. After what happened yesterday, I try not to look at her—I have a strong urge to jab my finger into the blue vein pulsating on her white neck. One jab would be enough to dispatch the loathsome creature. But, of course, that is one of those evil thoughts that a man must drive out of his head by an effort of will. By confiding my evil thoughts to this diary, I have managed to diminish the violence of my hatred a little.

The commissioner put Mme. Kleber in her place. "Please be quiet, madam," he said sternly. "Let us hear what other fantasies our diplomat has concocted."

Fandorin-san: "The entire story only makes sense if the stolen shawl is especially valuable in some way. That is one. According to what the professor told us, in itself the shawl is of no great value, so it is not a matter of the piece of silk, but of something else connected with it. That is two. As you already know, the shawl is connected with the final will and testament of the rajah Bagdassar, the last owner of the Brahmapur treasure. That is three. Tell me, Professor, was the rajah a zealous servant of the Prophet?"

Sweetchild-sensei (after a moment's thought): "I can't say, exactly . . . He didn't build mosques, and he never mentioned the name of Allah in my company. The rajah liked to dress in European clothes; he smoked Cuban cigars and read French novels . . . Ah, yes, he drank cognac after lunch! So he obviously didn't take religious prohibitions very seriously."

Fandorin-san: "Then that makes four: Although he is not overly devout, Bagdassar makes his son a final gift of a Koran, which for some reason is wrapped in a shawl. I suggest that the shawl was the most important part of this legacy. The Koran was included for the sake of appearances . . . Or possibly the notes made in the margins in Bagdassar's own hand contained instructions on how to find the treasure with the help of the shawl."

Sweetchild-sensei: "But why did it have to be with the help of the shawl? The rajah could have conveyed his secret in the marginalia!"

Fandorin-san: "He could have, but he chose not to. Why? Allow me to refer you to my argument number one: If the shawl were not immensely valuable in some way, it is unlikely that ten people would have been murdered for it. The shawl is the key to five hundred million francs or, if you prefer, fifty million pounds, which is approximately the same. I believe it is the greatest hidden treasure there has ever been in the whole of human history. And by the way, Commissioner, I must warn you that if you are not mistaken and the murderer really is on board the *Leviathan*, more people could be killed. Indeed, the closer you come to your objective, the more likely it becomes. The stakes are too high, and too great a price has already been paid for the key to the mystery."

These words were followed by deadly silence. Fandorin-san's logic seemed irrefutable, and I believe all of us felt shivers run up and down our spines. All of us except one.

The first to recover his composure was the commissioner. He gave a nervous laugh and said: "My, what a lively imagination you have, M. Fandorin. But as far as danger is concerned, you are right. Only you, gentlemen, have no need to quake in your boots. This danger threatens no one but old man Gauche, and he knows it very well. It is part of my profession. But I'm well prepared for it!" And he glanced around at us menacingly, as if he were challenging us to single combat.

The fat old man is laughable. Of everyone there, the only person whom he might be able to get the best of is the pregnant Mme. Kleber. In my mind's eye I glimpsed a tempting picture: The red-faced commissioner had flung the young witch to the floor and was strangling her with his hairy sausage fingers, and Mme. Kleber was expiring with her eyes popping out of her head and her malicious tongue dangling out of her mouth.

"Darling, I'm scared!" I heard the doctor's wife whisper in a thin, squeaky voice as she turned to her husband, who patted her shoulder reassuringly.

The redheaded freak M.S.-san (his name is too long for me to write it in full) raised an interesting question: "Professor, can you describe the shawl in more detail? We know the bird has a hole where its eye should be, and that it's triangle-shaped. Is there anything else remarkable about it?"

I should note that this strange gentleman takes part in the general conversation almost as rarely as I do. But, like the author of these lines, if he does say something, then it is always off the subject, and so the unexpected appropriateness of his question was all the more remarkable.

Sweetchild-sensei: "As far as I recall, apart from the hole and the unique shape there is nothing special about the shawl. It is about the size of a small fan, but it can easily be hidden in a thimble. Such remarkably fine fabric is quite common in Brahmapur."

"Then the key must lie in the eye of the bird and the triangular shape," Fandorin-san concluded with exquisite assurance.

He was truly magnificent.

The more I ponder on his triumph and the whole story in general, the more strongly I feel the unworthy temptation to demonstrate to all of them that Gintaro Aono is also no fool. I too could reveal things that would amaze them. For instance, I could tell Commissioner Gauche certain curious details about yesterday's incident involving the black-skinned savage. Even the wise Fandorin-san has admitted that the matter is not entirely clear to him as yet. What if the "wild Japanese" were suddenly to solve the riddle that is puzzling him? That could be interesting!

Yesterday's insults unsettled me and I lost my composure for a while. Afterward, when I had calmed down, I began comparing facts and weighing the situation up, and I have constructed an entire logical argument that I intend to put to the policeman. Let him work out the rest for himself. This is what I shall tell the commissioner.

First I shall remind him of how Mme. Kleber humiliated me. It was a highly insulting remark, made in public. And it was made at the precise moment when I was about to reveal what I had observed. Did Mme. Kleber perhaps wish to shut me up? This surely appears suspicious, monsieur commissioner.

To continue. Why does she pretend to be weak, when she is as fit as a sumo wrestler? You will say this is an irrelevant detail. But I shall tell you, monsieur detective, that a person who is constantly pretending must be hiding something. Take me, for instance. (Ha-ha. Of course, I shall not say that.)

Then I shall point out to the commissioner that European women have very delicate white skin. Why did the Negro's powerful fingers not leave even the slightest mark on it? Is that not strange?

And, finally, when the commissioner decides I have nothing to offer him but the vindictive speculations of an oriental mind bent on vengeance,

I shall tell him the most important thing, which will immediately make our detective sit up and take notice.

"M. Gauche," I shall say to him with a polite smile, "I do not possess your brilliant mind, and I am not attempting, hopeless ignoramus that I am, to interfere in your investigation, but I regard it as my duty to draw your attention to a certain circumstance. You yourself say that the murderer from the Rue de Grenelle is one of us. M. Fandorin has expounded a convincing account of how Lord Littleby's servants were killed. Vaccinating them against cholera was a brilliant subterfuge. It tells us that the murderer knows how to use a syringe. But what if the person who came to the mansion on the Rue de Grenelle were not a male doctor, but a woman, a nurse? She would have aroused even less suspicion than a man, would she not? Surely you agree? Then let me advise you to take a casual glance at Mme. Kleber's arms when she is sitting with her viper's head propped on her hand and her wide sleeve slips down to the elbow. You will observe some barely visible points on the inner flexure, as I have observed. They are needle marks, monsieur commissioner. Ask Dr. Truffo if he is giving Mme. Kleber any injections, and the venerable physician will tell you what he has already told me today: No, he is not, for he is opposed in principle to the intravenous injection of medication. And then, oh wise Gauche-sensei, you will add two and two, and you will have something for your gray head to puzzle over." That is what I shall tell the commissioner, and then he will take Mme. Kleber more seriously.

A European knight would say that I had behaved villainously, but that would merely demonstrate his own limitations. That is precisely why there are no knights left in Europe, but the samurai are still among us. Our lord and emperor may have set the different estates on one level and forbidden us to wear two swords in our belts, but that does not mean the calling of a samurai has been abolished. Quite the opposite; the entire Japanese nation has been elevated to the estate of the samurai in order to prevent us from boasting to one another about our noble origins. We all stand together against the rest of the world. Oh, you noble European knight (who has never existed except in novels)! In fighting with men, use the weapons of a man, but in fighting with women, use the weapons of a woman. That is the samurai code of honor, and there is nothing villainous in it, since women know how to fight every bit as well as men. What contradicts the honor of the samurai is to employ the weapons of a man against a woman or the weapons of a woman against a man. I would never sink as low as that.

I am still uncertain whether the maneuver I am contemplating is worthwhile, but my state of mind is incomparably better than it was yesterday. So much so that I have even managed to compose a decent haiku without any difficulty:

> *The moonlight glinting,*
> *Bright upon the steely blade,*
> *A cold spark of ice.*

Clarissa Stamp

CLARISSA GLANCED AROUND with a bored look on her face to see if anyone was watching, and only then did she peep cautiously around the corner of the deckhouse.

The Japanese was sitting alone on the quarterdeck with his legs folded up underneath him. His head was thrown back and she could see the whites of his eyes glinting horribly between the half-closed lids. The expression on his face was absolutely impassive—inhumanly dispassionate.

Br-r-r! Clarissa shuddered. What a strange specimen this Mr. Aono was. Here on the boat deck, located just one level above the first-class cabins, no one was taking the air except a gaggle of young girls skipping rope and two nursemaids exhausted by the heat who were sheltering in the shade of a snow-white launch. Who but children and a crazy oriental would be out in such scorching heat? The only structures higher than the boat deck were the control room, the bridge, and, of course, the funnels, masts, and sails. The white canvas sheets were swollen taut by a following wind, and *Leviathan* was making straight for the liquid-silver line of the horizon, puffing smoke into the sky as it went, while all around, the Indian Ocean lay spread out like a slightly crumpled tablecloth patterned in shimmering patches of bright bottle green. From up here she could see that the earth really was round: The rim of the horizon was clearly lower than the *Leviathan,* and the ship seemed to be running downhill toward it.

But Clarissa had not drenched herself in perspiration for the sake of the sea view. She wanted to see what Mr. Aono was up to. Where did he disappear to with such unfailing regularity after breakfast?

And she was right to have been curious. Look at him now, the very image of the inscrutable oriental! A man with such a motionless, pitiless mask for a face was capable of absolutely anything. The members of the yellow race were certainly not like us, and it was not simply a matter of the shape of their eyes. On the outside they looked very much like people, but on the inside they were a different species altogether. After all, wolves looked like dogs, didn't they, but their nature was quite different. Of course, the yellow-skinned races had a moral code of their own, but it was so alien to Christianity that no normal person could possibly understand it. It would be better if they didn't wear European clothes or learn how to use cutlery—that created a dangerous illusion of civilization, when there were things we couldn't possibly imagine going on under that slickly parted black hair and those yellow foreheads.

The Japanese stirred almost imperceptibly and blinked, and Clarissa hastily ducked back out of sight. Of course, she was behaving like an absolute fool, but she couldn't just do nothing! This nightmare couldn't be allowed to go on forever. The commissioner had to be nudged in the right direction; otherwise there was no way of telling how it all might end. Despite the heat, she felt a chill tremor run through her.

There was obviously something mysterious about Mr. Aono's character and behavior. Like the mystery of the crime in the Rue de Grenelle. It was strange that Gauche had still not realized that all the signs pointed to the Japanese as the main suspect.

What kind of officer was he? How could he have graduated from St. Cyr if he knew nothing about horses? One day, acting purely out of humanitarian motives, Clarissa had decided to involve the oriental in the general conversation and started talking about a subject that should have been of interest to a military man—training and racing horses, the merits and shortcomings of the Norfolk trotter. He was no officer! She had asked him: "Have you ever taken part in a steeplechase?" He replied that officers of the Imperial Army were absolutely forbidden to become involved in politics. He simply had no idea what a steeplechase was! Of course, who could tell what kind of officers they had in Japan—perhaps they rode around on sticks of bamboo—but how could an alumnus of St. Cyr possibly be so ignorant? No, it was quite out of the question.

She had to bring this to Gauche's attention. Or perhaps she ought to wait and see if she could discover something else suspicious?

And what about that incident yesterday? Clarissa had taken a stroll along the corridor past Mr. Aono's cabin after she heard some extremely strange noises. There was a dry crunching sound coming from inside the cabin, as if someone were smashing furniture with precise, regular blows. Clarissa had screwed up her courage and knocked.

The door had opened with a jerk and the Japanese appeared in the doorway—entirely naked except for a loincloth! His swarthy body was gleaming with sweat; his eyes were swollen with blood.

When he saw Clarissa standing there, he hissed through his teeth: "*Chikusho!*"

The question she had prepared in advance ("Mr. Aono, do you by any chance happen to have with you some of those marvelous Japanese prints I've heard so much about?") flew right out of her head, and Clarissa froze, stupefied. Now he would drag her into the cabin and throw himself on her! And afterward he would chop her into pieces and throw her into the sea. Nothing could be simpler. And that would be the end of Miss Clarissa Stamp, the well-brought-up English lady, who might not have been very happy, but had still expected so much from her life.

Clarissa mumbled that she had knocked at the wrong door. Aono stared at her without speaking. He gave off a sour smell.

Probably she ought to have a word with the commissioner, after all.

BEFORE AFTERNOON TEA she ambushed the detective outside the doors of the Windsor salon and began sharing her ideas with him, but the way the lout listened was very odd: He kept darting sharp, mocking glances at her, as though he were listening to a confession of some dark misdeed that she had committed.

At one point he muttered into his mustache: "Ah, how eager you all are to tell tales on one another."

When she had finished, he suddenly asked out of the blue: "And how are Mama and Papa keeping?"

"Whose, Mr. Aono's?" Clarissa asked in amazement.

"No, mademoiselle, yours."

"I was orphaned as a child," she replied, glancing at the policeman in alarm. Good God, this was no ship; it was a floating lunatic asylum.

"That's what I needed to establish," said Gauche with a nod of satisfaction, then the boor began humming a song Clarissa didn't know and walked into the salon ahead of her, which was incredibly rude.

That conversation had left a bad taste in her mouth. For all their much-vaunted gallantry, the French were not gentlemen. Of course, they could dazzle you and turn your head, make some dramatic gesture like sending a hundred red roses to your hotel room (Clarissa winced as she thought of that), but they were not to be trusted. Although the English gentleman might appear somewhat insipid by comparison, he knew the meaning of the words "duty" and "decency." But if a Frenchman wormed his way into your trust, he was certain to betray it.

These generalizations, however, had no direct relevance to Commissioner Gauche. And, moreover, the reason for his bizarre behavior was revealed at the dinner table in a most alarming manner.

Over dessert, the detective, who had thus far preserved a most untypical silence that had set everyone's nerves on edge, suddenly stared hard at Clarissa and said: "Yes, by the way, Mlle. Stamp" (although she had not said anything), "you were asking me recently about Marie Sanfon. You know—the little lady who was supposedly seen with Lord Littleby shortly before he died."

Clarissa started in surprise, and everyone else fell silent and began staring curiously at the commissioner, recognizing that special tone of voice in which he began his leisurely "little stories."

"I promised to tell you something about that individual at some time. And now the time has come," Gauche continued, his eyes still fixed on Clarissa, and the longer he looked, the less she liked it. "It will be a rather long story, but you won't be bored, because it concerns a quite extraordinary woman. And, in any case, we are in no hurry. Here we all are, sitting comfortably, eating our cheese and drinking our orangeade. But if anyone has business to attend to, do leave by all means; papa Gauche won't be offended."

No one moved.

"Then shall I tell you about Marie Sanfon?" the commissioner asked with feigned bonhomie.

"Oh, yes! You must!" they all cried.

Only Clarissa said nothing, aware that this topic had been broached for a reason; it was intended exclusively for her ears. Gauche did not even attempt to disguise the fact.

He smacked his lips in anticipation and took out his pipe without bothering to ask permission from the ladies.

"Then let me start at the beginning. Once upon a time in the Belgian town of Bruges there lived a little girl by the name of Marie. The little girl's parents were honest, respectable citizens who went to church, and they doted on their little golden-haired darling. When Marie was five years old, her parents presented her with a little brother, the future heir to the Sanfon and Sanfon brewery, and the happy family began living even more happily, until suddenly disaster struck. The infant boy, who was barely a month old, fell out of a window and was killed. The parents were not at home at the time; they had left the children alone with their nanny. But the nanny had gone out for half an hour to see her sweetheart, a fireman, and during her brief absence a stranger in a black cloak and black hat burst into the house. Little Marie managed to hide under the bed, but the man in black grabbed her little brother out of his cradle and threw him out the window. Then he simply vanished without trace."

"Why are you telling us such terrible things?" Mme. Kleber exclaimed, clutching at her belly.

"Why, I have hardly even begun," said Gauche, gesturing with his pipe. "The best—or the worst—is yet to come. After her miraculous escape, little Marie told Mama and Papa about the 'black man.' They turned the entire district upside down searching for him, and in the heat of the moment they even arrested the local rabbi, since he naturally always wore black. But there was one strange detail that kept nagging at M. Sanfon: Why had the criminal moved a stool over to the window?

"Oh, God!" Clarissa gasped, clutching at her heart. "Surely not!"

"You are quite remarkably perceptive, Mlle. Stamp," the commissioner said with a laugh. "Yes, it was little Marie who had thrown her own baby brother out the window."

"How terrible!" Mrs. Truffo felt it necessary to interject. "But why?"

"The girl did not like the way everyone was paying so much attention to the baby, while they had forgotten all about her. She thought that if she got rid of her brother, then she would be Mama and Papa's favorite again," Gauche explained calmly. "But that was the first and the last time Marie Sanfon ever left a clue and was found out. The sweet child had not yet learned to cover her tracks."

"And what did they do with the infant criminal?" asked Lieutenant Renier, clearly shaken by what he had heard. "They couldn't try her for murder, surely?"

"No, they didn't try her." The commissioner smiled craftily at Clarissa. "The shock, however, was too much for her mother, who lost her mind and was committed to an asylum. M. Sanfon could no longer bear the sight of the little daughter who was the cause of his family's calamitous misfortune, so he placed her with a convent of the Gray Sisters of St. Vincent, and the girl was brought up there. She was best at everything, in her studies and in her charity work. But most of all, they say, she liked to read books. The novice nun was just seventeen years old when a disgraceful scandal occurred at the convent." Gauche glanced into his file and nodded. "I have the date here. The seventeenth of July, 1866. The archbishop of Brussels himself was staying with the Gray Sisters when the venerable prelate's ring with a massive amethyst disappeared from his bedroom. It had supposedly belonged to St. Louis himself. The previous evening, the monseigneur had summoned the two best pupils, our Marie and a girl from Arles, to his chambers for a talk. Suspicion naturally fell on the two girls. The mother superior organized a search and the ring's velvet case was discovered under the mattress of the girl from Arles. The thief lapsed into a stupor and would not answer any questions, and she was escorted to the punishment cell. When the police arrived an hour later, they were unable to question the criminal—she had strangled herself with the belt of her habit."

"I've guessed it—the whole thing was staged by that abominable Marie Sanfon!" Milford-Stokes exclaimed. "A nasty story, very nasty!"

"Nobody knows for certain, but the ring was never found," the commissioner said with a shrug. "Two days later, Marie came to the mother superior in tears and said everyone was giving her strange looks and begged to be released from the convent. The mother superior's feelings for her former favorite had also cooled somewhat, and she made no effort to dissuade her."

"They should have searched the little dove at the gates," said Dr. Truffo with a regretful sigh. "You can be sure they would have found the amethyst somewhere in her skirts."

When he translated what he had said to his wife, she jabbed him with her elbow, evidently regarding his remark as somehow indecent.

"Either they didn't search her or they searched her and found nothing, I don't know which. In any case, after she left the convent, Marie chose to go to Antwerp, which, as you are aware, is regarded as the world capital of precious stones. The former nun suddenly grew rich and ever since has lived in the grand style. Sometimes, just occasionally, she has been left without a sou to her name, but not for long. With her sharp mind and brilliant skill as an actress, combined with a total lack of moral scruples [at this point the commissioner raised his voice and then paused] she has always been able to obtain the means required for a life of luxury. The police of Belgium, France, England, the United States, Brazil, Italy, and a dozen other countries have detained Marie Sanfon on numerous occasions on suspicion of all sorts of offenses, but no charges have ever been brought against her. Always it turns out that either no crime has actually been committed or there is simply not enough evidence. If you like, I could tell you about a couple of episodes from her distinguished record. Are you not feeling bored yet, Mlle. Stamp?"

Clarissa did not reply; she felt it was beneath her dignity. But in her heart she felt alarmed.

"Eighteen seventy," Gauche declared after another glance into his file. "The small but prosperous town of Fettburg in German-speaking Switzerland. The chocolate and ham industries. Eight and a half thousand pigs versus four thousand inhabitants. A land of rich, fat idiots—I beg your pardon, Mme. Kleber, I did not mean to insult your homeland," said the policeman, suddenly realizing what he had said.

"Never mind," said Mme. Kleber with a careless shrug. "I come from

French-speaking Switzerland. And anyway, the area around Fettburg really is full of simpletons. I believe I have heard this story; it is very funny. But never mind—carry on."

"Some might think it funny," Gauche sighed reproachfully, and suddenly he winked at Clarissa, which was going too far altogether. "One day the honest burghers of the town were thrown into a state of indescribable excitement when a certain peasant by the name of Möbius, who was known in Fettburg as an idler and a numskull, boasted he had sold his land, a narrow strip of stony wasteland, to a certain grand lady who styled herself the 'comtesse de Sanfon.' This damn fool of a countess had shelled out three thousand francs for thirty acres of barren land on which not even thistles would grow. But there were people smarter than Möbius on the town council, and they thought his story sounded suspicious. Why would a countess want thirty acres of sand and rock? Something fishy was going on. So they dispatched the very smartest of the town's citizens to Zurich to find out what was what, and he discovered that the comtesse de Sanfon was well known there as woman who knew how to enjoy life on a grand scale. Even more interesting, she often appeared in public in the company of Mr. Goldsilber, the director of the state railway company. The director and the countess were rumored to be romantically involved. Then, of course, the good burghers guessed what was going on. The little town of Fettburg had been dreaming for a long time of having its own railway line, which would make it cheaper to export its chocolate and ham. The wasteland acquired by the countess just happened to run from the nearest railway station to the forest, where the communal land began. Suddenly everything was clear to the city fathers: Having learned from her lover about plans to build a railway line, the countess had bought the key plot of land, intending to turn a handsome profit. An outrageously bold plan began to take shape in the good burghers' heads. They dispatched a deputation to the countess, which attempted to persuade her excellency to sell the land to the noble town of Fettburg. The beautiful lady was obstinate at first, claiming she knew nothing about any branch railway line, but when the burgomaster hinted subtly that the affair smacked of a conspiracy between her excellency and his excellency the director of state railways, which was a matter that fell within the competence of the courts, the woman's nerve finally gave way and she agreed. The wasteland was divided into thirty one-acre lots and auctioned off to the citizens of the town. The Fettburgers almost came to blows over it, and the price for some lots rose as high as fifteen thousand francs. Altogether the countess received . . ." The commissioner ran his finger along a line of print. "A little less than two hundred eighty thousand francs."

Mme. Kleber laughed out loud and gestured to Gauche as if to say: I'm saying nothing—go on, go on.

"Weeks went by, then months, and still the construction work had not started. The citizens of the town sent an inquiry to the government and received a reply that no branch line to Fettburg was planned for the next fifteen years. They went to the police and explained what had happened and said it was highway robbery. The police listened to the victims' story with sympathy, but there was nothing they could do about it: Mlle. Sanfon had said that she knew nothing about any railway line and she had not wanted to sell the land. The sales were properly registered; everything was perfectly legal. As for calling herself a countess, that was not a very nice thing to do, but unfortunately it was not a criminal offense."

"Very clever!" laughed Renier. "Indeed it was all perfectly legal."

"But that's nothing," said the commissioner, leafing through his papers again. "I have another story here—it is absolutely fantastic. The action is set in the Wild West of America in 1873. Miss Cleopatra Frankenstein, the world-famous necromancer and Grand Dragoness of the Maltese Lodge, whose name according to her passport is 'Marie Sanfon,' arrives in the goldfields of California. She informs the prospectors that she has been guided to this wild spot by the voice of Zarathushtra, who has ordered his faithful handmaiden to carry out a great experiment in the town of Golden Nugget. Apparently, at that precise longitude and latitude the cosmic energy was focused in such a way that on a starry night, with the help of a few cabbalistic formulae, it was possible to resurrect someone who had already crossed the Great Divide between the Kingdom of the Living and the Kingdom of the Dead. And Cleopatra intended to perform this miracle that very night, in public and entirely without charge, because she was no circus conjurer but the medium of the Supreme Spheres. And what do you think?" Gauche asked, pausing for effect. "Before the eyes of five hundred bearded onlookers, the Dragoness worked her magic over the burial mound of Red Coyote, the legendary Indian chief who had died a hundred years earlier, and suddenly the earth began to stir—it gaped asunder, you might say—and an Indian brave in a feather headdress emerged from the mound, complete with a tomahawk and painted face. The onlookers trembled, and Cleopatra, in the grip of her mystical trance, screeched: 'I feel the power of the cosmos in me! Where is the town cemetery? I will bring everyone in it back to life.' It says in this article," the policeman explained, "that the cemetery in Golden Nugget was vast, because in the goldfields someone was dispatched to the next world every day of the week. Apparently the headstones outnumbered the town's living inhabitants. When the prospectors imagined what would happen if all those troublemakers, drunks, and gallows-dancers suddenly rose from their graves, panic set in. The situation was saved by the justice of the peace, who stepped forward and asked politely whether the Dragoness would agree to halt her great experiment if the town's inhabitants gave her a saddlebag full of gold dust as a modest donation toward the needs of occult science."

"Well, did she agree?" chuckled the lieutenant.

"Yes. For two saddlebags of gold."

"And what became of the Indian chief?" asked Fandorin with a smile. He had a quite wonderful smile, except that it was too boyish, thought Clarissa. As they said in Suffolk: A grand pie, but not for your mouth.

"Cleopatra Frankenstein took the Indian chief with her," Gauche replied with a serious expression. "For purposes of scientific research. They say someone cut his throat during a drunken brawl in a Denver bordello."

"This Marie Sanfon really is a very interesting character," mused Fandorin. "Tell us more about her. It's a long way from all these clever frauds to cold-blooded mass murder."

"Oh, please, that's more than enough already," protested Mrs. Truffo, turning to her husband. "My darling, it must be awfully tiresome for you to translate all this nonsense."

"You are not obliged to stay, madam," said commissioner Gauche, offended by the English word "nonsense."

Mrs. Truffo batted her eyelids indignantly, but she had no intention of leaving.

"M. le Cosaque is right," Gauche acknowledged. "Let me try to dig out a more vicious example."

Mme. Kleber laughed and cast a glance at Fandorin, and, nervous as she was, even Clarissa was unable to restrain a smile—the diplomat was so very unlike a wild son of the steppe.

"Here we are—listen to this story about the black baby. It's a recent case, from the year before last, and we have a detailed report of the outcome." The detective glanced through several sheets of paper clipped together, evidently to refresh his memory of the story. He chuckled. "This is something of a masterpiece. I have all sorts of things in my little file, ladies and gentlemen." He stroked the black-calico binding lovingly with the stumpy fingers of his plebeian hand. "Papa Gauche made thorough preparations for his journey; he didn't forget a single piece of paper that might come in useful. The embarrassing events I am about to relate to you never reached the newspapers—what I have here is the police report. All right. In a certain German principality (I won't say which, because this is a delicate matter), a certain family of great note was expecting an addition to its number. It was a long and difficult birth. The delivering physician was a certain highly respected Dr. Vogel. Eventually the bedroom was filled with a sound of an infant wailing. The grand duchess lost consciousness for several minutes because she had suffered so much, and then she opened her eyes and said to the doctor: 'Ah, Herr Professor, show me my little child.' With an expression of extreme embarrassment, Dr. Vogel handed her highness the charming baby that was bawling so loudly. Its skin was the color of light coffee. When the grand duchess fainted again, the doctor glanced out the door and beckoned with his finger to the grand duke, which of course was a gross violation of court etiquette."

It was obvious the commissioner was taking great pleasure in telling this story to the prim and proper Windsorites. A police report was unlikely to contain such details—Gauche was clearly allowing himself to fantasize at will. He lisped when he spoke the countess's part and deliberately selected words that had a pompous ring to them: He obviously thought that made the tale sound funnier. Clarissa did not consider herself an aristocrat, but even she winced at the bad taste of his scoffing at royalty. Sir Reginald, a baronet and the scion of an ancient line, also knitted his brows in a scowl, but this reaction only seemed to inspire the commissioner to greater efforts.

"His highness, however, did not take offense at his physician, because this was a moment of tremendous pathos. Positively overwhelmed by a rising tide of paternal and conjugal feelings, he went dashing into the bedroom. You can imagine for yourselves the scene that followed: The crowned monarch swearing like a trooper, the grand duchess sobbing and making excuses and swooning by turns, the little Negro child bawling his lungs out, and the court physician frozen in reverential horror. Eventually his highness controlled himself and decided to postpone the investigation into her highness's behavior until later. In the meantime, the business had to be hushed up. But how? Flush the child down the toilet?" Gauche put his hand over his mouth, acting the fool. "I beg your pardon, ladies, it just slipped out. It was impossible to get rid of the child—the entire principality had been eagerly awaiting his birth. In any case, it would have been a sin. If he called his advisers together, they might let the cat out of the bag. What was he going to do? And then Dr. Vogel coughed deferentially into his hand and suggested a way of saving the situation. He said he knew a lady by the name of Fräulein von Sanfon who could work miracles—even pluck a phoenix from the sky for the prince if he needed it, let alone find him a newborn white baby. The fräulein knew how to keep her mouth shut, and, being a very noble individual, she would of course not take any money for her services, but she did have a great fondness for old jewels . . . Anyway, within a couple of hours a fine bouncing baby boy, whiter than a little suckling piglet, with white hair, was reposing on the satin sheets of the cradle, and the poor little Negro child was taken from the palace. They told her highness that the innocent child would be transported to southern climes and placed with a good family. And so everything was settled as well as could possibly be managed. The grateful duke gave the doctor a monogrammed diamond snuffbox for Fräulein von Sanfon, together with a note of gratitude and an oral request to depart the principality and never return. Which the considerate maiden immediately did." Gauche chuckled, unable to restrain himself. "The next morning, after a row that had lasted all night, the grand duke finally decided to take a closer look at his new son and heir. He squeamishly lifted the boy out of the cradle and turned him this way and that, and suddenly on his pink little backside—begging your pardon—he saw a birthmark shaped like a heart. His highness had one exactly like it on his own hindquarters, and so did his grandfather, and so on to the seventh generation. Totally confused, the duke sent for his physician, but Dr. Vogel had set out from the castle for parts unknown the previous night, leaving behind his wife and eight children." Gauche burst into hoarse laughter, then began coughing and waving his hands in the air. Someone else chuckled uncertainly, and Mme. Kleber put her hand to her mouth.

"The investigation that followed soon established that the court doctor had been behaving strangely for some time, and had even been seen in the gambling houses of neighboring Baden—in the company, moreover, of a certain young woman whose description closely matched that of Fräulein von Sanfon." The detective assumed a more serious expression. "The doctor was found two days later in a hospital in Strasbourg. Dead. He'd taken a fatal dose of laudanum and left a note: 'I alone am to blame for everything.' A clear case of suicide. The identity of the true culprit was obvious, but how could you prove it? As for the snuffbox, it was a gift from the grand duke, and there was a note to go with it. It would not have been worth their highnesses' while to take the case to court. The greatest mystery, of course, was how they managed to swap the newborn prince for the little Negro baby and where they could have found a chocolate-colored child in a country of people with blue eyes and blond hair. But then, according to some sources, shortly before the incident described, Marie Sanfon had a Senegalese maid in her service."

"Tell me, Commissioner," Fandorin said when the laughter stopped (four people were laughing: Lieutenant Renier, Dr. Truffo, Professor Sweetchild, and Mme. Kleber), "is Marie Sanfon so remarkably good-looking that she can turn any man's head?"

"No, she is nothing of the kind. It says everywhere that her appearance is perfectly ordinary, with absolutely no distinctive features." Gauche cast a lingering challenging glance in Clarissa's direction. "She changes the color of her hair, her behavior, her accent, and the way she dresses with the greatest of ease. But evidently there must be something exceptional about this woman. In my line of work, I've seen all sorts of things. The most devastating heartbreakers are not usually great beauties. If you saw them in a photograph, you would never pick them out, but when you meet them you can feel your skin creep. It's not a straight nose and long eyelashes that a man goes for; it's a certain special smell."

"Oh, Commissioner," Clarissa objected at this vulgar comment. "There are ladies present."

"There are certainly suspects present," Gauche parried calmly. "And you are one of them. How do I know that Mlle. Sanfon is not sitting at this very table?"

He fixed his eyes on Clarissa's face. This was becoming more and more like a bad dream. She could hardly catch her breath.

"If I have c-calculated correctly, then this person should be twenty-nine now?"

Fandorin's calm, almost indifferent question roused Clarissa to take a grip on herself, and casting female vanity aside, she cried out: "There is no point in staring at me like that, monsieur detective! You are obviously paying me a compliment that I do not deserve. I am almost ten years older than your adventuress! And the other ladies present are hardly suited to the role of Mlle. Sanfon. Mme. Kleber is too young and Mrs. Truffo, as you know, does not speak French!"

"For a woman of Marie Sanfon's skill, it is a very simple trick to add or subtract ten years from her age," Gauche replied slowly, staring at Clarissa as intently as ever. "Especially if the prize is so great and failure smacks of the guillotine. So, have you really never been to Paris, Mlle. Stamp? Somewhere in the region of the Rue de Grenelle, perhaps?"

Clarissa turned deathly pale.

"At this point, I feel obliged to intervene as a representative of the Jasper-Artaud Partnership," Renier interrupted irritably. "Ladies and gentlemen, I can assure you there is absolutely no way that any swindler or crook with an international reputation could have joined our cruise. The company guarantees there are no cardsharps or loose women on board the *Leviathan*, let alone adventuresses known to the police. You can understand why. A maiden voyage is a very great responsibility. A scandal is the very last thing we need. Captain Cliff and I personally checked and rechecked the passenger lists, and whenever necessary we made inquiries—including some to the French police, monsieur commissioner. The captain and I are prepared to vouch for everyone present here. We do not wish to prevent you from carrying out your professional duty, M. Gauche, but you are simply wasting your time. And French taxpayers' money."

"Well, now," growled Gauche, "that only time will tell."

Following which, to everyone's relief, Mrs. Truffo struck up a conversation about the weather.

Reginald Milford-Stokes

10 April 1878
22 hours, 31 minutes
In the Arabian Sea
17° 06' 28" N 59° 48' 14" E

My passionately beloved Emily,

This infernal ark is controlled by the forces of evil; I can sense it in every fiber of my tormented soul. Although I am not sure a criminal such as I can have a soul. Writing that has set me thinking. I remember that I have committed a crime, a terrible crime that can never ever be forgiven, but the strange thing is, I have completely forgotten what it was I did. And I very much do not want to remember.

At night, in my dreams, I remember it very well—otherwise how can I explain why I wake up in such a terrible state every morning? How I long for our separation to be over! I feel that if it lasts for even a little longer, I shall lose my mind. I sit in the cabin and stare at the minute hand of the chronometer, but it doesn't move. Outside on the deck I heard someone say, "It's the tenth of April today," and I couldn't grasp how it could possibly be April and why it had to be the tenth. I unlocked the trunk and saw that the letter I wrote to you yesterday was dated the ninth of April and the one from the day before yesterday was dated the eighth. So they're right. It is April. The tenth.

For several days now I have been keeping a close eye on Professor

Sweetchild (if he really is a professor). He is a very popular man with our group in Windsor, an inveterate old windbag who loves to flaunt his knowledge of history and oriental matters. Every day he comes up with new, fantastic stories of hidden treasure, each more improbable than the last. And he has nasty, shifty, piggy little eyes. Sometimes there is an insane gleam in them. If only you could hear how sensual his voice sounds when he talks about precious stones. He has a positive mania for diamonds and emeralds.

Today at breakfast Dr. Truffo suddenly stood up, clapped his hands loudly, and announced in a solemn voice that it was Mrs. Truffo's birthday. Everybody oohed and aahed and began congratulating her, and the doctor himself publicly presented his plain-faced spouse with a gift for the occasion, a pair of topaz earrings in exceptionally bad taste. What terrible vulgarity, to make a spectacle of giving a present to one's own wife! Mrs. Truffo, however, did not seem to think so. She became unusually lively and appeared perfectly happy, and her dismal features turned the color of a grated carrot. The lieutenant said: "Oh, madam, if we had known about this happy event in advance, we would certainly have prepared some surprise for you. You have only your own modesty to blame." The empty-headed woman turned an even more luminous shade and muttered bashfully: "Would you really like to make me happy?" The response was a general lazy mumble of goodwill. "Well, then," she said, "let's play my favorite game, lotto. In our family we always used to take out the cards and the bag of counters on Sundays and church holidays. It's such wonderful fun! Gentlemen, it will really make me very happy if you play!" It was the first time I had heard the doctor's wife speak at such length. For an instant I thought she was making fun of us, but no, Mrs. Truffo was entirely serious. There was nothing to be done. Only Renier managed to slip out, supposedly because it was time for him to go on watch. The churlish commissioner also attempted to cite some urgent business or other as an excuse, but everyone stared at him so reproachfully that he gave in with a bad grace and stayed.

Mr. Truffo went to fetch the equipment for this idiotic game and the torment began. Everyone dejectedly set out their cards, glancing longingly at the sunlit deck. The windows of the salon were wide open, but we sat there playing out a scene from the nursery. We set up a prize fund to which everyone contributed a guinea—"To make things more interesting" as the elated birthday girl said. Our leading lady should have had the best chance of winning, since she was the only one who was watching eagerly as the numbers were drawn. I had the impression that the commissioner would have liked to win the jackpot, too, but he had difficulty understanding the childish little rhymes that Mrs. Truffo kept spouting—for her sake on this occasion we spoke English.

The pitiful topaz earrings, which are worth ten pounds at the most, prompted Sweetchild to turn to his obsession again. "An excellent present, sir!" he declared to the doctor, who beamed in delight, but then Sweetchild spoiled everything with what he said next. "Of course, topazes are cheap nowadays, but who knows, perhaps their price will shoot up in a hundred years or so. Precious stones are so unpredictable! They are a genuine miracle of nature, unlike those boring metals, gold and silver. Metal has no soul or form, it can be melted down, while each stone has a unique personality. But it is not just anyone who can find them, only those who stop at nothing and are willing to follow their magical radiance to the ends of the earth, or even beyond, if necessary." These bombastic sentiments were accompanied by Mrs. Truffo calling out the numbers on the counters in her squeaky voice. While Sweetchild was declaiming, "I shall tell you the legend of the great and mighty conqueror Mahmud Gaznevi, who was bewitched by the brilliant luster of diamonds and put half of India to fire and the sword in his search for these magical crystals," Mrs. Truffo said: "Eleven, gentlemen. Drumsticks!" And so it went on.

But I shall tell you Sweetchild's legend of Mahmud Gaznevi anyway. It will give you a better understanding of this storyteller. I can even attempt to convey his distinctive manner of speech.

"In the year (I don't remember which) of our Lord Jesus Christ, which according to the Moslem chronology was (and of course I don't remember that), the mighty Gaznevi learned that in Sumnat on the peninsula of Guzzarat (I think that was it) there was a holy shrine that housed an immense idol worshiped by hundreds of thousands of people. The idol jealously guarded the borders of that land against foreign invasions, and anyone who stepped across them with a sword in his hand was doomed. This shrine belonged to a powerful Brahman community, the richest in all India. And these Brahmans of Sumnat also possessed an immense number of precious stones. But, unafraid of the power of the idol, the intrepid conqueror gathered his forces together and launched his campaign. Mahmud hewed off fifty thousand heads, reduced fifty fortresses to ruins, and finally burst into the Sumnat shrine. His soldiers defiled the holy site and ransacked it from top to bottom, but they could not find the treasure. Then Gaznevi himself approached the idol, swung his great mace, and smote its copper head. The Brahmans fell to the floor before their conqueror and offered him a million pieces of silver if only he would not touch their god. Mahmud laughed and smote the idol again. It cracked. The Brahmans began wailing more loudly than ever and promised this terrible ruler ten million pieces of gold. But the heavy mace was raised once again and it struck for a third time. The idol split in half and the diamonds and precious stones that had been concealed within it spilled out on to the floor in a gleaming torrent. The value of that treasure was beyond all calculation."

At this point Mr. Fandorin announced with a slightly embarrassed expression that he had a full card. Everyone except Mrs. Truffo was absolutely delighted and was on the point of leaving when she begged us so insistently to play another round that we had to stay. It started up again: "Thirty-nine—pig and swine! Twenty-seven—I'm in heaven!" and more drivel of the same kind.

But now Mr. Fandorin began speaking, and he told us another story in his gentle, rather ironic manner, an Arab fairy tale that he had read in an old book. Here is the fable as I remember it.

"Once upon a time three Maghreb merchants set out into the depths of the Great Desert, for they had learned that far, far away among the shifting sands, where the caravans do not go, there was a Great Treasure, the equal of which mortal eyes had never seen. The merchants walked for forty days, tormented by great heat and weariness, until they had only one camel each left—the others had all collapsed and died. Suddenly they saw a tall mountain ahead of them, and when they grew close to it they could not believe their eyes: The entire mountain consisted of silver ingots. The merchants gave thanks to Allah, and one of them stuffed a sack full of silver and set off back the way they had come. But the others said: 'We shall go farther.' They walked for another forty days, until their faces were blackened by the sun and their eyes were red and inflamed. Then another mountain appeared ahead of them, this time of gold. The second merchant exclaimed: 'Not in vain have we endured so many sufferings! Glory be to the Most High!' He stuffed a sack full of gold and asked his comrade: 'Why are you just standing there?' The third merchant replied: 'How much gold can you carry away on one camel?' The second said: 'Enough to make me the richest man in our city.' 'That is not enough for me,' said the third. 'I shall go farther and find a mountain of diamonds. And when I return home, I shall be the richest man in the entire world.' He walked on, and his journey lasted another forty days. His camel lay down and rose no more, but the merchant did not stop, since he was stubborn and believed in the mountain of diamonds, and everyone knows that a single handful of diamonds is more valuable than a mountain of silver or a hill of gold. Then the third merchant beheld a wondrous sight ahead of him: A man standing there doubled over in the middle of the desert, bearing a throne made of diamonds on his shoulders, and squatting on the throne was a monster with a black face and burning eyes. 'Joyous greetings to you, O worthy traveler,' croaked the doubled-over man. 'Allow me to introduce Marduf, the demon of avarice. Now you will bear him on your shoulders until another as avaricious as you and I comes to take your place.' "

The story was broken off at that point, because once again Mr. Fandorin had a full card, so our hostess failed to win the second jackpot, too. Five seconds later Mrs. Truffo was the only person left at the table—everyone else had disappeared in a flash.

I keep thinking about Mr. Fandorin's story. It is not as simple as it seems.

That third merchant is Sweetchild. Yes, when I heard the end of the story, I suddenly realized how dangerous a madman he is! An uncontrollable passion rages in his soul, and if anyone should know what that means, it is me. I have been gliding around after him like an invisible shadow ever since we left Aden.

I have already told you, my precious Emily, that I spent the time we were moored there very profitably. I'm sure you must have thought I meant I had bought a new navigational instrument to replace the one that was stolen. Yes, I now have a new sextant and I am checking the ship's course regularly once again, but what I meant was something quite different. I was simply afraid to commit my secret to paper. What if someone were to read it? For, after all, I am surrounded by enemies on all sides. But I have a resourceful mind, and I have invented a fine stratagem: Starting today I am writing in milk. To the eye of a stranger it will seem like a clean sheet of paper, quite uninteresting, but my quick-witted Emily will warm the sheets on the lamp shade to make the writing appear! What a fine dodge, eh?

Well then, about Aden. While I was still on the steamer, before they let us go ashore, I noticed that Sweetchild was nervous; more than simply nervous, he was positively jumping up and down with excitement. It began soon after Fandorin announced that the shawl stolen from Lord Littleby was the key to the mythical treasure of the Emerald Rajah. The professor became terribly agitated, started muttering to himself, and kept repeating: "Ah, I must get ashore soon." But what for, that was the question!

I decided to find out.

Pulling my black hat with the wide brim well down over my eyes, I set off to follow Sweetchild. It could not have gone better at first: He didn't glance round once and I had no trouble trailing him to the square behind the little customs house. But there I was in for an unpleasant surprise. Sweetchild called one of the local cabbies and drove off with him. His barouche was moving rather slowly, but I could not go running after it; that would have been unseemly. Of course, there were other barouches on the square, and I could easily have got into any of them, but you know, my dearest, how heartily I detest open carriages. They are the devil's own invention and only reckless fools ride in them. Some people (I have seen it with my own eyes more than once) even take their wives and innocent children with them. How long can it be before disaster strikes? The two-wheelers so popular at home in Britain are especially dangerous. Someone once told me (I can't recall who it was at the moment) that a certain young man from a very decent family, with a good position in society, was rash enough to take his young wife for a ride in one of those two-wheelers when she was eight months pregnant. It ended badly, of course: The mad fool lost control of the horses, which bolted, and the carriage overturned. The young man was all right, but his wife went into premature labor. They were unable to save her or the child. And all because of his recklessness. They could have gone for a walk or taken a ride in a boat. If it comes to that, one can take a ride on a train. In Venice they take rides in gondolas. We were there, remember? Remember how the water lapped at the steps of the hotel?

I am finding it hard to concentrate; I am constantly digressing. And so Sweetchild rode off in a carriage, and I was left standing beside the customs house. But do you think I lost my head? Not at all. I thought of something that calmed my nerves almost instantly. While I was waiting for Sweetchild, I went into a sailors' shop and bought a new sextant, even better than the old one, and a splendid navigational almanac with astronomical formulae. Now I can calculate the ship's position much faster and more precisely. See what a sly fellow I am!

I waited for six hours and thirty-eight minutes. I sat on a rock and looked at the sea, thinking about you.

When Sweetchild returned, I pretended to be dozing. He slipped past me, certain that I had not seen him.

The moment he disappeared round the corner of the customs house, I dashed across to his cabby. For six pence the Bengali told me where our dear professor had been. You must admit, my sweet Emily, that I handled this business most adroitly.

The information I received only served to corroborate my initial suspicions. Sweetchild had asked to be taken from the port directly to the telegraph office. He spent half an hour there, and then went back to the post office building another four times. The cabby said: "Sahib very-very worried. Run backward and forward. Sometimes say: Take me to bazaar, then tap me on back—take me back, post office, quick-quick." It seems quite clear that Sweetchild first sent off an urgent message to someone and then waited impatiently for an answer. The Bengali said that the last time he came out of the post office he was "not like himself, he wave paper" and told the cabby to drive him back to the ship. His reply must have arrived.

I do not know what was in it, but it is perfectly clear that the professor, or whoever he really is, has accomplices.

That was two days ago. Since then Sweetchild has been a changed man. As I have already told you, he speaks of nothing but precious stones all the time, and sometimes he suddenly sits down on the deck and starts drawing something, either on his cuff or his handkerchief.

This evening there was a ball in the grand salon. I have already described this majestic hall, which appears to have been transported here from Versailles or Buckingham Palace. There is gilt everywhere and the walls are covered from top to bottom with mirrors. The crystal electric chandeliers tinkle melodically in time to the gentle rolling of the ship. The orchestra (a perfectly decent one, by the way) mostly played Viennese waltzes, and as you know, I regard that dance as indecent, so I stood in the corner, keeping an eye on Sweetchild. He was enjoying himself greatly, inviting one lady after another to dance, skipping about like a goat and trampling on their feet outrageously, but he did not notice at all. I myself was even distracted, recalling how you and I once used to dance, and how elegant your arm looked in its white glove as it lay on my shoulder. Suddenly I saw Sweetchild stumble and drop his partner; then, without even bothering to apologize, he fairly raced across almost to the tables with the hors d'oeuvres, leaving his partner standing bewildered in the middle of the hall. I must admit that this sudden attack of uncontrollable hunger struck me as rather strange, too.

Sweetchild, however, did not even glance at the dishes of pies, cheese, and fruit. He grabbed a paper napkin out of a silver napkin holder, hunched over the table, and began furiously scribbling something on it. He has become completely obsessed, and obviously no longer feels it necessary to guard his secret, even in a crowded room! Consumed by curiosity, I began strolling casually in his direction. But Sweetchild had already straightened up and folded the napkin twice, evidently intending to put it in his pocket. Unfortunately, I was too late to glance at it over his shoulder. I stamped my foot furiously and was about to turn back when I noticed Mr. Fandorin coming over to the table with two glasses of champagne. He handed one to Sweetchild and kept the other for himself. I heard the Russian say: "Ah, my dear professor, how terribly absentminded you are! You have just put a dirty napkin in your pocket." Sweetchild was embarrassed; he took the napkin out, crumpled it into a ball, and threw it under the table. I immediately joined them and deliberately struck up a conversation about fashion, knowing the Indologist would soon grow bored and leave. Which is exactly what happened.

No sooner had he made his apologies and left us alone than Fandorin whispered to me conspiratorially: "Well, Sir Reginald, which of us is going to crawl under the table?" I realized that the diplomat was as suspicious of the professor's behavior as I was. We understood each other completely in an instant. "Yes, it is not exactly convenient," I agreed. Mr. Fandorin glanced around and then suggested: "Let us do this thing fairly and honestly. If one of us can come up with a reasonable pretext, the other will crawl after the napkin." I nodded and started thinking, but nothing appropriate came to mind. "Eureka!" whispered Fandorin, and with a movement so swift that I could barely see it, he unfastened one of my cuff links. It fell on the floor and the diplomat pushed it under the table with the toe of his shoe. "Sir Reginald," he said loudly enough for people standing nearby to hear, "I believe you have dropped a cuff link."

An agreement is an agreement. I squatted down and glanced under the table. The napkin was lying quite close, but the damned cufflink had skidded right across to the wall, and the table was rather wide. Imagine the scene: your husband crawling under the table on all fours, presenting the crowded hall with a view that was far from edifying. On my way back I got into a rather embarrassing fix. When I stuck my head out from under the table, I saw two young ladies directly in front of me, engaged in lively conversation with Mr. Fandorin. When they spotted my red head at the level of their knees, the ladies squealed in fright, but my perfidious companion merely said calmly: "Allow me to introduce Baronet Milford-Stokes." The ladies gave me a distinctly chilly look and left without saying a word. I leapt to my feet, absolutely bursting with fury, and exclaimed: "Sir, you deliberately stopped them so that you could make fun of me!" Fandorin replied with an innocent expression: "I did stop them deliberately, but not at all in order to make fun of you. It simply occurred to me that their skirts would conceal your daring raid from the eyes of the hall. But where is your booty?"

My hands trembled impatiently as I unfolded the napkin, revealing a strange sight. I am drawing it from memory.

What are these geometrical figures? What does the zigzagging line mean? And why are there three exclamation marks?

I cast a stealthy glance at Fandorin. He tugged at his earlobe and muttered something I didn't catch. I expect it was in Russian.

"What do you make of it?" I asked. "Let's wait for a while," the diplomat replied, a mysterious expression on his face. "He's getting close."

Who is getting close? Sweetchild? Close to what? And is it a good thing that he is getting close?

I had no chance to ask these questions, because at that moment there was a commotion in the hall and everyone started applauding. Then M. Driet, the captain's social director, began shouting deafeningly through a megaphone: "Ladies and gentlemen, the grand prize in our lottery goes to cabin number eighteen!" I had been so absorbed in the operation with the mysterious napkin that I had paid absolutely no attention to what was going on in the hall. It turned out that they had stopped dancing and set up the draw for the charity raffle in aid of fallen women (I wrote to you about this idiotic undertaking in my letter of the third of April). You are well aware how I feel about charity and fallen women, so I shall refrain from further comment.

The announcement had a strange effect on my companion—he frowned and ducked, lowering his head. I was surprised for a moment, and then I remembered that number eighteen is Mr. Fandorin's cabin. Just imagine that, he was the lucky winner again!

"This is becoming quite intolerable," our favorite of fortune mumbled, stammering more than usual. "I think I shall take a walk." He started backing away toward the door, but Mme. Kleber called out in her clear voice: "That's Mr. Fandorin from our salon! There he is, gentlemen! In the white dinner jacket with the red carnation! Mr. Fandorin, where are you going? You've won the grand prize!"

Everyone turned to look at the diplomat and began applauding more loudly than ever as four stewards carried the grand prize into the hall: an exceptionally ugly grandfather clock modeled after Big Ben. It was an absolutely repulsive construction of carved oak one and a half times the height of a man, and it must have weighed at least forty stone. I thought I caught a glimpse of something like horror in Mr. Fandorin's eyes. I must say I cannot blame him.

After that it was impossible to carry on talking, so I came back here to write this letter.

I have the feeling something terrible is about to happen; the noose is tightening around me. But you pursue me in vain, gentlemen, I am ready for you!

However, the hour is already late and it is time to take a reading of our position.

Good-bye, my dear, sweet, infinitely adored Emily.

Your loving

Reginald Milford-Stokes

Renate Kleber

RENATE LAY IN wait for the Watchdog (that was what she had christened Gauche once she discovered what the old bore was really like) outside his cabin. It was clear from the commissioner's wrinkled features and
tousled gray hair that he had only just risen from his slumbers—he must
have collapsed into bed immediately after lunch and snoozed into the evening.

Renate deftly grabbed hold of the detective's sleeve, lifted herself up
on tiptoe, and blurted out: "Wait till you hear what I have to tell you!"

The Watchdog gave her a searching look, crossed his arms, and said in
an unpleasant voice: "I shall be very interested to hear it. I've been meaning to have a word with you for some time, madam."

Renate found his tone of voice slightly alarming, but she decided it
didn't really mean anything—the Watchdog must be suffering from indi-
gestion, or perhaps he'd been having a bad dream.

"I've done your job for you," Renate boasted, glancing around to
make sure no one was listening. "Let's go into your cabin; we won't be interrupted there."

The Watchdog's abode was maintained in perfect order. The familiar
black file reposed impressively in the center of the desk, a neat pile of paper
and several precisely sharpened pencils lying beside it. Renate surveyed the
room curiously, turning her head this way and that, noting the shoe brush
and tin of polish and the shirt collars hung up to dry on a piece of string.
The man with the big mustache was obviously a penny-pincher—he pol-

ished his own shoes and did a bit of laundry to avoid having to give tips to the attendants.

"Right, then, out with it—what have you got for me?" the Watchdog growled irritably, clearly displeased by Renate's inquisitiveness.

"I know who the criminal is," she announced proudly.

This news failed to produce the anticipated effect on the detective. He sighed and asked: "Who is it?"

"Need you ask? It's so obvious a blind man could see it," Renate said, fluttering her hands as she sat down in an armchair. "All the newspapers said that the murder was committed by a lunatic. No normal person could possibly do anything so insane, could they? And now just think about the people we have sitting round our table. It's a choice collection of course, perfectly matching blooms, bores and freaks every last one of them, but there's only one lunatic."

"Are you hinting at the baronet?" asked the Watchdog.

"Finally you've got it!" said Renate with a pitying nod. "Why, it's as clear as day. Have you seen his eyes when he looks at me? He's a wild beast, a monster! I'm afraid to walk down the corridors. Yesterday I ran into him on the stairs when there wasn't a soul around. It gave me such a twinge in here!" She put one hand over her belly. "I've been watching him for a long time. At night he keeps the light on in his cabin and his curtains tightly closed. But yesterday they were open just a tiny little crack, so I peeped in. He was standing there in the middle of the cabin, waving his arms about and making ghastly faces and wagging his finger at somebody. It was so frightening! Later on, in the middle of the night, my migraine started up again, so I went out for a breath of fresh air, and there I saw the lunatic standing on the forecastle, looking up at the moon through some kind of metal contraption. That was when it dawned on me. He's one of those maniacs whose bloodlust rises with the full moon. I've read about them! Why are you looking at me as if I was some kind of idiot? Have you taken a look at the calendar recently?" Renate triumphantly produced a pocket calendar from her purse. "Look at this, I've checked it. On the fifteenth of March, when ten people were killed in the Rue de Grenelle, it was a full moon. See, it's written here in black and white: *pleine lune*."

The Watchdog looked, all right, but he didn't seem very interested.

"Why are you eyeing it like a dozy owl?" Renate asked angrily. "Don't you understand that today there's a full moon, too? While you're sitting around doing nothing, he'll go crazy again and brain somebody else. And I know who it will be—me. He hates me." Her voice trembled hysterically. "Everyone on this loathsome steamer wants to kill me! That African attacked me, that oriental of ours keeps glaring and grinding his teeth at me, and now it's this crazy baronet!"

The Watchdog merely gazed at her with his dull, unblinking eyes, and Renate waved her hand in front of his nose.

"Hallo! M. Gauche! You haven't fallen asleep, have you?"

The old man grabbed her wrist in a firm grip. He moved her hand aside and said sternly: "I'll tell you what, my dear. Stop playing the fool. I'll deal with our redheaded baronet, but I want you to tell me about your syringe. And no fairy tales—I want the truth!" He growled out the words so fiercely that she shrank back from him in alarm.

AT SUPPER SHE sat staring down into her plate. She always had an excellent appetite, but today she had hardly even touched her sautéed eels. Her eyes were red and swollen and every now and then her lips trembled slightly.

But the Watchdog was in a genial, even magnanimous mood. He looked at Renate frequently and with some severity, but his glance was fatherly rather than hostile. Commissioner Gauche was not as fierce as he liked to appear.

"A very impressive piece," he said with an envious glance at the Big Ben clock standing in the corner of the salon. "Some people have all the luck."

The monumental prize was too big to fit in Fandorin's cabin, and so it had been installed temporarily in Windsor. The oak tower continually ticked, jangled, and wheezed deafeningly, and on the hour it boomed out a noise that caught everyone by surprise, making them gasp. At breakfast, when Big Ben informed everyone (ten minutes late) that it was nine o'clock, the doctor's wife almost swallowed a teaspoon. In addition to all of this, the base of the tower was obviously a bit too narrow, and every strong wave set it swaying menacingly. Now, for instance, when the wind had freshened and the white curtains at the windows had begun waving in surrender, Big Ben's squeaky motions had become positively alarming.

The Russian seemed to take the commissioner's genuine admiration for irony and began making apologetic excuses.

"I t-told them to give the clock to fallen women, too, but M. Driet was adamant. I swear by Christ, Allah, and Buddha that when we g-get to Calcutta I shall leave this monster on the steamer. I won't permit that nightmare to be foisted on me!"

He squinted anxiously at Lieutenant Renier, who remained diplomatically silent. Then the diplomat turned to Renate for sympathy, but all she gave him in reply was a severe, sullen glance. In the first place, she was in a very bad mood; in the second, Fandorin had been out of favor with her for some time.

There was a story behind that.

It all started when Renate noticed that the sickly Mrs. Truffo positively blossomed whenever she was near the sweet little diplomat. And Mr. Fandorin himself seems to belong to that common variety of handsome males who manage to discover something fascinating in every dull woman they meet, and never neglect a single one. In principle Renate regarded this subspecies of men with respect, and actually found its members quite attractive. It would be very interesting to know what precious ore the blue-eyed, brown-haired Russian had managed to unearth in the dismal doctor's wife. There certainly could be no doubt he felt distinctly interested in her.

A few days earlier, Renate had witnessed an amusing scene played out by two actors: Mrs. Truffo (in the role of female vamp) and Mr. Fandorin (in the role of perfidious seducer). The audience had consisted of one young lady (quite exceptionally attractive, despite being in a certain delicate condition) who was concealed behind the tall back of a deck chair and following the action in her makeup mirror. The action was set at the stern of the ship. The time was a romantic sunset. The play was performed in English.

The doctor's wife had executed her lumbering approach to the diplomat with all the elephantine grace of a typical British seduction (both dramatis personae were standing at the rail, in profile to the aforementioned deck chair). Mrs. Truffo began, as was proper, with the weather.

"The sun is so very bright in these southern latitudes!" she bleated with passionate feeling.

"Oh, yes," replied Fandorin. "In Russia at this time of the year the snow has still not melted, and here the temperature is already thirty-five degrees Celsius, and that is in the shade. In the sunlight it is even hotter."

The preliminaries having been successfully concluded, Mrs. Goatface felt she could legitimately broach a more intimate subject.

"I simply don't know what to do!" she began in a modest tone appropriate to her theme. "I have such white skin! This insufferable sun will ruin my complexion or even, God forbid, give me freckles."

"The problem of f-freckles is one that worries me as well," the Russian replied in all seriousness. "But I was prudent and brought along a lotion made of extract of Turkish camomile. Look, my suntan is even and there are no freckles at all."

The cunning serpent presented his pretty little face temptingly to the respectable married woman.

Mrs. Truffo's voice trembled treacherously.

"Indeed, not a single freckle . . . And your eyebrows and eyelashes are barely bleached. You have a wonderful epithelium, Mr. Fandorin, quite wonderful!"

Now he'll kiss her, Renate predicted, seeing that the distance separating the diplomat's epithelium from the flushed features of the doctor's wife was a mere five centimeters.

But her prediction was mistaken.

Fandorin stepped back and said: "Epithelium? Are you familiar with the science of physiology?"

"A little," Mrs. Truffo replied modestly. "Before I was married, I had some involvement with medicine."

"Indeed? How interesting! You really must t-tell me about it!"

Unfortunately Renate had not been able to follow the performance all the way to its conclusion—a woman she knew had sat down beside her and she had been obliged to break off her surveillance.

However, the clumsy assault by the doctor's foolish wife had piqued Renate's own vanity. Why should she not ply her own charms on this nice-looking Russian bear cub? Purely out of sporting interest, naturally, and in order to maintain the skills without which no self-respecting woman could get by. Renate had no interest in the thrill of romance. In fact, in her present condition the only feeling that men aroused in her was nausea.

In order to while away the time (Renate's phrase was "to speed up the voyage"), she worked out a simple plan. Small-scale naval maneuvers, code name "Bear Hunt." In fact, of course, men were actually more like members of the canine family. Everybody knew they were primitive creatures who could be divided into three main types: jackals, sheepdogs, and gay dogs. There was a different approach for each type.

The jackal fed on carrion—that is, he preferred easy prey. Men of that kind went for the readily available.

And so the very next time they were alone together, Renate complained to Fandorin about M. Kleber, the tedious banker whose head was full of nothing but figures, the bore who had no time for his young wife. Any half-wit would have realized that here was a woman literally pining under the tedium of her empty life, ready to swallow any hook, even an unbaited one.

That didn't work, and she had to waste a lot of time parrying inquisitive questions about her husband's bank.

Very well, so next Renate set her trap for a sheepdog. This category of men loved weak, helpless women. All they really wanted was to be allowed to rescue and protect you. A fine subspecies, very useful to have around. The main thing here was not to overdo the physical weakness—men were afraid of sick women.

Renate had swooned a couple of times from the heat, slumping gracefully against the ironclad shoulder of her knight and protector. Once she had been unable to open the door to her cabin because the key had got stuck. On the evening of the ball, she had asked Fandorin to protect her from a tipsy (and entirely harmless) major of dragoons.

The Russian had lent her his shoulder, opened the door, and sent the dragoon packing, but he himself had not betrayed the slightest sign of amorous interest, the louse.

Could he in fact be a gay dog? Renate wondered. You certainly wouldn't think so to look at him. This third type of man was the least complicated, and entirely devoid of imagination. Only a coarsely sensual stimulus, such as a chance glimpse of an ankle, had any effect on them. On the other hand, many great men and even cultural luminaries belonged to precisely this category, so it was certainly worth a try.

With gay dogs the approach was elementary. Renate asked the diplomat to come and see her at precisely midday, so that she could show him her watercolors (which were nonexistent). At one minute to twelve the huntress was already standing in front of her mirror, dressed only in her bodice and pantaloons.

When there was a knock at the door she called out: "Come in, come in, I've been waiting!"

Fandorin stepped inside and froze in the doorway. Without turning round, Renate wiggled her rear at him and displayed her naked back to its best advantage. The wise beauties of the eighteenth century had discovered that it was not a dress open down to the navel that produced the strongest effect on men, but an open neck and a bare back. Obviously the sight of a defenseless spine roused the predatory instinct in the human male.

The diplomat seemed to have been affected. He stood there looking, not turning away. Pleased with the effect, Renate said capriciously: "What are you doing over there, Jenny? Come here and help me on with my dress. I'm expecting a very important guest any minute."

How would any normal man have behaved in this situation?

The more forward kind would have come up behind her without saying a word and kissed the soft curls on the back of her neck.

The average, fair-to-middling kind would have handed her the dress and giggled bashfully.

At that point Renate would have decided the hunt had been successfully concluded. She would have pretended to be embarrassed, thrown the insolent creature out, and lost all further interest in him. But Fandorin's response was unusual.

"It's not Jenny," he said in a disgustingly calm voice. "It is I, Erast Fandorin. I shall wait outside while you g-get dressed."

He was either one of the rare seduction-proof variety or a secret pervert. In the latter case, the Englishwomen were simply wasting their time and effort. But Renate's keen eye had not detected any of the characteristic

signs of perversion. Apart, that was, from his strange predilection for se-
cluded conversations with the Watchdog.

But this was all trivial nonsense. She had more serious reasons for
being upset.

AT THE VERY moment Renate finally decided to plunge her fork into the
cold sautée, the doors crashed open and the bespectacled professor burst
into the dining room. He always looked a little wild—either his jacket was
buttoned crookedly or his shoelaces were undone—but today he looked a
real mess: His beard was disheveled, his tie had slipped over to one side, his
eyes were bulging out of his head, and a suspender was dangling from
under the flap of his jacket. Obviously something quite extraordinary must
have happened. Renate instantly forgot her own troubles and stared curiously at the learned scarecrow.

Sweetchild spread his arms like a ballet dancer and shouted: "Eureka,
gentlemen! The mystery of the Emerald Rajah is solved!"

"Oh, no," groaned Mrs. Truffo. "Not again!"

"Now I can see how it all fits together," said the professor, launching abruptly into an incoherent explanation. "After all, I was there—why
didn't I realize it before? I kept thinking about it, going round and round in
circles, but it just didn't add up. In Aden I received a telegram from an acquaintance of mine in the French Ministry of the Interior. He confirmed
my suspicions, but I still couldn't make any sense of the eye, and most important, I couldn't work out who it could be. That is, I more or less know
who, but how? How was it done? But now it has suddenly dawned on me!"
He ran over to the window. A curtain fluttering in the wind enveloped him
like a white shroud, and the professor impatiently pushed it aside. "I was
standing at the window of my cabin, knotting my tie, and I saw the waves,
crest after crest all the way to the horizon. And then suddenly it hit me!
Everything fell into place—about the shawl, and about the son! It's a matter of clerical work pure and simple. Dig around in the registers at the
École Maritime and you'll find him!"

"I don't understand a word," growled the Watchdog. "You're raving.
What's this about some school or other?"

"Oh, no, this is very, very interesting," exclaimed Renate. "I just love trying to solve mysteries. But, my dear professor, this will never do. Sit down at the table, have some wine, catch your breath, and tell us everything from the beginning, calmly and clearly. After all, you have such a wonderful way with a story. But first someone must bring me my shawl so I don't catch a chill in this draft."

"Let me close the windows on the windward side, and the draft will stop immediately," Sweetchild suggested. "You are right, madam, I should tell you the whole thing starting from the beginning."

"No, don't close the windows—it will be too stuffy. Well, gentlemen?" Renate inquired capriciously. "Who will fetch my shawl from my cabin? Here is the key! Monsieur baronet?"

Of course the Ginger Lunatic did not stir, and Renier leapt to his feet.

"Professor, I implore you, do not start without me!" he said. "I shall be back in a moment."

"And I'll go get my knitting," said the doctor's wife with a sigh.

She got back first and began deftly clacking away with her needles. She waved her hand at her husband to tell him there was no need to translate.

Meanwhile Sweetchild was readying himself for his moment of triumph. Having taken Renate's advice to heart, he seemed determined to expound his discoveries as spectacularly as possible.

There was complete silence at the table, with everyone watching the speaker and following each movement he made.

Sweetchild took a sip of red wine and began walking backward and forward across the room. Then he halted, picturesquely posed in profile to his audience, and began.

"I have already told you about that unforgettable day when Rajah Bagdassar invited me into his palace in Brahmapur. It was a quarter of a century ago, but I remember everything quite clearly, down to the smallest detail. The first thing that struck me was the appearance of the palace. Knowing that Bagdassar was one of the richest men in the world, I had been expecting to see oriental luxury on a grand scale. But there was nothing of the kind. The palace buildings were rather modest, without any ornamental refinements. And the thought came to me that the passion for precious stones that was hereditary in this family, handed down from father to son, must have displaced every other vainglorious ambition. Why spend money on walls of marble when you could buy another sapphire or diamond instead? The Brahmapur palace was squat and plain, essentially the same kind of clay casket in which that indescribable distillation of magical luminescence was kept. No marble and alabaster could ever have rivaled the blinding radiance of those stones." The professor took another sip of wine and adopted a thoughtful pose.

Renier arrived, puffing and panting, respectfully laid Renate's shawl across her shoulders, and remained standing beside her.

"What was that about marble and alabaster?" he asked in a whisper.

"It's about the Brahmapur palace—let me listen," said Renate with an impatient jerk of her chin.

"The décor of the palace was also very simple," Sweetchild continued. "Over the centuries the halls and rooms had changed in appearance many times, and the only part of the palace that seemed interesting to me from a historical point of view was the upper level, consisting of four halls, each of which faced one of the points of the compass. At one time the halls had been open galleries, but during the last century they had been glassed in. At the same time the walls were decorated with quite fascinating frescoes depicting the mountains that surround the valley on all sides. The landscape is reproduced with astonishing realism, so that the mountains seem to be reflected in a mirror. From the philosophical point of view, this mirror imaging must surely represent the duality of existence and—"

Somewhere nearby a ship's bell began clanging loudly. They heard people shouting, and a woman screamed.

"My God, it's the fire alarm!" shouted the lieutenant, dashing for the door. "That's all we need now!"

They dashed after him in a tight bunch.

"What's happening?" the startled Mrs. Truffo inquired. "Have we been boarded by pirates?"

Renate sat there for a moment with her mouth open, then let out a bloodcurdling squeal. She grabbed the tail of the commissioner's coat and stopped him running out after the others.

"M. Gauche, don't leave me!" she begged him. "I know what a fire on board ship means, I've read about it! Now everyone will dash to the lifeboats and people will be crushed to death, and I'm a weak pregnant woman, I'll just be swept aside! Promise you'll look after me!"

"What's that about lifeboats?" the old man mumbled anxiously. "What kind of nonsense is that? I've been told the firefighting arrangements on the *Leviathan* are exemplary. Why, the ship even has a special fire officer. Stop shaking, will you? Everything will be all right." He tried to free himself, but Renate was clutching his coattail in a grip of iron. Her teeth were chattering loudly.

"Let go of me, little girl," the Watchdog said in a soothing voice. "I won't go anywhere. I'll just take a look at the deck through the window."

But no, Renate's fingers didn't release their grip.

The commissioner was proved right. After two or three minutes there was the sound of leisurely footsteps and loud voices in the corridor, and one by one the Windsorites began to return.

They had still not recovered from their shock, so they were laughing a lot and talking more loudly than usual.

The first to come in were Clarissa Stamp, the Truffos, and Renier, whose face was flushed.

"It was nothing at all," the lieutenant announced. "Someone threw a burning cigar into a litter bin that had an old newspaper in it. The fire spread to a door curtain, but the crew was alert and they put the flames out in a moment . . . But I see that you were all prepared for a shipwreck," he said with a laugh, glancing significantly at Clarissa.

She was clutching her purse and a bottle of orangeade.

"Well, orangeade in order not to die of thirst in the middle of the ocean," Renier guessed. "But what is the purse for? You wouldn't have much use for it in a lifeboat."

Renate giggled hysterically, and Miss Old Maid, embarrassed, put the bottle back on the table. The Truffos were also well equipped: The doctor had managed to grab his bag of medical instruments and his wife was clutching a blanket to her breast.

"This is the Indian Ocean, madam; you would hardly have frozen to death," Renier said with a serious expression, and the stupid goat idiotically nodded her head.

The Japanese appeared holding a pathetic, bright-colored bundle . . . What could he have in there, a traveling hara-kiri kit?

The lunatic came in looking disheveled, clutching a small box—the kind normally used for holding writing instruments.

"Who were you planning to write to, Mr. Milford-Stokes? Ah, I understand! When Miss Stamp had drunk her orangeade, we could have stuck a letter in the bottle and sent it floating off across the ocean waves," suggested the lieutenant, who was obviously acting so jovially out of a sense of relief.

Now everyone was there except the professor and the diplomat.

"M. Sweetchild is no doubt packing his scholarly works, and monsieur le Russe is lighting the samovar for a final cup of tea," said Renate, infected by the lieutenant's lighthearted mood.

And there was the Russian, speak of the devil. He stood by the door, his handsome face as dark as a storm cloud.

"Well, M. Fandorin, have you decided to take your prize with you in the boat?" Renate inquired provocatively.

Everyone roared with laughter except the Russian, who failed to appreciate the joke, even though it was rather witty.

"Commissioner Gauche," he said quietly. "Would you be so kind as to step out into the corridor? As quickly as you can."

It was strange, but when he spoke these words the diplomat did not stammer once. Perhaps the nervous shock had cured him? Such things did happen.

Renate was on the point of joking about that, too, but she bit her tongue. It would probably have been going too far.

"What's all the hurry?" the Watchdog asked gruffly. "Another teller of tales. Later, young man, later. First I want to hear the rest of what the professor has to say. Where has he got to?"

Fandorin looked at the commissioner expectantly, but when he realized the old man was feeling obstinate and had no intention of going out into the corridor, he shrugged and said: "The professor will not be joining us."

Gauche scowled.

"And why would that be?"

"What do you mean, he won't be joining us?" Renate put in. "He stopped just when it was getting interesting! It's not fair!"

"Professor Sweetchild has just been murdered," the diplomat announced coolly.

"What's that?" the Watchdog roared. "Murdered? What do you mean, murdered?"

"I believe it was done with a surgical scalpel," the Russian replied with remarkable composure. "His throat was cut very neatly."

Commissioner Gauche

⚭⚭⚭

"ARE THEY EVER going to let us go ashore?" Mme. Kleber asked plaintively. "Everyone else is out strolling round Bombay, and we're just sitting here doing nothing."

The curtains were pulled across the windows to keep out the searing rays of the sun that scorched the deck and made the air sticky and suffocating. But although it was hot and stuffy in the Windsor salon, everyone sat there patiently, waiting for the truth to be revealed.

Gauche took out his watch—a presentation piece with a profile portrait of Napoleon III on it—and replied vaguely.

"Soon, ladies and gentlemen. I'll let you out soon. But not all of you."

At least he knew what he was waiting for: Inspector Jackson and his men were conducting a search. The murder weapon itself was probably lying at the bottom of the ocean, but some clues might have been left. They must have been. Of course, there was plenty of circumstantial evidence, anyway, but hard evidence always made a case look better. It was about time Jackson put in an appearance . . .

The *Leviathan* had reached Bombay at dawn. Since the evening of the previous day, all the Windsorites had been confined to their cabins under house arrest, and immediately the ship arrived in port, Gauche had contacted the authorities, informed them of his own conclusions, and requested their assistance. They had sent Jackson and a team of constables. *Come on, Jackson, get a move on,* thought Gauche, wishing the inspector would stop dragging his feet. After a sleepless night, the commissioner's head felt as heavy as lead and his liver had started playing up, but despite everything he was feeling pleased with himself. He had finally unraveled the knots in this tangled thread, and now he could see where it led to.

At half past eight, after finalizing his arrangements with the local police and spending some time at the telegraph office, Gauche had ordered the detainees assembled in the Windsor salon—it would be more convenient for the search. He hadn't even made an exception for Renate, who had been sitting beside him at the time of the murder and could not possibly have cut the professor's throat. The commissioner had been watching over his prisoners for more than three hours now, occupying a strategic position in the deep armchair opposite his *client*, and there were two armed policemen standing outside the door of the salon, where they could not be seen from inside.

The detainees were all too sweaty and nervous to make conversation. Renier dropped in from time to time, nodded sympathetically to Renate, and went off again about his business. The captain looked in twice, but he didn't say anything—he just gave the commissioner a savage glance, as if this whole mess was papa Gauche's fault.

The professor's deserted chair was like the gap left by a missing tooth. The Indologist himself was ashore, in the chilly vault of the Bombay municipal morgue. The thought of the dark shadows and the blocks of ice almost made Gauche envy the dead man. Lying there, with all his troubles behind him, no sweat-drenched collar chafing into his neck . . .

The commissioner looked at Dr. Truffo, who did not seem very comfortable, either: The sweat was streaming down his olive-skinned face, and his English Fury kept whispering in his ear.

"Why are you looking at me like that, monsieur?" Truffo exploded when he caught the policeman's glance. "Why do you keep staring at me? It's absolutely outrageous! What right do you have? I've been a respectable medical practitioner for fifteen years," he almost sobbed. "What difference does it make if a scalpel was used? Anyone could have done it!"

"Was it really done with a scalpel?" Mlle. Stamp asked timidly.

It was the first time anyone in the salon had mentioned what had happened.

"Yes, only a very-good-quality scalpel produces such a clean incision," Truffo replied angrily. "I inspected the body. Someone obviously grabbed Sweetchild from behind, put one hand over his mouth, and slit his throat with the other. The wall of the corridor is splattered with blood just above the height of a man. That's because his head was pulled back—"

"No great strength would have been required, then?" asked the Russian (our homegrown criminologist!). "The element of surprise would have b-been enough?"

The doctor gave a despondent shrug.

"I don't know, monsieur. I've never tried it."

Aha—at last! The door half opened and the inspector's bony features appeared in the gap. The inspector beckoned to the commissioner, who grunted with the effort of hoisting himself out of his armchair.

There was a pleasant surprise waiting for the commissioner in the corridor. Everything had worked out quite splendidly: a thorough job, efficient and elegant. Solid enough to bring the jury in straightaway, no lawyer could demolish evidence like that. Good old papa Gauche, he could still give any young buck a hundred yards' head start. And well done Jackson for his hard work!

The four of them went back into the salon together: the captain, Renier, Jackson, with Gauche bringing up the rear. At this stage he was feeling so pleased with himself that he even started humming a little tune. And his liver had stopped bothering him.

"Well, ladies and gentlemen, this is it," Gauche announced cheerfully, stepping out into the very center of the salon. He put his hands behind his back and swayed on his heels. It was a pleasant feeling to know you were a figure of some importance—even, in your own way, a ruler of destinies. The road had been long and hard, but he had reached the end at last. Now for the most enjoyable part.

"Papa Gauche has certainly had to rack his old brains, but an old hunting dog will always sniff out the fox's den, no matter how confused the trail might be. By murdering Professor Sweetchild, our criminal has finally given himself away—it was an act of despair. I believe that under questioning the murderer will tell me all about the Indian shawl and many other things as well. Incidentally, I should like to thank our Russian diplomat, who without even knowing it helped to set me on the right track with several of his comments and questions."

In his moment of triumph, Gauche could afford to be magnanimous. He nodded condescendingly to Fandorin, who bowed his head without speaking. What a pain these aristocrats were, with all their airs and graces, always so arrogant; you could never get a civil word out of them.

"I shall not be traveling with you any farther. Thanks for the company, as they say, but all things in moderation. The murderer will also be going ashore: I shall hand him over to Inspector Jackson in a moment, here on board the ship."

Everyone in the salon looked warily at the morose, skinny Englishman standing there with his hands in his pockets.

"I am very glad this nightmare is over," said Captain Cliff. "I realize you have had to put up with much unpleasantness, but everything has been sorted out now. The head steward will find you places in different salons if you wish. I hope the remainder of your cruise on board the *Leviathan* will help you to forget this whole sad business."

"Hardly," said Mme. Kleber, answering for all of them. "This whole experience has been far too upsetting for all of us! But please don't keep us in suspense, monsieur commissioner. Tell us who the murderer is, quickly."

The captain was about to add something to what he had said, but Gauche raised his hand to stop him. This time he had earned the right to a solo performance.

"I must confess that at first my list of suspects included every single one of you. The process of elimination was long and difficult, but now I can reveal the most crucial point: Beside Lord Littleby's body we discovered one of the *Leviathan*'s gold emblems—this one here." He tapped the badge on his own lapel. "This little trinket belongs to the murderer. As you know, a gold badge could only have been worn by a senior officer of the ship or a first-class passenger. The officers were immediately eliminated from the list of suspects because they all had their badges and no one had requested the shipping line issue a new emblem to replace one that had been lost. But among the passengers there were four individuals who were not wearing a badge. Mlle. Stamp, Mme. Kleber, M. Milford-Stokes, and M. Aono. I have kept this quartet under particularly close observation. Dr. Truffo found himself here because he is a doctor, Mme. Truffo because husband and wife must not be set asunder, and our Russian diplomat because of his snobbish disinclination to appear like a janitor."

The commissioner lit his pipe and started pacing around the salon.

"I have erred, I confess. At the very beginning, I suspected monsieur le baronet, but I received timely information concerning his . . . circumstances and selected a different target. You, madam!" Gauche swung round to face Mlle. Stamp.

"As I observed," she replied coldly. "But I really cannot see what made me appear so suspicious."

"Oh, come now!" said Gauche, surprised. "In the first place, everything about you indicates that you suddenly became rich only very recently. That in itself is already highly suspicious. In the second place, you lied about never having been in Paris, even though the words 'Hotel Ambassadeur' are written on your fan in letters of gold. Of course you stopped carrying the fan, but old Gauche has sharp eyes. I spotted that trinket of yours straightaway. It is the sort of thing that expensive hotels give to their guests as mementos of their stay. The Ambassador happens to stand on the Rue de Grenelle, only a five-minute walk from the scene of the crime. It is a luxurious hotel, very large, and all sorts of people stay in it—so why is the mademoiselle being so secretive, I asked myself. There is something not right here. And I found I couldn't get the idea of Marie Sanfon out of my head . . ." The commissioner smiled disarmingly at Clarissa Stamp. "Well, I was casting around in the dark for a while, but eventually I hit upon the right trail, so I offer my apologies, mademoiselle."

Gauche suddenly noticed that the redheaded baronet had turned as white as a sheet: His jaw was trembling and his green eyes were glaring at the commissioner balefully.

"What precisely do you mean by . . . my 'circumstances'?" he said slowly, choking on the words in his fury. "What are you implying, mister detective?"

"Come, come," said Gauche, raising a conciliatory hand. "Above all else, you must remain calm. You must not become agitated. Your circumstances are your circumstances and they are no one else's business. I only mentioned them to indicate that you no longer figure among my potential suspects. Where is your emblem, by the way?"

"I threw it away," the baronet replied gruffly, his eyes still shooting daggers at Gauche. "It's repulsive! It looks like a golden leech! And—"

"And it was not fitting for the baronet Milford-Stokes to wear the same kind of name tag as a raggle-taggle bunch of nouveaux riches, was it?" the commissioner remarked shrewdly. "Yet another snob."

Mademoiselle Stamp also seemed to have taken offense.

"Commissioner, your description of exactly what it is that makes me such a suspicious character was most illuminating. Thank you," she said acidly, with a jerk of her pointed chin. "You have indeed tempered justice with mercy."

"When we were still in Aden, I sent a number of questions back to the prefecture by telegram. I could not wait for the replies, because the inquiries that had to be made took some time, but there were several messages waiting for me in Bombay. One of them concerned you, mademoiselle. Now I know that, from the age of fourteen, when your parents died, you lived in the country with a female cousin of your mother. She was rich but miserly. She treated you, her companion, like a slave and kept you on little more than bread and water."

The Englishwoman blushed and seemed to regret ever having made her comment. *Now, my sweet little bird,* thought Gauche, *let us see how deeply you blush at what comes next!*

"A couple of months ago, the old woman died and you discovered she had left her entire estate to you. It is hardly surprising that after so many years under lock and key, you should want to get out and travel a bit, to see the world. I expect you had never seen anything of life except in books?"

"But why did she conceal the fact that she had visited Paris?" Mme. Kleber interrupted rudely. "Because her hotel was on the street where all those people were killed? She was afraid you would suspect her, was that it?"

"No," laughed Gauche. "That was not it. Having suddenly become rich, Mlle. Stamp acted as any other woman would have done in her place—the first thing she did was visit Paris, the capital of the world. To admire the beautiful sights of Paris, to dress in the latest Paris fashion and also, well . . . for romantic adventures."

The Englishwoman had clenched her fingers together nervously. She was gazing at Gauche imploringly, but nothing was going to stop him now—this fine lady should have known better than to look down her nose at a commissioner of the Paris police.

"Mlle. Stamp found romance aplenty. In the Ambassador Hotel she made the acquaintance of an exceptionally suave and handsome gentleman, who is listed in the police files under the name of 'the Vampire.' A shady character who specializes in rich, aging foreign women. The flames of passion were ignited instantly and—as always happens with the Vampire—they were extinguished without warning. One morning, on the thirteenth of March to be exact, mademoiselle, you woke alone and forlorn in a hotel room that you could barely recognize, it was so empty. Your friend had made off with everything except the furniture. They sent me a list of the items that were stolen from you." Gauche glanced into his file. "Number thirty-eight on the list is 'a golden brooch in the form of a whale.' When I read that, I began to understand why Mlle. Stamp does not like to remember Paris."

The foolish woman was a pitiful sight now—she had covered her face with her hands and her shoulders were heaving.

"I never really suspected Mme. Kleber," said Gauche, moving on to the next point on his agenda, "even though she was unable to give a clear explanation of why she had no emblem."

"But why did you ignore what I told you?" the Japanese butted in. "I told you something very important."

"I didn't ignore it!" The commissioner swung round to face the speaker. "Far from it. I had a word with Mme. Kleber, and she gave me an explanation that accounted for everything. She suffered so badly during the first stages of her pregnancy that her doctor prescribed . . . certain sedative substances. Afterward the painful symptoms passed, but the poor woman had already become habituated to the medication, which she took for her nerves and insomnia. She was taking larger and larger doses, and the habit was threatening to get out of hand. I had a fatherly word with

Mme. Kleber, and afterward, under my watchful eye, she threw the vile narcotic into the sea." Gauche cast a glance of feigned severity at Renate, who had stuck out her lower lip like a sulking child. "Remember, my dear, you promised papa Gauche on your word of honor."

Renate lowered her eyes and nodded.

Clarissa erupted. "Ah, what touching concern for Mme. Kleber! Why could you not spare my blushes, monsieur detective? You have humiliated me in front of the entire company."

But the commissioner had no time for her now—he was still gazing at the Japanese, and his gaze was grave and unrelenting. The quick-witted Jackson understood without having to be told that it was time. There was a funereal gleam of burnished steel as he took his hand out of his pocket. He held the revolver with the barrel pointing straight at the oriental's forehead.

"I believe you Japanese think of us as ginger-haired monkeys?" Gauche said in a hostile voice. "I've heard that's what you call Europeans. We are hairy barbarians and you are cunning, subtle, and so highly cultured. White people are not even fit to lick your boots." The commissioner puffed out his cheeks sarcastically and blew out a thick cloud of smoke to one side. "Killing ten monkeys means nothing to you—you don't even think of it as wrong."

Aono sat there tense and still. His face was like stone.

"You accuse me of killing Rord Ritterby and his vassals . . . that is, servants?" the oriental asked in a flat, lifeless voice. "Why do you accuse me?"

"For every possible reason criminal science has to offer, my dear chap," the commissioner declared. Then he turned away from the Japanese, because the speech he was about to make was not intended for this yellow dog; it was intended for History. The time would come when they would print it in the textbooks on criminology.

"First, gentlemen, allow me to present the circumstantial evidence indicating that this person *could* have committed the crimes of which I accuse him." (Ah, but he shouldn't be giving this speech to an audience of ten people; he should be addressing a packed hall in the Palais de Justice!) "And then I shall present to you the evidence which demonstrates beyond all possible doubt that M. Aono not only could have, but actually did murder eleven people—ten on the fifteenth of March in the Rue de Grenelle and one yesterday, the fourteenth of April, on board the steamer *Leviathan*."

As he spoke, an empty space formed around Aono. The Russian was the only one left sitting beside the prisoner, and the inspector was standing just behind him, with his revolver at the ready.

"I hope nobody here has any doubt that the death of Professor Sweetchild is directly connected with the crime in the Rue de Grenelle. As our investigation has demonstrated, the goal of that murder most foul was to steal, not the golden Shiva, but the silk shawl." Gauche scowled sternly, as if to say: *Yes, indeed, the investigation has established the facts, so you can stop making that wry face, monsieur diplomat.* "And that is the key to the hidden treasure of Bagdassar, rajah of Brahmapur. We do not yet know how the accused came to learn the secret of the shawl, and we are all aware that the Orient holds many mysteries impenetrable to our European minds. However, the deceased professor, a genuine connoisseur of oriental culture, succeeded in solving this mystery. He was on the point of sharing his discovery with us when the fire alarm was sounded. Fate itself had sent the criminal a golden opportunity to stop Sweetchild's mouth forever. Afterward all would be silence again, just like at the Rue de Grenelle. But the killer failed to take into account one very important circumstance: This time Commissioner Gauche was on hand, and he is not one to be trifled with. It was a risky move, but it might have worked. The criminal knew that the scholar would dash straight to his cabin to save his papers—that is, his manuscripts. It was there, concealed by the bend in the corridor, that the murderer committed his foul deed. And there we have the first piece of circumstantial evidence." The commissioner raised a finger to emphasize his point. "M. Aono ran out of the salon and therefore he could have committed this murder."

"Not only I," said the Japanese. "Six other people ran out of the saron: M. Renier, M. and Mme. Truffo, M. Fandorin, M. Mirfor-Stokes, and Mlle. Stamp."

"Correct," Gauche agreed. "But I merely wished to demonstrate to the jury, by which I mean the present company, the connection between these two crimes, and also that you *could* have committed yesterday's murder. Now, let us return to the Crime of the Century. M. Aono was in Paris at the time, a fact of which there can be no doubt, and which is confirmed by a telegram I received."

"One and a half mirrion other people were also in Paris," the Japanese interjected.

"Perhaps, but nonetheless we now have our second piece of circumstantial evidence," said Gauche.

"Too circumstantial by far," put in the Russian.

"I won't dispute that." Gauche tipped some tobacco into his pipe before he made his next move. "However, the fatal injections were administered to Lord Littleby's servants by a medico of some sort, and there are certainly not one and a half million medics in Paris, are there?"

No one contested that, but Captain Cliff asked: "True, but what of it?"

"Ah, monsieur le capitaine," said Gauche, his eyes flashing brightly, "the point is that our friend Aono here is not a military man, as he introduced himself to all of us, but a qualified surgeon, a recent graduate from the medical faculty at the Sorbonne! I learned that from the same telegram."

A pause for effect. A muffled hum of voices in the hall of the Palais de Justice, the rustling of the newspaper artists' pencils on their sketch pads: "Commissioner Gauche Plays His Trump Card." Ah, but you must wait for the ace, my friends—the ace is yet to come.

"And now, ladies and gentlemen, we move from circumstantial evidence to hard facts. Let M. Aono explain why he, a doctor, a member of a respected and prestigious profession, found it necessary to pose as an army officer. Why such deception?"

A drop of sweat slithered down the waxen face of the Japanese. Aono said nothing—he certainly hadn't put up much of a fight.

"There is only one answer: He did it to divert suspicion from himself. The murderer was a doctor," the commissioner summed up complacently. "And that brings us to our second piece of hard evidence. Gentlemen, have you ever heard of Japanese boxing?"

"I've not only heard of it, I've seen it," said the captain. "One time in Macao, I saw a Japanese navigator beat three American sailors senseless. He was a puny little tyke, you'd have thought you could knock him over with a feather, but you should have seen the way he skipped around and flung his arms and legs around. He laid three hulking whalers out flat. He hit one of them on the arm with the edge of his hand and twisted the elbow the other way. Broke the bone, can you imagine it? That was some blow!"

Gauche nodded smugly.

"I have also heard that the Japanese possess the secret of killing with their bare hands in combat. They can easily kill a man with a simple jab of the finger. We have all seen M. Aono practicing his gymnastics. Fragments of a shattered gourd—a remarkably hard gourd—were discovered under the bed in his cabin. And there were several whole ones in a sack. The accused obviously used them for perfecting the precision and strength of his blow. I cannot even imagine how strong a man must be to smash a hard gourd with his bare hand, and into several pieces."

The commissioner surveyed his assembled audience before introducing his second piece of evidence.

"Let me remind you, ladies and gentlemen, that the skull of the unfortunate Lord Littleby was shattered into several fragments by an exceptionally strong blow with a blunt object. Now would you please observe the calluses on the hands of the accused."

The Japanese snatched his small, sinewy hands off the table.

"Don't take your eyes off him, Jackson. He is very dangerous," warned Gauche. "If he tries anything, shoot him in the leg or the shoulder. Now let me ask M. Aono what he did with his gold emblem. Well, have you nothing to say? Then let me answer the question myself: The emblem was torn from your chest by Lord Littleby the very moment you struck him a fatal blow to the head with the edge of your hand!"

Aono half opened his mouth, as though he was about to say something, but he only bit his lip with his strong, slightly crooked teeth and closed his eyes. His face took on a strange detached expression.

"And so the picture that emerges of the crime in the Rue de Grenelle is as follows," said Gauche, starting his summation. "On the evening of the fifteenth of March, Gintaro Aono went to Lord Littleby's mansion with the premeditated intention of killing everyone in the house and taking possession of the triangular shawl from the owner's collection. At that time he already had a ticket for the *Leviathan*, which was due to sail for India from Southampton four days later. The defendant was obviously intending to search for the Brahmapur treasure in India. We do not know how he managed to persuade the unfortunate servants to submit to an 'inoculation against cholera.' It is very probable that the accused showed them some kind of forged document from the mayor's office. That would have been entirely convincing because, as I have been informed by telegram, medical students in their final year at the Sorbonne are quite often employed in pro-phylactic public-health programs. There are quite a lot of orientals among the students and interns at the university, so the evening caller's yellow skin was unlikely to alarm the servants. The most monstrous aspect of the crime is the infernal callousness with which two innocent children were mur-dered. I have considerable personal experience dealing with the scum of society, ladies and gentlemen. In a fit of rage a criminal thug may toss a baby into a fire, but to kill with such cold calculation, with hands that do not even tremble . . . You must agree, gentlemen, that is not the French way, indeed it is not the European way."

"That's right!" exclaimed Renier, incensed, and Dr. Truffo supported him wholeheartedly.

"After that, everything was very simple," Gauche continued. "Once he was sure the poisonous injections had plunged the servants into a sleep from which they would never wake, the murderer walked calmly up the stairs to the second floor and into the hall where the collection was kept, and there he began helping himself to what he wanted. After all, he was certain the master of the house was away. But an attack of gout had pre-vented Lord Littleby from traveling to Spa, and he was still at home. The sound of breaking glass brought him out into the hall, where he was mur-dered in a most barbarous manner. It was this unplanned murder that shat-tered the killer's diabolical composure. He had almost certainly planned to take several items from the collection in order not to draw attention to the celebrated shawl, but now he had to hurry. We do not know; perhaps his lordship called out before he died and the killer was afraid his cries had been heard in the street. For whatever reason, he took only a golden Shiva that he did not need, then fled in haste without even noticing his *Leviathan* badge had been left behind in the hand of his victim. In order to throw the police off the scent, Aono left the house through the window of the con-servatory . . . No, that was not the reason!" Gauche slapped himself on the forehead. "Why did I not think of it before? He could not go back the way he had come if his victim had cried out! For all he knew, passersby were already gathering at the door of the mansion! That was why Aono smashed the window in the conservatory, jumped down into the garden, and then made his escape over the fence. But he need not have been so careful—at that late hour the Rue de Grenelle was empty. If there were any cries, no one heard them."

The impressionable Mme. Kleber sobbed. Mrs. Truffo listened to her husband's translation and blew her nose with some emotion.

Clear, convincing, and unassailable, thought Gauche. *The evidence and the investigative hypotheses reinforce each other perfectly. And old papa Gauche still hasn't finished with you yet.*

"This is the appropriate moment to consider the death of Professor Sweetchild. As the accused has quite rightly observed, in theory the murder could have been committed by six other people apart from himself. Please do not be alarmed, ladies and gentlemen!" The commissioner raised a reassuring hand. "I shall now prove that you did not kill the professor and that he was in fact killed by our slant-eyed friend here."

The blasted Japanese had completely turned to stone. Was he asleep, or what? Or was he praying to his Japanese god? Pray as much as you like, my lad, that old slut Mme. Guillotine will still have your head!

Suddenly the commissioner was struck by an extremely unpleasant thought. What if the English nabbed the Japanese for the murder of Sweetchild? The professor was a British subject, after all. Then the criminal would be tried in an English court and end up on a British gallows instead of under a French guillotine! Anything but that! The Crime of the Century could not be tried abroad! The trial must be held in the Palais de Justice and nowhere else! Sweetchild may have been killed on board an English ship, but there were ten bodies in Paris and only one here. And, in any case, the ship wasn't entirely British property—there were two partners in the consortium!

Gauche was so upset that he lost track of his argument. *Not on your life,* he thought to himself. *You will not have my client. I'll put an end to this farce and then go straight to the French consul. I'll take the murderer to France myself.* And immediately he could see it: the crowded quayside, the police lines, the journalists . . .

But first the case had to be brought to a conclusion.

"Now Inspector Jackson will tell us what was found when the defendant's cabin was searched."

Gauche gestured for Jackson to say his piece.

Jackson launched into a monotonous rigmarole in English, but the commissioner quickly put a stop to that.

"This investigation is being conducted by the French police," he said sternly, "and the official language of this inquiry is also French. Apart from which, monsieur, not everyone here understands your language. And most important of all, I am not sure the accused knows English. You must admit he has a right to know the results of your search."

The protest was made as a matter of principle, in order to put the English in their place right from the start. They had to realize they were the junior partners in this business.

Renier volunteered to act as interpreter. He stood beside the inspector and translated phrase by phrase, enlivening the Englishman's flat, truncated sentences with his own dramatic intonations and expressive gestures.

"Acting on instructions received, a search was carried out. In cabin number twenty-four. The passenger's name is Gintaro Aono. We acted in accordance with the Regulations for the Conduct of a Search in a Confined Space. A rectangular room with a floor area of two hundred square feet. Was divided into twenty squares horizontally and forty-four squares vertically." The lieutenant asked what that meant and then explained it to the others. "Apparently the walls also have to be divided into squares—they tap on them in order to identify secret hiding places, although I can't see how there could be any secret hiding places in a steamship cabin . . . The search was conducted in strict sequence: first vertically, then horizontally. No hiding places were discovered in the walls." At this point Renier gave an exaggerated shrug, as if to say: Who would ever have thought it? "During the examination of the horizontal plane, the following items relevant to the case were discovered. Item one: notes in a hieroglyphic script. They will be translated and studied. Item two: a long dagger of oriental appearance with an extremely sharp blade. Item three: a sack containing eleven Egyptian gourds. And finally, item five: a bag for carrying surgical instruments. The compartment for holding a large scalpel is empty."

The audience gasped. The Japanese opened his eyes and glanced briefly at the commissioner, but still did not speak.

He's going to crack any moment, thought Gauche, but he was wrong. Without getting up off his chair, the oriental swung round to face the inspector standing behind him and struck the hand holding the revolver a sharp blow from below. While the gun was still describing a picturesque arc through the air, the athletic Japanese had already reached the door, but when he jerked it open the two policemen standing outside jammed the barrels of their Colts into his chest. A split second later the inspector's weapon completed its trajectory, crashed down onto the center of the table, and went off with a deafening roar. A jangling sound, smoke, a scream.

Gauche quickly summed up the situation: The prisoner was backing toward the table; Mrs. Truffo was in a dead faint; there seemed to be no other casualties; there was a hole in Big Ben just below the dial and its hands weren't moving. The clock was jangling. The ladies were screaming. But all in all the situation was in hand.

The Japanese was returned to his seat and shackled with handcuffs; the doctor's wife was revived, and everyone returned to their seats. The commissioner smiled and began talking again, demonstrating his superior presence of mind.

"Gentlemen of the jury, you have just witnessed a scene that amounts to a confession of guilt, even though it was played out in a somewhat unusual manner."

He'd made that slip about the jury again, but he didn't bother to correct himself. After all, this was his dress rehearsal.

"As the final piece of evidence, it could not possibly have been more conclusive," Gauche summed up smugly. "And you, Jackson, may consider yourself reprimanded. I told you he was dangerous."

The inspector was as scarlet as a boiled lobster. That would teach him.

Yes, everything had turned out excellently.

The Japanese sat there with three guns pointing at him, pressing his shackled hands to his chest. He had closed his eyes again.

"That is all, Inspector. You can take him away. He can be kept in your lockup for the time being. When all the formalities have been completed, I shall take him to France. Good-bye, ladies and gentlemen—old papa Gauche is disembarking, I wish you all a pleasant journey."

"I am afraid, Commissioner, you will have to travel with us a little farther," the Russian said in his monotone voice.

For a moment Gauche thought he had misheard.

"Eh?"

"M. Aono is not guilty of anything, so the investigation will have to be continued."

The expression on Gauche's face must have looked quite ridiculous—eyes staring wildly, cheeks bright scarlet.

Before the outburst of fury came, the Russian continued with quite astonishing self-assurance.

"Captain, on b-board ship you are the supreme authority. The commissioner has just acted out a mock trial in which he took the part of prosecutor and played it with great conviction. However, in a civilized court, after the prosecution has made its case the defense is offered the floor. With your permission, I should like to take on that assignment."

"Why waste any more time?" the captain asked, surprised. "It all seems cut and dry to me. The commissioner of police explained everything very clearly."

"Putting a passenger ashore is a serious m-matter, and the responsibility is ultimately the captain's. Think what damage will be done to the reputation of your shipping line if it turns out you have made a mistake. And I assure you," said Fandorin, raising his voice slightly, "that the commissioner is mistaken."

"Nonsense!" exclaimed Gauche. "But I have no objections. It might even be interesting. Carry on, monsieur, I'm sure I shall enjoy it."

After all, a dress rehearsal had to be taken seriously. This boy was no fool; he might possibly expose some gaps in the prosecution's logic that needed patching up. Then, if the prosecutor made a mess of things during the trial, Commissioner Gauche would be able to help him out.

Fandorin crossed one leg over the other and clasped his hands around his knee.

"You gave a brilliant and convincing speech. At first sight your arguments appear conclusive. Your logic seems almost beyond reproach, although, of course, the so-called circumstantial evidence is worthless. Yes, M. Aono was in Paris on the fifteenth of March. Yes, M. Aono was not in the salon when the p-professor was killed. In themselves these two facts mean nothing, so let us not even take them into consideration."

"Very well," Gauche agreed sarcastically. "Let us move straight on to the hard facts."

"Gladly. I counted five more or less significant elements. M. Aono is a doctor, but for some reason he concealed that from us. That is one. M. Aono is capable of shattering a hard object, such as a gourd—and perhaps also a head—with a single blow. That is two. M. Aono does not have a *Leviathan* emblem. That is three. A scalpel, which might be the one that killed Professor Sweetchild, is missing from the defendant's medical bag. That is four. And, finally, five: We have just witnessed an attempted escape by the accused, which sets his guilt beyond all reasonable doubt. I don't think I have forgotten anything, have I?"

"There is a number six," put in the commissioner. "He is unable to offer an explanation for any of these points."

"Very well, let us make it six," the Russian readily agreed.

Gauche chuckled: "I'd say that's more than enough for any jury to send this little bird to the guillotine."

Inspector Jackson jerked his head up and growled in English: "To the gallows."

"No, to the gallows," Renier translated.

Ah, the perfidious English! He had nursed a viper at his bosom!

"I beg your pardon," fumed Gauche. "The investigation has been conducted by the French side. So our villain will go to the guillotine!"

"And the decisive piece of evidence, the missing scalpel, was discovered by the British side. He'll be sent to the gallows," the lieutenant translated.

"The main crime was committed in Paris. To the guillotine!"

"But Lord Littleby was a British subject. And so was Professor Sweetchild. It's the gallows for him."

The Japanese appeared not to hear this discussion, which threatened to escalate into an international conflict. His eyes were still closed and his face was completely devoid of all expression. *These yellow devils really are dif-*

ferent from us, thought Gauche. And just think of all the trouble they would have to take with him: a prosecutor, a defense attorney, a jury, judges in robes. Of course, that was the way it ought to be, democracy is democracy after all, but surely this was casting pearls before swine.

When there was a pause, Fandorin asked: "Have you concluded your debate? May I p-proceed?"

"Carry on," Gauche said gloomily, thinking about the battles with the British that lay ahead.

"And let us not d-discuss the shattered gourds, either. They also prove nothing."

This whole comedy was beginning to get on the commissioner's nerves.

"All right. We needn't waste any time on trifles."

"Excellent. Then that leaves five points: He concealed the fact that he is a doctor; he has no emblem; the scalpel is missing; he tried to escape; he offers no explanations."

"And every point enough to have the villain sent . . . for execution."

"The problem is, commissioner, that you think like a European, but M-mister Aono has a different, Japanese, logic, that you have not made any effort to fathom. I, however, have had the honor of conversing with this gentleman, and I have a better idea of how his mind works than you do. M. Aono is not simply Japanese, he is a samurai, and he comes from an old and influential family. This is an important point for this particular case. For five hundred years every man in the clan of Aono was a warrior. All other professions were regarded as unworthy of such a distinguished family. The accused is the third son in the family. When Japan decided to move a little closer to Europe, many noble families began sending their sons abroad to study, and M. Aono's father did the same. He sent his eldest son to England to study for a career as a naval officer, because the principality of Satsuma, where the Aono clan resides, provides officers for the Japanese navy. In Satsuma the navy is regarded as the senior service. Aono senior sent his second son to a military academy in Germany. Following the Franco-German War of 1870, the Japanese decided to restructure their army on the German model, and all their military advisers are Germans. This information about the clan of Aono was volunteered to me by the accused himself."

"And what the devil do we need all these aristocratic details for?" Gauche asked irritably.

"I observed that the accused spoke with pride about his older brothers, but preferred not to talk about himself. I also noticed a long time ago that, for an alumnus of St. Cyr, M. Aono is remarkably ignorant of military matters. And why would he have been sent to a French military academy when he himself had told me that the Japanese army was being organized along German lines? I have formed the following impression. In keeping with the spirit of the times, Aono senior decided to set his third son up in a peaceful, nonmilitary profession and make him into a doctor. From what I have read in books, in Japan the decision of the head of the family is not subject to discussion. The defendant traveled to France to take up his studies in the faculty of medicine, even though he felt unhappy about it. In fact, as a son of the martial clan of Aono, he felt disgraced by having to fiddle with bandages and tinker with clysters! That is why he said he was a soldier. He was simply ashamed to admit his true profession, which he regards as shameful. From a European point of view this might seem absurd, but try to see things through his eyes. How would your countryman D'Artagnan have felt if he had ended up as a physician after dreaming for so long of winning a musketeer's cloak?"

Gauche noticed a sudden change in the Japanese. He had opened his eyes and was staring at Fandorin in a state of obvious agitation, and crimson spots had appeared on his cheeks. Could he possibly be blushing? No, nonsense.

"Ah, how very touching," Gauche snorted. "But I'll let it go. Tell me instead, monsieur counsel for the defense, about the emblem. What did your bashful client do with it? Was he ashamed to wear it?"

"That is absolutely right," the self-appointed lawyer said with a nod. "That is the reason. He was ashamed. Look at what it says on the badge."

Gauche glanced down at his lapel.

"It doesn't say anything. There are just the initials of the Jasper-Artaud Partnership."

"Precisely." Fandorin traced out the three letters in the air with his finger. "J—A—P. The letters spell 'Jap,' the term of abuse that foreigners use for the Japanese. Tell me, Commissioner, how would you like to wear a badge that said 'Frog'?"

Captain Cliff threw his head back and burst into loud laughter. Even the sour-faced Jackson and standoffish Mlle. Stamp smiled. The crimson spots spread even farther across the face of the Japanese.

A terrible premonition gnawed at Gauche's heart. His voice was suddenly hoarse.

"And why can he not explain all this for himself?"

"That is quite impossible. You see—again, as far as I can understand from the books I have read—the main difference between the Europeans and the Japanese lies in the moral basis of their social behavior."

"That's a bit high-flown," said the captain.

The diplomat turned to face him.

"Not at all. Christian culture is based on a sense of guilt. It is bad to sin, because afterward you will be tormented by remorse. The normal European tries to behave morally in order to avoid a sense of guilt. The Japanese also strive to observe certain moral norms, but their motivation is different. In their society, moral restraints derive from a sense of shame. The worst thing that can happen to a Japanese is to find himself in a situation in which he feels ashamed and is condemned or, even worse, ridiculed by society. That is why the Japanese are so afraid of committing any faux pas that offends the social sense of decency. I can assure you that shame is a far more effective civilizing influence than guilt. From M. Aono's point of view, it would be quite unthinkable to speak openly of 'shameful' matters, especially with foreigners. To be a doctor and not a soldier is shameful. To confess that he has lied is even more shameful. And to admit that he, a samurai, could attach any importance to offensive nicknames—why, that is entirely out of the question."

"Thank you for the lecture," said Gauche, with an ironic bow. "And was it shame that made your client attempt to escape from custody, too?"

"That's the point," agreed Jackson, suddenly transformed from enemy to ally. "The yellow bastard almost broke my wrist."

"Once again you have guessed correctly, Commissioner. It is impossible to escape from a steamship; there is nowhere to go. Believing his position to be hopeless and anticipating nothing but further humiliation, my client—as you insist on calling him—undoubtedly intended to lock himself in his cabin and commit suicide according to samurai ritual. Is that not right, M. Aono?" Fandorin asked, addressing the Japanese directly for the first time.

"You would have been disappointed," the diplomat continued gently. "You must have heard that your ritual dagger was taken by the police during their search."

"Ah, you're talking about that—what's it called—hira-kira, hari-kari." Gauche smirked into his mustache. "Rubbish, I don't believe a man could rip his own belly open. If you've really had enough of this world, it's far better to brain yourself against the wall. But I'll let that pass too. There is one piece of evidence you can't shrug off—the scalpel missing from his set of medical instruments. How do you explain that? Do you claim the real culprit stole your client's scalpel in advance because he was planning the murder and wanted to shift the blame onto Aono? That just won't work! How could the murderer know the professor would decide to tell us about his discovery immediately after dinner? And Sweetchild himself had only just guessed the secret of the shawl. Remember the state he was in when he came running into the salon!"

"Nothing could be easier for me than to explain the missing scalpel. It is not even a matter of supposition, but of hard fact. Do you remember how things began disappearing from people's cabins after Port Said? The mysterious spate of thefts ended as suddenly as it had begun. And do you remember when? It was after our black stowaway was killed. I have given a lot of thought to the question of why he was on board the *Leviathan*, and this is my explanation. The Negro was probably brought here from darkest Africa by Arab slave traders, and naturally he arrived in Port Said by sea. Why do I think that? Because when he escaped from his masters, the Negro didn't simply run away; he boarded a ship. He evidently believed that since a ship had taken him away from his home, another ship could take him back."

"What has all this got to do with our case?" Gauche interrupted impatiently. "This Negro of yours died on the fifth of April, and Sweetchild was killed yesterday! To hell with you and your fairy tales! Jackson, take the prisoner away!"

The commissioner set off decisively toward the door, but the diplomat grabbed his elbow in a viselike grip and said in a repulsively obsequious voice: "My dear M. Gauche, I would like to follow my arguments through to their conclusion. Please be patient for just a little longer."

Gauche tried to break free, but this young whippersnapper had fingers of steel. After his second attempt failed, the commissioner decided not to make himself look even more foolish. He turned to face Fandorin.

"Very well, five more minutes," he hissed, glaring into the insolent youth's serene blue eyes.

"Thank you. Five minutes will be more than enough to shatter your final piece of hard evidence. I knew that the runaway slave must have a lair somewhere on the ship, so I looked for it. But while you were searching the holds and the coal bins, Captain, I started with the upper deck. The black man had only been seen by first-class passengers, so it was reasonable to assume he was hiding somewhere close by. I found what I was looking for in the third lifeboat from the bow on the starboard side: the remains of his food and a bundle of his belongings. There were several pieces of colored cloth, a string of beads, and all sorts of shiny objects, including a small mirror, a sextant, a pince-nez, and a large scalpel."

"Why should I believe you?" roared Gauche. His case was crumbling to dust before his very eyes.

"Because I am a disinterested party who is prepared to confirm his testimony under oath. May I continue?" The Russian smiled his sickening little smile. "Thank you. Our poor Negro was evidently a practical individual who did not intend to return home empty-handed."

"Stop, stop!" cried Renier, with a frown. "M. Fandorin, why did you not report your discovery to the captain and me? What right did you have to conceal it?"

"I did not conceal it. I left the bundle where it was. But when I came back to the lifeboat a few hours later, after the search, the bundle was gone. I was sure it must have been found by your sailors. But now it seems that the professor's murderer got there before you and claimed all the Negro's trophies, including M. Aono's scalpel. The c-criminal could have foreseen that he might need to take . . . extreme measures and carried the scalpel around with him as a precaution. It might help put the police off the scent. Tell me, M. Aono, was the scalpel stolen from you?"

The Japanese hesitated for a moment before reluctantly nodding.

"And you did not mention it because an officer of the Imperial Army could not possibly possess a scalpel, am I right?"

"The sextant was mine!" declared the redheaded baronet. "I thought . . . but that doesn't matter. So it turns out that savage stole it. Gentlemen, if someone's head is smashed in with my sextant, please bear in mind that it has nothing to do with me."

Bewildered by this final and absolute disaster, Gauche squinted inquiringly at Jackson.

"I'm very sorry, Commissioner, but it seems you will have to continue your voyage," the inspector said in French, twisting his thin lips into a smile of sympathy. "My apologies, M. Aono. If you would just hold out your hands . . . Thank you."

The handcuffs clinked mournfully as they were removed.

The silence that ensued was broken by Renate Kleber's frightened voice: "I beg your pardon, gentlemen, but then who is the murderer?"

PART THREE

BOMBAY TO
PALK STRAIT

Gintaro Aono

―――――∽∽∽―――――

The eighteenth day of the fourth month,
in view of the southern tip of the Indian peninsula

It is now three days since we left Bombay, and I have not opened my diary even once since then. It is the first time such a thing has happened to me since I made it a firm rule to write every day. But I decided upon the break deliberately. I had to come to terms with an overwhelming torrent of thoughts and feelings.

The essential significance of what has happened to me is best conveyed by a haiku that was born spontaneously the very moment the inspector of police removed the iron shackles from my wrists.

> *Lonely is the flight*
> *Of the nocturnal firefly,*
> *But stars throng the sky.*

I realized immediately that it was a very good poem, the best I have ever written, but its meaning is not obvious and requires elucidation. I have meditated for three days on the changes within my being, until I think I have finally discovered the truth.

I have been visited by the great miracle of which every man dreams— I have experienced satori, or catharsis, as the ancient Greeks called it. How many times has my Mentor told me that if satori comes, it comes when it will and on its own terms; it cannot be induced or impeded! A man may be righteous and wise, he may sit in the za-zen pose for many hours each day and read mountains of sacred texts, but still die unenlightened. And yet the radiant majesty of satori may be revealed to some idler who wanders aimlessly and foolishly through life, transforming his worthless existence in an instant! I am that idler. I have been lucky. At the age of twenty-seven I have been born again.

Illumination and purification did not come to me in a moment of spiritual and physical concentration, but when I was wretched, crushed, and empty, when I was reduced to no more than the wrinkled skin of a burst balloon. But the dull clanking of those irons signaled my transformation. Suddenly I knew with a clarity beyond words that I am not I, but . . . No, that is not it. That I am *not only I,* but also an infinite multitude of other lives. That I am not some Gintaro Aono, third son of the senior counselor to his Serene Highness Prince Shimazu: I am a small and yet precious particle of the One. I am in all that exists, and all that exists is in me. How many times I have heard those words, but I only understood them . . . no, I only experienced their truth on the fifteenth day of the fourth month of the eleventh year of Meiji, in the city of Bombay, on board an immense European steamship. The will of the Supreme is truly capricious.

What is the meaning of this tercet that was born of my inner intuition? Man is a solitary firefly in the gloom of boundless night. His light is so weak that it illuminates only a minute segment of space; beyond that lies cold, darkness, and fear. But if you turn your frightened gaze away from the dark earth below and look upward (you need only turn your head!), you see that the sky is covered with stars, shining with a calm, bright, eternal light. You are not alone in the darkness. The stars are your friends; they will help you. They will not abandon you in your distress. And a little while later one understands something else, something equally important: A firefly is also a star like all the others. Those in the sky above see your light, and it helps them endure the cold darkness of the Universe.

My life will probably not change. I shall be the same as I was before— trivial and absurd, at the mercy of my passions. But this certain knowledge will always dwell in the depths of my soul, my salvation and comfort in times of difficulty. I am no longer a shallow puddle that any strong gust of wind can spread across the ground. I am the ocean, and the storm that drives the all-destroying tsunami across my surface can never touch my inmost depths.

When my spirit was flooded with joy at this realization, I recalled that the greatest of virtues is gratitude. The first star I glimpsed glowing in the blackness around me was Fandorin-san. Thanks to him I know that the World is not indifferent to me, Gintaro Aono, that the Great Beyond will never abandon me in misfortune.

But how can I explain to a man from a different culture that he is my *onjin* for all time? The European languages do not have such a word. Today I plucked up my courage and tried to speak with him about this, but I feel that the conversation came to nothing.

I waited for Fandorin-san on the boat deck, knowing that he would come there with his weights at precisely eight.

When he appeared, wearing his striped tricot (I must inform him that loose clothes, not close-fitting ones, are best suited for physical exercise), I approached him and bowed low in obeisance. "Why, M. Aono, what's wrong?" he asked in surprise. "Why do you stay bent over and not straighten up?" Since it was impossible to make conversation in such a posture, I drew myself erect, although in such a situation I knew that I ought to maintain my bow for longer. "I am expressing my eternal gratitude to you," I said, greatly agitated. "Oh, forget it," he said, with a careless wave of his hand. This gesture pleased me greatly—Fandorin-san wished to belittle the significance of the boon he had bestowed on me and spare his debtor excessive feelings of gratitude. In his place any nobly raised Japanese would have done the same. But the effect was the reverse—my spirit was inspired with even greater gratitude. I told him that henceforth I was irredeemably in his debt. "Nothing irredeemable about it," he said with a shrug. "I simply wished to take that smug turkey down a peg or two." (A turkey is an ugly American bird whose pompous, strutting gait seems to express a risible sense of self-importance: figuratively speaking—a conceited and foolish person.) Once again I was struck by Fandorin-san's sensitivity and tact, but I had to make him understand how much I owed to him. "I thank you for saving my worthless life," I said and bowed again. "I thank you three times over for saving my honor. And I thank you an infinite number of times for opening my third eye, with which I see what I could not see before." Fandorin-san glanced (with some trepidation, it seemed to me) at my forehead, as if he were expecting another eye to open up and wink at him.

I told him that he is my *onjin*, that henceforth my life belongs to him, and that seemed to frighten him even more. "Oh, how I dream you might find yourself in mortal danger so that I can save your life, as you have saved mine!" I exclaimed. He crossed himself and said: "I think I would rather avoid that. If it is not too much trouble, please dream of something else."

The conversation was going badly. In despair I cried out: "Know that I will do anything for you!" And then I qualified my oath to avoid any subsequent misunderstanding: "If it is not injurious to my emperor, my country, or the honor of my family."

My words provoked a strange reaction from Fandorin-san. He laughed! I am certain I shall never understand the redheads. "All right, then," he said, shaking me by the hand. "If you insist, then by all means. I expect we shall be traveling together from Calcutta to Japan. You may repay your debt by giving me Japanese lessons."

Alas, this man does not take me seriously. I wished to be his friend, but Fandorin-san is far more interested in Senior Navigator Fox, a common man lacking in wisdom, than in me. My benefactor spends much time in the company of this windbag, listening attentively while he brags about his nautical adventures and amorous escapades. He even goes on watch with Fox! I must confess I feel hurt by this. Today I heard Fox's lurid description of his love affair with an "aristocratic Japanese lady" from Nagasaki. He talked about her small breasts and her scarlet mouth and all the other charms of this "dainty little doll." It must have been some cheap slut from the sailors' quarter. A girl from a decent family would not even have exchanged words with this foreign barbarian! The most hurtful thing of all was that Fandorin-san was clearly interested in these ravings. I was about to intervene, but just at that moment Captain Renier approached them and sent Fox off on some errand.

Oh yes! I have not mentioned a most important event that has taken place in the life of the ship! A firefly's feeble glow blinds his own eyes so that he cannot see his surroundings in their true proportions.

On the eve of our departure from Bombay, a genuine tragedy occurred, a calamity beside which my own sufferings pale into insignificance.

At half past eight in the morning, when the steamer had already weighed anchor and was preparing to cast off, a telegram was delivered from ashore to Captain Cliff. I was standing on the deck, looking at Bombay, the scene of such a crucial event in my life. I wanted that view to remain engraved on my heart forever. That was how I came to witness what happened.

The captain read the telegram, and his face underwent a startling transformation. I have never seen anything like it. It was as if an actor of the No theater had suddenly cast off the mask of the Fearsome Warrior and donned the mask of Insane Grief. The old sea dog's rough, weather-beaten face began to tremble. Then the captain uttered a groan that was also a sob and began pacing frantically around the deck. "Oh, God," he cried out in a hoarse voice. "My poor girl!" He dashed down the steps from the bridge and went to his cabin—as we discovered later.

The preparations for sailing were interrupted. Breakfast began as usual, but Lieutenant Renier was late. No one spoke of anything but the captain's strange behavior, and all tried to guess what could have been in the telegram. Renier-san looked into the salon as the meal was coming to an end. The first mate appeared distraught. He informed us that Cliff-san's only daughter (I have mentioned earlier that the captain doted on her) had been badly burned in a fire at her boarding school. The doctors feared for her life. The lieutenant said that Mr. Cliff was beside himself. He had decided to leave the *Leviathan* and return to England on the first available packet boat. He kept saying that he must be with his little daughter. The lieutenant repeated over and over again: "What is going to happen now? What an unlucky voyage!" We did our best to comfort him.

I must admit that I strongly disapproved of the captain's decision. I could understand his grief, but a man who has been entrusted with a task has no right to allow personal feelings to govern his actions. Especially if he is a captain in charge of a ship. What would become of society if the emperor or the president or the prime minister were to set personal concerns above their duty? There would be chaos. The very meaning and purpose of authority is to fight against chaos and maintain harmony.

I went back out on deck to see Mr. Cliff leave the ship that had been entrusted to him. And the Most High taught me a new lesson, the lesson of compassion.

Stooping low, the captain half walked and half ran across the gangway. He was carrying a travel bag in one hand and there was a sailor following him with a single suitcase. When the captain halted on the quayside and turned to face the *Leviathan*, I saw that his broad face was wet with tears. The next moment he began to sway and collapsed forward onto his face.

I rushed across to him. From his fitful breathing and the convulsive twitching of his limbs, I deduced that he had suffered a severe haemorrhagic stroke. When Dr. Truffo arrived he confirmed my diagnosis.

It often happens that the strident discord between the voice of the heart and the call of duty is too much for a man's brain to bear. I had wronged Captain Cliff.

After the sick man was taken away to a hospital, the *Leviathan* was detained at its mooring for a long time. Renier-san, ashen-faced with shock, drove to the telegraph office to conduct negotiations with the shipping company in London. It was dusk before he returned. He brought the news that Cliff-san had not recovered consciousness: Renier-san was to assume temporary command of the ship and a new captain would come aboard in Calcutta.

We sailed from Bombay after a delay of ten hours.

For days now I do not walk, I fly. I am delighted by the sunshine and the landscapes of the Indian coastline and the leisurely regularity of life on this great ship. Even the Windsor salon, which I used to enter with such a heavy heart, has now become almost like home to me. My companions at table behave quite differently toward me now—the antagonism and suspicion have disappeared. Everyone is very kind and considerate, and I also feel differently about them. Even Kleber-san, whom I was prepared to throttle with my bare hands (the poor woman!) no longer seems repulsive. She is just a young woman preparing to become a mother for the first time and entirely absorbed in the naïve egotism of her new condition. Having learned that I am a doctor, she plagues me with medical questions about all manner of minor complaints. Formerly her only victim was Dr. Truffo, but now we share the burden. And, almost unbelievably, I do not find it oppressive. On the contrary, I now possess a higher status than when I was taken for a military officer. It is astounding!

I hold a privileged position in the Windsor salon. Not only am I a doctor and an "innocent victim," as Mrs. Truffo puts it, of police brutality. I am—more important—"definitely not the murderer." It has been proved and officially confirmed. In this way I have been elevated to Windsor's highest caste—together with the commissioner of police and our new captain (whom we almost never see—he is very busy and a steward takes his food up to the bridge on a tray). We three are above suspicion and no one casts stealthy, frightened glances in our direction.

I feel sorry for the Windsor group, I really do. With my recently acquired spiritual vision, I can see clearly what none of them can see, even the sagacious Fandorin-san.

There is no murderer among my companions. None of them is suited to the role of a scoundrel. When I examine these people closely, I see that they have faults and weaknesses, but there is no black-hearted villain who could have killed eleven innocent victims, including two children, in cold blood. I would have detected the vile odor of that person's breath. I do not know whose hand felled Sweetchild-sensei, but I am sure it must have been someone else. The commissioner's assumptions are not entirely correct: The criminal is on board the steamship, but not in the Windsor salon. Perhaps he was listening at the door when the professor began telling us about his discovery.

If Gauche-san were not so stubborn and took a more impartial view of the Windsor group, he would realize he is wasting his time.

Let me run through all the members of our company.

Fandorin-san. It is obvious that he is innocent. Otherwise why would he have diverted suspicion from me when no one doubted I was guilty?

Mr. and Mrs. Truffo. The doctor is rather comical, but he is a very kind man. He would not harm a grasshopper. His wife is the very embodiment of English propriety. She could not have killed anyone, because that would simply be indecent.

M.S.-san. He is a strange man, always muttering to himself, and his manner can be sharp, but there is profound and genuine suffering in his eyes. People with eyes like that do not commit cold-blooded murders.

Kleber-san. Nothing could be clearer. First, it would be inhuman for a woman preparing to bring a new life into the world to snuff out other lives so casually. Pregnancy is a mystery that teaches us to cherish human life. Second, at the time of the murder Kleber-san was with the police commissioner.

And finally, Stamp-san. She has no alibi, but it is impossible to imagine her creeping up behind someone she knows, covering his mouth with one slim, weak hand, and raising my scalpel in the other . . . The idea is utter nonsense. Quite impossible.

Open your eyes, Commissioner-san. This path is a dead end.

Suddenly I find it hard to catch my breath. Could there be a storm approaching?

Commissioner Gauche

⁕

HIS DAMNED INSOMNIA was really getting out of hand now. Five nights of sheer misery, and it was getting worse all the time. And the Lord protect him if he did drop off just before the dawn; his dreams were so appalling that he woke up a broken man, his mind so numbed by his nocturnal visions that it invented all sorts of nonsense. Maybe it really was time to retire and just forget about everything. But he couldn't—nothing on earth was worse than a squalid old age spent in poverty. Someone here was all set to nab a treasure worth a billion and a half francs, and this old *flic* would have to live out the pitiful remainder of his days on a miserly hundred and twenty-five francs a month!

All night long the sheet lightning had flashed across the sky, the wind had howled in the masts, and the *Leviathan* had pitched ponderously to and fro on the heaving black rollers. Gauche lay in his bed, staring up at the ceiling, which was alternately dark and stark white—when it was lit up by lightning. The lashing rain drummed on the deck, and the glass that held his forgotten liver medicine skidded backward and forward across the table, the spoon tinkling inside it.

It was Gauche's first storm at sea, but he wasn't afraid—a sea monster like this couldn't possibly sink. It might get rattled and shaken about a bit, but certainly nothing more than that. His only problem was he couldn't get to sleep with the thunder booming away like that. The moment he started nodding off, there it went again—crash, boom!

But he must have fallen asleep somehow, because he suddenly jerked upright in bed, wondering what was happening. The cabin was echoing with the heavy, labored beating of his heart.

No, it wasn't his heart. It was someone pounding on the door.

"Commissioner!" (Bang-bang-bang.) "Commissioner!" (Bang-bang-bang-bang.) "Open up! Quickly!"

Whose voice was that? No, it couldn't be Fandorin!

"Who's there? What do you want?" cried Gauche, pressing his hand to the left side of his chest. "Have you gone out of your mind?"

"Open up, damn you!"

Oho! What kind of way was that for a diplomat to talk? Something really serious must have happened.

"Just a moment!"

Gauche pulled off his nightcap with the tassel (his old Blanche had knitted it for him), stuck his arms into the sleeves of his dressing gown, and slipped on his bedroom slippers.

When he peeped through the crack of the half-open door, he saw it really was Fandorin. In a frock coat and tie, holding a walking cane with an ivory knob. His eyes were blazing.

"What is it?" Gauche asked suspiciously, certain his nocturnal visitor could only have brought bad news.

The diplomat began speaking in an untypical jerky manner, but without stammering.

"Get dressed. Bring a gun. We have to arrest Captain Renier. Urgently. He's steering the ship onto the rocks."

Gauche shook his head—maybe it was just another of those awful dreams he'd been having?

"Monsieur le Russe, have you been smoking hashish?"

"I did not come alone," replied Fandorin.

The commissioner stuck his head out into the corridor and saw two other men standing beside the Russian. One was the half-mad baronet. But who was the other? The senior navigator, that's right. What was his name now . . . Fox.

"Pull yourself together!" said the diplomat, launching a new staccato assault. "There's not much time. I was reading in my cabin. There was a knock. Sir Reginald. He measured our position at one in the morning.

With his sextant. The course was wrong. We should go left of the Isle of Manar. We're going to the right. I woke the navigator. Fox, tell him."

The navigator stepped forward. He looked badly shaken. "There are shoals there, monsieur," he said in broken French. "And rocks. Sixteen thousand tons, monsieur. If it runs aground it will break in half like a French loaf. A baguette, you understand? Another half hour on this course and it will be too late to turn back!"

Wonderful news! Now old Gustave had to be a master mariner and lift the curse of the Isle of Manar!

"Why don't you just tell the captain that . . . that he's following the wrong course?"

The navigator glanced at the Russian.

"Mr. Fandorin says we shouldn't."

"Renier must have decided on one last desperate gamble." The Russian began jabbering away again. "He's capable of anything. He could have the navigator arrested. For disobeying orders. He could even use a gun. He's the captain. His word is law on board the ship. Only the three of us know what's happening. We need a representative of authority. You, commissioner. Let's get up there!"

"Wait, wait!" Gauche pressed his hands to his forehead. "You're making my head spin. Has Renier gone insane, then?"

"No. But he's determined to destroy the ship. And everyone on board."

"What for? What's the point?"

No, no, this couldn't really be happening. It was all a dream, a nightmare.

Realizing the commissioner wasn't going to be lured out of his lair so easily, Fandorin began speaking more slowly and clearly.

"I have only a hunch to go on. An appalling suspicion. Renier wants to destroy the ship and everyone on it to conceal his crime and cover his tracks. Hide all the evidence on the bottom of the ocean. If you find it hard to believe anyone could snuff out thousands of lives so callously, then think of the Rue de Grenelle and remember Sweetchild. In the hunt for the Brahmapur treasure, human life is cheap."

Gauche gulped.

"In the hunt for the treasure?"

"Yes," said Fandorin, controlling himself with an effort. "Renier is Rajah Bagdassar's son. I'd guessed, but I wasn't sure. Now there can be no doubt."

"What do you mean, his son? Rubbish! The rajah was Indian, and Renier is a pure-blooded Frenchman."

"Have you noticed he doesn't eat beef or pork? Do you realize why? It's a habit from his childhood. In India the cow is regarded as a sacred animal, and Moslems do not eat pork. The rajah was an Indian, but he was a Moslem by religion."

"That proves nothing!" Gauche said with a shrug. "Renier said he was on a diet."

"What about his dark complexion?"

"A suntan from sailing the southern seas."

"Renier has spent the last two years sailing the London–New York and London–Stockholm routes. Renier is half Indian, Gauche. Think! Rajah Bagdassar's wife was French, and at the time of the Sepoy Mutiny their son was being educated in Europe. Most probably in France, his mother's homeland. Have you ever been in Renier's cabin?"

"Yes, he asked me in. He asked everybody in."

"Did you see the photograph on the table? 'Seven feet under the keel . . . Françoise B.'?"

"Yes, I saw it. It's his mother."

"If it's his mother, then why 'B' instead of 'R'? A son and his mother should have the same surname."

"Perhaps she married a second time."

"Possibly. I haven't had time to check that. But what if 'Françoise B.' means 'Françoise Bagdassar'? In the European manner, since Indian rajahs don't have surnames."

"Then where did the name Renier come from?"

"I don't know. Let's suppose he took his mother's maiden name when he was naturalized."

"Conjecture," Gauche retorted. "Not a single hard fact. Nothing but 'what if' and 'let's suppose.' "

"I agree. But surely Renier's behavior at the time of Sweetchild's murder was suspicious? Remember how the lieutenant offered to fetch Mme. Kleber's shawl? And he asked the professor not to start without him. I think the few minutes Renier was away were enough for him to set fire to the litter bin and pick up the scalpel from his cabin."

"And why do you think he was the one who had the scalpel?"

"I told you, the Negro's bundle disappeared from the boat after the search. And who was in charge of the search? Renier!"

Gauche shook his head skeptically. The steamer swung over hard and he struck his shoulder painfully against the doorpost, which didn't help improve his mood.

"Do you remember how Sweetchild began?" Fandorin continued. He took a watch out of his pocket, glanced at it, and began speaking faster. " 'Suddenly it hit me! Everything fell into place—about the shawl, and about the son! It's a matter of clerical work pure and simple. Dig around in the registers at the École Maritime and you'll find him!' Not only had he guessed the secret of the shawl; he had discovered something about the rajah's son as well. For instance, that he studied at the École Maritime in Marseille. A training school for sailors. Which our Renier also happens to have attended. Sweetchild mentioned a telegram he sent to an acquaintance of his in the French Ministry of the Interior. Perhaps he was trying to find out what became of the child. And he obviously did find out something, but he didn't guess that Renier is the rajah's son. Otherwise he would have been more careful."

"And what did he dig up about the shawl?" Gauche asked eagerly.

"I think I can answer that question as well. But not now—later. We're running out of time!"

"So you think Renier himself set the fire and took advantage of the panic to shut the professor's mouth?" Gauche mused.

"Yes, damn it! Use your brains! I know there's not much hard evidence, but we have only twenty minutes left before *Leviathan* enters the strait!"

But the commissioner still wasn't convinced.

"The arrest of a ship's captain on the high seas is mutiny. Why did you believe what this gentleman told you?" He jerked his chin in the direction of the crazy baronet. "He's always talking nonsense."

The redheaded Englishman laughed disdainfully and looked at Gauche as if he were some kind of pill bug or flea. He didn't dignify his comment with a reply.

"Because I have suspected Renier for a long time," the Russian said rapidly. "And because I thought what happened to Captain Cliff was strange. Why did the lieutenant need to negotiate for so long with the shipping company over the telegraph? It means they did not know that Cliff's daughter had been injured in a fire. Then who sent the telegram to Bombay? The directors of the boarding school? How would they know the *Leviathan*'s route in such detail? Perhaps Renier himself sent the message? My guidebook says Bombay has at least a dozen telegraph offices. Sending a telegram from one to another would be very simple."

"And why in damnation's name would he want to send such a telegram?"

"To gain control of the ship. He knew that if Cliff received news like that he would not be able to continue the voyage. The real question is, why did Renier take such a risk? Not out of idle vanity—so that he could command the ship for a week and then to hell with everything! There is only one possible explanation: He did it so he could send the *Leviathan* to the bottom with all the passengers and crew on board. The investigation was getting too close for comfort; he could feel the noose tightening around his neck. He must know the police will carry on hounding all the suspects. But if there's a shipwreck with all hands lost, the case is closed. And then there's nothing to stop him picking up the casket at his leisure."

"But he'll be killed along with the rest of us!"

"No he won't. We've just checked the captain's launch, and it is ready to put to sea. It's a small craft, but sturdy. It can easily weather a storm. It has a supply of water and a basket of provisions and something else rather touching—a travel bag all packed and ready to go. Renier must be planning to abandon ship as soon as the *Leviathan* has entered the narrow channel and can no longer turn back. The ship will be unable to swing around; even if the engines are stopped the current will still carry it onto the rocks. A few people might be saved, since we are not far from the shore, but everyone who disappears will be listed as lost at sea."

"Don't be such a stupid ass, monsieur policeman!" the navigator butted in. "We've wasted far too much time already. Mr. Fandorin woke me up and said the ship was on the wrong course. I wanted to sleep and I told Mr. Fandorin to go to hell. He offered me a bet—a hundred pounds to one that the captain was off course. I thought, *The Russian's gone crazy, everyone knows how eccentric the Russians are, this will be easy money.* I went up to the bridge. Everything was in order. The captain was on watch, the pilot was at the helm. But for the sake of a hundred pounds I checked the course anyway and then I started sweating, I can tell you! But I didn't say a word to the captain. Mr. Fandorin had warned me not to say anything. And that"—the navigator looked at his watch—"was twenty-five minutes ago."

Then he added something in English that was obviously uncomplimentary about the French in general and French policemen in particular. The only word Gauche could understand was "frog."

The sleuth hesitated for one final moment before making up his mind. Immediately he was transformed; he began getting dressed with swift, precise movements. Papa Gauche might be slow off the mark, but once on the move he needed no further urging.

As he pulled on his jacket and trousers, he said to the navigator: "Fox, bring two sailors up on to the top deck, with carbines. The captain's mate should come, too. No, better not, there's no time to explain everything all over again."

He put his trusty Lefaucheux in his pocket and offered the diplomat a four-cylinder Marietta.

"Do you know how to use this?"

"I have my own, a Herstal-Agent," replied Fandorin, showing him a handsome, compact revolver unlike any Gauche had ever seen before. "And this as well."

With a single rapid movement he drew a slim, pliable sword out of his cane.

"Then let's go."

Gauche decided not to give the baronet a gun—who could tell what the lunatic might do with it?

The three of them strode rapidly down the long corridor. The door of one of the cabins opened slightly and Renate Kleber glanced out, a shawl over her brown dress.

"Gentlemen, why are you stamping about like a herd of elephants?" she exclaimed angrily. "I can't get any sleep as it is with this awful storm."

"Close the door and don't go anywhere," Gauche told her sternly, shoving her back into the cabin without even slowing his stride. This was no time to stand on ceremony.

The commissioner thought he saw the door of cabin number twenty-four, which belonged to Mlle. Stamp, tremble and open a crack, but he had no time now to worry about minor details.

On deck the wind drove the rain into their faces. They had to shout in order to hear one another.

There were the steps leading to the wheelhouse and the bridge. Fox was already waiting at the bottom with two sailors from the watch.

"I told you to bring carbines!" shouted Gauche.

"They're in the armory!" the navigator yelled in his ear. "And the captain has the key!"

"Never mind, let's go up," Fandorin communicated with a gesture. Raindrops glistened on his face.

Gauche looked around and shuddered: In the flickering lightning the rain glittered like steel threads in the night sky and the waves frothed and foamed white in the darkness. It was an awesome sight.

Their heels clattered as they climbed the iron steps, their eyes half-closed against the lashing rain. Gauche went first. At this moment he was the most important person on the whole *Leviathan*, this colossal two-hundred-meter monster drifting unsuspectingly toward disaster. The detective's foot slipped on the top step and he grabbed hold of the banister only just in time. He straightened up and caught his breath.

They were up. There was nothing above them now but the funnels spitting out occasional sparks and the masts, almost invisible in the darkness.

There was the metal door with its steel rivets. Gauche raised his finger in warning: Quiet! The precaution was not really necessary—the sea was so loud that no one in the wheelhouse could have heard a thing.

"This is the door to the captain's bridge and the wheelhouse!" shouted Fox. "No one enters without the captain's permission!"

Gauche took his revolver out of his pocket and cocked it. Fandorin did the same.

"You keep quiet!" the detective warned the overenterprising diplomat. "I'll do the talking! Oh, I should never have listened to you!" He gave the door a determined shove.

But of course the damned thing didn't budge.

"He's locked himself in," said Fandorin. "Say something, Fox."

The navigator knocked loudly and shouted in English: "Captain, it's me, Jeremy Fox! Please open up! It's an emergency!"

They heard Renier's muffled voice from behind the door: "What's happened, Jeremy?"

The door remained closed.

The navigator glanced at Fandorin in consternation. Fandorin pointed at the commissioner, then put a finger to his own temple and mimed pressing the trigger. Gauche didn't understand what the pantomime meant, but Fox nodded and roared at the top of his voice: "The French cop's shot himself!"

The door immediately swung open and Gauche presented his wet but living face to Renier. He trained the barrel of his Lefaucheux on the captain.

Renier screamed and leapt backward as if he had been struck. Now that was real hard evidence for you: A man with a clear conscience wouldn't shy away from a policeman like that. Gauche grabbed hold of the sailor's tarpaulin collar.

"I'm glad you were so distressed by the news of my death, my dear rajah," the commissioner purred, then barked out the words known and feared by every criminal in Paris. "Get your hands up in the air! You're under arrest."

The most notorious cutthroats in the city had been known to faint at the sound of those words.

The helmsman froze at his wheel, with his face half turned toward them.

"Keep hold of the wheel, you idiot!" Gauche shouted at him. "Hey you!"—he prodded one of the sailors from the watch with his finger—

"bring the captain's mate here immediately so he can take command. In the meantime, you give the orders, Fox. And look lively about it! Give the command 'halt all engines' or 'full astern' or whatever; don't just stand there like a dummy!"

"Let me take a look," said the navigator, leaning over a map. "Maybe it's not too late to just swing hard to port."

Renier's guilt was obvious. The fellow didn't even pretend to be outraged; he just stood there hanging his head, with his hands raised in the air and his fingers trembling.

"Right, then, let's go and have a little talk, shall we?" Gauche said to him. "Ah, what a lovely little talk we'll have."

Renate Kleber

————

RENATE ARRIVED FOR breakfast later than everyone else, so she was the last to hear about the events of the previous night. Everyone threw themselves on her, desperate to tell her the incredible, nightmarish news.

Apparently Captain Renier was no longer captain.

Apparently Renier was not even Renier.

Apparently he was the son of that rajah.

Apparently he was the one who had killed everybody.

Apparently the ship had almost run aground in the night.

"We were all sound asleep in our cabins," whispered Clarissa Stamp, her eyes wide with terror, "and meanwhile that *man* was sailing the ship straight onto the rocks. Can you imagine what would have happened? The sickening scraping sound, the impact, the crunching as the metal plating ripped away! The shock throws you out of bed onto the floor and for a moment you can't understand what's happening. Then the shouting, the running feet. The floor heeling over farther and farther. And the terrible realization that the ship isn't moving, it has stopped! Everyone runs out on deck, half dressed . . ."

"Not me!" the doctor's wife declared resolutely.

"The sailors try to lower the lifeboats," Clarissa continued in the same hushed, mystical voice, ignoring Mrs. Truffo's comment, "but the crowds of passengers milling around on the deck get in their way. Every new wave throws the ship farther over on to its side. Now we are struggling to stay on our feet, we have to hold on to something. The night is pitch-black, the sea is roaring, the thunder rumbles in the sky . . . One lifeboat is finally lowered, but so many people crazed by fear have packed into it that it capsizes. The little children . . ."

Fandorin interrupted the word artist gently but firmly. "P-please, no more."

"You should write novels about the sea, madam," the doctor remarked with a frown.

But Renate had frozen motionless with one hand over her heart. She was already pale from lack of sleep and now she had turned quite green at all the news.

"Oh!" she said, and then repeated it: "Oh!"

Then she rebuked Clarissa with a stern face. "Why are you saying such awful things? Surely you know I mustn't listen to them, in my condition?"

The Watchdog was not at the table. It was unlike him to miss breakfast.

"But where is M. Gauche?" Renate asked.

"Still interrogating his prisoner," the Japanese told her. In the last few days he had stopped being so surly and given up glaring at Renate like a wild thing.

"Has M. Renier really confessed to all these appalling crimes?" she gasped. "He is slandering himself! He must be confused in his mind. You know, I noticed some time ago that he was not quite himself. Did he himself say he is the rajah's son? Well, I suppose it's better than being Napoleon's son. It's obvious the poor man has simply gone mad."

"Yes, that, too, madam, that, too," Commissioner Gauche's weary voice said behind her.

Renate had not heard him come in. But that was only natural—the storm was over, but the sea was still running high, the ship was rolling on the choppy waves, and every moment something squeaked, clanged, or cracked. Big Ben's pendulum had stopped working since the clock had been hit by a bullet, but the clock itself was swaying to and fro—sooner or later the oaken monstrosity was bound to keel over, Renate thought in passing, then concentrated her attention on the Watchdog.

"What's going on? Tell me!" she demanded.

The policeman walked unhurriedly across to his chair and sat down. He gestured to the steward to pour him some coffee.

"Oof, I am absolutely exhausted," the commissioner complained. "What about the passengers? Do they know?"

"The whole ship is buzzing with the news, but so far not many know the details," the doctor replied. "Mr. Fox told me everything, and I considered it my duty to inform everyone here."

The Watchdog looked at Fandorin and the Ginger Lunatic, then shook his head in surprise.

"I see that you gentlemen, however, are not inclined to gossip."

Renate didn't understand the meaning of his remark, but it was irrelevant to the matter in hand.

"What about Renier?" she asked. "Has he really confessed to all these atrocities?"

The Watchdog took a sip from his cup, relishing it. There was something different about him today. He no longer looked like an old dog that barks but doesn't bite. This dog looked as though it would go for you. And if you weren't careful, it would even take a bite out of you. Renate decided to rechristen the commissioner "the Bulldog."

"A nice drop of coffee," the Bulldog said appreciatively. "Yes, he confessed, of course he did. What else could he do? It took a bit of coaxing, but old Gauche has plenty of experience in such matters. Your Renier is sitting writing out his confession as we speak. He's got into the flow of it; there's just no stopping him. I left him there to finish the job."

"Why is he my Renier?" Renate asked in alarm. "Don't be ridiculous. He's just a considerate man who gave a pregnant woman a helping hand. And I don't believe that he is such a monster."

"When he's finished his confession, I'll let you read it," the Bulldog promised. "For old times' sake. All those hours we've spent sitting at the same table. And now it's all over, the investigation's concluded. I trust you won't be acting for my client this time, M. Fandorin? There's no way this one can avoid the guillotine."

"The insane asylum, more likely," said Renate.

The Russian was also on the point of saying something, but he held back. Renate looked at him curiously. He looked as fresh and fragrant as if he had spent the whole night dreaming sweetly in his own bed. And, as always, he was dressed impeccably: a white jacket and a silk waistcoat with a pattern of small stars. He was a very unusual character; Renate had never met anyone like him before.

The door burst open so violently that it almost came off its hinges, and a sailor with wildly staring eyes appeared on the threshold. When he spotted Gauche, he ran over and whispered something to him, waving his arms about despairingly.

Renate listened, but she could only make out the words "bastard" and "by my mother's grave."

"Now what's happened?"

"Doctor, please come out into the corridor." The Bulldog pushed away the plate with his omelette on it with a gesture of annoyance. "I'd like you to translate what this lad is muttering about for me."

The three of them went out.

"WHAT!" THE COMMISSIONER'S voice roared in the corridor. "Where were you looking, you numskull?"

There was a sound of hasty footsteps retreating into the distance, then silence.

"I'm not going to set foot outside this room until M. Gauche comes back," Renate declared firmly.

The others seemed to feel much the same.

The silence that descended in the Windsor salon was tense and uncomfortable.

THE COMMISSIONER AND Truffo came back half an hour later. Both looked grim.

"What we ought to have expected has happened," the diminutive doctor announced, without waiting for questions. "This tragic story has been concluded. And the final word was written by the criminal himself."

"Is he dead?" exclaimed Renate, jumping abruptly to her feet.

"He has killed himself?" asked Fandorin. "But how? Surely you took precautions?"

"In a case like this, of course I took precautions," Gauche said in a dispirited voice. "The only furniture in the cell where I interrogated him is a table, two chairs, and a bed. All are bolted to the floor. But if a man has really made up his mind to die, there's nothing you can do to stop him. Renier crushed his forehead in against the corner of the wall. There's a place in the cell where it juts out. And he was so cunning about it that the sentry didn't hear a thing. They opened the door to take in his breakfast, and he was lying there in a pool of blood. I ordered him not to be touched. Let him stay there for a while."

"May I take a look?" asked Fandorin.

"Go ahead. Gawk at him as long as you like; I'm going to finish my breakfast." And the Bulldog calmly pulled his cold omelette toward himself.

Four of them went to look at the suicide: Fandorin, Renate, the Japanese, and, strangely enough, the doctor's wife. Who'd have thought the prim old nanny goat would be so curious?

Renate's teeth chattered as she glanced into the cell over Fandorin's shoulder. She saw the familiar body with it broad shoulders stretched out diagonally across the floor of the cell, its dark head toward the projecting corner of the wall. Renier was lying facedown, his right arm twisted into an unnatural position.

Renate did not enter the cell; she could see well enough without that. The others went in and squatted down beside the corpse.

The Japanese raised the dead man's head and touched the bloodied forehead with his finger. Oh, yes, he was a doctor, wasn't he?

"O Lord, have mercy on this sinful creature," Mme. Truffo intoned piously in English.

"Amen," said Renate, turning her eyes away from the distressing sight.

Nobody spoke as they walked back to the salon.

They got back just in time to see the Bulldog finish eating, wipe his greasy lips with a napkin, and pull over his black file.

"I promised to show you the testimony of our former dining companion," he said impassively, setting out three pieces of paper on the table: two full sheets and a half sheet, all covered with writing. "It turns out it is his letter of farewell as well as his confession. But that doesn't really make any difference. Would you like to hear it?"

There was no need to repeat the invitation—they all gathered round the commissioner and waited with bated breath. The Bulldog picked up the first sheet, held it away from his eyes, and began reading.

To Commissioner Gustave Gauche
Representative of the French police

19 April 1878, 6.15 A.M.
On board the *Leviathan*

I, Charles Renier, do hereby make the following confession of my own free will and without duress, solely and exclusively out of a desire to unburden my conscience and clarify the motives that have led me to commit heinous criminal acts.

Fate has always treated me cruelly . . .

"Well, that's a song I've heard a thousand times," remarked the commissioner. "No murderer, thief, or corrupter of juveniles has ever told a court fate had showered its gifts on him but he had squandered them all, the son of a bitch. All right, then, let us continue."

Fate has always treated me cruelly, and if it pampered me at the dawn of my life, it was only in order to torment me all the more painfully later on. I was the only son and heir of a fabulously rich rajah, a very good man who was steeped in the wisdom of the East and the West. Until the age of nine I did not know the meaning of anger, fear, resentment, or frustrated desire. My mother, who was homesick for her own country, spent all her time with me, telling me about *la belle France* and gay Paris, where she grew up. My father fell head over heels in love the first time he saw her at the Bagatelle Club, where she was the lead dancer. Françoise Renier (that was my mother's surname, which I took for my own when I became a French citizen) could not resist the temptation of everything that marriage to an oriental sovereign seemed to promise, and she became his wife. But the marriage did not bring her happiness, although she genuinely respected my father and has remained faithful to him to this day.

When India was engulfed by a wave of bloody rebellion, my father sensed danger and sent his wife and son to France. The rajah had known for a long time that the English coveted his cherished casket of jewels and would not hesitate to resort to some underhanded trick in order to obtain the treasure of Brahmapur.

At first my mother and I were rich—we lived in our own mansion in Paris, surrounded by servants. I studied at a privileged lycée, together with the children of crowned monarchs and millionaires. But then everything changed and I came to know the very depths of poverty and humiliation.

I shall never forget the black day when my mother wept as she told me I no longer had a father, or a title, or a homeland. A year later, the only inheritance my father had left me was finally delivered via the British embassy in Paris. It was a small Koran. By that time my mother had already had me christened and I attended Mass, but I swore to myself that I would learn Arabic so I could read the notes made in the margins of the Holy Book by my father's hand. Many years later I fulfilled my intention, but I shall write about that below.

"Patience, patience," said Gauche with a cunning smile. "We'll get to that later. This part is just the lyrical preamble."

We moved out of the mansion as soon as we received the terrible news. At first to an expensive hotel. Then to a cheaper hotel. Then to furnished apartments. The number of servants grew less and less until finally the two of us were left alone. My mother had never been a practical person, either during the wild days of her youth or later. The jewels she had brought with her to Europe were enough for us to live on for two or three years, and then we fell into genuine poverty. I attended an ordinary school, where I was beaten and called "darky." That life taught me to be secretive and vengeful. I kept a secret diary in which I noted the names of everyone who offended me, in order to take my revenge on every one of them. And, sooner or later, the opportunity always came. I met one of the enemies of my unhappy adolescence many years later. He did not recognize me—by that time I had changed my name and no longer resembled the skinny, persecuted "hindoo" (the name they used to taunt me with in school). One evening I lay in wait for my old acquaintance as he was on his way home from a tavern. I introduced myself by my former name and then cut short his cry of amazement with a blow of my penknife to his right eye, a trick I picked up in the drinking dens of Alexandria. I confess to this murder because it can hardly make my position any more desperate.

"Well, he's quite right there," the Bulldog agreed. "One corpse more or less doesn't make much difference now."

When I was thirteen years old, we moved from Paris to Marseille because it was cheaper to live there and my mother had relatives in the city. At sixteen, after an escapade I do not wish to recall, I ran away from home and enlisted as a cabin boy on a schooner. For two years I sailed the Mediterranean. It was a hard life, but it was useful experience. I became strong, supple, and ruthless, and later this helped me become the best cadet at the École Maritime in Marseille. I graduated from the college with distinction and ever since I have sailed on the finest ships of the French merchant fleet. When applications were requested for the post of first lieutenant on the super-steamship *Leviathan* at the end of last year, my service record and excellent references guaranteed me success. But by that time I had already acquired a Goal.

As he picked up the second sheet of paper, Gauche warned his listeners: "This is the point where it starts to get interesting."

I was taught Arabic as a child, but my tutors had been too indulgent with the heir apparent and I did not learn much. Later, when my mother and I were in France, the lessons stopped altogether and I rapidly forgot the little that I knew. For many years the Koran with my father's notes in it seemed to me like an enchanted book written in a magical script no mere mortal could ever decipher. How glad I was later that I never asked anyone who knew Arabic to read the jottings in the margins! I had decided that I must fathom this mystery for myself, no matter what it cost me. I took up Arabic again while I was sailing to Maghreb and the Levant, and gradually the Koran began speaking to me in my father's voice. But many years went by before the handwritten notes—ornate aphorisms by Eastern sages, extracts from poems, and worldly advice from a loving father to his son—began hinting to me that they made up a kind of code. If the notes were read in a certain order, they acquired the sense of precise and detailed instructions, but that could only be understood by someone who had committed the notes to memory and engraved them on his heart. I struggled longest of all with a line from a poem that I did not know:

> *Death's emissary shall deliver unto you*
> *The shawl dyed crimson with your father's blood.*

One year ago, as I was reading the memoirs of a certain English general who boasted of his "feats of courage" during the Great Mutiny (the reason for my interest in the subject should be clear), I read about the gift the rajah of Brahmapur had sent to his son before he died. The Koran had been wrapped in a shawl! The scales seemed to fall from my eyes. Several months later, Lord Littleby exhibited his collection in the Louvre. I was the most assiduous of all the visitors to that exhibition. When I finally saw my father's shawl, the meaning of the following lines was revealed to me:

> *Its tapering and pointed form*
> *Is like a drawing, or a mountain.*

And:

> *The blind eye of the bird of paradise*
> *Sees straight into the secret heart of mystery.*

What else could I dream of during all those years of exile if not the clay casket that held all the wealth in the world? How many times in my dreams had I seen that coarse earthen lid swing open to reveal, once again, as in my distant childhood, the unearthly glow that filled the entire universe?

The treasure was mine by right; I was the legitimate heir! The English had robbed me, but they had gained nothing by their treachery. That repulsive vulture Littleby, who prided himself on his plundered "rarities," was really no better than a common dealer in stolen goods. I felt not the slightest doubt that I was in the right, and the only thing I feared was that I might fail at the task I had set myself.

But I made several terrible, unforgivable blunders. The first was the death of the servants, and especially of the poor children. Of course I did not wish to kill those people, who were entirely innocent. As you have guessed, I pretended to be a doctor and injected them with tincture of morphine. I only wished to put them to sleep, but due to my inexperience and fear that the soporific would not work, I miscalculated the dose.

A shock awaited me upstairs. When I broke the glass of the display case and pressed my father's shawl to my face with fingers trembling in reverential awe, one of the doors into the room suddenly opened and the master of the house came limping in. According to my information, his lordship was supposed to be away from home, but suddenly there he was in front of me with a pistol in his hand! I had no choice. I grabbed a statuette of Shiva and struck the English lord on the head with all my might. Instead of falling backward, he slumped forward, clutching me in his arms and splashing blood on my clothes. Under my white doctor's coat I was wearing my dress uniform—the dark-blue sailor's trousers with red piping are very similar to the trousers worn by the municipal medical service. I was very proud of my cunning, but in the end it was to prove my undoing. In his death throes, my victim tore the *Leviathan* emblem off the breast of my jacket under the open white coat. I noticed that it was gone when I returned to the steamship. I managed to obtain a replacement, but I had left behind a fatal clue.

I do not remember how I left the house. I know I did not dare go out through the door, and I recall climbing the garden fence. When I recovered my wits, I was standing beside the Seine. In one bloody hand I was holding the statuette, and in the other the pistol—I have no idea why I took it. Shuddering with revulsion, I threw them both into the water. The shawl lay in the breast pocket of my uniform jacket, where it warmed my heart.

The following day I learned from the newspapers that I had murdered nine other people as well as Lord Littleby. I will not describe here how I suffered because of that.

"I should think not," the commissioner said with a nod. "This stuff is a bit too sentimental already. Anybody would think he was addressing the jury: I ask you, gentlemen, how could I have acted in any other way? In my place, you would have done the same. Phooey." He carried on reading.

The shawl drove me insane. That magical bird with a hole instead of an eye acquired a strange power over me. It was as if I were not in control of my actions, as if I were obeying a quiet voice that would henceforth guide me in all I did.

"There he goes, building toward a plea of insanity," the Bulldog said, laughing. "It's an old trick; we've heard that one before."

The shawl disappeared from my writing desk when we were sailing through the Suez Canal. I felt as if it had abandoned me to the whim of fate. It never even occurred to me that the shawl had been stolen. By that time I was already so deeply in thrall to its mystical influence that I thought of the shawl as a living being with a soul of its own. I was absolutely devastated. The only thing that prevented me from taking my own life was the hope that the shawl would take pity on me and come back. The effort required to conceal my despair from you and my colleagues was almost more than I could manage.

And then, on the eve of our arrival in Aden, a miracle happened! When I heard Mme. Kleber's frightened cry and ran into her cabin, I saw a Negro who had appeared out of nowhere, wearing my lost shawl round his neck. Now I realize the Negro must have taken the bright-colored piece of cloth from my cabin a few days before, but at the time I experienced a genuine holy terror, as if the Angel of Darkness in person had appeared from the underworld to return my treasure to me!

In the tussle that followed, I killed the black man, and while Mme. Kleber was still in a faint I surreptitiously removed the shawl from the body. Since then I have always worn it on my chest, never parting with it for a moment.

I murdered Professor Sweetchild in cold blood, with a calculated deliberation that exhilarated me. I attribute my supernatural foresight and rapid reaction entirely to the magical influence of the shawl. I realized from Sweetchild's first enigmatic words that he had solved the mystery of the shawl and picked up the trail of the rajah's son—my trail. I had to stop the professor from talking, and I did. The silk shawl was pleased with me—I could tell from the way its warmth soothed my poor, tormented heart.

But by eliminating Sweetchild I had done no more than postpone the inevitable. You had me hemmed in on all sides, Commissioner. Before we reached Calcutta you, and especially your astute assistant, Fandorin . . .

Gauche chuckled grimly and squinted at the Russian.

"My congratulations, monsieur, on earning a compliment from a murderer. I suppose I must be grateful he has at least made you my assistant, and not the other way around."

The Bulldog would obviously have been only too happy to cross out that line so his superiors in Paris would not see it. But a song isn't a song without the words. Renate glanced at the Russian. He tugged on the pointed end of his mustache and gestured for the policeman to continue.

. . . assistant, Fandorin, would undoubtedly have eliminated all the suspects one by one until I was the only one left. A telegram to the naturalization department of the Ministry of the Interior would have been enough to discover the name now used by the son of Rajah Bagdassar.

And the student records of the École Maritime would have shown that I joined the college under one name and graduated under another.

I realized that the road through the blank eye of the bird of paradise did not lead to earthly bliss, but to the eternal Abyss. I decided I would not depart this world as an abject failure, but as a great rajah. My noble ancestors had never died alone. They were followed onto the funeral pyre by their servants, wives, and concubines. I had not lived as a ruler, but I would die as a true sovereign should—as I had decided. And I would take with me on my final journey not slaves and handmaidens, but the flower of European society. My funeral carriage would be a gigantic ship, a miracle of European technical progress! I was enthralled by the scale and grandeur of this plan. It is a prospect even more vertiginous than limitless wealth!

"He's lying here," Gauche interjected sharply. "He was going to drown us, but he had the boat all ready for himself."

The commissioner picked up the final sheet, or rather half sheet.

I admit that the trick I played on Captain Cliff was vile. I can only offer the partial excuse that I did not anticipate such a tragic outcome. I regard Cliff with genuine admiration. Although I wished to seize control of the *Leviathan*, I also wished to save the grand old man's life. I knew that his concern for his daughter would make him suffer, but I thought he would soon discover she was all right. Alas, malicious fate dogs my steps relentlessly. How could I have foreseen the captain would suffer a stroke? That cursed shawl is to blame for everything!

I burned the bright-colored triangle of silk on the day the *Leviathan* sailed from Bombay. I have burned my bridges.

"He burned it!" gasped Clarissa Stamp. "Then the shawl has been destroyed?"

Renate stared hard at the Bulldog, who shrugged indifferently and said, "And thank God it's gone. To hell with the treasure, that's what I say, ladies and gentlemen. We'll all be far better off without it."

The new Seneca had pronounced judgment. Renate rubbed her chin and thought hard.

> Do you find it hard to believe? Well, then, to prove my sincerity I shall tell you the secret of the shawl. There is no point in hiding it now.

The commissioner broke off and cast a cunning glance at the Russian.

"As I recall, monsieur, last night you boasted of having guessed that secret. Share your guess with us, and we shall see if you are as astute as our dead man thought."

Fandorin was not in the least taken aback.

"It is not very c-complicated," he said casually.

He's bluffing, thought Renate, *but he does it very well. Can he really have guessed?*

"Very well, what do we know about the shawl? It is triangular, with one straight edge and two that are rather sinuous. That is one. The picture on the shawl shows a mythical bird with a hole in place of its eye. That is two. I am sure you remember the description of the Brahmapur palace, in particular its upper level: a mountain range on the horizon, reflected in a mirror image on the wall. That is th-three."

"We remember, but what of it?" asked the Ginger Lunatic.

"Oh, come now, Sir Reginald," the Russian exclaimed in mock surprise. "You and I both saw Sweetchild's little sketch. It contained all the clues required to guess the truth: the triangular shawl, the zigzag line, the word 'palace.' "

He took a handkerchief out of his pocket and folded it along a diagonal to make a triangle.

"The shawl is the key that indicates where the treasure is hidden. The shape of the shawl corresponds to the outline of one of the mountains depicted in the frescoes. All that is required is to position the upper corner of the shawl on the peak of that mountain—thus." He put the triangle on the table and ran his finger round its edge. "And then the eye of the bird Kalavinka will indicate the spot where one must search. Not on the painted mountain, of course, but on the real one. There must be a cave or something of the kind there. Have I got it right, Commissioner, or am I mistaken?"

Everyone turned toward Gauche, who thrust out his thick lips and knitted his bushy eyebrows so that he looked exactly like a gruff old bulldog.

"I don't know how you pull these things off," he grumbled. "I read the letter back there in the cell and I haven't let it out of my hands for a second . . . All right then, listen to this."

In my father's palace are four halls that were used for official ceremonies: Winter ceremonies were held in the North Hall, summer ceremonies in the South Hall, spring ceremonies in the East Hall, and autumn ceremonies in the West Hall. You may remember the deceased Professor Sweetchild speaking about this. The murals in these halls do indeed portray the mountainous landscape that can be seen through the tall windows stretching from the floor to the ceiling. Even after all these years, if I close my eyes I can still see that landscape before me. I have traveled far and seen many things, but nowhere in the world is there any sight more beautiful! My father buried the casket under a large brown rock on one of the mountains. To discover which mountain peak it is, you must set the shawl against each of the mountains depicted on the walls in turn. The treasure is on the mountain with the outline that perfectly matches the form of the shawl. The place where the rock should be sought is indicated by the empty eye of the bird of paradise. Of course, even if someone knew in which general area to look, it would still take him many hours, or even days, to find the stone—the search would have to cover many square meters of ground. But there can be no possibility of confusion. There are many brown boulders on the mountains, but there is only one in that particular area of the mountainside. "A mote lies in the single eye, A lone brown rock among the gray," says the note in the Koran. How many times I have pictured myself pitching my tent on that mountainside and searching for that mote? But it is not to be.

The emeralds, sapphires, rubies, and diamonds are fated to lie there until an earthquake sends the boulder tumbling down the mountain. It may not happen for a hundred thousand years, but the precious stones can wait—they are eternal.

But my time is ended. That cursed shawl has drained all my strength and addled my wits. I am crushed; I have lost my reason.

"Well, he's quite right about that," the commissioner concluded, laying the half sheet of paper on the table. "That's all—the letter breaks off at that point."

"I must say that Renier-san has acted correctly," said the Japanese. "He lived an unworthy life, but he died a worthy death. Much can be forgiven him for that, and in his next birth he will be given a new chance to atone for his sins."

"I don't know about his next birth," said the Bulldog, carefully gathering the sheets of paper together and putting them into his black file, "but this time around my investigation is concluded, thank God. I shall take a little rest in Calcutta and then go back to Paris. The case is closed."

But then the Russian diplomat presented Renate with a surprise.

"The case is certainly not closed," he said loudly. "You are being too hasty again, Commissioner." He turned to face Renate and trained the twin barrels of his cold blue eyes on her. "Surely Mme. Kleber has something to say to us?"

Clarissa Stamp

THIS QUESTION CAUGHT everyone by surprise. But no, not everyone—Clarissa was astonished to realize the mother-to-be was not at all disconcerted. She turned a little paler and bit her plump lower lip for a moment, but she replied in a loud, confident voice with barely any hesitation.

"You are right, monsieur, I do have something to tell. But not to you; only to a representative of the law."

She glanced helplessly at the commissioner and implored him: "In God's name, sir, I should like to make my confession in private."

Gauche did not seem to have anticipated this turn of events. The sleuth blinked and cast a suspicious glance at Fandorin. Then he thrust out his double chin pompously and growled.

"Very well—we can go to my cabin, if it's so important to you."

Clarissa had the impression that the policeman had no idea what Mme. Kleber intended to confess to him.

But then the commissioner could hardly be blamed for that—Clarissa herself had been struggling to keep up with the rapid pace of events.

The moment the door closed behind Gauche and his companion, Clarissa glanced inquiringly at Fandorin, who seemed to be the only one who really knew what was going on. It had been a whole day since she had dared to look at him so directly, instead of stealing furtive glances or peering at him from under lowered eyelids.

She had never before seen Erast (oh, yes, she could call him that to herself) looking so dismayed. There were wrinkles on his forehead and alarm in his eyes; his fingers were drumming nervously on the table. Could it be that even this confident man, with his lightning-fast reactions, was no longer in control of the situation? Clarissa had seen him unsettled the previous night, but only for the briefest of moments, and then he had rapidly recovered his self-control.

It was after the Bombay catastrophe.

She had not appeared in public for three whole days. She told the maid she was not well, took her meals in her cabin, and went out walking only under cover of darkness, like a thief in the night.

There was nothing wrong with her health, but how could she show herself to these people who had witnessed her shame, and especially *him*? That scoundrel Gauche had made her a general laughingstock, humiliated her, destroyed her reputation. And the worst thing was that she couldn't even accuse him of lying—it was all true, every last word of it. Yes, as soon as she came into possession of her inheritance, she had gone dashing off to Paris, the city she had heard and read so much about. Like a moth to a flame. And she had singed her wings. Surely it was enough that the shameful affair had deprived her of her final shred of self-respect—why did everyone else have to know that Miss Stamp was a loose woman and gullible fool, the contemptible victim of a professional gigolo?

Mrs. Truffo had visited her twice to inquire about her health. Of course, she wanted to gloat over Clarissa's humiliation. She gasped affectedly and complained about the heat, but there was a gleam of triumph in her beady, colorless eyes: *Well, my darling, which of us is the lady now?*

The Japanese called in and said it was the custom in his country to pay a visit of condolence when someone was unwell. He offered his services as a doctor and looked at her with sympathy.

Finally Fandorin had come knocking. Clarissa had spoken to him sharply and not opened the door—she told him she had a migraine.

Never mind, she said to herself as she sat there all alone, picking listlessly at her beefsteak. Only nine days until Calcutta. Nine days was no great time to spend behind closed doors. It was child's play if you had been imprisoned for almost a quarter of a century. And it was better here than in her aunt's house. Alone in her comfortable cabin with good books for company. And once she reached Calcutta, she would quietly slip ashore and turn over a brand-new leaf.

But in the evening of the third day she began having very different thoughts. Oh, how right the Bard had been when he penned those immortal lines:

> *Such sweet release new freedom does beget,*
> *When cherished bonds are shed without regret.*

Now she really did have nothing to lose. Late that night (it was already after twelve), Clarissa had resolutely arranged her hair, powdered her face lightly, put on the ivory-colored Parisian dress that suited her so well, and stepped out into the corridor. The ship's motions tossed her from one wall to the other.

Clarissa halted outside the door of cabin number eighteen, trying not to think about anything. When she raised her hand, it faltered—but only for a moment, just a single brief moment. She knocked on the door.

Erast opened it almost immediately. He was wearing a blue Hungarian robe with cord fastenings and his white shirt showed through the wide gap in the front.

"G-good evening, Miss Stamp," he said, speaking quickly. "Has something happened?"

Then, without waiting for a reply, he added: "Please wait for a moment and I'll get changed."

When he let her in, he was already dressed in a frock coat with an impeccably knotted tie. He gestured for her to take a seat.

Clarissa sat down, looked him in the eyes, and began.

"Please do not interrupt me. If I lose the thread, it will be even worse . . . I know I am a lot older than you. How old are you? Twenty-five? Less? It doesn't matter. I am not asking you to marry me. But I like you. I am in love with you. My entire upbringing was designed to ensure that I would never under any circumstances say those words to any man, but at this moment I do not care. I do not want to lose any more time. I have already wasted the best years of my life. I am fading away without ever having blossomed. If you like me even a little, tell me so. If not, then tell me that also. Nothing could be more bitter than the shame I have already endured. And you should know that my . . . adventure in Paris was a nightmare, but I do not regret it. Better a nightmare than the stupor in which I have spent my entire life. Well, then, answer me—don't just sit there!"

My God, how could she have said those things aloud? It was something she could feel proud about.

For an instant Fandorin was taken aback; he even blinked those long lashes in a most unromantic fashion. Then he began to speak, stammering more than usual.

"Miss Stamp . . . C-Clarissa . . . I do like you. I like you very much. I admire you. And I envy you."

"You envy me? For what?" she asked, amazed.

"For your courage. For the fact that you are not afraid to b-be refused and appear ridiculous. You see, I am b-basically very timid and uncertain of myself."

"You, timid?" Clarissa asked, even more astounded.

"Yes. There are two things I am really afraid of: appearing foolish or ridiculous and . . . dropping my guard."

No, she couldn't understand this at all.

"Your guard?"

"You see, I learned very early what it means to lose someone, and it frightened me badly—probably for the rest of my life. While I am alone, my defenses against fate are strong, and I fear nothing and nobody. For a man like me, it is best to be alone."

"I have already told you, Mr. Fandorin, that I am not laying claim to a place in your life, or even a place in your heart. Let alone attempting to penetrate your defenses."

She said no more, because everything had already been said.

And just at that very moment, of course, someone started hammering on the door. She heard Milford-Stokes's agitated voice in the corridor.

"Mr. Fandorin, sir! Are you awake? Open up! Quickly! It's a conspiracy!"

"Stay here," Erast whispered. "I shall be back soon."

He went out into the corridor. Clarissa heard muffled voices, but she couldn't make out what they were saying. Five minutes later Fandorin came back. He took some small, heavy object out of a drawer and put it in his pocket, then he picked up his elegant cane and said in an anxious voice: "Wait here for a while and then go back to your cabin. Things seem to be coming to a head."

She knew now what he had meant by that. Later, when she was back in her cabin, Clarissa had heard footsteps clattering along the corridor and the sound of excited voices, but of course it had never even entered her head that death was hovering over the masts of the proud *Leviathan*.

"What is it Mme. Kleber wants to confess?" Doctor Truffo asked nervously. "M. Fandorin, please tell us what is going on. How can she be involved in all this?"

But Fandorin simply assumed an even gloomier expression and said nothing.

Rolling in time to the regular impact of the waves, *Leviathan* was sailing northward, full speed ahead, carving through the waters of the Palk Strait, which were still murky after the storm. The coastline of Ceylon was a green stripe on the distant horizon. The morning was overcast and close. From time to time a gust of hot air blew a whiff of decay in through the open windows on the windward side of the salon, but the draft could find no exit and foundered helplessly, barely even ruffling the curtains.

"I think I have made a mistake," Erast muttered, taking a step toward the door. "I'm always one step or half a step behind . . ."

When the first shot came, Clarissa did not immediately realize what the sound was—it was just a sharp crack, and any number of things could make such a sound on a ship sailing a rough sea. But then there was another.

"Those are revolver shots!" exclaimed Sir Reginald. "But where from?"

"The commissioner's cabin!" Fandorin snapped, dashing for the door. Everybody rushed after him.

There was a third shot, and then, when they were only about twenty steps away from Gauche's cabin, a fourth.

"Stay here!" Fandorin shouted without turning around, pulling a small revolver out of his back pocket.

The others slowed down, but Clarissa was not afraid; she was determined to stay by Erast's side.

He pushed open the door of the cabin and held the revolver out in front of him. Clarissa stood on her tiptoes and peered over his shoulder.

The first thing she saw was an overturned chair. Then she saw Commissioner Gauche. He was lying on his back on the other side of the polished table that stood in the center of the room. Clarissa craned her neck to get a better look at him and shuddered: Gauche's face was hideously contorted, and there was dark blood bubbling out of the center of his forehead and dribbling onto the floor in two narrow rivulets.

Renate Kleber was in the opposite corner, huddled against the wall. She was sobbing hysterically and her teeth were chattering. There was a large black revolver with a smoking barrel in her trembling hand.

"Aaa! Ooo!" howled Mme. Kleber, pointing to the dead body. "I . . . I killed him!"

"Yes, I noticed," Fandorin said coolly.

Keeping his revolver trained on the Swiss woman, he went up to her and deftly snatched the gun out of her hands. She made no attempt to resist.

"Dr. Truffo!" Erast called, following Renate's every move closely. "In here!"

The diminutive doctor glanced into the gunsmoke-filled cabin with timid curiosity.

"Examine the body, if you please," said Fandorin.

Muttering some lamentation to himself in Italian, Truffo knelt beside the dead Gauche.

"A fatal wound to the head," he reported. "Death was instantaneous. But that's not all . . . There is a gun wound to the right elbow. And one here, to the left wrist. Three wounds in all."

"Keep looking. There were four shots."

"There are no more wounds. One of the bullets must have missed. No, wait! Here it is, in the right knee!"

"I'll tell you everything," Renate babbled, shuddering and sobbing. "Only take me out of this awful room!"

Fandorin put his little revolver in his pocket and the big one on the table.

"Very well, let us go. Doctor, inform the head of the watch what has happened here and have him put a guard on this door. And then rejoin us. There is no one but us now to conduct the investigation."

"What an ill-starred voyage!" Truffo gasped as he walked along the corridor. "Poor *Leviathan*!"

IN THE WINDSOR salon Mme. Kleber sat at the table, facing the door, and everyone else sat facing her. Fandorin was the only one who took a chair beside the murderess.

"Gentlemen, do not look at me like that," Mme. Kleber said in a pitiful voice. "I killed him, but I am the innocent victim. When I tell you what happened, you will see . . . But, for God's sake, give me some water."

The solicitous Japanese poured her some lemonade—the table had not yet been cleared after breakfast.

"So what happened?" asked Clarissa.

"Translate everything she says," Mrs. Truffo sternly instructed her husband, who had already returned. "Everything, word for word."

The doctor nodded, wiping his bald head with his handkerchief to remove the perspiration caused by walking so fast.

"Don't be afraid, madam. Just tell the truth," Sir Reginald said encouragingly to Renate. "This person is no gentleman—he has no idea how to treat a lady. But I guarantee you will be treated with respect."

These words were accompanied by a glance in Fandorin's direction—a glance filled with such fierce hatred that Clarissa Stamp was taken aback. What on earth could have happened between Erast and Milford-Stokes since the previous day to cause this hostility?

"Thank you, dear Reginald," Renate sobbed.

She drank her lemonade slowly, sniffling and moaning under her breath. Then she looked imploringly at her interrogators and began speaking.

"Gauche is no guardian of the law! He is a criminal, a madman! That loathsome shawl has driven everybody insane! Even a police commissioner!"

"You said you had something to confess to him," Clarissa reminded her in a cold, unfriendly voice. "What was it?"

"Yes, there was something I was hiding . . . something important. I was going to confess everything, but first I wanted to expose the commissioner!"

"Expose him? As what?" Sir Reginald asked sympathetically.

Mme. Kleber stopped crying and solemnly declared: "A murderer. Renier did not kill himself. Commissioner Gauche killed him!"

Seeing how astounded her listeners were by this claim, she continued rapidly. "It's obvious! You try smashing your skull by running at the wall in a room only six square meters! It can't be done. If Charles had decided to kill himself, he would have taken off his tie, tied it to the ventilation grill, and jumped off a chair. No, Gauche killed him! He struck him on the head with some heavy object and then made it look like suicide by smashing the dead man's head against the wall."

"But why would the commissioner want to kill Renier?" Clarissa asked with a skeptical shake of her head. Mme. Kleber was obviously talking nonsense.

"I told you—greed had driven him completely insane! That shawl is to blame for everything. Either Gauche was angry with Charles for burning the shawl, or he didn't believe him—I don't know which. But anyway, it's quite clear that Gauche killed him. And when I told him so to his face, he didn't try to deny it. He took out his pistol and started waving it about and threatening me. He said that if I didn't keep my mouth shut, I'd go the same way as Renier . . ." Renate began sniffling again and then—miracle of miracles—the baronet offered her his handkerchief.

What mysterious transformation was this? He had always shunned Renate like the plague.

"Then he put the pistol on the table and started shaking me by the shoulders. I was so afraid, so afraid! I don't know how I managed to push him away and grab the gun from the table. It was terrible! I ran away from him and he started chasing me round the table. I turned and pressed the trigger. I kept pressing it until he fell . . . and then M. Fandorin came in."

Renate began sobbing loudly. Milford-Stokes patted her shoulder tentatively, as if he were touching a rattlesnake.

Clarissa started when the silence was suddenly broken by the sound of loud clapping.

"Bravo!" said Fandorin with a mocking smile, still clapping his hands. "Bravo, Mme. Kleber. You are a great actress."

"How dare you!" exclaimed Sir Reginald, choking with indignation, but Erast cut him short with a wave of his hand.

"Sit down and listen. I shall tell you what really happened." Fandorin was absolutely calm and seemed quite certain he was right. "Mme. Kleber is not only a superb actress; she is quite exceptionally talented in every respect. She possesses true brilliance and breadth of imagination. Unfortunately, her greatest talent lies in the criminal sphere. You are an accomplice to a whole series of murders, madam. Or rather, not an accomplice, but the instigator, the leading lady. It was Renier who was *your* accomplice."

"Look," Renate appealed plaintively to Sir Reginald. "Now he's gone crazy, too. And he was so calm and quiet."

"The most amazing thing about you is the superhuman speed with which you react to a situation," Erast continued, as though she hadn't even spoken. "You never defend yourself—you always strike first, Mlle. Sanfon. You don't mind if I call you by your real name, do you?"

"Sanfon! Marie Sanfon? Her?" Dr. Truffo exclaimed.

Clarissa realized she was sitting there with her mouth open. Milford-Stokes jerked his hand away from Renate's shoulder. Renate herself looked at Fandorin pityingly.

Fandorin said: "Yes, you see before you the legendary, brilliant, ruthless international adventuress Marie Sanfon. Her style is breathtakingly daring and inventive. She leaves no clues or witnesses. And, last but not least, she cares nothing for human life. The testimony of Charles Renier, which we shall come to later, is a mixture of truth and lies. I do not know, my lady, when you met him or under what circumstances, but two things are beyond all doubt. First, Renier genuinely loved you and tried to divert suspicion from you until his very last moment. And second: It was you who persuaded the son of the Emerald Rajah to go in search of his inheritance— otherwise why would he have waited for so many years? You made Lord Littleby's acquaintance, acquired all the information you required, and worked out a p-plan. Obviously at first you had counted on obtaining the shawl by cunning and flattery—after all, his lordship had no idea of the significance of that scrap of cloth. But you soon became convinced it would never work: Littleby was absolutely fanatical about his collection and he would never have agreed to part with any of his pieces. It was not possible to obtain the shawl by stealth, either—there were armed guards constantly on duty beside the display case. So you decided to keep the risk to a minimum and leave no traces, the way you always prefer to do things. Tell me, did you know Lord Littleby had not gone away, that he was at home on that fateful evening? I am sure you did. You needed to bind Renier to you with blood. It was not he who killed the servants—you did."

"Impossible!" said Dr. Truffo, throwing his hand in the air. "Without medical training and practice, no woman could give nine injections in three minutes! It's quite out of the question."

"First, she could have prepared nine loaded syringes in advance. And second . . ." Erast took an apple from a dish and cut a piece off it with an elegant flourish. "M. Renier may have had no experience in using a syringe, but Marie Sanfon does. Do not forget that she was raised in a convent of the Gray Sisters of St. Vincent, an order founded to provide medical assistance to the poor, and their novices are trained from an early age to work in hospitals, leper colonies, and hospices. These nuns are highly qualified nurses—and, as I recall, young Marie was one of the best."

"But of course. I forgot. You're right," the doctor said, lowering his head penitently. "Please continue. I shall not interrupt you again."

"Well then, Paris, the Rue de Grenelle, the evening of the fifteenth of March. T-two people arrive at the mansion of Lord Littleby: a young doctor with a dark complexion and a nurse with the cowl of her gray nun's habit pulled down over her eyes. The doctor presents a piece of p-paper with a seal from the mayor's office and asks for everyone in the house to gather together. He probably says it is getting late and they still have a lot of work to do. The inoculations are given by the nun—deftly, quickly, painlessly. Afterward the pathologist will not discover any sign of bruising at the sites of the injections. Marie Sanfon has not forgotten what she learned in her charitable youth. What happened after that is clear, so I shall omit the details: The servants fall asleep, the criminals climb the stairs to the second floor, Renier has a brief tussle with the master of the house. The murderer fails to notice that his gold *Leviathan* badge has been left behind in Lord Littleby's hand. Which meant that afterward, my lady, you had to give him yours—it would be easier for you to avoid suspicion than the captain's first mate. And I expect you had more confidence in yourself than in him."

Up to this point Clarissa had been gazing spellbound at Erast, but now she glanced briefly at Renate. She was listening carefully, an expression of offended amazement on her face. If she was Marie Sanfon, she had not given herself away yet.

"I began to suspect both of you from the day that poor African supposedly fell on top of you," Fandorin said to Renate. He bit off a piece of the apple with his even white teeth. "That was Renier's fault, of course—he panicked and got carried away. You would have invented something more cunning. Let me try to reconstruct the sequence of events, and you can correct me if I get any of the details wrong. All right?"

Renate shook her head mournfully and propped her plump cheek on her hand.

"Renier saw you to your cabin—you certainly had things to discuss, since your accomplice states in his confession that the shawl had mysteriously disappeared only a short while before. You went into your cabin, saw the huge Negro rifling through your things, and for a moment you must have been frightened—if you are acquainted at all with the feeling of fear. But a second later your heart leapt when you saw the precious shawl on the Negro's neck. That explained everything: When the runaway slave was searching Renier's cabin, the colorful piece of material had caught his eye and he decided to wear it round his massive neck. When you cried out, Renier came running in, saw the shawl, and, unable to control himself, pulled out his dirk. You had to invent the story about the mythical attack—to lie down on the floor and hoist the Negro's hot, heavy body onto yourself. I expect that was not very pleasant, was it?"

"I protest, this is all pure invention!" Sir Reginald exclaimed heatedly. "Of course the Negro attacked Mme. Kleber, it is obvious! You are fantasizing again, mister Russian diplomat!"

"Not in the least," Erast said mildly, casting a look of either sorrow or pity at the baronet. "I told you I had seen slaves from the Ndanga people before, when I was a prisoner of the Turks. Do you know why they are valued so highly? Because, for all their great strength and stamina, they are exceptionally gentle; they have absolutely no aggressive instinct. They are a tribe of farmers, not hunters; they have never fought a war against anyone. The Ndanga could not possibly have attacked Mme. Kleber, not even if he was frightened to death. M. Aono was surprised, at the time, that the savage's fingers had left no bruises on the delicate skin of your neck. Surely that is strange?"

Renate bowed her head thoughtfully, as though she herself were amazed at the oversight.

"Now let us recall the murder of Professor Sweetchild. The moment it became clear that the Indologist was close to solving the mystery, you, my lady, asked him not to hurry, but to tell the whole story in detail from the beginning, and meanwhile you sent your accomplice out, supposedly to fetch your shawl, but in actual fact to make preparations for the murder. Your partner understood what he had to do without being told."

"It's not true!" Renate protested. "Gentlemen, you are my witnesses! Renier volunteered of his own accord! Don't you remember? M. Milford-Stokes, I swear I'm telling the truth. I asked you first, do you remember?"

"That's right," confirmed Sir Reginald. "That was what happened."

"A t-trick for simpletons," said Fandorin, with a flourish of the fruit knife. "You knew perfectly well, my lady, that the baronet could not stand you and never indulged your caprices. Your little operation was carried through very deftly—but on this occasion, alas, not quite neatly enough. You failed to shift the blame onto M. Aono, although you came very close to succeeding." At this point Erast lowered his eyes modestly to allow his listeners to recall precisely who had demolished the chain of evidence against the Japanese.

He is not entirely without vanity, thought Clarissa, but to her eyes this characteristic appeared quite charming and only seemed to make the young man even more attractive. As usual, it was poetry that provided the resolution of the paradox:

> *For even the beloved's limitation*
> *Is worthy, in love's eyes, of adoration.*

Ah, mister diplomat, how little you know of Englishwomen. I believe you will be making a protracted stay in Calcutta.

Fandorin maintained his pause, as yet quite unaware that his faults were worthy of adoration, or that he would arrive at his new post later than planned, and then continued.

"Now your situation has become genuinely perilous. Renier described it quite eloquently in his letter. And so you take a terrible decision that is nonetheless, in its own way, a stroke of genius: to sink the ship together with the punctilious commissioner of police, the witnesses, and a thousand others. What do the lives of a thousand people mean to you, if they are preventing you from becoming the richest woman in the world? Or, even worse, if they pose a threat to your life and liberty?"

Clarissa looked at Renate with horrified fascination. Could this young woman, who was rather bitchy but otherwise seemed perfectly ordinary, really be so utterly wicked? It couldn't be true! But not to believe Erast was also impossible. He was so eloquent and so handsome!

A huge tear the size of a bean slithered down Renate's cheek. Her eyes were filled with mute appeal: *Why are you tormenting me like this? What did I ever do to you?* The martyr's hand slipped down to her belly and her face contorted in misery.

"Fainting won't help," Fandorin advised her calmly. "The best way to bring someone around is to massage the face with a slap. And don't pretend to be weak and helpless. Dr. Truffo and Dr. Aono consider you as strong as an ox. Sit down, Sir Reginald!" There was a steely ring to Erast's voice. "You will have your chance to intervene on behalf of your damsel in distress—afterward, when I am finished. Meanwhile, ladies and gentlemen, you should know that we have Sir Reginald to thank for saving all our lives. If not for his . . . unusual habit of taking the ship's position every three hours, we would have been breakfasting on the b-bottom of the sea today. Or rather others would have been breakfasting on us."

"Where's Polonius?" the baronet blurted out with a laugh. "At supper. Not where he eats, but where he is eaten." Very funny.

Clarissa shuddered. A larger wave than usual had struck the side of the ship, clinking the dishes against one another on the table and setting Big Ben swaying ponderously to and fro.

"Other people are no more than extras in your play, my lady, and the extras have never really meant anything to you. Especially in a matter of some fifty million pounds. A sum like that is hard to resist. It led poor Gauche astray, for instance. But how clumsy our master detective was as a murderer! You are right, of course—the unfortunate Renier did not commit suicide. I would have realized that for myself if your assault tactics had not thrown me off-balance. What force does a letter of f-farewell carry on its own? From the tone of the letter, it is clearly not a final testament—Renier is still playing for time, hoping to plead insanity. Above all, he is relying on you, Mlle. Sanfon; he has grown used to trusting you implicitly. Gauche calmly tore off a third of a page at the point he thought was best suited for an ending. How clumsy! The prospect of the treasure of Brahmapur had driven our commissioner completely insane. After all, it was his salary for three hundred thousand years!" Fandorin gave a sad chuckle. "Do you remember how enviously Gauche told us the story of the gardener who sold his stainless reputation to a banker for such a good price?"

"But why kill M. Renier?" asked the Japanese. "The shawr had been burned."

"Renier very much wanted the commissioner to believe that; to make his story more convincing, he even gave away the shawl's secret. But Gauche did not believe him," said Fandorin. He paused for a moment and said: "And he was right not to."

You could have heard a pin drop in the salon. Clarissa had just breathed in, but she forgot to breathe out. She wondered why her chest felt so tight; then she realized and released her breath.

"Then the shawl is safe?" the doctor asked tentatively, as though afraid of startling a rare bird. "But where is it?"

"That scrap of fine material has changed hands three times this morning. At first Renier had it. The commissioner did not believe what was in the letter, so he searched his prisoner and f-found the shawl on him. The thought of the riches that were almost in his grasp deranged him, and he committed murder. The temptation was too great. Everything fitted together so neatly: It said in the letter that the shawl had been burned; the murderer had confessed to everything; and the steamer was heading for Calcutta, which is only a stone's throw from Brahmapur. So Gauche went for broke. He struck his unsuspecting prisoner on the head with some heavy object, rigged things to look like a suicide, and came back here to wait for the sentry to discover the body. But then Mlle. Sanfon played her hand and outsmarted both of us—the commissioner and myself. You are a most remarkable woman, my lady," said Erast, turning toward Renate. "I had expected you to start making excuses and blaming your accomplice for everything now that he is dead. It would have been very simple, after all. But no, that is not your way. You guessed from the way the commissioner was behaving that he had the shawl, and your first thought was not to defend, but to attack. You wanted to get back the key to the treasure, and you did!"

"Why must I listen to this nonsense?" Renate exclaimed in a tearful voice. "You, monsieur, are nobody and nothing. A mere foreigner! I demand that my case be handled by one of the ship's senior officers!"

The little doctor suddenly straightened his shoulders, stroked a strand of hair forward across his olive-skinned bald patch, and declared: "There is a senior ship's officer present, madam. You may regard this interrogation as sanctioned by the ship's command. Continue, M. Fandorin. You say this woman managed to get the shawl away from the commissioner?"

"I am certain of it. I do not know how she managed to get hold of Gauche's revolver. The poor fool was probably not afraid of her at all. But somehow she managed to and demanded the shawl. When the old man wouldn't give it to her, she shot him, first in one arm, then in the other, then in the knee. She tortured him! Where did you learn to shoot like that, madam? Four shots, all perfectly placed. I'm afraid it is rather hard to believe that Gauche chased you round the table with a wounded leg and two useless arms. After the third shot he couldn't stand any more pain and he gave you the shawl. Then you finished your victim off with a shot to the center of his forehead."

"Oh, God!" Mrs. Truffo exclaimed unnecessarily.

But Clarissa was more concerned about something else.

"Then she has the shawl?"

"Yes," said Erast with a nod.

"Nonsense! Rubbish! You're all crazy!" Renate (or Marie Sanfon?) laughed hysterically. "Lord, this is such grotesque nonsense!"

"This is easy to check," said the Japanese. "We must search Mme. Kleber. If she does not have the shawr, then M. Fandorin is mistaken. In such cases in Japan, we cut our berries open."

"No man's hands shall ever search a lady in my presence!" declared Sir Reginald, rising menacingly to his feet.

"What about a woman's hands?" asked Clarissa. "Mrs. Truffo and I will search this person."

"Oh, yes, it would take no time at all," the doctor's wife agreed eagerly.

"Do as you like with me," said Renate, pressing her hands together like a sacrificial victim. "But afterward you will be ashamed."

The men went out and Mrs. Truffo searched the prisoner with quite remarkable dexterity. She glanced at Clarissa and shook her head.

Clarissa suddenly felt afraid for poor Erast. Could he really have made a mistake?

"The shawl is very light," she said. "Let me have a look."

It was strange to feel her hands on the body of another woman, but Clarissa bit her lip and carefully examined every seam, every fold, and every gather in the underwear. The shawl was not there.

"You will have to get entirely undressed," she said resolutely. It was terrible, but it was even more terrible to think that the shawl wouldn't be found. What a blow for Erast! How could he bear it?

Renate raised her arms submissively to make it easier to remove her dress and said timidly: "In the name of all that is holy, Mlle. Stamp, do not harm my child."

Gritting her teeth, Clarissa set about unfastening Renate's dress. When she reached the third button, there was a knock at the door and Erast's cheerful voice called out: "Ladies, stop the search! May we come in?"

"Yes, yes, come in!" Clarissa shouted, quickly fastening the buttons.

The men had a mysterious air about them. They took up a position by the table without saying a word. Then, with a magician's flourish, Erast spread out on the tablecloth a triangular piece of fabric that shimmered with all the colors of the rainbow.

"The shawl!" Renate screeched.

"Where did you find it?" asked Clarissa, feeling totally confused.

"While you were searching Mlle. Sanfon, we were busy, too," Fandorin explained, looking smug. "It occurred to me that this prudent individual could have hidden the incriminating clue in the commissioner's cabin. But she only had a few seconds, so she could not have hidden it too well. It did not take long to find the crumpled shawl where she had thrust it under the edge of the carpet. So now we can all admire the famous bird of paradise, Kalavinka."

Clarissa joined the others at the table and they all gazed spellbound at the scrap of cloth for which so many people had died.

The shawl was shaped like an isosceles triangle, with sides no longer than about twenty inches. The colors of the painting were brilliant and intense: a strange creature with pointed breasts, half woman and half bird like the sirens of ancient times, stood with its wings unfurled against a background of brightly colored trees and fruit. Her face was turned in profile, and instead of an eye the long curving lashes framed a small hole that had been painstakingly trimmed with stitching of gold thread. Clarissa thought she had never seen anything more beautiful in her life.

"Yes, it's the shawl, all right," said Sir Reginald. "But how does your find prove Mme. Kleber's guilt?"

"What about the travel bag?" Fandorin asked in a low voice. "Do you remember the travel bag we found in the captain's launch yesterday? One of the things I saw in it was a cloak we have often seen on the shoulders of Mme. Kleber. The travel bag is now part of the material evidence in the case. No doubt other items belonging to our good friend here will also be found in it."

"What reply can you make to that, madam?" the doctor asked Renate.

"The truth," she replied, and in that instant her face changed beyond all recognition.

Reginald Milford-Stokes

⸺∞⸺

. . . THEN SUDDENLY HER face was transformed beyond all recognition, as though someone had waved a magic wand and the weak, helpless little lamb crushed by a cruel fate was instantly changed into a ravening she-wolf. She straightened her shoulders and lifted her chin, her eyes suddenly ablaze and her nostrils flaring as if the woman before us had turned into a deadly predator—no, not a she-wolf, one of the big cats, a panther or lioness who has scented fresh blood. I recoiled; I could not help it. My protection was certainly no longer required here!

The transformed Mme. Kleber cast Fandorin a glance of searing hatred that pierced even that imperturbable gentleman's defenses. He shuddered.

I could sympathize entirely with this strange woman's feelings. My own attitude to the contemptible Russian has also changed completely. He is a terrible man, a dangerous lunatic with a fantastic, monstrously depraved imagination. How could I ever have respected and trusted him? I can hardly even believe it now!

I simply do not know how to tell you this, my sweet Emily. My hand is trembling with indignation as it holds the pen. At first I intended to conceal it from you, but I have decided to tell you after all. Otherwise it will be hard for you to understand the reason for the metamorphosis in my feelings toward Fandorin.

Yesterday night, after all the shocks and upheavals I have described above, Fandorin and I had an extremely strange conversation that left me feeling both perplexed and furious. The Russian approached me and thanked me for saving the ship, and then, positively oozing sympathy and stammering over every word, he began talking the most unimaginable, monstrous drivel. What he said was literally this—I remember it word for word: "I know of your grief, Sir Reginald. Commissioner Gauche told me everything a long time ago. Of course, it is none of my business, and I have thought long and hard before deciding to speak to you about it, but when I see how greatly you are suffering, I cannot remain indifferent. The only reason I dare say all this is that I have suffered a similar grievous loss, and my reason was also undermined by the shock. I have managed to preserve my reason, and even hone its edge to greater sharpness, but the price I had to pay for survival was a large piece of my heart. But, believe me, in your situation there is no other way. Do not hide from the truth, no matter how terrible it might be; do not seek refuge in illusion. And, above all, do not blame yourself. It is not your fault that the horses bolted, or that your pregnant wife was thrown out of the carriage and killed. This is a trial, a test ordained for you by fate. I cannot understand what need there could possibly be to subject a man to such cruelty, but one thing I do know: If you do not pass this test, it means the end, the death of your very soul."

At first I simply could not understand what the scoundrel was getting at. Then I realized! He imagined that you, my precious Emily, were dead! That you were the pregnant lady who was thrown from a carriage and killed! If I had not been so outraged, I should have laughed in the crazy diplomat's face! How dare he say such a thing, when I know that you are waiting there for me beneath the azure skies of the islands of paradise! Every hour brings me closer to you, my darling Emily. And now there is nobody and nothing that can stop me.

Only—it is very strange—I cannot for the life of me remember how you came to be in Tahiti, alone without me. There certainly must have been some important reason for it. No matter. When we meet, my dear friend, you will explain everything to me.

But let me return to my story.

Mme. Kleber straightened up, suddenly seeming taller (it is amazing how much the impression of height depends on posture and the set of the head), and began speaking, for the most part addressing Fandorin.

"All these stories you have hatched up here are absolute nonsense. There is not a single piece of proof or hard evidence. Nothing but assumptions and unfounded speculation. Yes, my real name is Marie Sanfon, but no court in the world has ever been able to charge me with any crime. Yes, my enemies have often slandered me and intrigued against me, but I am strong. Marie Sanfon's nerve is not so easily broken. I am guilty of only one thing—of loving a criminal and a madman to distraction. Charles and I were secretly married, and it is his child that I am carrying under my heart. It was Charles who insisted on keeping our marriage secret. If this misdemeanor is a crime, then I am willing to face a judge and jury—but you may be sure, mister homegrown detective, that an experienced lawyer will scatter your chimerical accusations like smoke. What charges can you actually bring against me? That in my youth I lived in a convent with the Gray Sisters and eased the suffering of the poor? Yes, I used to give myself injections, but what of that? The moral suffering caused by a life of secrecy and a difficult pregnancy led me to become addicted to morphine, but now I have found the strength to break free of that pernicious habit. My secret but entirely legitimate husband insisted I should embark on this voyage under an assumed name. That was how the mythical Swiss banker Kleber came to be invented. The deception caused me suffering, but how could I refuse the man I loved? I had absolutely no idea about his other life and his fatal passion, or his insane plans!

"Charles told me it was not appropriate for the captain's first mate to take his wife with him on a cruise, but he was concerned for the health of our dear child and could not bear to be parted from me. He said it would be best if I sailed under a false name. What kind of crime is that, I ask you?

"I could see that Charles was not himself, that he was in the grip of strange passions I did not understand, but never in my worst nightmare could I have dreamed he committed that terrible crime in the Rue de Grenelle! And I had no idea he was the son of an Indian rajah. It comes as a shock to me that my child will be a quarter Indian. The poor little mite, with a madman for a father. I have no doubt at all that Charles has been completely out of his mind for the last few days. How could anyone sane attempt to sink a ship? It is obviously the act of a sick mind. Of course I knew nothing at all about that insane plan!"

At this point Fandorin interrupted her and asked with a hideous little grin: "And what about your cloak, packed so thoughtfully in the travel bag?"

Mme. Kleber—Miss Sanfon—that is, Mme. Renier . . . or Mme. Bagdassar? I do not know what I ought to call her. Very well, let her remain Mme. Kleber, since that is what I am used to. Mme. Kleber replied to her inquisitor with great dignity: "My husband evidently packed everything ready for our escape and was intending to wake me at the last minute."

But Fandorin was unrelenting. "But you were not asleep," he said with a haughty expression on his face. "We saw you when we were walking along the corridor. You were fully clothed and even had a shawl on your shoulders."

"I could not sleep because I felt strangely alarmed," replied Mme. Kleber. "I must have felt in my heart that something was wrong . . . I was shivering and I felt cold, so I put on my shawl. Is that a crime?"

I was glad to see that the amateur prosecutor was stumped. The accused continued with calm self-assurance: "The idea that I supposedly tortured that other madman, M. Gauche, is absolutely incredible. I told you the truth. The old blockhead went insane with greed and he threatened to kill me. I have no idea how I managed to hit him with all four bullets. But it is pure coincidence. Providence itself must have guided my hand. No, sir, you cannot make anything of that, either!"

Fandorin's smug self-assurance had been shattered. "I beg your pardon!" he cried excitedly. "But we found the shawl! You hid it under the carpet!"

"Yet another unfounded assertion!" retorted Mme. Kleber. "Of course the shawl was hidden by Gauche, who had taken it from my poor husband. And despite all your vile insinuations, I am grateful to you, sir, for returning my property."

And so saying, she calmly stood up, walked over to the table, and took the shawl!

"I am the legitimate wife of the legitimate heir of the Diamond Rajah," declared this astonishing woman. "I have a marriage certificate. I am carrying Bagdassar's grandson in my womb. It is true that my deceased husband committed a number of serious crimes, but what has that to do with me and our inheritance?"

Miss Stamp jumped to her feet and tried to grab the shawl from Mme. Kleber.

"The lands and property of the rajah of Brahmapur were confiscated by the British government," my fellow countrywoman declared resolutely. "That means the treasure belongs to her majesty Queen Victoria!"—and there was no denying that she was right.

"Just a moment!" our good Dr. Truffo put in. "Although I am Italian by birth, I am a citizen of France and I represent her interests here. The rajah's treasure was the personal property of his family and did not belong to the principality of Brahmapur, which means its confiscation was illegal! Charles Renier became a French citizen of his own free will. He committed a most heinous crime on the territory of his adopted country. Under the laws of the French Republic, the punishment for such crimes, especially when committed out of purely venal motives, includes the expropriation of the criminal's property by the state. Give back the shawl, madam! It belongs to France." And he also took a defiant grip on the edge of the shawl.

The situation was a stalemate, and the crafty Fandorin took advantage of it. With the Byzantine cunning typical of his nation, he said loudly: "This is a serious dispute that requires arbitration. Permit me, as the representative of a neutral power, to take temporary possession of the shawl so that you do not tear it to pieces. I shall place it over here, a little distance away from the contending parties."

And so saying, he took the shawl and carried it across to the side table on the leeward side of the salon, where the windows were closed. You will see later, my beloved Emily, why I mention these details.

And so the bone of contention, the shawl, was lying there on the side table, a bright triangle of shimmering color sparkling with gold. Fandorin was standing with his back to the shawl in the pose of a guard of honor. The rest of us were bunched together at the dining table. Add to this the rustling of the curtains on the windward side of the room, the dim light of an overcast afternoon, and the irregular swaying of the floor beneath our feet, and the stage was set for the final scene.

"No one will dare to take from the rajah's grandson what is his by right!" Mme. Kleber declared, her hands set on her hips. "I am a Belgian subject and the court hearing will take place in Brussels. All I need to do for the jury to decide in my favor is promise that a quarter of the inheritance will be donated to charitable work in Belgium . . . A quarter of the inheritance is eleven billion Belgian francs, five times the annual income of the entire kingdom of Belgium!"

Miss Stamp laughed in her face: "You underestimate Britannia, my dear. Do you really think your pitiful Belgium will be allowed to decide the fate of fifty million pounds? With that money we shall build hundreds of mighty battleships and triple the size of our fleet, which is already the greatest in the world! We shall bring order to the entire planet!"

Miss Stamp is an intelligent woman. Indeed, civilization could only benefit if our treasury were enriched by such a fantastic sum. Britain is the most progressive and freest country in the world. All the peoples of the earth would benefit if their lives were arranged after the British example.

But Mr. Truffo was of a different opinion entirely. "This sum of a billion and a half French francs will not only finance France's recovery from the tragic consequences of the war with Germany, but will allow her to create the most modern and well-equipped army in the whole of Europe. You English have never been Europeans. You are islanders! You do not share in the interests of Europe. M. de Perier, who until recently was the captain's second mate and is now in temporary command of the *Leviathan,* will not allow the shawl to go to the English. I shall bring M. de Perier here immediately, and he will place the shawl in the captain's safe!"

Then everyone began talking at once, all trying to shout one another down. The doctor became so belligerent that he even dared push me in the chest, and Mme. Kleber kicked Miss Stamp on the ankle.

Then Fandorin took a plate from the table and smashed it on the floor with a loud crash. As everyone gazed at him in amazement, the cunning Byzantine said: "We shall not solve our problem in this way. You are getting too heated, ladies and gentlemen. Why don't we let a bit of fresh air into the salon? It has become rather stuffy in here."

He went over to the windows on the leeward side and began opening them one by one. When Fandorin opened the window above the side table on which the shawl was lying, something startling happened: The draft immediately snatched at the feathery material, which trembled and fluttered and suddenly flew up into the air. Everyone gasped in horror as the silk triangle went flying away across the deck, swayed twice over the handrails—as if it were waving good-bye to us—and sailed off into the distance, gradually sinking lower and lower. We all stood there, dumbfounded, following its leisurely flight until it ended at some distant point among the lazy white-capped waves.

"How very clumsy I am," said Fandorin, breaking the deadly silence. "All that money lost at sea! Now neither Britain nor France will be able to impose its will on the world. What a terrible misfortune for civilization. And it was half a billion rubles. Enough for Russia to repay its entire foreign debt."

That was when things really started moving.

With a war cry, halfway between a whistle and a hiss, that made my skin crawl, Mme. Kleber grabbed a fruit knife from the table and made a mad dash at the Russian. The sudden attack caught him by surprise. The blunt silver blade swung through the air and stabbed Fandorin just below his collarbone, but I do not think it went very deep. The diplomat's white shirt was stained red with blood. My first thought was: God does exist, and he punishes scoundrels. As he staggered backward, the villainous Byzantine dodged to one side, but the enraged Fury was not satisfied with the damage she had inflicted, and, taking a firmer grip on the handle, she raised her hand to strike again.

And then our Japanese colleague, who had so far taken no part in the discussion and remained almost unnoticed, astonished us all. With a piercing cry like the call of an eagle, he leapt up almost as high as the ceiling and struck Mme. Kleber on the wrist with the toe of his shoe! Not even in the Italian circus have I ever seen a trick to match it!

The fruit knife went flying into the air, the Japanese landed in a squatting position, and Mme. Kleber staggered backward with her face contorted, clutching her injured wrist.

But still she would not abandon her bloodthirsty intent! When she felt her back strike the grandfather clock (I have already written to you about that monster), she suddenly bent down and lifted up the hem of her dress. I was already dazed by the speed of events, but this was too much! I caught a glimpse (forgive me, my sweet Emily, for mentioning this) of a slim ankle clad in a silk stocking and the frills of a pair of pink pantaloons, and a second later, when Mme. Kleber straightened up, a pistol had appeared out of nowhere in her left hand. It was very small and double-barreled, finished in mother-of-pearl.

I do not dare repeat to you word for word exactly what this creature said to Fandorin—you probably do not know the meaning of such expressions, anyway. The general sense of her speech, which was most forceful and expressive, was that the "rotten pervert" (I employ euphemisms, for Mme. Kleber expressed herself rather more crudely) would pay for his lousy trick with his life. "But first I shall neutralize this venomous yellow snake!" cried the mother-to-be: She took a step forward and fired at Mr. Aono, who fell on his back with a dull groan.

Mme. Kleber took another step and pointed her pistol straight at Fandorin's face. "I really do never miss," she hissed. "And I'm going to put a bullet right between those pretty blue eyes of yours."

The Russian stood there, pressing his hand to the red patch spreading across his shirt. He was not exactly quaking in fear, but he was definitely pale.

The *Leviathan* heeled over harder than usual—a large wave had struck it amidships—and I saw that ugly monstrosity, Big Ben, lean farther and farther over, and then . . . it collapsed—right onto Mme. Kleber! There was a dull thud as the hard wood struck the back of her head and the irrepressible woman fell flat on her face, pinned down by the heavy oak tower.

Everyone dashed across to Mr. Aono, who was still lying on the floor with a bullet in his chest. The wounded man was conscious and kept trying to get up, but Dr. Truffo squatted down beside him and pressed on his shoulders to make him lie back. The doctor cut open his clothes to examine the entry wound and frowned.

"It is nothing," the Japanese said in a low voice through clenched teeth. "The rung is barery grazed."

"And the bullet," Truffo asked in alarm. "Can you feel it, my dear colleague? Where is it?"

"I think the burret is stuck in the right shoulder brade," replied Mr. Aono, adding with astonishing composure, "The rower reft quadrant. You will have to section the bone from the back. That is very difficult. Please forgive me for causing you such inconvenience."

Then Fandorin did something very mysterious. He leaned over the wounded man and said in a quiet voice: "Well, now, Aono-san, your dream has come true—now you are my *onjin*. I am afraid the free Japanese lessons will have to be canceled."

Mr. Aono, however, seemed to understand this gibberish perfectly well and he even managed a feeble smile.

When the Japanese gentleman had been bandaged up and carried away on a stretcher by sailors, the doctor turned his attention to Mme. Kleber.

We were really surprised to discover that the solid oak had not smashed her skull in; it had only given her a substantial bump on the head. We pulled the stunned criminal out from under London's finest sight and moved her to an armchair.

"I'm afraid the baby will not survive the shock," sighed Mrs. Truffo. "The poor little thing is not to blame for his mother's sins."

"The baby will be all right," her husband assured her. "This . . . lady possesses such tremendous vitality that she will certainly have a healthy child, with an easy birth at full term."

Fandorin added, with a cynicism that I found offensive: "There is reason to hope that the birth will take place in a prison hospital."

"It is terrible to think what will be born from that womb," Miss Stamp said with a shudder.

"In any case, the pregnancy will save her from the guillotine," remarked the doctor.

"Or from the gallows," laughed Miss Stamp, reminding us of the bitter wrangling between Commissioner Gauche and Inspector Jackson.

"The most serious threat she faces is a short prison sentence for the attempted murder of Mr. Aono," Fandorin remarked with a sour face. "And extenuating circumstances will be found for that: temporary insanity, shock, the pregnancy. As she herself demonstrated quite brilliantly, it will be absolutely impossible to prove anything else. I assure you, Marie Sanfon will be at liberty again very soon."

It is strange, but none of us mentioned the shawl, as if it had never even existed, as if the scrap of silk that had carried off into oblivion a hundred British battleships and the French *revanche* had also taken with it the feverish stupor that had shrouded our minds and souls.

Fandorin stopped beside his fallen Big Ben, which was now fit for nothing but the rubbish dump: The glass was broken, the mechanism was smashed, and the oak panel was cracked from top to bottom.

"A magnificent clock," said the Russian, confirming yet again the well-known fact that the Slavs have no artistic taste whatever. "I shall certainly have it repaired and take it with me."

The *Leviathan* gave a mighty hoot on its whistle, no doubt in greeting to some passing vessel, and I began thinking that soon, very soon, in just two or three weeks, I shall arrive in Tahiti and we shall meet again, my adored little wife. Everything else is mere fog and vapor, an insubstantial fantasy.

We shall be together and we shall be happy in our island paradise, where the sun always shines.

> In anticipation of that joyful day,
> I remain your tenderly loving
>
> Reginald Milford-Stokes

MURDER ON THE LEVIATHAN

BORIS AKUNIN

A Reader's Guide

Questions for Discussion

1. What criteria does Gustave Gauche use in assembling his list of suspects? Are his inferences about the golden whale badge sound? Also, discuss what is at stake for Gauche in solving this case. Did you ever sympathize with his ambitions?

2. Evaluate the varying structure of the novel. Describe how its changing narrative viewpoints, and its digressions and seemingly trivial details (for instance, the news report on cholera), become important throughout the course of the investigation. Also, why do you think Akunin chooses to narrate the story from the perspectives of Gauche, Renate, Clarissa, Milford-Stokes, and Aono, but not from that of Professor Sweetchild, the Truffos, or even Fandorin?

3. Renate Kleber complains that her tablemates are "a choice collection of . . . blooms, bores and freaks . . . [and] one lunatic" (126). How does Boris Akunin cast suspicion on each of the characters assembled in the Windsor Salon? What secrets are they each trying to hide?

4. Papa Gauche is proud of his title as "Investigator for Especially Important Cases" (54). Discuss the appropriateness of the detective's name, and also how his ego and cultural prejudices thwart his progress. How does Gauche take a simplistic view of people and events?

5. Reginald Milford-Stokes calls the *Leviathan* a "miracle of a ship" (35). Describe this colossal ship and evaluate the significance of its name. Consider what features of a cruise ship—such as confinement, exoticism, luxury, and social stratification—make it a particularly good setting for a mystery.

6. Erast Fandorin cuts quite a dashing figure on board the *Leviathan*. Describe his appearance and the effect of his manners on the company assembled in the Windsor Salon. When and why does he stutter? What are his vulnerabilities, as confessed to Clarissa Stamp? And to what personal tragedy does he refer when he offers unwelcome comfort to Reginald Milford-Stokes?

7. Gauche claims that the Paris police conducts its work "in accordance with the very latest advances in scientific method" (29). What tools do the inspectors have at their disposal? What is the Bertillon method, and what forensic advancement does Fandorin suggest instead? Compare the early work of detectives to our modern practices; how have scientific advancements such as forensics and DNA changed the nature of crime solving? On the flipside, how has detective work remained the same?

8. Compare Fandorin's logical method of detection with Gauche's approach. Do you think it is unusual for a murder mystery to feature two detectives? What does this rivalry add to the plot?

9. Gintaro Aono claims that the Rajah Bagdassar's jewels are the "greatest hidden treasure there has ever been in the whole of human history" (95). Describe the Brahmapur treasure and its unfortunate fate, the mystery of its location, and the importance of Lord Littleby's pilfered shawl.

10. Discuss the diagram drawn by Professor Sweetchild, which Reginald rescues from beneath the table in the grand salon. What did you initially make of the "palace" sketch, and what is the true meaning of the puzzle?

11. Many of the Windsorites display cultural prejudices common in their time. How does this chauvinism increase suspicion among the passengers, and how does it lead to false accusations and bungled investigations? More generally, discuss the theme of national pride in the novel.

12. Why does M. Aono try to commit suicide rather than defend himself against Gauche's circumstantial charges? Why is honor so important to the samurai, and how do the Eastern and Western philosophies differ? What occasions Aono's enlightenment, and how does he fulfill his "debt" to Erast Fandorin?

13. Who is the real rue de Grenelle killer, and what complicates the murderer's unveiling? Was this the outcome you suspected, or did you peg another Windsorite as the murderer?

14. Do you think the colorful shawl possesses some sort of mystical power? Describe its hold on Renate, Renier, Gauche, and the rest of the Windsorites. Did you agree with Fandorin's decision to "accidentally" lose the shawl through the ship's window, or would you have kept it? Why are the others ultimately content to see the shawl disappear? Finally, what is the significance of Erast Fandorin's parable of the three Maghreb merchants (page 118) in relation to the treasure?

ENJOY ALL THE ERAST FANDORIN MYSTERIES BY BORIS AKUNIN

Filled with delicious detail, ingenious plotting, and subtle satire, the internationally bestselling Erast Fandorin mysteries confirm Boris Akunin's status as a master of the historical thriller—and Erast Fandorin as a fictional detective for the ages.

The Winter Queen

Set in 1870s Moscow, St. Petersburg, and London, *The Winter Queen* introduces American readers to the brilliant young sleuth, Erast Fandorin. In his first case, he investigates a wave of student suicides, falls deeply in love, and finds himself in the center of a deadly world conspiracy.

"Elaborate, intricate, profoundly czarist, and Russian to its bones, as though Tolstoy had sat down to write a murder mystery." —*Alan Furst*

"A nonstop array of plot twists to rival the best detective tales . . . *The Winter Queen* is an energetic hands-down winner." —*People*

The Turkish Gambit

In 1877, Erast Fandorin finds himself at the Bulgarian front, during the war between Russia and the Ottoman Empire. There, he finds and rescues Varya, a daring Russian woman who has risked her life to join her fiancé, a decoder in the Russian army who has been wrongly accused of espionage. Can Fandorin clear Varya's lover and find the true culprit?

"An exquisitely filigreed thriller . . . delicious."
—*Entertainment Weekly*

Murder on the Leviathan

Set in 1878, in Paris, and aboard a luxury liner headed for Calcutta, Erast Fandorin joins forces with police commissioner "Papa" Gauche to determine which of ten suspicious passengers, now trapped on the ship, is guilty of a rising number of despicable murders.

"With a cast of eccentrics [and] a plot bristling with surprises . . . this is a novel that does Christie, Collins, and Conan Doyle proud."
—*The Washington Post Book World*

SAVE YOUR JOB, SAVE OUR COUNTRY

WHY NAFTA MUST BE STOPPED—NOW!

BY

ROSS PEROT

WITH PAT CHOATE

NEW YORK

Why U.S. Companies are Moving to Mexico

Minimum Wage
Average Manufacturing Wage
Maquiladora Wage

$16.17

$4.25

$0.58 $2.35 $1.64

Mexico   United States

What can you do?

1. Understand that you own this country

2. Realize that *you* can make the difference

3. Read this book

4. Share it with friends and fellow workers

5. Mail the ballots in the back of this book to your Representative and Senators

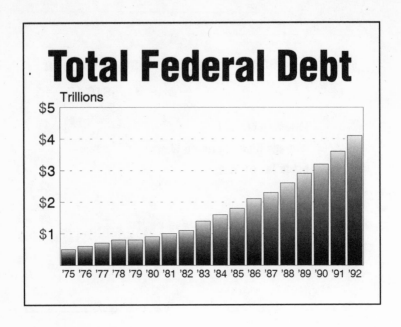

Total Federal Debt

Trillions

$5

$4

$3

$2

$1

'75 '76 '77 '78 '79 '80 '81 '82 '83 '84 '85 '86 '87 '88 '89 '90 '91 '92

At this critical time, we must do nothing that will lower the standard of living of the American worker.

In United We Stand America, every issue must pass through one filter —

Is it good for our country?

As you read this book, repeatedly ask yourself this question.

Contents

United We Stand America

The purpose of United We Stand America is to give the people a voice.

You own United We Stand America.

The goals of United We Stand America are:

- To re-create a government that comes from the people — not at the people.
- To reform the federal government at all levels to eliminate fraud, waste, and abuse.
- To have a government where the elected, appointed, and career officials come to serve and not to cash in.
- To get our economy moving and put our people back to work.
- To balance the budget.
- To pay off our nation's debt.
- To build an efficient and cost effective health care system.
- To get rid of foreign lobbyists.
- To get rid of political action committees.
- To make our neighborhoods and streets safe from crime and violence.
- To create the finest public schools in the world for our children.
- To pass on the American Dream to our children, making whatever fair shared sacrifices are necessary.

To The Reader,

Imagine for a moment that the President of the United States and the Congress were to decide that one state, such as California, was so badly in need of investment and jobs that it — and it alone — would be exempted from the laws that govern work and life in America. Let's assume that the state of California reduced its minimum wage to 58 cents an hour, exempted itself from child labor laws, expanded the work week, and reduced protections for health, safety, pension rights, and the environment. Then imagine that the goods and services produced by the California companies would still have unlimited access to the markets of the other 49 states. Ridiculous? Of course. The other states would never allow such a drastic and unfair scheme.

Yet, none of this is imaginary. The state is Mexico. President Clinton, virtually every state governor, most U.S. Senators, and almost a majority of the members of the U.S. House of Representatives support a recently negotiated trade agreement that will make this scenario a reality. It is known as the North American Free Trade Agreement (NAFTA), and if it is passed, the trade agreement will pit American and Mexican workers in a race to the bottom. In this race, millions of Americans will lose their jobs.

It seems bizarre that our public servants would put our jobs at risk.

The North American Free Trade Agreement is really less about trade than it is about investment. Its principal goal is to protect U.S. companies and investors operating in Mexico.

The text of the agreement is contained in two volumes covering more than 1,100 pages. The text is mind-numbingly dull. Large portions of it are written in the type of obscure legal terms found in the fine print on the back of an insurance policy. Buried

i

in the fine print are provisions that will give away American jobs and radically reduce the sovereignty of the United States.

The deal was negotiated under a special congressional authorization that gave extraordinary powers to the president. He alone was given the authority to decide whether to proceed, set the U.S. strategy, select who would be involved as advisers, and negotiate in complete secrecy.

NAFTA is the ultimate insider deal. A completed pact was announced on August 13, 1992, but the text of the agreement was kept out of the hands of the American people until January 20, 1993.

In October 1992, presidential candidate Bill Clinton announced his support for NAFTA. He accepted the basic agreement as negotiated by the Bush Administration. In addition, he asked for side agreements on worker rights, environmental protection, and restraints against cheap imports. The side agreements will be submitted to Congress along with NAFTA. These side agreements have also been negotiated in wartime-like secrecy.

Before NAFTA can go into effect, it must be approved by a simple majority in both the U.S. Senate and the U.S. House of Representatives.

The government of Mexico and Mexican corporations have hired dozens of former U.S. trade negotiators, American diplomats, political party officers, and U.S. cabinet members to get this deal through our Congress. It is the most expensive foreign lobbying campaign in U.S. history.

The Mexican efforts, moreover, are boosted by the lobbying of the largest corporations in the United States, most of which have already moved thousands of American jobs to Mexico and want the guarantees provided by this pact so that they can move even more jobs.

The objective of this book is to explain to the working people of the United States just what is contained in the North American Free Trade Agreement, how it will cost millions of American jobs, and why the agreement is not in our national interest. At the

TO THE READER

same time, this book outlines what should be involved in the right kind of deal with Mexico.

Mexico is our neighbor, its people are good, and we want them to prosper. But NAFTA is not the way.

The present deal must be scrapped and negotiators put to work to develop a long-term economic relationship between Mexico, Canada, and the United States that is in our mutual interest.

If the administration pursues its plan to have NAFTA in place by the end of 1993, then American voters must take action. First, they must examine for themselves what is in this deal and decide if they support the agreement as it now stands. If they agree that NAFTA should be rejected, then millions of citizens must contact their senators and representatives and stop it. Their addresses, telephone numbers, and fax numbers are found in the back of the book.

Never forget, this is our country. We own it. Congress works for us.

Dallas, Texas
September 6, 1993

How Other Countries See Washington, D.C.

The Japanese, in the
Japan Economic Journal, *say:*

Influence in Washington is just like Indonesia — it's for sale.

The British,
in The Economist, *say:*

Washington's culture of influence for hire is uniquely open to all buyers, foreign and domestic. Its lawful ways of corrupting public policy remain unrivaled.

The Dutch writer,
Karel van Wolferen, says:

A big part of the problem is that Americans can be bought so easily.

Chapter 1

Out Traded – Again

On November 1, 1992, President Carlos Salinas de Gortari addressed the Congress of Mexico. He appeared as a conquering hero, having just concluded the most successful trade negotiation in Mexican history — the North American Free Trade Agreement.

With pride, President Salinas explained how Mexico had out negotiated the United States. Under NAFTA, he said, Mexican manufacturers would have immediate access to the rich U.S. and Canadian markets, yet Mexico would be able to keep vital parts of its market closed to American and Canadian companies for another 15 years. He also said:

Exports to Canada and the United States will increase following the elimination of quotas and duties — some to be eliminated immediately and others gradually. Mexico will also open its market, but will do so more slowly, starting with those products that we [Mexico] do not produce, or productions with which we are better prepared to compete. In those sectors in which we are less efficient, we were granted longer terms to open our markets, which range between 5 and 15 years, and allowed time to modernize, produce and distribute more efficiently, and thus compete more successfully. This procedure takes into account the different degrees of development in the three countries. This is why 84 percent of our exports will immediately be free from import duties to enter the [U.S. and Canadian] market. We, in turn, will initially be open to 42 percent of the products they send us, which consist mainly of raw materials and capital goods that are not manufactured in Mexico.

The Salinas address was televised throughout Mexico. In the days that followed, the government-dominated media praised the agreement and repeated over and over the benefits that NAFTA would bring to the people of Mexico.

The media, however, did not identify the tiny handful of people in Mexico who would gain the very most from this trade pact. They are the 36 businessmen who own Mexico's 39 largest conglomerates. Collectively, their companies control more than 54 percent of Mexico's Gross National Product. These companies dominate virtually every sector of the Mexican economy of any consequence — banking, insurance, steel, transport, manufacturing, engineering, construction, real estate, and telecommunications, among many others. When the Mexican government sold off big chunks of Mexico's state-run companies in the late 1980s and early 1990s, this tiny handful of people quickly acquired control.

In late February 1993, President Salinas hosted a private dinner in Mexico City for 29 of these Mexican elite. Over smoked salmon, beef medallions, and wine, an aide to President Salinas pointed out that each of the men at the table had benefited from the present political system. Each of them had profited from the economic reforms of the Salinas administration, and all would benefit from the new trade agreement. The aide spelled out the details of a political slush fund that President Salinas wished to create.

Then President Salinas spoke. He told the businessmen that when he leaves office in 1994 (Mexico's president has a six-year term limit), he intends to leave his ruling political party, the PRI, strongly in control of Mexico's government, as it has been since 1929. But to do so, Salinas said, required money. He asked each of the 29 businessmen to make a $25 million political contribution.

One by one, they responded. All said that they would contribute. One businessman said, "I have won so much money in these past years that I commit myself to contribute a greater amount." He, alone, pledged $70 million.

A $25 million political contribution is serious money. But for these men, it would be money well invested because NAFTA would guarantee the advantages that President Salinas had gained for them.

Advantages of NAFTA for Mexico

Trucking

More than 80 percent of the trade between Mexico and the United States moves by truck. If NAFTA is enacted, that freight volume will double and then double again within this decade. The owners of the trucking companies, terminals, and warehouses will reap enormous profits.

NAFTA gives Mexican investors, such as the 29 elite businessmen at the Salinas dinner, a distinct competitive advantage in the U.S.-Mexican trucking industry. The agreement, for instance, does not allow U.S.-owned trucks to cross into Mexico for three years, even though Mexican trucks already are allowed to move goods into U.S. border areas.

NAFTA also permits Mexican investors to hold one hundred percent of the stock of U.S. international trucking companies (those authorized to do business in both countries) just three years after the deal is ratified. Yet, U.S. investors cannot hold a one hundred percent ownership in a similar Mexican company until the 11th year of the agreement.

Because of these unequal investment rights embodied in NAFTA, Mexican trucking companies can assure their U.S. and Mexican customers a guaranteed level of service from pickup to delivery, and will do so almost from the day that NAFTA is enacted. By contrast, U.S. trucking companies must wait ten years before they can offer the same service.

More important, NAFTA jeopardizes the safety of American travelers. In order to make U.S. highways safe, U.S. trucks must comply with federal standards concerning weight, size, maintenance, and engine emissions levels. Very strict regulations are also imposed on American truck drivers. These regulations set tough standards which cost American trucking companies money, but are necessary to keep U.S. highways safe.

NAFTA makes a mockery of these safety standards by opening U.S. roads to trucks and drivers who do not meet U.S. minimum safety standards. U.S. trucks, for instance, are required to have front brakes, but Mexican trucks are not. U.S. trucks must meet tough repair and maintenance regulations, but Mexican trucks do not.

The United States imposes an 80,000 pound weight limit on a truck; Mexico's weight limit is 170,000 pounds. U.S. highways, bridges, and tunnels are designed for U.S. weight standards, not Mexican weight standards. Under NAFTA, Americans can expect to see overloaded Mexican trucks that will crush our highways and reduce the usable lives of our bridges and tunnels. U.S. taxpayers, of course, will foot the repair bill.

Federal and state agencies are supposed to keep overloaded, unsafe trucks off the U.S. highways. But these agencies are so understaffed that adequate inspection is simply impossible. At the Laredo, Texas border crossing, for example, there are only two inspectors from the Texas Department of Public Safety. Yet, more than 700 trucks a day cross into the United States. This equals one truck every four minutes per inspector. And that's if they arrived evenly spaced over the entire twenty-four hour day — which they don't.

Once inside the United States, the Mexican trucks will be subject to U.S. weight limits. Roadside weight inspection stations are used to enforce these weight limits. However, truckers share information with one another about the location of the weigh stations, and they frequently change their routes to avoid weigh stations and safety inspections.

Many of the drivers of these Mexican trucks will not meet the minimum safety qualifications required of U.S. truck drivers. American truck drivers, for instance, must be 21 years old before they are eligible to get a commercial driver license. Mexican truck drivers need only be 18 years old. American truck drivers must pass tough, standardized licensing tests. The Mexican tests are much easier. American truck drivers are subject to random drug tests, Mexican truck drivers are not. To prevent fatigue, American truck drivers can only drive 10 hours per day and no more than 60 hours per week. Mexican truck drivers can drive an unlimited number of hours per day or week. The driving records of American truck drivers can be accessed immediately by law officials anywhere in the United States. The records of Mexican truck drivers operating in the United States cannot be accessed.

Finally, U.S. truck drivers are required to have a working knowledge of English before they can get a commercial license. The ability to quickly read road signs is vital. Yet, Mexican truck drivers intending to drive in the United States do not have to read English to get a Mexican commercial license authorizing them to drive in the United States.

Not surprisingly, many Mexican trucking companies already take advantage of Mexico's low standards and almost total lack of enforcement. A check of 271 Mexican truck drivers operating inside the commercial zones of Arizona and New Mexico found that 19 percent had no commercial drivers license, and that 81 percent of their vehicles did not have a certificate of registration required by the Interstate Commerce Commission. In essence, four out of every five vehicles was unregistered, and one of every five drivers was unlicensed. Do you suppose they had insurance? When the United States has attempted to enforce its highway safety laws on Mexican trucks, Mexico's border officials have retaliated against American citizens, and Mexican truck drivers have blocked the borders.

Even if the U.S. and Mexico develop some common standards for trucks, drivers, and highway safety — as they are supposed to do under NAFTA — it is doubtful that they will, or can, be enforced.

Under NAFTA, therefore, Mexican truck drivers — qualified or not, fatigued or not, able to read English or not — and their Mexicans trucks — overloaded or not, well-maintained or not — will soon be on U.S. highways. These Mexican trucks can already come into the commercial areas on the U.S.-Mexican border. Within three years, they will have full access to the states of California, Arizona, New Mexico, and Texas. Within six years, they can go anywhere in the continental United States. Do we really want this to happen?

As difficult as it is to believe, highway safety is only part of the problem with the NAFTA truck provisions. Under NAFTA, smuggling drugs into the United States will become much easier.

Mexico is the principal staging area for the shipment of illegal drugs into the United States. The *New York Times* reported that up to 70 percent of the cocaine consumed in this country is slipped across the U.S.-Mexican border by smugglers working with Colombia's Medellin and Cali drug cartels.

Today, much of this drug movement is done by illegal immigrants carrying the contraband across the border. Drugs are also smuggled under the border through tunnels. For instance, in early June 1993, U.S. and Mexican officials discovered a partially completed 1,450 foot tunnel for smuggling drugs. It was concrete-lined, fully-lighted, air conditioned, and it extended from a warehouse in Tijuana, Mexico to just outside of San Diego.

If NAFTA is enacted, drug smugglers won't have to go to so much trouble or expense. They can just transport their illegal goods across the border in trucks, and do so with very little fear of being caught. U.S. customs officials are already so overworked that they often have less than five minutes to inspect the cargo in trucks crossing the border from Mexico. This is an open invitation to smuggle.

Colombian and Mexican drug traffickers are accepting the invitation. According to the same *New York Times* article, U.S. drug enforcement officials report that these dealers have bought factories and trucking companies that they can use as fronts for smuggling operations. Once NAFTA is passed and Mexican trucks have easy access into the United States and Canada, drugs will be hidden in goods and shipped throughout the continent. Drug dealers operating out of Mexico will soon be able to offer door-to-door delivery anywhere in the United States and Canada. Is overnight service far behind?

Here is the really amazing part. The *New York Times* also reports that U.S. NAFTA negotiators had "foreseen the possibility that drug traffickers would take advantage of the trade pact [but] the problem was not raised during the negotiations." The United States spends $10 billion per year fighting the drug wars and to keep drugs out of the United States. Why wasn't this a central part of the NAFTA negotiations?

Real Estate

The United States has long permitted foreign investors, including those from Mexico, to own one hundred percent of virtually any type of real estate within its boundaries. On the other hand, Mexico has long restricted foreign ownership of real estate within its boundaries. One of the alleged objectives of NAFTA was to open the markets of both nations to foreign investment. If this was the goal, it was not met. Under NAFTA, Mexican investors, such as those at the Salinas dinner, will continue to enjoy a distinct advantage over U.S. investors.

Trade and investment in agriculture, livestock, and lumber, for instance, is a key part of U.S.-Mexican trade. Mexican investors will still be allowed to own one hundred percent of farms, forests, and other real estate in the United States. But U.S. investors are restricted to owning no more than 49 percent of any enterprise that owns agricultural or forest land in Mexico. Only Mexicans are allowed to own controlling interest of land in Mexico that is used for agriculture, livestock, and lumber production.

U.S. investors are forced to find a controlling Mexican partner, while Mexican investors are free to act on their own in the United States.

Communications

NAFTA also favors Mexican investors in the communications sector. Mexican investors, for instance, can hold one hundred percent ownership of U.S. cable television systems or companies that provide cable television services in the United States.

Under NAFTA, however, U.S. investors in Mexico can only own, directly or indirectly, up to 49 percent of similar enterprises. What's more, only Mexican citizens or enterprises are permitted to operate a cable television system in Mexico. Again, Americans wanting to invest in Mexico's cable television industry need a well-connected, and controlling, Mexican partner.

Construction

According to the NAFTA proponents, the agreement will stimulate a major construction boom in both the United States and Mexico. But under NAFTA, Mexican investors will be better able to profit from this new activity than their U.S. counterparts.

Why? Because NAFTA allows Mexican investors to own one hundred percent of construction companies doing business in the United States, but limits U.S. investors to 49 percent ownership in Mexican construction companies for the first five years of the agreement.

In exceptional cases, U.S. investors can own a majority interest in a construction company doing business in Mexico, but approval by the Mexican government is required on a case-by-case basis. Having a Mexican partner in such instances is an unofficial obligation.

Banking

As part of Mexico's economic reforms, President Salinas sold 18 government-owned banks. They were bought by Mexico's economic elite. NAFTA ensures that these new owners retain a tight grip over Mexican banking for at least another decade.

Today, only one U.S. financial institution — Citicorp — has a deposit-taking operation in Mexico, and it only has $500 million of Mexican deposits. Meanwhile, there are at least six Mexican banks operating in the United States, with U.S. deposits of more than $5.6 billion.

Under NAFTA, Mexico keeps its largest banks "off limits" to U.S. investors by limiting all foreign ownership of the bank's common stock to no more than a total of 30 percent. NAFTA allows U.S. banks to establish operations in Mexico, but limits all foreign banks from controlling more than eight percent of the entire Mexican banking sector. This market share would increase to no more than 15 percent by 1999. However, if non-Mexican banks reach the point where they hold 25 percent of the Mexican market between the years 2000 and 2004, Mexico can freeze the foreign-owned market share at that level until 2007.

Even if NAFTA is enacted, U.S. banks will be prohibited from enjoying the full benefits of NAFTA until the year 2007. There will be a total lack of banking reciprocity between the U.S. and Mexico for another 13 years. Who negotiated this one?

So why are U.S. banks such strong supporters of NAFTA? Because banking operations in Mexico are not subject to the same strict regulations as U.S. banks — the regulations that are designed to protect U.S. depositors from speculative investments by the institutions that are holding their money. For example, a bank operating in Mexico may participate with more freedom in securities-related investment activities. This means that U.S. banks will have every incentive to get their U.S. business customers to establish affiliates in Mexico. Once the customer is doing business in Mexico, the banks can take an equity position in these enterprises and provide a wide array of very speculative and potentially very profitable services that are prohibited by U.S. laws.

Auto Trade

Clearly, the Mexican negotiators out-traded the U.S. negotiating team in the areas of land ownership, communications, shipping, and banking. But it didn't stop there. The U.S. negotiators stuck to their strategy and gave away more American jobs.

Auto trade among Mexico, the United States, and Canada accounts for *more trade than any other single product.* One of the reported U.S. goals in the NAFTA negotiations was to eliminate Mexican and Canadian restrictions on the production and sale of cars.

If that was the goal, the U.S. negotiating team failed spectacularly. By the end of the negotiations, the U.S. team had agreed to let Canada continue to require U.S. automakers who sell in Canada to manufacture most of their vehicles there. The U.S. team also agreed to allow Mexico to keep most of its auto investment and production restrictions in place for another ten years. Meanwhile, the U.S. auto market remains virtually open.

Even worse, the United States also agreed to immediately drop its tariffs on automobiles imported from Mexico regardless of whether they are manufactured by European, Japanese, Mexican, or American companies while allowing Mexico to keep half its tariffs on vehicles produced in the United States. The remaining Mexican tariffs would be phased out over a ten-year period.

The bottom line is that NAFTA will allow U.S. automakers to replace American workers with low-wage Mexican workers. At the same time, European and Japanese manufacturers will gain easy access to the U.S. markets. Northern Mexico will replace Detroit as the car production center of North America.

Agriculture

The NAFTA deal on agricultural trade is just as bad. Under NAFTA, only Mexicans can own land that is used for agricultural production in Mexico.

Also, NAFTA allows Canadian wheat producers to keep the price and marketing advantages over U.S. producers that were negotiated in the 1988 Canadian Free Trade Agreement. In wheat markets, just a small price advantage makes a big difference in sales.

The U.S. citrus industry will also suffer under NAFTA. The United States must immediately cut its tariffs on the import of frozen concentrated citrus from Mexico in half. In contrast, Mexico only has to phase out its 20 percent duty on imports of U.S. citrus *over an extended period of time*. NAFTA will accelerate investment in Mexico's citrus export operations. In the process, Florida's citrus industry will be devastated. Today, Florida's citrus industry employs 145,000 workers in the growing, processing, distribution, and marketing of citrus products.

NAFTA also exempts Mexico from the U.S. Meat Import Act, which limits the amount of imported beef that can enter U.S. markets. At the same time, the agreement will give Mexico unrestricted access to U.S. and Canadian feed grains, which it needs to develop a large scale cattle-feeding and beef-processing industry. The result will be a massive shift of the U.S. beef industry from the United States to Mexico as investors rush to take advantage of cheap wages, low safety standards, and lax sanitation practices. As a result, more American jobs will be lost. Remember, each lost job causes a triple-dip: loss of needed income taxes; loss of social security payments; and increased unemployment compensation payments.

The Real Deal

Just after the private Salinas dinner in February 1993, the event and the pledges became a major U.S. and Mexican news story. Soon afterwards, President Salinas agreed not to accept the promised political funds. The source of the news leak has never been identified. The most likely explanation is that it was one of the elite 29 Mexican businessmen at the dinner who didn't want to make a $25 million political contribution to President Salinas. Besides, each of the businessmen already has most of what he wanted included in NAFTA.

Ultimately, NAFTA is not a trade agreement but an investment agreement. NAFTA's principal goal is to protect the investment of U.S. companies that build factories in Mexico. This is accomplished by reducing the risk of nationalization, by permitting the return of profits to U.S. businesses, and by allowing unlimited access to the American markets for goods produced in Mexico.

11

SAVE YOUR JOB, SAVE OUR COUNTRY

The eventual elimination of Mexican tariffs on U.S. goods going to Mexico, which average only about ten percent, will mean little to most U.S. companies and workers. The reason is simple: Mexico's market is small — less than five percent of the size of the U.S. market — and Mexican consumers are poor. Mexicans have per capita incomes that are less than $2,500 a year, or roughly one-tenth that of someone in the United States. A person making that little can't buy very much.

Does anyone from the United States benefit from NAFTA? Yes, the owners of labor intensive companies that move their factories to Mexico. They can save a minimum of $10,000 for every job they move from the United States to Mexico. In the process, they can avoid U.S. environmental, health, and safety regulations.

Indeed, this job shift is already happening. Today, more than 1,300 U.S. companies are operating more than 2,200 factories in Mexico. They employ more than 500,000 Mexican workers. Most of these jobs were once held by American workers.

Today, thousands more U.S. companies are being urged to move their factories to Mexico by the Mexican government, by banks that want a foothold in Mexico, and by junk bond dealers. If NAFTA passes, it will remove any final doubts for those companies.

A person can only wonder why and how a trade agreement so harmful to U.S. interests was negotiated, and whose interest was foremost in the minds of the U.S. negotiating team.

Chapter 2

A Secret Deal

The world almost had a bank panic over the weekend of August 14 and 15, 1982, when the Mexican government suspended payments on its international debts.

To forestall a world financial panic, a Mexican bailout package was stitched together over that weekend by the U.S. Treasury, the International Monetary Fund, and the World Bank. But there was a price. Mexico had to commit to privatize its state enterprises, lower wages, reduce imports, expand exports, and attract more foreign investment.

Subsequently, the strategy was ruthlessly pursued. In quick order, Mexico slashed its public expenditures and cut its imports. Mexico also sold off dozens of state-owned enterprises.

To attract foreign-owned factories, Mexico reduced the wages of its workers and promoted its Maquiladora Program. This program allows foreign investors in specially designated areas of Mexico to hold one hundred percent ownership of factories. These factories produce mainly for export, and most of their products go to the United States. Yet, Mexico kept most of the Mexican economy "off limits" to foreigners.

When President Salinas came to power in 1988, Mexico accelerated its economic reform program. Salinas also accelerated Mexico's efforts to attract foreign factories. In 1989 and early 1990, he met with European and Japanese corporations. Salinas expected that Mexico's economic reforms would make his country attractive to these investors, but instead he was politely rebuffed — Mexico's domestic market was too small and too poor. The keys to Japanese and European investment at the levels Mexico wanted, he was told, were expanded protection for investors and guaranteed access to the vast U.S. market.

13

President Salinas got the message. In June 1990, he met with President Bush in Washington and proposed that the United States and Mexico negotiate a free trade and investment agreement that would open up all of Mexico to foreign investment in much the same manner as the border area was opened to foreign investment under the Maquiladora Program. President Bush quickly agreed. The two men then called Canadian Prime Minister Brian Mulroney and invited Canada to join in these negotiations. Despite some well-founded reservations, Prime Minister Mulroney eventually consented. Before negotiations began in June 1991, there was one item that President Bush needed to get from Congress.

Getting on the Fast Track

The most bitter Congressional fight of 1991 was over an obscure little piece of legislation called "fast track." It gave President George Bush the authority to negotiate the North American Free Trade Agreement in complete secrecy and without the participation of either Congress or the U.S. public.

The fact that a Republican president won this battle with a Congress controlled by Democrats could lead to speculation as to how the victory was achieved. For the moment, let's defer the speculation on the "how" and turn our attention to the "what" — as in what was achieved in this victory.

The term "fast track" refers to a process whereby Congress turns over to the President its authority to regulate foreign commerce — a power granted to Congress in Article I, Section 8 of the Constitution. Operating under the "fast track" designation, President Bush had the authority to:

- Enter into negotiations with Mexico and Canada on a trade agreement at his sole discretion;
- Set the agenda on which items would be negotiated and the negotiating objective for each item;

14

- Select all the private sector advisers that would be used to guide the negotiations and establish the way that their advice would be used, if at all;
- Conduct the entire negotiations in secrecy and make side agreements which could remain a secret among the three governments;
- Restrict Congress' access to materials about the agreement during the negotiations, and force Members of Congress to pledge neither to take notes on materials they were permitted to see nor to share that information with anyone;
- Determine when, or if, any materials about the agreement, including the final text, would be released to the public and the manner and form in which it would be made available; and
- Send a final agreement to Congress that could not be amended, and therefore, had to be accepted or rejected as presented.

Congress also agreed to make the agreement a top priority and vote on it within 90 days after receiving it from the President. Congress agreed, moreover, to limit any debate to 20 hours in the House and 20 hours in the Senate. To make certain the path was completely clear, "fast track" did not allow a Senate filibuster. For the Senate to forgo its right to filibuster is unusual. Since 1960, the Senate has approved or ratified 25 treaties, conventions, and agreements — including nuclear nonproliferation treaties — all without "fast track."

Congress gave President Bush "fast track" authority for NAFTA in late May of 1991. But there was a catch — these extraordinary powers would expire at the end of 24 months. Contrary to expectations, the pact was not sent to Congress within that time period. Thus, the "fast track" powers expired on June 1, 1993.

By this time it was clear the only way NAFTA would ever pass Congress would be under the limited-debate, no-filibuster, up-or-down vote restrictions imposed by "fast track." This was a problem to which there was only one answer — Congress had to pass another "fast track" bill. Rather than replay the bitter legislative fight of 1991, congressional allies of the Clinton Administration quietly slipped legislation into the one thousand page budget reconciliation package that was rushed to a House vote late in the evening on May 27, 1993. Not a word was said about "fast track" during the abbreviated debate on the budget bill. Days later, House members learned that while they were passing the budget bill they were also reauthorizing "fast track" status for NAFTA.

To prevent a similar stealth-like vote in the Senate, several anti-NAFTA senators forced a public debate and vote for the record. They lost 76 to 16. Congress extended President Clinton's "fast track" powers until December 15, 1993.

Not The Way To Negotiate

The question is, of course, how could U.S. negotiators be out smarted so badly? The answer is that Mexico was better focused, better staffed, and better organized. Its negotiators knew what they wanted and worked closely with Mexican business to get it.

Mexico had the edge in the negotiations from day one. Why? Because the Bush Administration wanted a deal done quickly so it could brag about it in the 1992 Presidential elections. The Bush administration was willing to make concessions to get any deal, and Mexico's negotiators knew it.

In contrast, the earlier trade agreement between the United States and Canada had taken almost four years to complete, despite the fact that Canada and the United States have almost equal income levels, possess similar institutions, and share a common heritage. Yet, President Bush instructed the U.S. negotiators to complete NAFTA in only 14 months — a much more complex deal with a country that is far less developed than the United States, possesses far different political and economic institutions, and does not share a common heritage.

The Advisers

Together, Mexico's corporations and government hired an army of Washington insiders to gather intelligence, provide negotiating advice, supply contacts, and lobby the U.S. negotiating team. These insiders included 33 former high-ranking federal officials — people who once represented the United States in similar negotiations, but who were now paid handsomely to represent a foreign government, Mexico, against their former employer, the American people. These 33 former U.S. government officials who now work as foreign lobbyists are identified in Appendix A.

Mexico's U.S. Advisers

Mexico's chief legal adviser in the NAFTA negotiations was a former Under Secretary of Trade at the U.S. Commerce Department. Mexico's principal trade adviser during the NAFTA negotiations used to be the United States Trade Advisor from 1981 to 1985 and is still widely known as the "father of NAFTA." Mexico's chief technical adviser had formerly been responsible for U.S.-Mexican trade at the Office of the United States Trade Representative during the late 1980s.

The U.S. team, on the other hand, was composed of bureaucrats from various federal agencies. The team leader, the United States Trade Representative, had served in both the Nixon and Ford Administrations, and in between this public service, had worked as a Washington lawyer and a foreign lobbyist for Canadian, Korean, and Japanese interests. The USTR's deputy, a former State Department official in the Nixon Administration, also had been a foreign lobbyist for U.S., Canadian, and Japanese interests in the 1980s.

Some of the bureaucrats on the U.S. negotiating team were experienced, but many were not. One participant reports that when the trade talks began not a single person in the U.S. Commerce Department's Office of Mexico spoke Spanish. He says that during one inter-agency session, only two of the 14 members of the U.S. negotiating team knew that key sectors of the Mexican economy, such as petroleum, had once been American-owned before they were nationalized by the Mexican government. He also reports that only five percent of the Mexican documents, such as copies of proposed regulations and administrative procedures, received by the U.S. negotiating team were ever translated for review.

The President's Advisers

Even though Congress gave up a large measure of its authority with the "fast track" authorization, it did not surrender complete control of the treaty negotiating process. Under the 1974 Trade Act, Congress directed the Office of the U.S. Trade Representative to seek advice and counsel from private advisory panels during any treaty negotiations, including NAFTA. For the most part, it never happened. The Bush White House, for instance, announced the completion of the agreement on August 12, 1992, but refused to give its own Labor Advisory Committee the text to review until September 8.

The 29 official U.S. trade advisory committees, involving more than 825 industry representatives, were created by Congress to ensure that U.S. goals and bargaining positions in trade talks, such as NAFTA, would be guided by advisers who represent the broad interests of the United States. *This balanced review did not occur during the NAFTA negotiations.* The advisory committees were dominated by companies and industries with a direct interest in an agreement that would protect and stimulate more U.S. investment in Mexico. *The deck was stacked against the American people.*

The most important of these advisory committees was the Advisory Committee on Trade Policy and Negotiations (ACTPN). Its 45 members were appointed by the president. None were confirmed by Congress. Each member of this Committee was required to have a security clearance. Each member was prohibited from sharing information outside the group. The ACTPN meetings were exempt from the sunshine provisions of the Federal Advisory Committee Act, which require that the public's business be conducted in public. The ACTPN recom-

18

mendations were labeled "secret" and shared with only a handful of administration insiders.

Of the 45 members of the ACTPN panel, 38 were senior officers of major U.S. corporations, banks, and insurance companies, and four led trade associations. On the other hand, only two were union officials, and one was a business consultant. Of the 38 corporations represented, 27 had extensive business investments in Mexico. Today, these are the same companies that are leading the charge to get NAFTA approved by Congress. Is anyone surprised?

Behind Closed Doors

U.S. trade negotiators have a long tradition of trading away American jobs. To get Turkey to join the Persian gulf coalition against Iraq in 1990, for instance, the Bush Administration agreed to increase the quota of Turkish apparel, fabric, and yarn that could be exported from Turkey into the United States. What kind of negotiation is it when the United States agrees to pay Turkey to allow the United States to defend Turkey from a mad dictator? The Europeans just laughed when Turkey asked them for the same deal.

The deal with Turkey, though, is not unusual. In the 1970s, U.S. negotiators traded away big parts of high-wage industries such as steel, consumer electronics, and automobiles for foreign policy reasons. In the 1980s, U.S. negotiators were unwilling to defend American jobs from subsidized and predatory competition from Asia. In addition, European competitors pulled U.S. jobs from other high-paying industries such as aircraft, hi-tech electronics, and machine tools.

Remember, most of these trade deals are made behind closed doors. When trade agreements are released to the public, they often have what are known as "side letters," which are government-to-government deals that often counteract the public document. Many are kept secret forever, but all are binding.

In these closed negotiations, the U.S. negotiating team has the authority to put virtually anything on the table. It can, for instance, trade away jobs in U.S. agriculture to get strong provisions for U.S. investors. Trade treaty negotiations are much like a giant game of Monopoly, but played for real with U.S. industries, companies, and jobs. This happened in the NAFTA negotiations.

But more than just jobs were traded away. The U.S. negotiating team also accepted provisions that will ultimately lower U.S. health, safety, and environmental standards and regulations.

After the trade pact was completed, one of the U.S. negotiators explained to an audience of federal regulators that although changes in most domestic regulations normally require notice and public comment, secret trade negotiations (such as NAFTA) could alter these same regulations without need for notice and public comment. The negotiator said, "I have seen specific instances where USTR staff denied copies of U.S. negotiating positions which would require overturning Federal regulations from the staff of the agency issuing those regulations."

As the negotiations proceeded, the U.S. negotiating team was constantly lobbied by special interests to use NAFTA as a vehicle to weaken long-standing U.S. regulations. Chemical and food processing companies, for example, were able to get provisions into NAFTA that will lead to the import of food produced with pesticides that are outlawed in the United States. This was all done secretly, of course.

In a similar manner, the NAFTA negotiations played with the future of dozens of U.S. industries, particularly industries that were not represented on the advisory committees or did not hire well-connected, special-interest lobbyists. A typical example is what happened to the U.S. broom industry, which will disappear if Congress enacts NAFTA.

The broom industry is made up of small, family-owned companies that employ between ten and two hundred workers. Production is labor intensive, and therefore, the industry is particularly vulnerable to low-wage Mexican imports.

A SECRET DEAL

Early in the NAFTA negotiations, William Libman of the Libman Company, a leading U.S. manufacturer of brooms, was assured by U.S. trade officials that the industry would be granted the maximum protection — that is, a 15-year phase-out of tariffs.

Throughout the negotiations, the Libman Company and the other companies in the broom industry were assured that they would receive the 15-year phase-out so that they would have time to adjust. Nonetheless, Libman suggested to U.S. officials that the U.S. broom industry negotiate its portion of the agreement with its Mexican counterparts. But the U.S. Trade Representative prohibited industry-to-industry negotiations, saying that the deal would be made by the governments, not by the affected industries.

Toward the end of the negotiations, the U.S. trade negotiators contacted Libman and asked "whether or not the broom industry had contacted Mexican manufacturers to co-produce products in Mexico for distribution in the United States as other labor-intensive industries — such as ceramic tile, watches, and rubber footwear — had."

Libman was shocked to learn his own government was encouraging U.S. companies to move American jobs to Mexico. He told the U.S. negotiating team, "the industry had no intention of moving production to Mexico, and that the industry was dedicated to maintaining employment in the United States for the thousands of quality American craftsmen — many of whom are second- and third-generation broom makers."

Libman's problem was that the U.S. negotiators were, at best, amateurs, but they held the fate of his industry in their hands. The U.S. negotiators kept him and anyone else who had specific knowledge about the industry out of the negotiations.

Mexico operated differently, of course. Its negotiators in this area were guided by Mexico's leading broom manufacturer. During the final negotiations, the Mexican broom manufacturer came to Washington to advise the Mexican delegation on the type of provisions he would like to see in the agreement. The U.S.

negotiating team did not invite Libman or any other representative of his industry to participate in the negotiations.

The broom portion of the NAFTA deal was made behind closed doors by the U.S. negotiators, the Mexican negotiators, and the Mexican industrialist. The Mexican broom industry scored a major victory. *It will be permitted to export 1.2 million brooms duty-free into the United States.*

If NAFTA is enacted, U.S. broom factories will be forced out of business. More than one hundred small Midwestern communities will lose jobs. In many of these towns, the local broom factory is the major provider of jobs. Libman asks, "If their jobs move to Mexico, how will these skilled master broom makers, who have devoted the greater part of their lives to their craft, be retrained; what high paying jobs will they be retrained for; and where will these jobs be located?"

Unfortunately, the experience of the U.S. broom industry in the NAFTA negotiations is neither unique nor extreme. The inexperienced U.S. negotiators kept dozens of industries, such as trucking, and sugar, in the dark as Mexican industries were working hand in glove with Mexico's negotiators.

Keeping the U.S. Public in the Dark

What's worse, our trade negotiators refused to share the text of the agreement with the American people even after the deal was supposedly completed.

When President Bush announced on August 12, 1992 — just before the Republican Party's national convention — that NAFTA had been completed, the American public was given only a 44-page public relations handout instead of the text of the more than 1,100-page agreement.

When the agreement was initialed by the three government leaders on October 18, 1992 — two weeks before the U.S. presidential election — the American public was handed a short, marked-up version of the agreement.

A SECRET DEAL

When the agreement was officially signed on December 18, 1992, no additional information was provided to the American public.

The complete text of NAFTA was finally released to the American people on the afternoon of January 20, 1993.

The Government Printing Office now sells the two-volume document for $41. It is not a big seller. A private publisher has reprinted the book, and is selling it for $10. Only a handful of people outside of Washington know what is actually in the agreement, and working people whose jobs are being put at risk have had little information prior to this book.

The goal of all this secrecy, of course, is to keep the American people in the dark about NAFTA. Until recently, it has worked.

The Wall Street Journal
on
Mexico's NAFTA Lobbying Campaign
in the United States

*Mexico is bankrolling a nationwide
campaign to sell the trade accord, and
Mexico, to Americans... Mexico
government and business interests have
hired no fewer than 24 lobbying, public
relations and law firms to negotiate and
promote the trade pact... it has treated 76
congressional aides to Mexican junkets to
meet with government and business leaders.
Other Mexican lobbyists have arranged
tours for lawmakers and U.S. business
officials. ... Indeed, no opportunity for
influence seems too remote for
Mexico's legion of lobbyists.*

The Wall Street Journal, May 20, 1993

Chapter 3

American Jobs Matter

Only a tiny handful of working people are ever asked to testify before the U.S. Congress. Scarlett Bachman is one of those few. In April 1993, she appeared before the U.S. Senate to describe what happens to workers when a small town's principal employer moves to Mexico.

Scarlett and her husband live in a modest home in Dowagiac, Michigan. For 23 years, the 49-year-old wife, mother, and grandmother worked at the local Sundstrand Heat Transfer factory, which makes the copper tubing used in refrigeration and air conditioning units.

In the late 1980s, Sundstrand, a large aerospace conglomerate and government contractor headquartered in Rockford, Illinois, decided to boost corporate profits by shifting a portion of the work from its Dowagiac plant to a new, low-wage facility in Nuevo Laredo, Mexico.

When the Mexican plant fell behind on its production schedule, Scarlett and the remaining Dowagiac workers pitched in so the company wouldn't lose its customer orders. She told the Senate, "Hoping we could prove that we were still needed, our dedication to our lifetime jobs prevailed, but we only prolonged our devastation."

Within a few months, the Mexican plant met its production schedules as well as the company's quality standards. More work was shifted from the plant in Dowagiac where Scarlett worked to the plant in Mexico. Scarlett and the skeleton crew left in Dowagiac then had to clean up, crate, and load the equipment they used to operate for shipment to Mexican workers at the new plant in Mexico. The last big job Scarlett and her co-workers had was to send the tools of their trade to someone willing to do their work for a fraction of their pay. That's the American nightmare, not the American dream.

In 1990, Sundstrand reorganized itself and sold its heat transfer division to the Modine Manufacturing Company, a 75-year old Wisconsin corporation. Less than four months later, Scarlett, with 23 years of devoted service to the company, was laid off. She was making $10.37 per hour at the time. Her husband, who worked at Modine, was also laid off. The company gave them 60 days notice but no severance pay. Scarlett and her husband drew unemployment benefits for awhile, but payments on their monthly bills soon fell behind, and their savings were wiped out.

Scarlett went back to school at age 47. It was tough, she says, but she worked hard and made the Dean's List. After graduation, she got a job at the Lee Memorial Hospital making $5.88 per hour. Her husband also found a job, but it only pays $5.00 per hour, and he doesn't know how long the work will last. Together, the Bachman's pay is now only half what it was, and their benefits are only a quarter of what they had before their jobs were shipped to low-wage Mexican employees.

When Scarlett began working at the heat transfer factory in 1968, it employed more than 1,200 people. Now the American factory has less than 80 production workers.

Scarlett made the sacrifice and effort needed to acquire new skills in the hope of gradually restoring her family's standard of living. However, that is not what happened. About the only jobs available to her were ones that pay scarcely better than the minimum wage and have little or no potential for advancement. But Scarlett considers herself lucky because so many of her former co-workers still haven't found jobs. Their benefits have run out, many have lost their homes, some have lost their families, and most can't afford medical insurance.

Mexican workers now fill the jobs that were once in Dowagiac, Michigan. Modine Manufacturing Company refuses to reveal how much it pays its Mexican workers, but wages in Mexico are low.

Mexico's legal minimum wage is only 58 cents per hour. The Mexican state of Yucatan claims to have an abundance of workers available at $1.00 per hour, including all benefits. Even the best paying jobs in Mexico don't pay much more. For instance, the average hourly wage for manufacturing workers in Mexico is only $2.35 per hour, and that includes their pay for time worked, pay for holidays and vacations, bonuses, and any employer payments for insurance or mandated benefits. But most of the Mexican workers employed by U.S. companies in border factories, called maquiladoras, are paid an average of only $1.64 per hour, including all benefits. Thus, Scarlett whose pay was more than $10 per hour plus benefits, was pitted against a worker in Mexico whose pay was less than $2 per hour including all benefits.

Life is hard for low-paid Mexican workers in the maquiladora factories. They have very few, if any, work-related benefits. Their hours are long. Their houses are small, crowded, and often without indoor toilets or electricity. The roads and streets are unpaved. Often, all of their earnings go for feeding, clothing, and sheltering their families.

And what happened to Modine Manufacturing? In 1992, Modine Manufacturing had record sales and paid its investors a record dividend. The CEO was paid a salary of $292,000. He was also given a cash bonus of $175,000, restricted stock worth $273,000, and stock options worth another $36,000. The company also paid $21,000 into his corporate 401(k) and other retirement plans. The CEO of Modine Manufacturing Company received $797,000 in total compensation for 1992.

Ironically, Scarlett's government is actively encouraging U.S. companies, such as Sundstrand and Modine, to move manufacturing jobs such as hers into Mexico and other less-developed nations. Somehow, a succession of U.S. presidents and a majority in the United States Congress have failed to grasp the fact that manufacturing jobs such as Scarlett's are irreplaceable. Perhaps if they listened to the people who have first-hand experience, they would understand. When Scarlett testified in April 1993, only Carl Levin, the one Senator who sponsored her, was present for her testimony.

Manufacturing Matters

If for no other reason, manufacturing is vitally important for this reason: without the ability to manufacture, the United States cannot defend itself.

Manufacturing is important because it provides the greatest number of high-paying U.S. jobs. These are the types of jobs that U.S. workers need if they are to buy a house, build a retirement nest egg, and create a better future for themselves. It also matters because each one hundred manufacturing jobs creates, on average, another 421 support jobs.

Even the lowest paid U.S. manufacturing jobs create more secondary employment than the highest paid U.S. business service jobs. The Economic Policy Institute, a Washington research organization, reports that every one hundred manufacturing jobs in the:

- apparel industry creates 207 secondary jobs;
- textile industry creates 267 secondary jobs;
- iron and steel industry creates 368 secondary jobs;
- non-electrical machinery industry creates 289 secondary jobs;
- aerospace industry creates 388 secondary jobs; and
- automobile manufacturing creates 691 secondary jobs.

By contrast, one hundred retail jobs only create 94 secondary jobs. And one hundred business service jobs, such as banking or insurance, generate only 147 secondary jobs. Thus, hundreds of new service jobs must be created to offset the loss of even one hundred low-paying manufacturing jobs such as those in the apparel industry.

These job multipliers also work in reverse. When a community such as Dowagiac, Michigan loses 1,100 jobs, many of the 4,200 secondary jobs they support are lost somewhere else in the country.

Take a look at the graph on Page 30. It should come as no surprise that the percentage of manufacturing jobs in the United States has decreased over the past 25 years. In 1965, manufacturing provided 27 percent of all U.S. jobs. Today, it provides 17 percent. More people in the United States are now employed by federal, state, and local government than in all manufacturing.

By contrast, German and Japanese trade officials work to keep their manufacturing jobs at home. In 1965, manufacturing provided 36 percent of German jobs; today it's 32 percent. In 1965, 21 percent of Japanese jobs were in manufacturing; today, it's 25 percent.

It is just plain wrong to think that "progress" as a nation requires shifting from a manufacturing economy to a service economy. The fact that so many of our leaders support this concept explains why incomes and living standards are rising in Germany and Japan while they are falling in the United States.

The Endangered Jobs List

NAFTA will accelerate the loss of manufacturing jobs in the United States. Some companies will move factories to Mexico to take advantage of low-cost Mexican labor. Others will move to Mexico to escape U.S. regulations. Many American companies will move to Mexico, not because they want to, but because their competitors have moved, and they must move to compete. Eventually, companies that choose to stay in the U.S. will need to reduce employee wages and benefits in order to lower prices to compete with cheaper Mexican imports. No product, no company, and no community is immune from the effects of NAFTA.

And which jobs are at risk?

Virtually all U.S. manufacturing jobs are ultimately vulnerable, but some jobs are in more immediate danger than others. A guide-

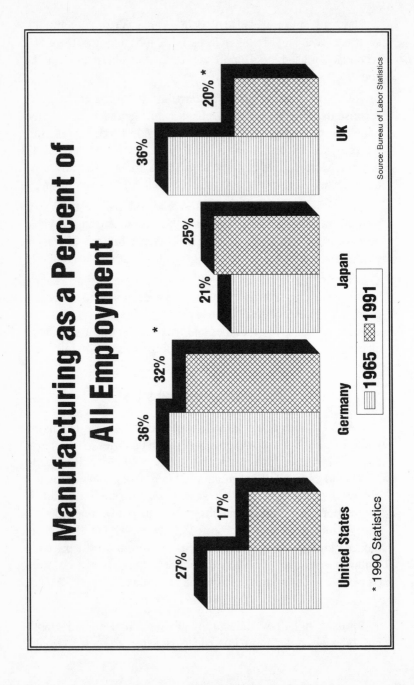

post for determining the Americans jobs that are at risk is provided by the shift in Mexican products exported to the United States.

A decade ago, roughly half of Mexico's exports to the United States consisted of minerals, fuels, and foodstuffs. Now they make up only 25 percent. Today, Mexican exports to the United States are dominated by the flow of high-profit electrical machinery, machinery parts, automobiles, automobile parts, trucks, televisions, radios, apparel, telecommunications equipment, and office machinery. Of these products, most come from U.S.-owned plants operating in Mexico under the Maquiladora Program. These U.S. companies still employ millions of American workers. These companies have demonstrated that they will close U.S. factories, fire American workers, and move their plants to Mexico. If NAFTA is enacted, there will be many new advantages and even fewer obstacles for U.S. companies to relocate more American jobs to Mexico.

On this endangered U.S. jobs list, the auto industry ranks close to the top. Mexican autoworkers make one-seventh the pay of their U.S. counterparts, and this includes any benefits provided to the Mexican workers. However, the health care costs for Mexican autoworkers is negligible. In U.S. auto plants, health care expenses exceed the cost of steel used to manufacture the automobiles.

Mexico provides automakers an easy escape hatch from the high costs of operating in the United States, and they are taking advantage of it. Remember, as shown on page 28, the U.S. auto industry creates more secondary American jobs than any other industry. The combined impact of losing the auto industry jobs and the secondary jobs would be enormous.

Five hundred thousand vehicles were manufactured in Mexico in 1988. More than one million will be produced there in 1993. Within seven years, automakers in Mexico will be producing more than three million units per year. This is one of the reasons why dozens of U.S. auto factories are closing and tens of thousands of American auto manufacturing and secondary jobs are disappearing.

These job losses are increasing as auto parts suppliers move their factories to Mexico as well. In many cases, these U.S. auto parts makers, particularly the smaller companies, are draftees. Big Three U.S. automakers are quietly requiring U.S. suppliers to serve their Mexican auto assembly operations from Mexican parts factories. This allows Ford, Chrysler, and General Motors to squeeze price reductions out of their suppliers while employing low-cost Mexican workers. The supplier's parts production also gets credited toward the auto manufacturers' satisfaction of Mexico's "domestic content" regulations, which force foreign companies that sell in Mexico to produce in Mexico. NAFTA does not significantly alter Mexico's long-standing requirement that a high percentage of a vehicle sold in Mexico must be made in Mexico. European and Japanese car makers will also be required to buy parts from factories operating in Mexico.

Mexico's domestic content restrictions should have been eliminated during the NAFTA negotiations. Instead, U. S. negotiators agreed that Mexico could continue to apply these unfair restrictions, slightly modified, for another ten years.

Ironically, the biggest — and quietest — boosters for keeping Mexico's domestic content rules were the Big Three U.S. automakers. They want to move even more of their U.S. operations to Mexico, but they also want to avoid the blame for firing tens of thousands of U.S. workers and destroying the economies of hundreds of U.S. communities. This way, they can blame the relocation of American jobs on Mexico's domestic content regulations.

Apparel and textile jobs are also close to the top of the endangered U.S. jobs list. Already, tens of thousands of apparel jobs have been moved from the U.S. to Mexico. Today, 129 U.S. apparel companies employing more than 30,000 Mexican workers are operating 222 factories in Mexico. The jobs of many of the remaining 830,000 American apparel workers, who are paid an average of $6.94 per hour, will vanish under NAFTA. Mexican workers are paid an average of $1.64 an hour for this type of work.

NAFTA will permit a virtual free flow of apparel products from Mexico into the United States. U.S. apparel makers will face an uncomplicated choice: stay in the United States and go broke; or fire U.S. workers, go to Mexico, and boost profits. Guess which alternative most U.S. manufacturers will choose?

Textile jobs will follow the apparel jobs to Mexico. Because NAFTA limits the import of textiles made outside North America, foreign textile producers are already building factories in Mexico. Eventually, U.S. textile companies will have to relocate to Mexico to remain competitive enough to keep their customers. If NAFTA is enacted, many of the remaining 540,000 U.S. textile jobs — which pay an average of $8.53 an hour — will go to Mexican textile workers making an average of $1.64 per hour.

High-wage, skilled electrical workers are also on the NAFTA-endangered U.S. jobs list. In the 1970s, most jobs in the U.S. consumer electronics industry moved to Asia and Mexico. Now big chunks of the U.S. electrical equipment industry are being shifted to Mexico. These are factories that employ workers to produce motors, transformers, generators, relay switches, and other sophisticated electrical products.

The International Brotherhood of Electrical Workers reports that between 1985 and 1990 more than 25,000 of its members' jobs were moved from the U.S. to Mexico. The companies that moved these jobs, such as AT&T, Johnson Controls, Westinghouse, General Electric, and Cooper Industries, still employ hundreds of thousands of electrical workers in the United States whose pay averages $15.08 per hour, including benefits. Many of these remaining jobs could be profitably shifted to Mexico, where comparable work earns $1.64 per hour, including benefits once NAFTA is ratified by Congress.

Millions of jobs in dozens of other industries are now on the NAFTA-endangered U.S. jobs list. Industries that produce products like metalworking machinery, partitions, fixtures, metal forgings, clay products, office furniture, fabricated metal products, aircraft, aircraft parts, aircraft repairs, concrete products, lighting equipment, electrical wiring equipment, and luggage, among many others, are on the NAFTA-endangered U.S. jobs list.

The Endangered Place List

Different manufacturing industries in the United States tend to be concentrated in different parts of the country. When an industry suffers or loses jobs, specific areas of the country and the people who live there suffer the greatest financial strain.

The auto assembly and parts industries, for example, are heavily concentrated in the states of Michigan, Illinois, Wisconsin, Ohio, and Indiana. Not surprisingly, then, these states will lose disproportionately more auto and secondary industry jobs if the auto industry moves more of its factories to Mexico.

Local and state governments will lose revenue from property taxes, income taxes, and sales taxes. The lost revenue, combined with increased government expenditures for unemployment benefits and uninsured health care, drive the taxes up on the industries that remain and the workers who are still employed.

Similarly, almost 90 percent of the U.S. apparel and textile industries are concentrated in only eight states — New York, New Jersey, California, Texas, Tennessee, North Carolina, South Carolina, and Georgia. These are the states that have the most to lose if more apparel and textile jobs are moved out of the United States.

The biggest potential losers are the nation's largest urban areas. Millions of manufacturing jobs have already disappeared from our cities. According to the U.S. Commerce Department, between the 1970 census and 1990 census, 19 of the largest American cities lost more than 2.3 million manufacturing jobs. Since the 1990 census, these metropolitan areas have lost even more jobs.

Many of these urban manufacturing jobs have gone to Mexico. The University of Illinois at Chicago, for instance, has identified 67,088 jobs and 42 factories that moved from Illinois to Mexico between 1980 and 1990. More than 47,000 of those jobs came from the Chicago metropolitan area. The researchers say that the actual job losses are much higher since they only counted those job relocations for which there is some public record.

Large-scale job losses are devastating U.S. cities. A job in manufacturing has long been a first step on the ladder out of urban poverty. Not surprisingly, the cities that lost these 2.3 million manufacturing jobs are the very same cities that have some of the highest urban unemployment, highest welfare, highest crime, and highest infant mortality rates.

How can Congress consider NAFTA, which will destroy urban jobs, at the same time that it is considering the Clinton Administration's urban empowerment program, which will try to create urban jobs by spending $800 million a year of taxpayers' money over the next five years to provide incentives for businesses to locate in urban areas?

The United States is swapping good manufacturing jobs for lower paying service jobs. For instance, the University of South Carolina reports that between 1978 and 1990 South Carolina lost more than 58,000 manufacturing jobs. At the same time, the biggest job gains in South Carolina were in restaurants, bars, and grocery stores — more than 72,000 service jobs were created in such establishments. It's a bad trade-off. *The lost manufacturing jobs paid an average of $279 per week. The replacement service jobs pay only $127 a week — less than half as much.* The result: the living standards of working men and women are declining, and America is becoming a nation of hamburger-flippers.

The Endangered People List

As NAFTA endangers some industries and places more than others; some American workers are more at risk than others.

Working men and women, recent immigrants, and urban dwellers are at great risk from NAFTA. For example, the sons and daughters of sharecroppers who moved north in the 1940s and 1950s to improve their lives can't get work because manufacturing jobs have gone to low-wage southern states, overseas, or to Mexico.

The loss of manufacturing jobs has the greatest impact on urban minorities. Half of all the manufacturing jobs that disappeared in Chicago during the 1980s were lost by minorities and women.

With the decline of U.S. manufacturing, the country is increasingly unable to provide good entry-level jobs for its youth. As a result, the earning power of young people has fallen over the past decade. In 1980, for instance, 18 percent of 18- to 24-year-old men earned less than $12,000 per year. In 1990, more than 40 percent earned less than $12,000 per year. And because of inflation, $12,000 in 1980 was worth far more than $12,000 in 1990.

During that same decade, young women, who started out in a worse position than their male peers, suffered similar losses in earnings. In 1980, more than 29 percent of 18- to 24-year-old women made less than $12,000. But by 1990, more than 48 percent had incomes of less than $12,000. No doubt about it, this country is not meeting its responsibility to provide the young people with job opportunities.

NAFTA puts at risk many of the very industries that can provide badly-needed jobs. The Texas Department of Commerce did a detailed analysis of the employment effects of NAFTA. They report that the Texas industries that will "lose" under this pact employ one-third more workers in the state than the projected "winners." The "loser" industries include fabricated metals, lumber and paper, primary metals, fresh fruits and vegetables, livestock, distribution services, transportation equipment, leather and leather products, apparels and textiles. These are industries that employ high numbers of semi-skilled workers.

The same pattern is found in New York City. The New York metropolitan area lost 725,000 manufacturing jobs over the past two decades. Many of the jobs that remain, such as the 60,000 in the apparel industry, pay less than $7.00 per hour. If NAFTA is ratified by Congress, these jobs will be at risk.

AMERICAN JOBS MATTER

In study after study, the U.S. Department of Labor has found that displaced workers have an increasingly difficult time finding new jobs. The Labor Department reports that:

- The lower the skill of the displaced workers, the less likely they are to be reemployed *ever*.
- Blacks and Hispanics are less likely to find new jobs than whites.
- Women are less likely than men to find new jobs and more likely to drop out of the work force.

The Congressional Budget Office (CBO) reports that of every one hundred American workers who lost their jobs in the 1980s, that at least 61 had not reached the same standard of living they had before losing their job. The hard fact of life is that a majority of the American workers who will be thrown out of work if NAFTA is passed will have to take less pay and fewer benefits to get another job — and that's if they can find someone willing to hire them. See the chart on page 38 for more details.

Even the strongest NAFTA supporters now acknowledge that the agreement will cost U.S. jobs. NAFTA advocates argue the solution is for the federal government (i.e., the U.S. taxpayers) to provide more worker retraining for the unemployed (i.e., the former U.S. taxpayers). The unanswered question, of course, is for what type of job will U.S. workers be retrained? Nobody can articulate the "jobs of the future" for which American workers would be retrained. By definition, a job of the future may not even exist yet. Every day that a working American remains unemployed, it is a crushing defeat to the person, the family, the community, and the country. The impact of job loss and unemployment cannot be dealt with in an abstract manner.

Let's look at it another way. Job retraining for a displaced worker is unnecessary if the worker's job never leaves the United States in the first place.

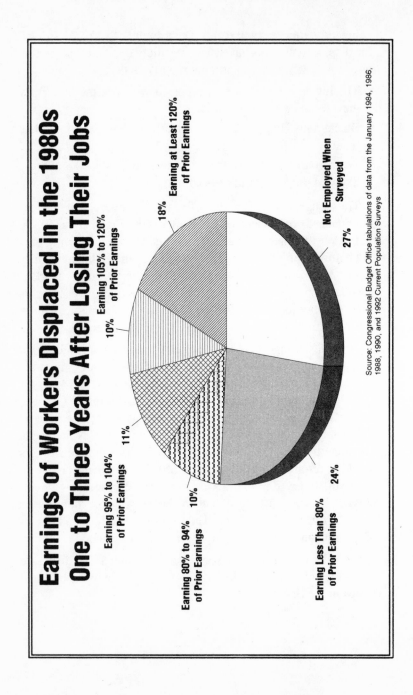

Earnings of Workers Displaced in the 1980s
One to Three Years After Losing Their Jobs

Earning at Least 120%
of Prior Earnings

18%

Earning 105% to 120%
of Prior Earnings

10%

Earning 95% to 104%
of Prior Earnings

11%

Earning 80% to 94%
of Prior Earnings

10%

Earning Less Than 80%
of Prior Earnings

24%

Not Employed When
Surveyed

27%

Source: Congressional Budget Office tabulations of data from the January 1984, 1986, 1988, 1990, and 1992 Current Population Surveys

An Endangered Nation

In her testimony to the U.S. Senate, Scarlett Bachman said that the whole community had suffered when most of the factory jobs from her town were moved to Mexico.

The Warren Act required the company to send out a list 60 days before a person lost their job, she said, but that didn't mean that in 60 days you could pick up the pieces and go on with your life. Some people saw their names on this list four or more times before they actually lost their jobs. Many people who were once friends ended up bitter enemies. It was like throwing a raw bone to 50 dogs and see who was going to come out on top. Imagine 1,200 people employed in 1968 and now, 1993, only 75-80 left as factory workers.

This pitting of one employee against another to preserve their family income is being magnified thousands of times across the nation. As America loses its job base, destructive social divisions are forced on the nation — the elderly who depend on social security and government medical assistance are pitted against the young who must pay; minorities who lack jobs are pitted against majorities who are barely hanging on to theirs; a declining middle class versus a tiny minority who grow increasingly wealthy.

Again, the Illinois study reveals what is happening. Between 1977 and 1988, the 84 percent of the Illinois population that earned less than $50,000 annually had a loss in taxable, inflation-adjusted income of more than eight percent. The 16 percent of the Illinois population that earned more than $50,000 increased their inflation-adjusted income by more than 50 percent.

The solution, of course, is not to take away the wealth and opportunities for the 16 percent who prospered, but to assure the other 84 percent that they will have access to more and better jobs — such as the ones lost to other countries.

Viewed another way, the United States is now more than $4 trillion in debt. Every day, the national debt grows by another $1 billion. In 1992, just the interest cost on the federal debt was $199 billion. At the same time, the total payroll for all U.S. manufacturing jobs was $266 billion. At the current rate of the federal debt growth and manufacturing job losses, the annual interest on the federal debt will exceed the salaries paid to all U.S. manufacturing workers by the year 1996.

These federal deficits are irresponsible beyond imagination. Proposals such as NAFTA that would destroy the good jobs that produce the taxes that the country needs to pay its bills and build a sound future for American children.

Chapter 4

A Giant Sucking Sound

One million Mexicans enter the work force each year. They need jobs.

To get those jobs, President Salinas and his government have deliberately kept wages down to attract foreign investment. Mexico has vastly expanded its vocational training programs to improve worker skill levels. The Mexican government also offers low-cost loans and tax benefits to companies that build factories in Mexico.

Mexico's national development strategy is reminiscent of strategies used by Japan, Korea, and Taiwan a generation ago. Like the strategies used by those countries, Mexico's strategy depends on taking jobs from the United States.

Good Workers at Low Wages

Mexico has a three-fold attraction to U.S. companies: it provides good workers at low wages; its government is decidedly pro-business; and Mexico is located next to the largest and richest consumer market in the world — the United States.

For more than a year, the Mexican state of Yucatan has capitalized on these advantages by running an advertising campaign offering U.S. companies a plentiful supply of high-quality, loyal Mexican workers at $1 per hour, including benefits. The ad promises a worker turnover rate of less than five percent a year and a savings of over $15,000 a year per worker for every U.S. job moved to the Mexican state of Yucatan.

Look at the chart on page 43. The wage differential between the United States and Mexico could not be more obvious. The United States Department of Labor reports that, even when mandated non-wage benefits are counted, manufacturing labor costs in Mexico are only 15 percent of those found in the United States — $2.35 per hour versus $16.17. What's more, despite all the supposed prosperity in Mexico during the last 12 years, the Mexican workers' standard of living has remained stagnant. The same low wages that are being used by the Mexican government to lure businesses are at the same time exploiting the majority of Mexican workers.

The *New York Times* reports that the skills of Mexican workers already match the skills of 70 percent of the labor force in the United States. Once properly trained, Mexican workers' productivity and work quality equals that of anyone, anywhere in the world.

The experiences of U.S., Japanese, and German automakers illustrate just how good the Mexican workers can be. Ford, GM, Chrysler, and Nissan now operate high-volume engine plants in Mexico. Last year, they exported more than 1.2 million engines, making Mexico the largest engine exporter in the world.

In a Congressional study released in June 1993, auto expert Harley Shaiken compared the productivity and quality of work in Mexican plants with their counterparts in the United States and elsewhere. He found that Mexican workers in one engine plant reached 85 percent of the productivity of their U.S. counterpart plant within two years; 89 percent within eight years; and 97 percent within nine years. This is impressive by any measure.

Even more impressive, the product quality in the Mexican plant surpassed that of the counterpart U.S. plant in four of the six years for which they had data. In 1991, the quality in the Mexican plant exceeded the U.S. facility by 32 percent.

The eye opener is that the U.S. and Mexican plants had similar equipment, but the technology in the Mexican facility was more advanced. The message is simple: Mexican workers can master

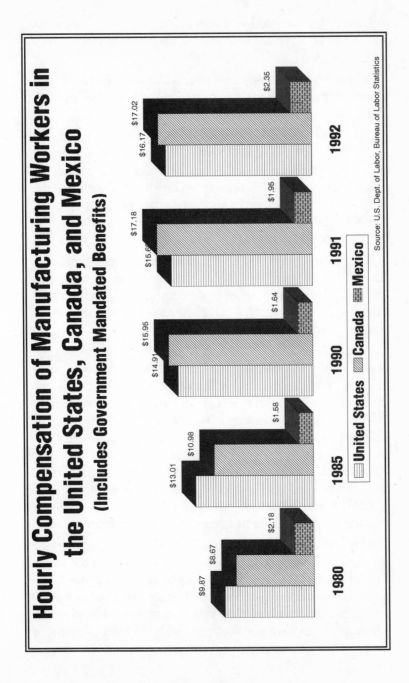

Hourly Compensation of Manufacturing Workers in the United States, Canada, and Mexico
(Includes Government Mandated Benefits)

United States   Canada   Mexico

1980: $9.87 $8.67 $2.18
1985: $13.01 $10.98 $1.58
1990: $14.91 $15.95 $1.64
1991: $15.6 $17.18 $1.95
1992: $16.17 $17.02 $2.35

Source: U.S. Dept. of Labor, Bureau of Labor Statistics

high technology and deliver the goods when given a chance. No one should be surprised to learn that the Mexican plant is now being expanded.

Nissan reports that its engine plant in Aguascalientes, Mexico is now producing the fewest number of defects per engine of any of the company's worldwide plants.

Only three years after Ford Motor Company opened its auto assembly plant in Hermosillo, Mexico, its cars were virtually equal in quality to the Honda Civic, the highest quality small car sold in the United States. Shaiken reports that the quality of the vehicles assembled in Ford's Mexican factory was superior to the highly-regarded Nissan Sentra and Toyota Corolla made in Japan by experienced Japanese autoworkers.

High quality work by Mexican workers is not limited to automaking. Sanyo reports that its Mexican plants are as productive and its products as defect-free as any of its U.S. or Japanese factories. Sony's plant in Tijuana, Mexico has won worldwide quality awards for the company.

Despite their accomplishments, Mexican workers are paid low wages. Unlike the middle-class U.S. family displaced by these low wage jobs, the majority of the work force in Mexico — the lower class — has little hope of greatly improving its standard of living. The standard factory earnings in the Mexican state of Chihuahua, for instance, are $1 per hour. In very modern Mexican factories, such as the Ford, GM, Chrysler, Volkswagen, and Nissan plants, production workers start at only $1.25 to $1.50 per hour. When benefits are included, the average total compensation in 1992 for Mexican autoworkers was $3.33 per hour — one-seventh the $24.21 per hour that was paid their U.S. counterparts.

There are a number of reasons for the vast wage gap. One of the primary reasons is that since 1987, Mexico has fixed wages through a complex government-business-labor arrangement. The goal: hold inflation down and keep Mexico attractive to foreign investors. As a result of this arrangement, known as *el pacto*, Mexican wages have not kept pace with inflation. In terms of absolute purchasing power, Mexican workers are now making less than half of what they made a decade ago, according to The Economic Policy Institute, a Washington, D.C.-based research organization. Mexico's real wages have gone down despite the fact that they are producing superior products in some of the most advanced factories of the world's largest companies.

Of course, manufacturing companies look for more than just cheap labor when deciding upon a location for a new plant. They must consider access to transportation facilities, reliability of power systems, proximity to their suppliers, and political stability. No one seriously contends that Mexico is superior to the United States in any of these categories. Yet, even after factoring in these components, Mexico still wins a large percentage of plant relocations. Why? Cheap labor can offset all of the areas where Mexico is still deficient. Although Mexico is deficient in certain categories right now, there is no reason to believe that it will remain deficient in these areas in the future.

The CEO of Zenith recently told the *New York Times*, "When I factor in other non-labor costs — less heat, cheaper land and cheaper construction — there is no question that Mexico's lower labor costs are decisive." Over the past decade and a half, Zenith has moved thousands of jobs from the United States to Mexico.

In theory, Mexican unions could stop the exploitation of the workers they represent. Certainly, the Mexican Constitution gives workers the right to organize their own unions and the right to strike. The catch is this: unions must be certified by the Mexican government. The government only recognizes unions affiliated with the Institutional Revolutionary Party (PRI), which has governed Mexico under one-party rule for more than 60 years. Unions that are not registered with the government cannot exist, and if a union is created and strikes, the Minister of Labor for the government will probably send in the police and army to restore order.

If Mexican workers protest these strike-breaking tactics, they can expect swift and severe retaliation. In the summer of 1992, for example, the Mexican government upheld the firing of more than 14,000 workers who had turned down a contract negotiated by the government-dominated union. The government and the company allowed most of the fired employees to slink back to work at company-set wages; some employees were forbidden from ever returning.

Yet, these workers were far luckier than the Mexican workers who struck against Ford Motor Company in 1987. In a bitter two-month strike, Ford tore up its union contract, fired 3,400 workers, and cut wages by 45 percent. When workers rallied around their union leaders, gunmen from the official government-sanctioned union went into the plant and randomly shot people. Then, more than one thousand state police came into the plant to restore order and enforce the company-dictated union contract.

Mexican workers got the message. So too did foreign companies — the Mexican government will keep pay low and workers in line. With Mexican wages kept artificially low, how can the United States expect Mexicans to buy high-priced, American products? How much can 36 wealthy Mexican families be expected to buy?

Low wages and tame unions are only part of what attracts factories to Mexico. Foreign companies operating in Mexico under NAFTA, for instance, have unimpeded access to the rich U.S. consumer market. Not surprisingly, President Salinas constantly emphasizes this access to the U.S. market as a selling point to European and Asian companies. To sweeten the deal for foreign investors, Mexico provides financing for these foreign investors. In 1992, for instance, the Mexican government's import-export banks signed an agreement to sponsor Chinese investment in Mexico. This will allow Chinese textile and apparel companies to secure an exemption from U.S. quotas and duties. Duty-free access to the U.S. market is a very attractive business proposition. This roundabout entry into the U.S. market couldn't be more blatant. After all, why would China, with two billion people, invest in Mexico? To sell to Mexicans? No. The rich markets of the U.S. and Canada are the real prize.

A GIANT SUCKING SOUND

A move to Mexico also allows companies to avoid paying benefits and mandated U.S. payroll taxes. The arithmetic tells the story: benefits and mandates now increase U.S. labor costs by more than 28 percent. Viewed another way, top quality Mexican workers can be hired for less per hour than just the cost of mandated taxes on U.S. pay alone.

Mexico keeps its wages low, of course, to attract foreign investment. This strategy has worked. *Business Week* reports that since 1988 Mexico has attracted more than $26 billion of foreign investment, much of which went to finance new plants and upgrade existing ones. In the process, more than two million Mexican jobs have been created, while hundreds of thousands of U.S. manufacturing jobs have quietly disappeared.

Many of these Mexican jobs were once held by U.S. workers. While the U.S. government refuses to collect data on factory or job relocations to Mexico, private researchers have been able to identify hundreds of U.S. plants that were moved to Mexico in the late 1980s and early 1990s. Their U.S. companies include AT&T, Allied Signal, Cooper Industries, General Electric, Mallinckrodt Medical, Quaker Oats, Unisys, United Technologies, and Westinghouse, among many others.

Besides low wages, another attraction for companies to relocate to Mexico is the loose enforcement of its health, safety, and environmental standards. Mexico provides U.S. companies an escape hatch from increasingly expensive U.S. regulations. For instance, the U.S. General Accounting Office reported to Congress in 1992 that the Mexican government has neither the staff, funds, nor systems it needs to identify the new companies locating there, let alone monitor and enforce its environmental laws. A survey of six U.S. plants operating in Mexico found that all the plants were operating without required environmental licenses. This lack of government enforcement is neither unique nor extreme in Mexico.

The futility of the NAFTA side agreements is obvious: Mexico already has laws it does not enforce. Why should new environmental regulations assure future compliance?

In addition to the U.S. companies that are relocating some of their facilities to Mexico, many of the foreign plants so eagerly recruited by U.S. communities over the past two decades are now choosing to locate in Mexico. Among them are factories owned by Thomson, Goldstar, Phillips, and Sanyo. It seems that companies from other countries are just as attracted to Mexico's low wages as U.S. companies are, providing they can ship goods to the U.S. market.

Most of these U.S. and foreign companies already in Mexico are operating under Mexico's Maquiladora Program, which allows Mexican and foreign investors to own one hundred percent of factories if the factories are located in designated parts of Mexico and if they manufacture mainly for export. Not surprisingly, the finished and semi-finished goods made in these factories are exported primarily to the United States. The Mexican government charges no duty on the imported machinery, raw materials, or components used in these facilities. The Mexican government closely watches the finished products to ensure that they *do not* enter the Mexican market, where they might compete with similar goods produced by Mexican companies.

To encourage U.S. companies to operate in Mexico, the U.S. government subsidizes companies in Mexico that ship products to the U.S. by removing import fees (taxes). These factories are known as "maquiladoras."

Hundreds of U.S. companies have quietly shifted jobs and factories into Mexico. The numbers tell the story:

- In 1980, Mexico had 620 maquiladora plants employing 119,550 workers.
- By 1991, there were 1,925 maquiladoras employing 467,000 workers.
- Today, there are more than 2,200 maquiladoras factories employing more than 500,000 Mexicans.

The chart on page 49 shows the explosive growth of employment in the maquiladoras during the last 17 years. At this growth rate, production in such Mexican factories will expand 400 per-

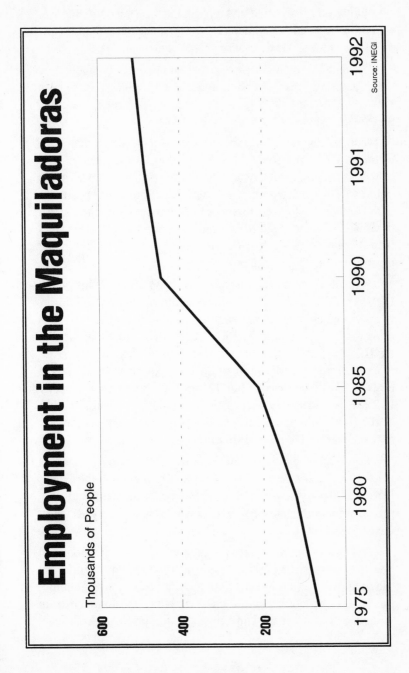

Employment in the Maquiladoras

Thousands of People

Source: INEGI

49

cent by the end of the 1990s. And Mexico has enough workers to meet the demand — remember, more than one million new workers enter the Mexican work force each year.

U.S. multinational corporations created almost as many new manufacturing jobs in Mexico under the Maquiladora Program between 1986 and 1990 as they created in the United States — 92,000 jobs versus 97,000 jobs.

Most of the goods produced in Mexico by these new manufacturing jobs are shipped into the U.S. market. Consequently, most of the so-called trade between the United States and Mexico is not trade as trade is commonly understood. Rather, it is primarily U.S. companies shipping their own machinery, components, and raw materials across the border into their Mexican factories and then shipping their finished or semi-finished goods back over the border into the United States.

Again, the numbers tell the story: In 1992, almost a third of all U.S. exports to Mexico went directly into maquilidora factories whose products were either shipped back into the United States or to markets outside of Mexico. Altogether, more than half of the U.S. "exports" to Mexico never entered Mexico's domestic market. More than 30 percent of the U.S. exports to Mexico were tools and machines used to build more Mexican factories, mostly U.S. owned and mostly maquiladoras. Finally, less than $8 billion of the $40.6 billion of U.S. exports to Mexico in 1992 actually entered Mexico's consumer market.

The point of all these numbers is this: Mexico is a small consumer market, largely because its per capita income is less than $2,500 per year. But it is a large and growing manufacturing platform for companies that want cheap labor and easy access to the U.S. market.

As if the United States government were not doing enough to help move American jobs to Mexico, a growing army of so-called "facilitators" has sprung up to lend a hand. Now you might think this is a group composed of the chambers of commerce from various Mexican cities. Unfortunately, the group is American, including many lawyers, real estate promoters, and investment bankers — the same bunch that was in the middle of the S&L bailout and leveraged buy-out excesses of the 1980s. The name of their game is to find a U.S. company that is considering a relocation to Mexico. For a fee, the facilitator will maneuver a client company through the official and unofficial channels required to set up a business in Mexico.

In June 1993, several of these facilitators were featured at a Washington, D.C. meeting of the National Association of Corporate Real Estate Executives, an organization of more than 2,000 corporate officials who select factory sites for their companies. In workshops and presentations before hundreds of these executives, the facilitators extolled the many advantages of moving their company to Mexico. *The facilitators' two big selling points were low wages and passive unions.*

Another member of the facilitators fraternity is the American Industry Relocation Services, Inc. This organization publishes a worksheet that can be used to calculate the approximate labor savings for a U.S.-based company that relocates to Mexico. The worksheet states, "you can substitute your own labor & fringe costs, plus total number of employees to arrive at your actual savings." The sample worksheet shows a U.S. company with labor and fringe costs of $15.00 per hour. It shows labor and fringe costs of $1.00 per hour for a Mexican relocation. The worksheet concludes, "Bottom Line: Labor costs in Mexico average about $1.00 U.S. per hour. If you operate a labor intensive manufacturing facility, you will increase your profits by relocating to Mexico."

One facilitator told the Washington *Post* that, "Hourly labor costs are one-tenth that of the United States. There it's $1 to $1.50 an hour, and that's a fully loaded rate." The *Post* also quoted other facilitators as saying, "Not only are wages in Mexico low, but workers are unlikely to organize there to demand better pay, in contrast to workers in eastern European countries who expect a comparable living standard to western, industrialized nations."

Earlier in 1993, the National Association of Corporate Real Estate Executives, in a survey of its members, found that one hundred large U.S. companies plan to expand or relocate operations in Mexico within the next 24 months. These results are similar to the results of a poll done by *The Wall Street Journal* in late 1992, in which 182 of the top U.S. executives said that their companies were leaning toward investing in Mexico in the near future.

The Mexican Buyout

The flow of U.S. companies voluntarily moving factories to Mexico under the Maquiladora Program threatens to become a flood under NAFTA. Well-financed investors are beginning to buy established U.S. companies and move them south to take advantage of Mexico's low wages. The technique is simple: the investors buy marginally profitable U.S. manufacturing companies that are labor intensive, move the factories to Mexico, fill the jobs with low-wage Mexican workers, boost corporate earnings, and then sell the companies at big profits. This "Mexican Buyout" promises to do even more harm to the U.S. economy and American workers in the 1990s than leveraged buyouts (LBOs) did in the 1980s.

An illustration of this strategy is the prospectus of the AmeriMex Maquiladora Fund, a financial group controlled by U.S. and Mexican investors and initially backed by Nafinsa, Mexico's largest national development bank.

According to the AmeriMex prospectus:

The Fund will purchase established domestic United States companies suitable for maquiladora acquisitions, wherein a portion or all of the manufacturing operations will be relocated to Mexico to take advantage of the cost of labor.

The Fund will seek to acquire companies where labor is a significant component of a company's cost of goods sold. It is anticipated that within six to 18 months after a company has been acquired by the Fund, the designated portion of the company's manufacturing operations will be relocated to Mexico to take advantage of reduced labor costs.

We anticipate that manufacturing companies that experience fully loaded, gross labor costs in the $7-$10 per hour range in the U.S. may be able to utilize labor in a Mexico maquiladora at fully loaded, gross labor cost of $1.15-$1.50 per hour. Though each situation may vary, it is estimated that this could translate into annual savings of $10,000-$17,000 per employee involved in the relocated manufacturing operations.

It is anticipated that most investments will be retained for three to eight years, but some investments may be realized earlier or later.

These AmeriMex-type buyouts can be enormously profitable. Under the AmeriMex estimates, investors can save $10 million to $17 million per year for every one thousand manufacturing jobs that they shift to Mexico. One year's savings alone would fully finance severance payments to the fired American workers, the training of the Mexican workers, and the construction of the new Mexican factory.

The most profitable aspect of these deals, of course, is the potential "earnings multiple." Low-wage Mexican labor translates into even bigger profits for investors when the company is sold. The reason is that manufacturing companies are typically worth at least five to ten times their annual earnings. Thus, a $10 million to $17 million boost in annual profits will increase a company's value by $50 million to $170 million.

Which U.S. companies are most at risk for a Mexican buyout? Companies with moderate to good growth, low- to mid-technology operations, and a labor component of 20 percent or more of the cost of goods sold.

Today, 75 U.S. manufacturing industries fit these criteria. They employ more than 5.9 million U.S. production workers. Their payrolls to U.S. workers exceed $138 billion a year. The tables on pages 56 and 57 indicate the jobs at risk on a state-by-state basis using the above criteria. Not all these jobs will be lost — but all will be vulnerable if NAFTA is ratified by Congress.

Making Mexico Investor-Safe

Many U.S. companies have already located or expanded their operations in Mexico primarily under the U.S. taxpayer-subsidized Maquiladora Program. For them, the vagaries of Mexico's judicial and political system are not an obstacle to investment. Other investors, however, have doubts about the political stability of Mexico and their continued right to do business there and, therefore, remain on the fence. NAFTA is designed to calm their fears. Its principal goal is to assure foreign investors that their capital investments and plants will be safeguarded in Mexico.

One NAFTA provision assures investors that if either their plants or capital investment is nationalized or expropriated by the Mexican government, the investors will get a quick reimbursement at market rates. For many U.S. investors who have a knowledge of Mexico's long history of nationalizing foreign companies, this is a vital protection.

NAFTA also guarantees foreign investors and companies that they can take their profits, dividends, and capital gains out of Mexico. In addition, NAFTA guarantees the convertibility of pesos at market rates.

Another NAFTA provision gives foreign investors and companies in Mexico the same protection for their intellectual properties — patents, copyrights, and trademarks — that they now have in the United States. NAFTA discourages counterfeiting and theft of intellectual properties, while simultaneously encouraging foreign companies to shift their best, most advanced technologies into Mexico.

Most important, NAFTA creates a dispute settlement mechanism that is out of the hands of the Mexican court system. It works through binding arbitration undertaken by trinational panels of experts.

A GIANT SUCKING SOUND

As a final assurance to skittish investors, all of these new protections are locked up in an international agreement that is beyond the reach of Mexican, Canadian, and U.S. politicians.

Thus, NAFTA makes Mexico investor friendly — a place where U.S. companies can operate under lax government regulations and with high-quality, low-wage workers kept in line by a tough Mexican government.

For both investors and companies, NAFTA is a terrific deal. But at a price — the loss of millions of jobs that the United States sorely needs. Middle-class American careers and standards of living are sacrificed and Mexican workers are exploited — all in the name of increasing profits.

SAVE YOUR JOB, SAVE OUR COUNTRY

AMERICAN MANUFACTURING JOBS AT RISK BY STATE – Using AmeriMex Criteria			
State	Total Manufacturing Employment	Fit AmeriMex Relocation Criteria	Annual Mfg Payroll (In Millions)
United States	18,061,900	5,988,200	$138,563
Alabama	363,300	120,000	2,359
Arizona	173,500	35,800	811
Arkansas	220,200	15,900	282
California	1,961,800	747,600	17,495
Colorado	176,200	35,500	917
Connecticut	338,600	101,200	2,679
Delaware	62,400	3,000	83
Florida	473,100	164,500	3113
Georgia	545,100	69,000	1,341
Idaho	60,500	8,700	189
Illinois	976,100	305,900	7,585
Indiana	594,100	177,700	4,583
Iowa	224,000	396,800	927
Kansas	187,000	61,900	1,446
Kentucky	272,900	85,400	1,828
Louisiana	174,800	38,100	972
Maine	97,800	42,000	937
Maryland	200,600	42,000	1,079
Massachusetts	489,700	144,800	3,559
Michigan	858,200	239,500	7,458
Minnesota	384,500	103,300	2,401
Mississippi	237,200	88,000	1,499
Missouri	401,400	88,600	1,977
Montana	19,800	6,800	160
Nebraska	100,500	25,600	514
Nevada	25,600	5,200	105
New Hampshire	85,800	42,100	995
New Jersey	590,900	173,800	4,247
New Mexico	40,700	9,300	182
New York	1,054,000	265,900	6,195

A GIANT SUCKING SOUND

AMERICAN MANUFACTURING JOBS AT RISK BY STATE – Using AmeriMex Criteria			
State	Total Manufacturing Employment	Fit AmeriMex Relocation Criteria	Annual Mfg Payroll (In Millions)
North Carolina	801,900	180,000	3,317
North Dakota	17,200	N/A	N/A
Ohio	1,045,400	323,900	28,776
Oklahoma	168,600	51,200	1,165
Oregon	208,400	47,800	1,094
Pennsylvania	962,000	349,500	8,120
Rhode Island	94,600	32,500	613
South Carolina	352,600	70,700	1,395
South Dakota	30,300	6,000	104
Tennessee	493,000	172,100	3,404
Texas	922,700	226,200	5,312
Utah	101,800	22,800	462
Vermont	42,800	18,400	400
Virginia	408,400	94,900	2,006
Washington	353,800	49,400	1,261
West Virginia	78,100	12,000	297
Wisconsin	533,000	178,000	4,206
Wyoming	9,800	1,700	40

Abraham Lincoln
on
Informing the American People

I am a firm believer in the people. If given the truth, they can be depended upon to meet any national crisis. The great point is to bring them the real facts.

Chapter 5

"Selling" NAFTA – Myth vs. Reality

In June 1990, the United Nations-sponsored Economic Commission for Latin America and the Caribbean published a handbook for its members about how to lobby the U.S. government. It serves as an interesting analysis of how the government of the United States really works.

The Commission reports that in other nations "attempts by foreigners at influencing decision-making processes are commonly understood as interference in internal affairs." But in the United States, the Commission says, "lobbying constitutes a lawful opportunity available to [foreign] interest groups to exert influence and to have an impact on policy."

Actually, influence over the decision-making process in Washington is for sale to the highest bidder.

As the Commission report makes clear, foreign interests can buy the knowledge, contacts, and advice of "both famous and not-so-famous former government officials and Members of Congress — Washington's so-called revolving door, as well as lawyers, public relations specialists, coalition builders, marketing experts, communicators, consultants, and many others who have experience in government or on Capitol Hill."

These Washington insiders provide a variety of services to foreign governments. As the Commission handbook points out, the cafeteria of influence-peddling options provided by one prominent Washington law firm includes, "legal services, Washington lobbying, grassroots lobbying, coalition building, public relations, media strategies, economic consulting, management consulting, political fund raising, issues monitoring, and event planning. In addition, other firms offer media production, direct mail, political consulting, and opinion polling."

In short, Washington is a political bazaar where foreign interests can buy virtually everything they need to alter the actions of the U.S. government to suit their needs.

What is especially troubling about foreign lobbying is not just that it is so widespread and completely legal, but that the United Nations is using U.S. taxpayers' money to teach the rest of the world how to take advantage of the American people.

Mexico Comes to Washington

In June 1990, President Bush and President Salinas agreed to negotiate a trade and investment agreement. Two months later, the Mexican government sent Herminio Blanco, its chief trade negotiator, to Washington to do what he called "lobbyist shopping."

Blanco came to Washington with an open checkbook, and he did not go home empty-handed. In a ground-breaking study of foreign lobbying, the Center for Public Integrity reports that among the foreign agents he hired are 33 former high-ranking officials of the U.S. government (see Appendix A). Some examples are:

- Robert Herzstein, a former U.S. Under Secretary of Commerce for International Trade, is now Mexico's lead U.S. legal counsel for NAFTA. Also, the Center for Public Integrity reports that Mexico paid his law firm $5.2 million between August 1991 and January 1993.

- William Brock, the former United States Trade Representative (USTR), is now Mexico's principal U.S. trade and political advisor on NAFTA. While serving as USTR in 1982, he initiated discussions with Mexico about a trade and investment agreement. Later, Mexico paid Brock's firm $191,000 between January 1991 and December 1992.

- Timothy Bennett, the former deputy assistant USTR for Mexico, is now the Mexican negotiating team's technical advisor. Mexico paid his firm $223,000 between August 1991 and December 1992.

- Charls Walker, a former Deputy Secretary of the Treasury, now collects political intelligence from the U.S. Congress on behalf of Mexico. In addition, he is lobbying the new Members of Congress elected in 1992 to support NAFTA. For his services, Mexico paid Walker's firm $727,000 between July 1991 and December 1992.

- Joseph O'Neill is now a key lobbyist for Mexico. O'Neill is the former assistant to the Senate Finance Committee that oversees all trade legislation. O'Neill is now charged by Mexico with the task of getting Congress to ratify NAFTA. Mexico paid O'Neill's firm $455,000 between June 1991 and October 1992.

In addition to its foreign lobbying effort, Mexico has mounted a massive public relations campaign inside the United States to sell NAFTA. Since the beginning of the NAFTA negotiations in 1991, Mexico has paid one public relations firm more than $5.4 million. It has paid another more than $250,000.

Mexico has also hired many prominent Hispanic-Americans to be its NAFTA spokespersons. One spokesperson, Toney Anaya, formerly served as Governor of New Mexico. Another, Gabriel Guerra-Mondragon, served as a top aide to the U.S. Ambassador to Mexico, and, more recently, as a member of the Clinton Presidential Transition Team. A third spokesman, Edward Hidalgo, was once Secretary of the Navy. Their job now is to convince their fellow Americans — especially Hispanic-Americans — that NAFTA will benefit them.

The Center estimates that Mexico will spend more than $30 million on its NAFTA campaign. The Center also notes that this $30 million is probably a low estimate because it is based only on lobbying expenditures that have to be reported under the federal government's Foreign Agents Registration Act. This law is riddled with loopholes. Other experts on lobbying believe that the $30 million estimate is less than half the amount that Mexico will actually spend to attempt to get the United States Congress to ratify NAFTA.

Mexico's political campaign in Washington is extraordinarily well organized. Early on, the Mexican government established a separate NAFTA office in Washington and put a skilled Mexican businessman in charge. He and the Mexican ambassador tightly control their army of Washington insiders.

To help in this process, Mexico has staffed its Washington, D.C. NAFTA office with enough people to monitor every phase of their lobbying campaign. One staffer coordinates Mexico's lobbying efforts with the U.S. corporations that are also advocating passage of NAFTA. Another Mexican official closely monitors the position of each Member of Congress on NAFTA. This allows Mexico to concentrate its lobbying on the Members who are still undecided about how to vote on the agreement.

Another Mexican official manages the "Hispanic outreach" program in the United States. As a measure of Mexico's thoroughness, it also has an official assigned to coordinate the lobbying of U.S. environmental groups.

In addition to managing its Washington team, Mexico's NAFTA office arranges for Mexican officials to visit prestigious forums throughout the United States. Over the past two years, the President of Mexico and his cabinet have spoken before dozens of U.S. audiences. The Mexican message is always the same: American workers have nothing to fear from NAFTA.

The Mexican lobbying coordinators meet with their top Washington agents at least once a week. At these meetings, Mexico's "Team NAFTA" shares information and coordinates its efforts to persuade Congress.

Mexico is aided by many prominent and well-connected Americans who have financial interests in Mexico. These influential Americans contact newspaper publishers, editorial writers, and reporters. Again, the message is the same: NAFTA is good for the United States. To help the influential Americans working on behalf of Mexico keep their message consistent, Mexico's U.S. public relations team distributes talking points about NAFTA and stands ready to write articles that can be signed and submitted for publication by the influential Americans.

Mexico has left nothing to chance in their campaign to convince the U.S. Congress to ratify NAFTA. Mexico has hired a well-known former senate aide to escort key congressional staff members to Mexico, all expenses paid by the Mexican government. Since Mexico began its campaign to persuade the U.S. Congress to ratify NAFTA, more than 76 senior congressional staffers have taken all-expense paid trips to Mexico where they are wined, dined, and lobbied. Mexico knows that individual members of Congress will depend on the advice of their aides about how to vote on the ratification of NAFTA.

Mexico is a good neighbor and a friend of the United States, but the U.S. should not be subjected to foreign political campaigns and foreign lobbying. Former public officials should be prohibited from cashing in on their public service, as so many are doing in this NAFTA campaign. Finally, if it is absolutely necessary for U.S. public officials — whether appointed, elected, or staff — to travel anywhere on government business, the complete tab should be paid by the U.S. Government. U.S. public officials should never be beholden to anyone, particularly not to foreign interests.

Big Business Wants NAFTA

Multinational corporations have had their eye on Mexico for years — not as a market of any real consequence, but as a locale for an unlimited supply of cheap, high-quality labor with weak unions and a sympathetic central government. Until recently, the principal obstacle to this corporate dream has been Mexico's fierce resentment of both the United States and the multinational corporations.

For more than a decade, these companies and many public opinion makers have quietly, but persistently, worked on the idea of integrating the U.S. and Mexican economies. They have done studies, persuaded Mexican officials to sign "framework" investment agreements, conducted conferences, written editorials, and done all of the things that shape public opinion and debate. NAFTA is the culminating event.

U.S. corporations are spending as much as the Mexican government to persuade Congress to ratify NAFTA. These expenditures are far less visible than Mexican expenditures, however, because domestic companies are not required to report nearly as much information about their lobbying efforts as are foreign interests. However, the enormity of this effort is apparent.

The U.S. corporate lobbying campaign to ratify NAFTA is led by a newly-formed lobbying group called USA*NAFTA. It has more than one thousand members, but the group's money comes from fewer than one hundred of those members. The CEOs of many of USA*NAFTA companies served as advisers to the U.S. negotiating team during the NAFTA negotiations. Most of the USA*NAFTA companies will profit greatly if Congress ratifies NAFTA.

USA*NAFTA has publicly stated that it is raising $2 million to spend on pro-NAFTA lobbying. This, too, is the tip of a larger political iceberg. Most of the sponsoring companies also maintain full-time lobbying offices in Washington. These lobbyists are working hard to get NAFTA approved.

But there is more. These same companies also provide major funding for the key business and trade associations in Washington, D. C., such as the United States Chamber of Commerce, the National Association of Manufacturers, the Business Roundtable, and dozens of others. All these organizations and their lobbyists are working hard to get Congress to ratify NAFTA.

Most of these U.S. corporations and trade associations also have large Political Action Committees (PACs) that have donated heavily to the NAFTA advocates in Congress.

Finally, the largest lobbying organization in the United States is doing all that it can to persuade Congress to ratify NAFTA. That organization is the executive branch of the federal government.

It is illegal for the executive branch to lobby Congress, but the White House and the dozens of agencies under its control employ hundreds of people in a category called "congressional relations." It's the same thing as lobbying, but it doesn't pay as well.

The president's "congressional relations" staff is backed by the premier public relations machine in the world — the White House. The congressional relations staff also has the services of economists, statisticians, librarians, and clerks who can quickly find any piece of information needed to sell this agreement to Congress.

NAFTA Myths

A strange thing happens in the executive branch of our government when the president adopts a position on legislation — facts suddenly don't matter. The only goal is to get the legislation through Congress. The debate over NAFTA has reached that stage. The administration's team has one goal — get NAFTA ratified by Congress. In pursuit of that objective, a huge public relations effort is underway.

To sell this agreement, NAFTA proponents are using dozens of sales pitches. If one pitch won't work, then another is tried. But much of what is being presented as fact by NAFTA advocates in speeches and editorials crumbles upon closer examination. Here are some of the premier NAFTA myths:

Myth 1 — NAFTA Critics Are Racists

The quickest way to discredit a critic, discount an argument, or intimidate an opponent in U.S. politics is to label that person a "racist." It happens time and again because it works. Once a prominent official makes the smear, it is repeated by the media, and the victims are then forced to prove they are not bigots. The accusers are rarely criticized by the media.

The "racist" card is already being played by the pro-NAFTA advocates. High-level administration officials are telling reporters in "off the record" interviews that NAFTA opponents are racists. Several Members of Congress are making similar slurs in public. It is, of course, all planned and coordinated. Politicians who claim otherwise should be asked to explain such demagoguery to their constituents.

The fact that American workers don't want their jobs moved to Mexico is not "racist."

Myth 2 — NAFTA Will Create More and Better U.S. Jobs

When NAFTA negotiations began in 1991, advocates claimed NAFTA would create more jobs for Americans. In 1992, during the middle of the negotiations, the U.S. Secretary of Labor testified before Congress that NAFTA would cost 150,000 American jobs. In July 1993, the Congressional Budget Office reported that the total number of lost American jobs would be "well under half a million." Notice a trend here?

The reason that most U.S. policymakers are so blind to the job shifting that will occur if NAFTA is ratified is that they rely on the dozens of "reputable" academic studies that say it won't happen.

Yet, these studies are based on unrealistic assumptions and flawed mathematical models. Most of these models assume, for instance, that the United States is operating at full employment, meaning that anyone losing a job has the skills and resources to get a comparable job almost immediately. They also assume that Mexico will not become an export platform into the United States for Asian and European manufacturers.

As absurd as these assumptions are, they are the least of the weaknesses found in the studies. Specifically, the International Trade Commission, the federal agency that analyzes the economic effects of U.S. trade agreements, reported to Congress in February 1993 that the most prominent of the NAFTA studies, including its own earlier reports, are based on mathematical models that are unable to "capture" the effects of key elements of the agreement. One element is "the elimination of trade balancing requirements in the automotive sector, and rules-of-origin requirements in the computer, automotive, and textiles sectors." Yet computers, automobiles, and textiles are a major component of U.S.-Mexico trade.

In addition, the International Trade Commission concluded that these models were unable to satisfactorily calculate the effects of NAFTA on key agricultural sectors, like sugar, because of "special factors such as changes in government price support programs in both the Mexican and U.S. sectors as well as liberalization under NAFTA of quota on imports of downstream products in the sugar-containing products sector." But agriculture is also a major component of U.S.-Mexico trade in this agreement.

Most important, the International Trade Commission reports that the mathematical models do not "incorporate potential increases in Mexican investment resulting from NAFTA." In plain English, this means these models cannot calculate whether NAFTA will result in U.S. companies moving to Mexico. And since these model makers cannot do the calculations, they assume that U.S. companies will not relocate. These mathematical model studies are worthless.

Let's be clear about this: these studies certainly do not provide a basis on which Congress can make an informed decision about NAFTA.

Myth 3 — U.S. Companies Will Relocate to Mexico With or Without NAFTA

It is true that many U.S. companies have already moved some of their operations to Mexico under the Maquiladora Program. For these U.S. companies, the risk associated with Mexico's court system and political system is not an obstacle. For many other U.S. companies, these legal obstacles are too large. NAFTA is the ticket for this latter group. It guarantees quick payment for nationalized properties at market prices, protects the intellectual property rights of investors, ensures currency convertibility, and allows foreigners to take their profits out of Mexico. Disputes will be settled by a new institution that is beyond the reach of Mexican courts. All these investor protections are in an international agreement that is beyond the reach of Mexican politicians.

If a U.S. company has been sitting on the fence trying to decide whether to move its manufacturing operations to Mexico, then NAFTA removes most of the remaining impediments and doubts.

In other words, if NAFTA is ratified, the stream of U.S. factories flowing to Mexico will become a flood.

Myth 4 — Low Mexican Wages Don't Matter

Dozens of speeches and editorials by NAFTA advocates have included the following message, "If low wage rates mattered in determining where to locate factories, Haiti would be the most industrialized country in the hemisphere." Sometimes, Bangladesh is substituted for Haiti. The real reason U.S. manufacturers do not go to Haiti or Bangladesh is that these countries don't have the political stability or investment guarantees of NAFTA.

The argument made by these advocates is that Mexico's low wages reflect low productivity, giving companies little reason to relocate.

This argument is wrong on three counts. First, Mexican workers are very good. Dozens of articles in leading publications, such as the *New York Times* and *Business Week* document that although overall U.S. productivity is much greater than Mexico's, the productivity of the new Mexican plants operated by U.S. corporations is fully competitive with plants located anywhere in the world.

Second, the vital link of workers getting more pay for greater productivity has been broken by the Mexican government's wage controls. This is why real wages in Mexico have dropped by more than 50 percent over the past decade, even as Mexican workers in the export industries have dramatically increased their productivity. Mexico's government is deliberately using low wages to lure foreign manufacturers.

Finally, labor costs are the principal cost of production for most U.S. manufacturers. They have few means to cut the costs of interest, taxes, supplies, components, energy, and other factors of production. But management can cut labor costs. In the 1980s, most U.S. companies eliminated entire layers of workers. Now, a large and growing number of companies are cutting labor costs by using low-wage, temporary workers and denying them any benefits. Other manufacturers are moving to Mexico in search of cheap labor.

The arithmetic of relocation is awesome. The Internal Revenue Service reports that U.S. manufacturers have average taxable profits of three to five percent on sales. A quick way to boost those profits is to find workers who will do the same work for less pay. By moving factories to Mexico, companies can cut their costs of labor by 80 percent or more. If labor is 20 percent of the total cost of production in the United States (which it is for half of all U.S. manufacturers), a shift to Mexico means a savings of 16 percent on total production costs. For most companies, just one year's savings on labor will pay for the cost of relocation. Thereafter, most of these savings translate to increased profits.

The question, therefore, is this: will large numbers of U.S. manufacturers abandon their American workers and relocate to Mexico if they can generate cost savings and vastly increase their profits under the protection of NAFTA?

Myth 5 — Mexico Is A Vast Market For U.S. Exports

The raw statistics of U.S.-Mexican trade give the mistaken impression that Mexico is a vast and growing market for American exports. A closer look, however, reveals a far different picture.

Of the $40.6 billion of U.S. exports to Mexico in 1992, $15.5 billion was capital goods — that is, factories. For example, when Smith Corona closed its typewriter factory in Cortland, New York last year and shipped its manufacturing equipment to Tijuana, Mexico the transfer of equipment counted as an "export" from the United States. At this rate, the U.S. will go bankrupt running up trade surpluses.

More than $6.7 billion of the $40.6 billion in U.S. exports were auto parts shipped to U.S. automakers in Mexico for final assembly. These final assembly jobs once belonged to American autoworkers.

Another $9.4 billion of U.S. exports were for industrial supplies that were used in the manufacturing of products — a large portion of which were shipped back to the United States.

So, of the $40.6 billion of U.S. exports, less than $8 billion actually entered the Mexican market as consumer goods, food, and beverages. Most of the so-called U.S. exports to Mexico are little more than "work-in-process" inventory that is returned for sale in the United States.

During 1992 the largest category of U.S. exports to Mexico was capital goods — machinery and equipment that will be used to manufacture items that were once manufactured in the U.S. by American workers. The graph on page 71 tells the story.

Myth 6 — NAFTA Creates a Vast New North American Market

NAFTA advocates constantly argue that "Once ratified, NAFTA presents great economic opportunities to all three countries — the United States, Canada, and Mexico — and creates an estimated $7 trillion market for 362 million people."

This myth omits one important fact. The United States *is* the market. The U.S. economy constitutes more than 85 percent of the North American market, while Mexico's economy is only four percent of the market. There is no doubt about it — Mexico has a lot of people. Of the 362 million people in North America, almost 90 million are in Mexico — approximately 25%. But Mexican consumers do not have the money to buy American or Canadian exports. The annual per capita income in Mexico is less than $2,500. The goods Mexican consumers might buy, such as radios and stereos, are made in Asia. What Mexico really offers certainly *is not* a large consumer market but *is* a plentiful supply

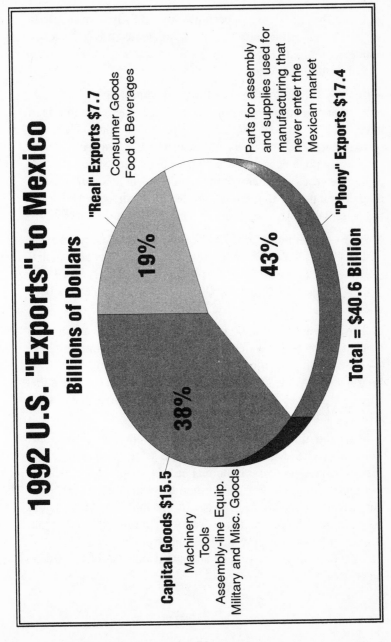

1992 U.S. "Exports" to Mexico

Billions of Dollars

"Real" Exports $7.7
Consumer Goods
Food & Beverages

19%

Parts for assembly
and supplies used for
manufacturing that
never enter the
Mexican market

"Phony" Exports $17.4

43%

38%

Capital Goods $15.5
Machinery
Tools
Assembly-line Equip.
Military and Misc. Goods

Total = $40.6 Billion

of low-wage workers. The graph on page 73 explains these relationships.

The only significant opportunity the U.S. has to export to Mexico is the opportunity to sell capital goods to U.S. factories relocated in Mexico. The grim reality of this arrangement is the loss of millions of American jobs.

Myth 7 — NAFTA Will Reduce Illegal Immigration

As manufacturing in northern Mexico expands, hundreds of thousands of Mexican workers will be drawn north. They will quickly find that wages in the Mexican maquiladora plants cannot compete with wages anywhere in the United States. Out of economic necessity, many of these mobile workers will consider illegally migrating into the United States. In short, NAFTA has the potential to increase illegal immigration, not decrease it.

Myth 8 — Rejection of NAFTA Will Cost 400,000 American Jobs

The United States Trade Representative and other administration officials have testified that if Congress rejects NAFTA, the United States will lose 400,000 jobs. This estimate has been widely repeated. It is nonsense.

The estimate of 400,000 lost jobs is based on the assumption that U.S. exports to Mexico will rise by almost one-third by 1995 — a $13.4 billion increase — if NAFTA passes, or to about a $54 billion level. At the same time, the administration estimates that exports will fall by a quarter if NAFTA is rejected — that is, from $40.6 billion today to $31 billion.

How did the administration get that 400,000 job figure? Economist Thea M. Lee was asked the same question by Congress. She punctured this balloon. Lee told Congress that the drop of exports from $40.6 to $31 billion accounts for 161,000 jobs. But, when Congress asked, "Where do the other 239,000 lost jobs come from," she responded as follows: the loss of 400,000 jobs is not measured from current levels, but from the mythical height of 900,000, which is never actually attained, but only assumed to be possible.

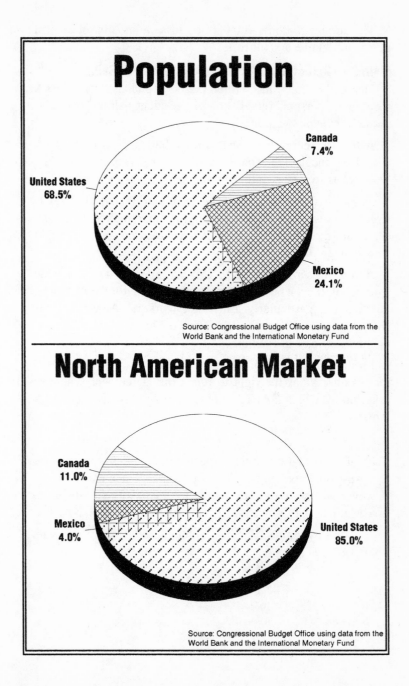

Population

United States
68.5%

Canada
7.4%

Mexico
24.1%

Source: Congressional Budget Office using data from the
World Bank and the International Monetary Fund

North American Market

Canada
11.0%

Mexico
4.0%

United States
85.0%

Source: Congressional Budget Office using data from the
World Bank and the International Monetary Fund

The administration's 400,000 job loss claim is baseless; just more blue smoke and mirrors.

Myth 9 — Rejection Of NAFTA Is A Rejection Of Salinas

One U.S. Senator has written that a "repudiation of NAFTA would be a personal repudiation of President Salinas, who first requested the negotiations."

A former Secretary of State writes that "Defeat of NAFTA would do incalculable harm to the reform process President Salinas has so successfully begun."

Administration officials argue in private that if NAFTA is rejected, President Salinas might not be able to choose his successor and the ruling PRI's dominance of Mexico's politics might be endangered.

Again, let's be clear here. This is supposed to be a trade agreement. It must be evaluated on what is best for the American people, and particularly American workers. American jobs should not be used as a foreign policy device to take sides in the upcoming Mexican elections.

From the beginning of negotiations, everyone has understood that Congress has the right to reject this agreement. The sole criterion by which NAFTA should be judged is "is it good for America?"

Each of these myths is being repeated in countless forms as the Congressional vote on NAFTA approaches. Upon examination, however, all the myths are merely rationalizations designed to give Members of Congress an excuse to vote "Yes" on NAFTA.

It is up to you, the American voters, to tell Congress to vote "No" on NAFTA.

Chapter 6

What's in NAFTA

As the battle over the federal budget began to heat up in July 1993, the national media got a copy of a White House memorandum that told administration officials what to say about the president's budget proposal. They were instructed to skip the details and simply state that the plan will "be good for the country, good for the economy and good for middle-class working families."

The president's staff was also advised to project "optimism, energy, and enthusiasm." The memo said, "Even your most cynical critics will walk away impressed with your commitment... Your body language, attitude and confidence will be infectious."

NAFTA is being sold in a similar manner — skip the details and make optimistic, but vague, claims; all presented with energy, enthusiasm and positive body language, whatever that is.

Is it any surprise, therefore, to learn that only a few Members of Congress have read NAFTA or understand its implications? It shouldn't be. Most Members of Congress are learning about NAFTA from foreign lobbyists, special interests, or from the short summaries of the trade agreement prepared by the special interests and the governments of the United States, Canada, and Mexico.

America's business should not be conducted this way. But the reality of the situation is that the elected servants must deal with an enormous volume of information and documentation. In one sense, they are the victims of their own creation — a huge bureaucracy that is capable of producing more legislative proposals than any one person can possibly comprehend.

While there is no substitute for reading the actual agreement, it is unlikely that very many Members of Congress will take the time or make the effort to read it before they must cast their vote. Reading and understanding a 1,100-page document with language similar to a life insurance policy is something that few people have time to do.

Yet, elected servants bear the burden to ensure that they are hearing all sides of a particular issue and know what they are doing when they vote, particularly on something as dangerous to America's economic future as NAFTA.

The remainder of this chapter is devoted to a summary of NAFTA. Special attention is focused on the provisions affecting American jobs and U.S. sovereignty.

The Basic NAFTA Document

The North American Free Trade Agreement is a two-volume document with a blue cover. The 570 pages in Volume I present the key provisions of the agreement between Mexico, Canada and the United States.

Volume II consists of 450 pages. Of these pages, 147 are devoted to "exceptions" to NAFTA. Another name for an exception might be a "special treatment provision." If you've just finished negotiating a deal with someone, you might judge your negotiating success on the number of "special treatment provisions" to the contract that you were able to get — the more the better. We've already seen several examples of one country or two countries receiving special treatment or exceptions under NAFTA. We'll see several more exceptions in this chapter.

The NAFTA document conveniently summarizes the exceptions on a country-by-country basis. It shouldn't come as any surprise to learn that the United States has the fewest pages of exceptions — a total of 21. Canada has twice as many pages —

42. Mexico has twice as many pages of exceptions as Canada—a total of 84. If you've ever traveled in Mexico and tried to buy anything, you quickly learned not to accept the first offer that someone gave you. Maybe the U.S. negotiators didn't spend enough time in Mexico before they began negotiating.

Because NAFTA incorporates virtually all the provisions of the 1988 Canada Free Trade Agreement, very few changes in trade between Canada and the United States will occur if NAFTA is ratified by Congress. As a result, the North American Free Trade Agreement basically defines Mexico's new relationship with its two northern neighbors. NAFTA integrates a very under-developed country with two very developed countries.

NAFTA — Volume I

Part One — General Matters

Volume I is divided into eight parts and 22 chapters. Part One is very short. In only seven pages, which are divided into two chapters, Part One describes the six basic objectives of the agreement, defines the terms that are used, identifies NAFTA's relationship to existing international trade and environmental agreements, and states the obligations that each nation assumes once the agreement is adopted.

Of the six objectives, *three are concerned with the principal goal of the agreement — protecting foreign investors who do business in Mexico.*

Extent of Obligations — The most important provision in Part One is Article 105 which defines the obligations of the three countries if NAFTA is enacted. It states *that each government* "shall ensure that all necessary measures are taken in order to give effect to the provisions of this Agreement, including their observance, except as otherwise provided in this Agreement, by state and provincial governments."

This is a very, very broad commitment on the part of the United States if NAFTA is ratified by Congress. Not only will the United

States be bound to change its federal laws that conflict with NAFTA, but it will also make a commitment to see that any state laws that conflict with NAFTA are changed. Many existing laws and regulations at all levels of government will be superseded by NAFTA.

Equally important, NAFTA gives Mexico and Canada the right to challenge the legality of our federal, state, and local laws as illegal trade barriers. Any challenge will be considered in secret by a panel of international trade bureaucrats. There is no appeal process involving the U.S. justice system. The third branch of U.S. government, the judiciary, and the American right to due process have been negotiated away. What happened to the system of checks and balances? If the United States loses a decision before this board of international arbitrators, the United States is obligated to change its laws or pay a penalty to the other nations.

The impact of this provision on U.S. sovereignty is neither trivial nor far-fetched. In the late 1980s, the United States banned tuna imports from Mexico under the provisions of the U.S. Marine Mammal Protection Act, which protects dolphins from lethal fishing methods. Mexico challenged the legality of the U.S. law under the General Agreement on Tariffs and Trade (GATT), the world trade agreement. In August 1991, a GATT panel ruled that the U.S. law is an illegal trade barrier. An appeal of the matter is still pending.

In 1990, Canada challenged U.S. excise taxes on beer, wine, and cider. As part of its opinion in this case, a GATT panel of arbitrators established a significant precedent with respect to the effect of both U.S. federal law and state law. The international panel declared that, "GATT law is part of the United States federal law and, being based on the Commerce Clause of the Constitution, overrides, as a general matter, inconsistent state law." GATT ruled that the U.S. federal government must take all measures within its constitutional authority to force compliance with GATT by each of its state governments.

As these examples suggest, NAFTA obligates the United States in ways that are only dimly understood. An international agreement of such importance to the United States should never have been negotiated in secrecy or in haste. Congress should not attempt to ignore the impact of NAFTA on the United States by limiting itself to only 20 hours of debate in the House and 20 hours of debate in the Senate as provided by "fast track." This is reckless and irresponsible. What's the hurry?

Part Two — Trade in Goods

Part Two of NAFTA specifies the rules that will be used to guide trade between Mexico, Canada, and the United States. In 151 pages, which is divided into eight chapters, Part Two defines the future for thousands of U.S. companies and millions of American workers.

National Treatment and Market Access for Goods — Chapter Three describes in great detail the goods that can be traded under NAFTA, the duties that can be charged, the restrictions that can be imposed, and the exceptions. The net effect of this section is to quickly open the U.S. market to goods shipped from Mexico.

Under NAFTA, the United States must eliminate all of its tariffs on automobiles imported from Mexico, while Mexico only has to reduce its tariffs on autos made in the United States over a ten-year period. Mexico and Canada can impose domestic content restrictions on auto makers requiring that significant portions of all vehicles sold in their countries must be made there. *No reciprocal right exists for the United States.* NAFTA makes Mexico a very attractive manufacturing center for U.S., Japanese, and European automakers.

The U.S. apparel market is further opened under NAFTA to producers operating out of Mexico. Open access to U.S. markets will speed the flight of American apparel companies out of the United States in search of low-wage Mexican labor. U.S. and Canadian negotiators won an exception in this part of the agreement requiring that a substantial portion of the apparel made in Mexican factories must use yarn, thread, and fabric manufactured in North America. The intent is to protect U.S. and Canadian textile jobs. However, *Chinese and other foreign textile makers have already figured a way around this provision by building their own factories in Mexico.* U.S. textile makers who want to be competitive will be forced to move jobs to Mexico or go out of business.

For the next ten years, Mexico can prohibit the import of 95 types of used equipment. The equipment that cannot be shipped into Mexico includes virtually every type of construction equipment imaginable, such as scrapers, graders, draglines, cranes, and tamping machines. Mexican manufacturers and foreign equipment makers with Mexican factories are protected from inexpensive imports of used equipment. Assuming that new construction equipment produced in the United States cannot compete from a price standpoint, the sale of used equipment would have been the only hope for U.S. equipment manufacturers. As a result of this NAFTA restriction on U.S. equipment manufacturers, only construction equipment produced in Mexico will be used in the post-NAFTA building boom. It's a cozy little arrangement nicely protected under NAFTA. Whose interests were the U.S. negotiators looking out for?

Rules of Origin — Chapter Four establishes rules that deny preferential treatment for goods produced outside of North America. The way for a Japanese or European company to get preferential treatment, of course, is to build a factory in Mexico. This is exactly what the Mexican government is encouraging investors from outside of North America to do.

Customs Procedures — Chapter Five requires each nation to provide assurances that a product exported to one of the other two participating countries was produced in the country that exported it. The idea is to make certain that Mexico does not become a transshipment station into the United States and Canada for goods manufactured outside of Mexico.

The problem, of course, is enforcement. The flow of trucks across the Mexican border has grown far faster than the capacity of the U.S. Customs Service to inspect the goods. The state of California reports that the volume of commercial traffic entering

California from Mexico increased from 391,000 vehicles in 1983 to more than 786,000 in 1990. The volume will expand even more if NAFTA is ratified by Congress.

According to the General Accounting Office, the United States had 1,800 inspectors along the border in 1990 when their work load demanded 2,500. If traffic increases again by another one hundred percent, as it surely will, the U. S. Customs Service will need an additional 2,500 inspectors. The likely result is not enough inspectors to cope with a flood of imports across the U.S.-Mexico border.

Take this situation a step further. Assume that the United States could put enough customs agents along the border to inspect every item exported from Mexico to the United States. Are those customs agents going to be able to tell the difference between a shirt made by prison labor in China and a shirt made in Mexico?

Energy and Basic Petrochemicals — Under Part Two, Chapter Six of NAFTA, Mexico retains its constitutional prohibitions on foreign ownership of its energy resources. While citizens of Mexico can own oil companies in the United States, the reverse is not true in Mexico. The agreement does allow U.S. companies to export natural gas and petrochemicals into Mexico, and to participate in ownership of companies that generate electricity and provide contract services to Mexico's state-owned energy monopolies. For the most part, however, Mexico kept energy, one of its principal industries, off the NAFTA negotiating table.

Agriculture, Sanitary, and Phytosanitary Measures — Chapter Seven is one of the most important parts of NAFTA. The negotiations on this section were handled in the worst possible way. First, Canada refused to negotiate jointly with the United States and Mexico because it didn't want to risk losing any part of the very good deal they struck in the 1988 Canadian Free Trade Agreement. Mexico negotiated one deal with Canada and another deal with the United States. The U.S.-Canadian negotiations simply reaffirmed the existing trade pact between the two countries.

NAFTA's text contains one agreement that applies to agricultural trade only between Canada and Mexico, and another agreement that applies only to Mexico and the United States. In each agreement, new tariffs are specified on a product-by-product basis for dozens of agricultural products.

Two of the most important provisions, however, concern the export of wheat and corn to Mexico. Under NAFTA, Mexico's market will be opened to U.S. and Canadian exports of both commodities. But, U.S. wheat farmers will be at a price disadvantage because the 1988 Canada Free Trade Agreement already permits Canada to subsidize the wheat production of its farmers.

Perhaps the greatest dangers from NAFTA are contained in the food hygiene standards. NAFTA's lax standards undermine existing U.S. health and environmental standards. Rather than adopt the highest possible food hygiene levels, NAFTA adopts standards developed by something called the Codex Alimentarius Commission, plus those of the International Office of Epizootics, the International Plant Protection Convention, and the North American Plant Protection Organization.

The Codex, a United Nations organization, is a standards-setting body whose members are national governments. It meets every two years to ratify standards — such as those on pesticides, residues, and meats — that are proposed by its committees.

The Codex delegations create a problem because they rely heavily upon the expertise of executives from the very industries that are to be regulated. Again, the numbers reveal a lot: the U.S. Advisory Panel to the Codex Alimentarius at a recent standards review was composed of representatives from 14 food and chemical companies, six food and chemical trade associations, but only two consumer groups.

As in other parts of the U.S. government, the revolving door is once again a problem. The leader of the U.S. Codex team until 1991 was the Under Secretary for Agriculture. In August 1991, he cashed in on his government service and became the chief lobbyist for the National Food Processors Association.

A comparison of the Codex standards with standards of the Food and Drug Administration (FDA) and the Environmental Protection Agency (EPA) reveals the recklessness of the American negotiators in adopting those standards. For example, the Codex allows five times more heptachlor on broccoli than the FDA, ten times more DDT on carrots, three times more aldrin on lettuce, and 50 times more DDT on peaches. The Codex also allows 25 times more benomyl on carrots than the EPA, 40 times more permethryn on apples, three times more lindane on strawberries, and almost two times more aldicarb on bananas.

The Codex and other United Nations' standard-setting bodies are a quick and easy way to get around U.S. hygiene standards. It's really simple:

- Load the Codex committees with representatives from industry;
- Have the industry officials set weak standards;
- Get the standards adopted by the Codex;
- Persuade governments to use the Codex standards in their trade agreements;
- Use the exemptions provided by the trade agreements to enter the U.S. market with foods that would never meet the U.S. hygiene standards.

NAFTA is back-door deregulation of U.S. health and environmental standards.

Part Two, Chapter Eight is supposed to provide any one country protection from a flood of imports from one or both of the other two countries if an industry in the one country is seriously threatened. The provision only remains in force for ten years. However, its administrative procedures are so slow and bureaucratic that a U.S. industry asking for relief would be financially dead by the time any relief action were taken.

Part Three —Technical Barriers to Trade

Chapter Nine, which is only 22 pages long, comprises all of Part Three. It defines the standards that will be used for trade under NAFTA, excluding those for food hygiene which are defined in Chapter Seven.

The objective of Chapter Nine is to equalize the standards used by the three nations in a vast array of areas such as labeling, pharmaceutical testing, communications, health standards, and transportation safety among others. While the goal should be to raise Mexico's standards, which are lower than those of the United States, NAFTA uses international standards as the foundation for setting rules in the future. Many of these international standards are lower than existing standards in either Canada or the United States.

An apparent U.S.-inspired provision (probably from a pang of conscience) allows each of the three nations to establish higher domestic standards, and to exclude imports that fail to meet these higher standards. However, any standard stronger than the official international standard can be challenged as an unfair trade barrier. The challenge will be decided by a trinational panel of trade bureaucrats operating in secrecy.

Put another way, NAFTA forces the United States to justify its domestic regulations to Mexico and Canada. Instead of bringing the Mexican standards up, NAFTA will lower U.S. standards on health, safety, and the environment. U.S. trade negotiators should never have put the American consumer in this position.

Part Four — Government Procurement

This 79-page chapter opens country's government procurement operations to suppliers from the other two countries. NAFTA specifies which government agencies will accept foreign bids, provides equal competitive opportunities to bid, and makes certain that the rules are fair for all.

The big gain for the United States is that U.S. companies will be permitted to do work for PEMEX, Mexico's giant petroleum industry. But the price is high. For instance, NAFTA will nullify the federal *Buy America Act*, which provides that federal outlays will be used to buy competitive U.S. products. NAFTA will also undermine the *Buy America* laws of 35 states and hundreds of cities. NAFTA allows Mexico and Canada to challenge *Buy America* laws as illegal trade barriers.

There is another consideration — government procurement in the United States is more than five times greater than that of Mexico and Canada combined. Hence, Mexican and Canadian suppliers get access to a big market and U.S. suppliers get access to a little market. Some deal.

Part Five — Investment, Services, and Related Matters

Make no mistake about it: this is the core chapter of NAFTA. Although it lies neatly buried in the middle of the document, this really should be the first chapter — everything else is sort of incidental. This chapter is comprehensive, and the exceptions to the agreement are defined in exquisite detail. The U.S. negotiators obviously gave these provisions a great deal of time and thought.

Investment — The protections provided in this pact cover not only investors from the three signatory countries, but also investors from other nations that do business in North America. Foreign investors already have these protections in the United States and Canada. NAFTA extends protection for foreign investors to Mexico, thereby increasing Mexico's attraction to European and Asian investors.

The investment chapter defines a series of commitments, mostly for Mexico, that will make doing business in Mexico much like doing business in either Canada or the United States. In the process, Mexico surrenders many of the restrictions that it once imposed on the operation of foreign businesses and allows foreign investors to operate in industries that were once reserved to Mexican citizens.

In NAFTA, Mexico agrees to allow foreign investors to take home any profits, dividends, interest, capital gains, royalty payments, management fees, and other monies derived from investment in Mexico. This new ability to take money out of Mexico is very important to foreign investors.

In NAFTA, Mexico agrees not to nationalize or expropriate foreign investments. However, in the event Mexico does nationalize or expropriate foreign investments, NAFTA protects the foreign investors by requiring compensation to be paid in full, without delay, and at a rate equivalent to the fair market value of the expropriated property.

The question that investors must ask themselves, of course, is this: if the promise not to nationalize foreign investments is broken, what are the chances that the promise to reimburse the foreign owners will be kept? The most likely remedy for American investors would be to get the U.S. government to impose high import tariffs that can be used for compensation and also permit fast tax write-offs — all of which will come out of the pockets of U.S. taxpayers.

Under NAFTA, investor disputes will be handled by a new institution that is beyond the reach of Mexico's judicial system and the United States' judicial system. Foreign investors will go to international arbitration to seek binding awards for any violations of NAFTA, and secure those awards under both NAFTA and other international treaties.

Finally, with its status as an international agreement, NAFTA's investor protections are beyond the reach of Mexico's politicians. NAFTA is intended to create political stability where it might not exist.

NAFTA also makes some important exceptions for foreign investment, most of which are at the expense of the United States. Canada, for instance, is allowed to review the direct acquisition by foreigners of all Canadian business assets over $5 million and the indirect investment of more than $50 million in uranium, oil and gas, financial services, transportation, and the entertainment industry. Mexico is allowed to review foreign investments over $25 million, an amount that will rise over time.

Mexico and Canada want to know who is investing in their country and whether those investments are in their national interest. Mexico and Canada reserve the right to limit or prohibit foreign investors. The United States does not have this same right under NAFTA.

Canada can also require U.S. investors to transfer technology to Canada as a condition of doing business within its borders. NAFTA prohibits the United States from imposing the same conditions on Canadian investors.

Mexico and Canada's entertainment industries (movie and television production, for example) have important exclusions under NAFTA. Similar exclusions are not available to the United States.

NAFTA allows Mexico and Canada to protect certain industries and to exclude U.S. investors (both individuals and corporations) at their discretion.

Cross-Border Trade in Services — The service industries of the United States are among the strongest in the world. NAFTA will provide U.S. service industries access to Mexico's closed market. At the same time, Mexican service providers will also gain full access to the rich U.S. market.

It is the intent of this section of NAFTA to eventually allow service providers to practice anywhere in North America. It also commits the United States to negotiate the removal of restrictions, licensing provisions, and performance measures that might exclude citizens of Mexico or Canada from providing services in the United States.

NAFTA commits the United States to ensure that the licensing of professionals or service providers is based on competence to provide the service and does not constitute a disguised trade barrier. NAFTA forces the United States to eliminate any citizenship and permanent residency requirements for professional service providers, such as doctors, lawyers, and accountants.

NAFTA is a threat to more than blue-collar jobs. Today, more than 15 million Americans work in professional occupations. All professionals have a major stake in ensuring the standards of their profession. Under NAFTA, those standards will be subject to a challenge which will be heard by an international panel. U.S. professionals will soon be competing with lower wage Mexican professionals in the U.S. service market.

Telecommunications — U.S. companies that move to Mexico may require top quality computer, data processing, and electronic data base services. The telecommunications section of NAFTA ensures that foreign companies in Mexico will have full access to public telecommunications networks, including privately leased lines, on reasonable and non-discriminatory terms. The goal of this provision is to allow foreign investors to have the same level of telecommunications services in Mexico that they can get in the United States or Canada.

Financial Services — Under NAFTA, Mexico can restrict foreign banks from controlling more than eight percent of the entire banking market. Mexico will have to allow this limit to rise to 15 percent by 1999. If foreign banks achieve 25 percent of the Mexican banking market between the years 2000 and 2004, Mexico can freeze foreign financial affiliate's market share at that level. This freeze may not remain in effect for more than three years. Mexico can restrict foreign banks to controlling no more than one-quarter of the Mexican banking market until as late as the year 2007.

The important result of NAFTA's financial provisions is they provide a safe haven for U.S. and Japanese banks that want to avoid banking restrictions in their own countries. The International Trade Commission explains how:

> NAFTA will likely have a modestly beneficial impact on long-term [banking] investment in Mexico. In the absence of U.S. domestic regulatory reform, however, long-term investment in Mexico's universal banking system will be particularly attractive to U.S. and Japanese banks. Once established as financial groups in Mexico, they will be able to operate commercial banking, investment banking, insurance, leasing, and factoring businesses simultaneously. The

United State's Glass-Steagall Act and Japan's Article 65 separate commercial banking and investment banking in these two countries. Both regulations have provided incentives for U.S. and Japanese commercial banks to establish overseas operations, where they may participate more freely in securities-related activities.

In plain English, this means that U.S. banks will have every incentive to get their U.S. customers to establish affiliates in Mexico. Once the U.S. banks are doing business with their U.S. customers in Mexico, the banks can take an equity position in these enterprises and provide a wide array of high-risk investment services that are prohibited by U.S. laws. Japanese banks can do the same. No one should be surprised that U.S. banks are among NAFTA's strongest supporters — U.S. banks can make a great deal of money if the U.S. companies they serve move factories and jobs to Mexico.

While the United States has long permitted direct foreign investment in its insurance industry, Mexico has not. In one of NAFTA's more beneficial provisions, Mexico opens its insurance market to U.S. and Canadian companies. Today, only 20 percent of Mexico's cars are insured, and less than eight percent of Mexico's homes have household insurance.

Under NAFTA, U.S. and Canadian investors are permitted to own a majority position in Mexican insurance companies. Initially, the collective market share of the foreign insurance companies will be limited, but these restrictions are supposed to disappear within seven years.

U.S. insurance companies, to no one's surprise, are among NAFTA's biggest supporters.

Competition Policy, Monopolies, and State Enterprises — Both Mexico and Canada operate state enterprises that enjoy monopoly status within their countries. While the United States has an antitrust agreement with Canada, it does not have an antitrust agreement with Mexico. The basic intent of this provision is to establish a trinational working group that within five years will produce a set of recommendations to the three countries on how to equalize antitrust laws and regulations in North America.

If the other sections of NAFTA are any indication, there will be well-organized and well-financed attempts to use this trinational report as a means to weaken U.S. laws on monopolies and predatory business practices. This antitrust language should be spelled out prior to ratifications by Congress. This is Negotiation 101!

Temporary Entry for Business Persons — This is one of the most important and most overlooked sections of NAFTA. Today, foreign professional workers can enter the U.S. labor market, but only "temporarily" and only if an employer gets a certification that a qualified U.S. worker cannot be found. Also, the existing U.S. immigration laws place a numerical limit on the number of temporary workers. Put another way, American workers have a priority for American jobs.

NAFTA radically alters this entire concept. Under NAFTA, Mexican and Canadian workers in 63 designated categories may be hired in the United States, *even if qualified American workers are available.*

NAFTA also eliminates, by stages, any numerical limits on the number of these professionals who can work in the United States. In year one of the agreement, only 5,500 professional "temporary" workers from Mexico and Canada can enter the United States. After the first year, NAFTA obligates the United States to consider raising the ceiling. But in any case, another 5,500 can enter in the second year, and another 5,500 in the third year.

If any ceilings remain at the end of three years, the United States must enter into negotiations with Canada and Mexico. At the end of ten years, NAFTA allows an unlimited number of Mexican and Canadian professionals to enter the U.S. labor market on a "temporary" status.

WHAT'S IN NAFTA

63 PROFESSIONS That Will Lose Under NAFTA

GENERAL
1 Accountant
2 Architect
3 Computer Systems Analyst
4 Disaster Relief Insurance Claims Adjuster
5 Economist
6 Engineer
7 Forester
8 Graphic Designer
9 Hotel Manager
10 Industrial Designer
11 Interior Designer
12 Land Surveyor
13 Landscape Architect
14 Lawyer
15 Librarian
16 Management Consultant
17 Mathematician (including Statistician)
18 Range Manager/ Range Conservationalist
19 Research Assistant
20 Scientific Technician/ Technologist
21 Social Worker
22 Sylviculturist (including Forestry Specialist)
23 Technical Publications Writer
24 Urban Planner (including Geographer)
25 Vocational Counselor

MEDICAL/ ALLIED
26 Dentist
27 Dietician
28 Medical Laboratory Technologist/Medical Technologist
29 Nutritionist
30 Occupational Therapist
31 Pharmacist
32 Physician
33 Physiotherapist/ Physical Therapist
34 Psychologist
35 Recreational Therapist
36 Registered Nurse
37 Veterinarian

SCIENTIST
38 Agriculturist (including Agronomist)
39 Animal Breeder
40 Animal Scientist
41 Apiculturist
42 Astronomer
43 Biochemist
44 Biologist
45 Chemist
46 Dairy Scientist
47 Entomologist
48 Epidemiologist
49 Geneticist
50 Geologist
51 Geochemist
52 Geophysicist (including Oceanographer)
53 Horticulturist
54 Meteorologist
55 Pharmacologist
56 Physicist (including Oceanographer)
57 Plant Breeder
58 Poultry Scientist
59 Soil Scientist
60 Zoologist

TEACHER
61 College
62 Seminary
63 University

Source: North American Free Trade Agreement, Appendix 1603.D.1, Chapter 16, page 14.

There is more. Once "temporary" workers from Canada and Mexico begin to work in the United States, their "temporary" status can be extended for an unlimited number of years.

NAFTA also expands the concept of "business worker" — which previously meant the owner or executive-level employee of a company doing international business. The expanded concept includes business visitors who are paid from a non-U.S. source. Mexican and Canadian professionals, whether or not they have anything to do with international trade, can work in the United States so long as they are paid from a company in either Mexico or Canada.

Under NAFTA, Mexican and Canadian entrepreneurs will be able to provide U.S. drug stores with pharmacists, hotels with managers, builders with architects, schools with teachers, companies with accountants, hospitals with nurses, and manufacturers with engineers. As a result, hundreds of thousands of professional and semi-professional American workers are going to be put under intense pressure to cut their wages and benefits. Tens of thousands of other American workers are not going to be so lucky. They're going to lose their jobs to low-paid foreign contract workers from Mexico and Canada.

While no one was watching, U.S. NAFTA negotiators radically revised the nation's immigration laws.

Part Six — Intellectual Property

Intellectual property is a short way of saying the economic rights of the owners of patents, copyrights and trademarks. NAFTA provides these holders with strong protections.

The unstated goal of this section of NAFTA is to improve Mexico's laws until they are as strong and as rigidly enforced as those of the United States and Canada. The concern is real because Mexico has long been a transshipment point into the United States for counterfeit goods made elsewhere in the world, and its protections of intellectual property rights are weak. To provide the assurances wanted by the United States and Canada,

Mexico agreed to abide by the provisions of the principal international agreements on intellectual property rights.

NAFTA describes in great detail the procedures and standards that will be used to protect copyrights, computer programs, data, photos, sound recordings, encrypted programs on satellites, trademarks, patents, layouts of semiconductor integrated circuits, trade secrets, and industrial designs. The real question is: can these procedures be enforced?

As with other parts of NAFTA, the underlying goal of this section is to make operating within Mexico as safe for investors as operating within either the United States or Canada. While there is certainly nothing wrong with protecting intellectual property rights, it is a two-edged sword — it will protect U.S. and Canadian artists, inventors, scientists, and engineers, but it will offer additional incentives for moving operations and jobs to Mexico.

Part Seven — Administrative and Institutional Provisions

This part of the agreement defines how NAFTA will be administered and how disputes will be settled. It proposes some radical changes to the rights of U.S. citizens.

Publication, Notification, and Administration of Laws — This section of NAFTA is only three pages long. It binds each nation to establish tribunals that can review and, if necessary, adjust any final administrative actions taken to implement NAFTA. Each country is required to promptly provide the other two countries with information about any proposed action that might affect any provisions of NAFTA.

Review and Dispute Settlement in Antidumping and Countervailing Duty Matters — In simple language, NAFTA takes away the constitutional right of American citizens to seek redress in U.S. courts if they are harmed by several types of international economic crimes, such as "dumping." Dumping is a predatory business practice in which foreign industries sell their products at cutthroat prices often below the selling price for the same goods in the predator's domestic market or even below the cost of production. The purpose of dumping is to unfairly destroy competitors and take away their market share. Although this is illegal in the United States, Mexican and Canadian companies have engaged in these practices many times in the past.

NAFTA is crystal clear on this issue in Chapter 19 which states "As provided in this Article, each Party [nation] shall replace judicial review of final antidumping and countervailing duty determinations with binational panel review."

In the past, the Canadian and Mexican governments have also subsidized many of their companies, which gives them an unfair advantage in international competition. In those cases, the United States can still impose a tariff — a tax on the imported goods — that is equal to the amount of the government subsidy, thereby leveling the playing field.

Over the past several decades, the United States has often been the target of dumping and subsidized exports. Time and again, crime has paid. Dozens of industries, thousands of companies, and millions of American jobs have been lost to these illegal acts. The most visible of these losses is consumer electronics, which was destroyed by dumping in the 1960s and 1970s.

Subsequently, protections have been built into U.S. laws and victims have access to expedited methods to deal with these predators in U.S. courts. NAFTA would wipe out these rights and procedures. The NAFTA procedures are modeled after the procedures incorporated in the 1988 Canada Free Trade Agreement. They have received virtually no attention. Here's how they work:

If U.S. judicial procedures find that Mexican or Canadian firms are either dumping goods in the U.S. market or are being subsidized by their governments, the Mexican and Canadian governments can appeal the ruling by requesting the formation of a binational panel.

The rulings of the international panel are final. Ultimately, U.S. citizens and corporations are denied the protection of American laws within the United States.

The international panels are composed of people appointed by the respective governments. Moreover, a majority of these panelists must be lawyers — a job protection provision conveniently inserted by the U.S. lawyers who negotiated NAFTA.

A panel is composed of five people. The two nations each identify two panelists, and the four panelists then pick the fifth from a list. The U.S. panelists are selected from a list prepared by the White House.

In the spring of 1989, the White House identified a pool of 25 American trade experts from which the U.S. panelists would be selected under the CFTA. Of the 25 potential panelists, 14 were either registered foreign agents or senior partners in Washington law firms that serve as lawyer/lobbyists for foreign interests, including those from Canada.

The list of panelists is now kept secret. These panelists, who in effect serve as international judges, are not confirmed by the senate. Indeed, like the American public, the Senate does not even know who is on this list.

The work of the panel is done in secret, and the proceedings are not released to the public. The only appeal from a decision of a panel is to another international panel, and that panel's decisions are final. These are modern-day Star Chambers — secret courts empowered to decide matters of enormous consequence to Americans.

The authors of this kangaroo court system went a step further to discourage any challenge to their decisions. The CFTA implementing legislation states that, "in the event the provisions providing for the creation and operation of these binational panels is declared unconstitutional by the Appellate Court of the District of Columbia or by the Supreme Court, then the President is authorized on behalf of the United States to accept, as a whole, the decision of the binational panel...." Any action taken by the President "shall not be subject to judicial review, and no court of the United States shall have power or jurisdiction to review such action on any question of law or fact by an action in the nature of mandamus or otherwise."

Furthermore, as one of Ronald Reagan's last acts as President, he signed Executive Order 12662, dated December 31, 1988, which stipulates that in the event the Supreme Court finds that the dispute resolution procedure contained in the CFTA is unconstitutional, the United States accepts as a whole, all decisions of the binational panels. This Executive Order is still in effect. So much for the American system of checks and balances.

After four years of experience with CFTA, there is evidence of how this panel process will work. Canadian interests have appealed the decision of 16 rulings of the U.S. International Trade Commission (ITC). Binational panels were created, and ten out of 16 times they reversed the ITC ruling in favor of the Canadians. U.S. industry has appealed three dumping decisions made by the Canadian government. Panels were formed, and three out of three times they ruled in favor of the Canadians. Of the 16 panels that reviewed ITC decisions, ten had one or more U.S. panelists who was either a registered foreign agent or from a law firm that represents foreign interests.

No one should be surprised to learn that these panels reversed 67 percent of the U.S. dumping and countervailing duty rulings brought before them. In the process, these lawyer/lobbyists established legal precedents that will favorably affect their clients in other cases.

By contrast, the Court of International Trade, which is an independent judiciary and handles all other trade appeals in the United States other than those in CFTA, has a reversal rate of only seven percent. It is a glaring difference.

The dispute resolution mechanism imposed on the United States is sufficient reason to reject NAFTA.

Institutional Arrangements and Dispute Settlement Procedures — NAFTA establishes a trinational Free Trade Commission that will supervise NAFTA's implementation and resolve disputes other than disputes concerned with dumping and countervailing duties. The agreement requires that the U.S. representative be a cabinet-level appointee. Mexico, Canada, and the United States also agreed to form a new trade bureaucracy that would assist in the administration of NAFTA. This is just what the U.S. taxpayers need — another international agency to support.

The Free Trade Commission, its staff, and its mandate are the undefined features of NAFTA, yet this Commission will wield substantial power over U.S., Canadian, and Mexican trade. The Commission is responsible to staff binational or trinational panels that will resolve any disputes over the agreement. These panels would be drawn from a roster of 30 people, who must be approved by each of the three governments, and who will serve a term of three years. These panelists may be reappointed.

Dispute settlement panels will be composed of five people. But the three governments cannot select anyone from the roster of 30 who are from their own country. If the United States has a dispute with Mexico over some point in NAFTA, the United States must select panelists from either Mexico or Canada.

If a panel rules against the United States, the United States would be required to pay some form of compensation to either Mexico, Canada, or both countries. The net effect of this new supranational commission is to shift the judicial power over vital jobs-related issues from the hands of the U.S. Government and U.S. courts into the hands of international bureaucrats.

What's worse, the rules of procedure for this new bureaucracy will not even be available until January 1,1994. Congress and the American people are being asked to accept a powerful new quasi-judicial bureaucracy before they are told its rules and procedures. As with the trade negotiations, the American people are being kept in the dark about something that will have a profound impact on their jobs and future.

Exceptions — Chapter 21 tried to clean up the agreement by clarifying several exceptions. One exception, for instance, is that none of the three nations is required to provide information that will undermine its national security or impede law enforcement. Another provision specifies that if anything in NAFTA is inconsistent with any international tax agreement that deals with double taxation, the international agreement shall prevail.

Final Provisions — Chapter 22 is only two pages long, but it has four very important provisions.

The first provision is that the three nations may modify or add to the agreement.

The second provision is that NAFTA shall take effect on January 1, 1994. It cannot take effect, however, until it is ratified by a majority vote in both the U.S. House of Representatives and the U.S. Senate.

The third provision — and this is important — is the *accession provision,* which provides that any country or group of countries may become participants to this agreement. The presidents of Mexico and the United States have both stated that they hope to have South American countries join NAFTA once the United States Congress ratifies NAFTA. This provision gets very little attention.

Finally, Article 2205 of NAFTA permits any nation to withdraw from NAFTA six months after it provides written notice to the other parties. At least there is an escape hatch.

NAFTA'S MISSING PARTS

On paper, American and Mexican workers have virtually the same rights. In reality, they do not.

- American workers, for instance, have the right to bargain collectively. Mexican workers do not.
- American workers have minimum wage structures that can provide a basic living. Mexican workers do not.
- American workers have health and safety protections. Mexican workers do not.
- American workers have child labor protections. Mexican workers do not.

The glaring differences in labor rights should have been addressed if the goal of NAFTA is to integrate the U.S., Mexican, and Canadian economies.

Likewise, both the United States and Mexico have strong environmental laws. They are strictly enforced in the United States, but only loosely enforced in Mexico. Major investments will be required to clean up the pollution in Mexico. No one knows precisely how much the environmental clean-up of Mexico will cost, but some estimates have run as high as $20 billion.

The further industrialization of Mexico will require additional billions of dollars to be spent modernizing its environmental infrastructure such as the water and waste water treatment facilities, utility emissions, and solid waste disposal systems, among others.

NAFTA does not address these necessary and costly environmental issues. It merely suggests that no nation should use weak enforcement of its environmental laws as a means of attracting foreign investment. Yet, Mexico has consistently done this for many years, and continues to do so.

To correct these labor rights and environmental deficiencies in NAFTA, side agreements have been requested by the U.S. government. Canada and Mexico have both insisted that any such agreements have weak mechanisms of enforcement. This brings into question the international commitment to the enforcement of side agreements.

Many Members of Congress have taken the position that they will reserve their judgment of whether or not to vote against NAFTA depending on the final form of the side agreements. For most of these elected officials, this is just an excuse for them to wait and see what the political winds will be at the time they have to vote on NAFTA. It is vitally important that you let your congressmen and senators know your views. Forms are included at the back of this book.

In summary, each of these three weaknesses is a reason to reject NAFTA:

- A flawed dispute resolution system;
- The lack of enforceable worker protection laws; and
- Inadequate environmental protection enforcement.

Even with the strongest possible side agreements and the strongest possible enforcement mechanisms, the basic NAFTA pact is so flawed that it requires rejection.

Good side agreements must not be used as an excuse to approve a bad trade agreement.

Just as the president's staff was instructed to sell his budget package by skipping the details and telling how it will "be good for the country, good for the economy and good for middle-class working families," it is now adopting the same tactics to sell NAFTA. The White House is aided in its lobbying efforts by the Mexican government and profit-driven corporations from both nations.

The pro-NAFTA campaign is the largest lobbying campaign on a single issue in U.S. history.

Chapter 7

How to Make NAFTA Work

Inevitably, the economies of the United States and Mexico will become more entwined with each other. The question is, how?

Ultimately, there are two basic routes. One is to pit the workers of each nation against the other in a race to the bottom for wages and benefits. The other is to create a complementary relationship in which the people of both nations improve their jobs, wages, and living standards — a positive situation for both countries. This is the choice before the American people and the U.S. Congress.

To adopt NAFTA is to choose the first alternative — destructive competition. NAFTA will pull down the wages and standards in the United States while doing little more than exploiting many of Mexico's workers and their families. NAFTA is a losing proposition for both sides.

To move forward in a positive manner, Congress and the president can take the following common sense actions.

What Is Required Of Congress

The Constitution of the United States gives Congress the power to regulate foreign commerce. While the president negotiates trade agreements, it is done within the instructions given to the executive branch by the legislature. Congress alone makes the ultimate decision whether a trade agreement should be adopted or rejected. Many people in Washington seem to have forgotten these provisions of the Constitution of the United States.

SAVE YOUR JOB, SAVE OUR COUNTRY

For more than 50 years, Congress has handed over the power to negotiate trade agreements to the executive branch, giving one president after another a blank check in trade negotiations. As a result, one president after another has used that blank check to give away entire U.S. industries and American jobs to meet foreign policy objectives. Now that the Cold War is over, the time has come to stop giving away the jobs that belong to the American people.

Trade is really about jobs and wages. Other nations realize this and give trade negotiations a top priority. Japan, Germany, Italy, Switzerland, Sweden, and other advanced industrialized nations would never consider throwing away either the high- or low-wage jobs of their people. The United States must do the same.

Members of Congress must understand they will be held accountable, individually, and as a group, by American voters, based on whether or not Congress faces up to its constitutional trade authority.

At a minimum, Congress should never enact the types of "fast track" authorities that it has given recent presidents. Congress should never put into place a mechanism that in any way alleviates Congress's duty to debate and amend trade agreements. Congress should never allow the president to conduct treaty negotiations in secrecy as was the case during NAFTA talks. Most important, Congress should never again permit itself to be made a "potted plant."

Any trade agreement that can't stand full public scrutiny by Congress before, during, and after the negotiations is not worth having.

Let's make certain this is perfectly clear: you, the American people — the owners of this country — now understand that the U.S. government has been reckless with the jobs of the American people. The American people are now closely watching Congress and will not stand for such negligence again.

The first action that is required of Congress is to reject NAFTA. Congress' second action should be to reauthorize the president to negotiate a win-win trade deal with Mexico. But this time, Congress should give the president a clear mandate on the type of trade agreement that is acceptable.

Give the President Instructions with Clear Limits and Goals

In recent years, the trade mandate from Congress to the President can be summarized as "do whatever you want and we will rubber stamp it." All too often, this permission has been slipped into other bills, as the "fast track" extension was in the House of Representatives on May 27, 1993, with no discussion or thought. It is ridiculous to sneak trade, or any language, into a non-germane bill. If a public policy is "good for America," the public policy should stand on its own merits.

Any future initiation of trade discussions should include extensive public hearings to present diverse views. The purpose of these hearings and, ultimately, a debate in Congress, is to define U.S. goals in specific trade negotiations and the limits that will be imposed on American negotiators. In short, no more blank checks.

Ten Basic Principles of Congressional Mandate

At a minimum, any congressional mandate for a new round of trade negotiations with Mexico should include the following ten basic principles:

1. A Coherent, Long-Term U.S. Trade Strategy

Any trade deals with Mexico, or any other nation, must be considered in the context of how they fit into the long-term U.S. trade strategy. The United States must develop a trade strategy that reflects these realities:

- The Cold War is over.
- The United States does not have enough good jobs.

- The U.S. is $4 trillion dollars in debt and must not do anything to damage its tax base.
- Every other nation plays by a different set of rules.

The questions, therefore, are: how does the United States expand trade with other nations in a way that neither punishes the other nations for their successes nor destroys jobs or industries in America? How do individual agreements, such as a new NAFTA, fit into the overall U.S. trade strategy? And most important, how can trade be used to create more and better jobs in the United States?

As a nation, the danger of failing to think strategically about trade is measured by the fact that the U.S. trade deficit in 1993 will be close to $100 billion. A trade deficit of this magnitude means a loss of 1.9 million to two million good U.S. jobs. A total overhaul of America's approach to trade is critical. It is not too late.

2. Negotiate With Complete Integrity

To ensure that any new NAFTA negotiations are done with total integrity, the Congressional authorization should prohibit all U.S. officials and former U.S. officials from ever working as foreign lobbyists after they leave office. In fact, the U.S. should eliminate foreign lobbyists entirely. They are an embarrassment to the country. Trade negotiations are so vital to jobs and the national well being that the country must demand the best deal from the U.S. trade negotiators. The fact that Mexico's negotiators for NAFTA were advised at every step by former U.S. officials is an outrage that must never be permitted to happen again.

In the future, all countries must be prohibited from mounting the type of foreign lobbying campaign that Mexico has launched in Washington and around the country to persuade the U.S. Congress to ratify NAFTA. The government of Mexico would consider that kind of politicking inside Mexico to be raw, foreign interference in its internal affairs. So should the United States. Mexico's interests can be represented in the United States by its ambassador and embassy. The American people own their country, and only the American people should decide who gets to participate in American political decisions.

America needs a fundamental change in government. The owners of this country must erect large signs in front of Congress, the White House, and every government office that read *NOT FOR SALE AT ANY PRICE.*

3. Do Not Violate National Sovereignty

In the current version of NAFTA, the sovereignty of all three nations is negotiated away to international panels, commissions, and other authorities, including sub-units of the United Nations and the organization in Geneva that administers the General Agreement on Tariffs and Trade (GATT).

International trade bureaucrats, operating in secret, will have the authority to review U.S. laws and regulations to determine if they violate the provisions of NAFTA. Any adverse rulings, moreover, will create substantial financial penalties for U.S. taxpayers.

As a matter of basic principle, the United States should never surrender its national sovereignty. Nor should the U.S. ask Mexico, Canada, or any other nation to surrender its sovereignty.

4. Uphold the Legal Rights of U.S. Citizens

In its current form, NAFTA removes an American citizen's right to judicial review of many matters from U.S. courts and puts dispute resolution in the hands of binational panels whose work is done in secret and whose decisions cannot be appealed.

U.S. negotiators must be clearly instructed that any new foreign treaty or agreement must protect and safeguard the Constitution of the United States and the rights it bestows on U.S. citizens.

5. Increase Jobs and Wages for American Workers

NAFTA permits Mexico to offer foreign investors highly productive, low-wage labor, and lax regulation of business. In addition, Mexico's on-going investment in telecommunications basic support systems they can find in either the United States or Canada.

Already, hundreds of U.S. companies have moved facilities to Mexico. Many more are using the possibility of relocating to Mexico as a bargaining tool to force their American workers to take less pay and to work harder.

If enacted, NAFTA will accelerate the downward spiral of U.S. wages. An unfair trade agreement pits workers from one country against workers from another. Unfair trade is contrary to the U.S. goal in any trade negotiation: to expand the U.S. job base and increase the wages and benefits of American workers.

To stem the on-going hemorrhage of American job loss, future access to the U.S. consumer market should be conditioned on imports meeting basic requirements. One basic requirement should be that imports from Mexico and other developing nations be produced by workers whose wages reflect their productivity and value. To ensure this condition, the United States can impose a "social tariff" at a level that is equal to the difference between the wage paid in the developing nation and the wage paid in the United States for comparable work. Social tariffs should apply to the imports from both foreign-owned or U.S.-owned companies.

A social tariff has a number of advantages. A social tariff constructively uses the enormous power of the U.S. consumer market. It does not interfere in the internal affairs of other nations — if they want to do business with the United States, they can play by the rules; if other nations don't want to play by the rules, they can find other markets for their products. The choice is entirely theirs. A social tariff allows U.S. companies to move production anywhere in the world, but limits their power to exploit low-wage production through U.S. import laws. Social tariffs create an incentive for U.S. companies to keep jobs in the United States and improve the productivity of American workers. They give American consumers an assurance their tax dollars will no longer be used to exploit poorly-paid workers in Mexico or other developing countries, as they are now.

6. Increase Jobs and Wages for Mexican Workers

The people of Mexico are good and they deserve a better life. Any new trade agreement should include provisions that will help Mexican workers improve their jobs, wages, and standard of living. The current version of NAFTA does none of this for the people of Mexico.

Again, the principal attraction of the United States is its wealth and market size. If the government of Mexico truly wants companies operating from within its borders to have greater access to the U.S. market, the United States should require that exports from Mexico to the United States be produced by workers who:

- Possess the right to organize independent unions and bargain collectively;
- Have working conditions — hours, minimum wages, workplace safety, and health care — that are equal to those found in the United States;
- Have the right of association; and
- Are not exploited by age or sex.

These standards will reduce the economic incentives of companies to exploit Mexican workers. Moreover, if the United States establishes a set of standards for imports, the U.S. will not be interfering with Mexico's internal affairs. If Mexico wants access to the U.S. market, then Mexico knows the conditions. The same requirements, of course, must apply to all nations.

The imposition of workers rights standards is nothing new. Several existing U.S. laws contain workers rights provisions. Among them are the Caribbean Basin Economic Recovery Act of 1986, the Generalized System of Preferences Act of 1986, the Overseas Private Investment Corporation statute of 1986, and the 1988 Omnibus Trade and Competitiveness Act. The problem is the workers rights provisions in these laws are not enforced. Now they must be enforced.

7. Do Not Make Mexico an Export Platform into the United States

Any future trade agreement should include full assurance that Mexico will not become a low-wage manufacturing platform for other nations that want unimpeded access to the rich U.S. market. Otherwise, foreign manufacturers will attempt to send products made by 30-cent-per-hour labor in Asia into the United States through Mexico. Strict rules of origin must be required and enforced on all U.S. imports to ensure that they meet the new proposed standards on wages and working conditions. Again, enforcement is critical.

8. Protect the Health and Safety of All Parties

Any new trade agreement with Mexico should enforce the highest health and safety standards. The current NAFTA seeks to use international standards that are often substantially lower than standards now used in the United States. For instance, these reduced standards would permit the import of farm products to the U.S. grown with chemicals that are now outlawed in the United States, such as DDT.

9. Protect the Environment

For many years, one of Mexico's principal economic attractions has been the government's lax enforcement of its environmental laws. Over the past two decades, hundreds of U.S. companies have moved to the maquiladora area of Mexico to evade the more strict U.S. environmental regulations which are enforced. In the process, companies in the maquiladora area have done enormous damage to the environment of Mexico.

The U.S. Department of Commerce estimates that over the next decade $20 billion will be needed for sewage-treatment centers, environmental cleanup projects along the Mexican border, and other basic infrastructure such as roads, bridges, and power plants.

Currently, NAFTA contains a weak provision that supposes to prohibit Mexico from luring foreign investment by loosely enforcing its environmental regulations. This provision is meaningless. The proposed side agreement on the environment, though more explicit, is still effectively unenforceable.

If the environment is to be protected, the agreement must contain adequate enforcement provisions. The standard is simple: products cannot be imported into the United States from Mexico that are produced in factories or by companies that violate either U.S. or Mexican environmental standards. No exceptions. Again, the U.S. market is the carrot. If Mexico chooses not to enforce its rules, that is Mexico's sovereign right. Goods produced under conditions which violate environmental standards should be prohibited in the United States. That's America's sovereign right!

10. The Agreement Must Be Enforced

The United States has a history of making trade agreements that contain strong but unenforceable provisions. Too often, no attempt is even made to enforce provisions of a trade agreement. This practice must cease.

Any trade agreement with Mexico or any other nation must be constructed in such a way that it can be enforced. Then, the resources must be made available to enforce it.

This means having enough well-trained customs agents. It means providing the customs agents with sufficient tools and technology to do their job. It means punishing violators of American laws, whether they are individuals, corporations, or governments.

In the future, the standard of the United States should be this: The American people will only accept trade agreements that are good for the American people and that can be strictly enforced.

The Bottom Line

The bottom line is: the North American Free Trade Agreement is not in the best interest of the American people. Therefore, NAFTA must be rejected when it goes to a vote in Congress.

SAVE YOUR JOB, SAVE OUR COUNTRY

A win-win trade deal with Mexico is possible. To become a reality, Congress must fully accept its responsibility to regulate foreign commerce and provide clear, principled goals for U.S. trade negotiators. Any agreement presented for ratification by Congress must be examined in its entirety with the full participation of the American people.

The American people deserve nothing less.

Acknowledgements

This book is dedicated to the thousands of Americans who suffered from the midwest floods of 1993. United We Stand America salutes the brave, selfless volunteers who worked endless hours to save lives, minimize injuries, and protect their neighbor's property from the ravages of the floods.

Among the many people who helped to bring about this book, I would like to give special recognition to Mike Poss for his leadership, tireless efforts, and creative talents.

This book reflects many hours of work by people dedicated to informing you, the reader, in a fair manner. I want to especially thank Russell Verney and Jeff Zucker for their contribution to the research and organization of the material contained in this book.

A special debt of gratitude goes to Bobbie Van Pelt, Christy Kurtz, and Bill Fisher for their many hours of administrative support and creativity. Without their tireless help, the book would not have been produced in a timely manner.

I would also like to thank Dan Routman, Shari Guthrie, and Eric Grafstrom for their attention to detail in reviewing the many manuscripts.

Ross Perot

The New York Times
on
Mexico's NAFTA Lobbying Campaign in the United States

The Mexican Trade and Foreign Ministries — since their successful push last year for approval in the United States of the "fast track" legislation that authorizes the Bush Administration to negotiate an agreement that Congress cannot amend — have built one of the biggest and most expensive teams of lobbyists and public relations agents of any foreign mission in Washington.

The New York Times, August 12, 1992

Notes

Chapter 1   Out Traded – Again

1. **Exports to Canada and the United States:** President Carlos Salinas de Gortari, State of the Nation Address to the People of Mexico, 11 November 1992.

2. **In the days that followed:** Andres Oppenheimer, "Mexican Government Pays Media to Guarantee Favorable Coverage," Journal of Commerce, August 3, 1992.

2. **Collectively, their companies:** "Purported PRI Financiers Are Among the Richest Men In the Country: Elite Controlled Over 54% Of The GDP This Year," El Pais, Mexico City, Mexico, March 7, 1993.

2. **When the Mexican Government:** Stephen Baker, "The Friends of Carlos Salinas, The President encourages rich cronies to buy state companies and toughen up their own." Business Week, July 22, 1991.

2. **In late February 1993:** Rafael Rodriquez Castaneda, "29 Tycoons And The President," El Proceso, Mexico City, Mexico, March 6, 1993.

2. **He asked each:** John Rice, "Big Business Donations To Mexico's Ruling Party Causing Row," Associated Press, March 6, 1993.

3. **More than 80 percent:** Thomas J. Donohue, "What Truckers Want From Mexico," Journal of Commerce, September 28, 1992.

3. **The agreement, for instance,:** "Potential Impact on the U.S. Economy and Selected Industries of the North American Free Trade Agreement," U.S. International Trade Commission, (hereafter called ITC Study) Washington, D.C., January 1993, p. 40-2 North American Free Trade Agreement, Volume II, (hereafter called NAFTA Text II), p. IU19.

3. **NAFTA also permits:** NAFTA Text II, p. IU20 & p. IM63.

4. **The United States imposes:** The Threat to Trucking Safety Under NAFTA, Citizens For Reliable and Safe Highways, San Francisco, CA.

5. **Mexican truck drivers:** U.S. Federal Highway Administration, Commercial Drivers License Reciprocity with Mexico, Final Rule, July 16, 1992. This U.S. FHWA grants reciprocity to the Licencia Federal de Conductor (LFC) issued by the Government of Mexico, which states that the LFC satisfies U.S. commercial driver testing and licensing standards of the "Commercial Motor Vehicle Safety Act of 1986," 49 U.S.C. Sections 27012718.

6. **These Mexican trucks**: NAFTA Text II, p. IU20.

6. **The New York Times reported**: Tim Weiner and Tim Golden, "Free-Trade Treaty May Widen Traffic in Drugs, U.S. Says", New York Times, May 24, 1993.

7 **Mexicans Investors will still be**: NAFTA Text II, p. IM9.

7. **Only Mexicans**: NAFTA Text II, p. IM1.

8. **In exceptional cases**: NAFTA Text II, p. IM22.

8. **As part of Mexico's economic**: ITC Study, p. 423.

9. **Under Nafta, Mexico**: NAFTA Text II, p. VIIM1 and p. VIIM13.

9. **Nafta allows U.S. banks**: ITC, footnote 15, p. 422.

10. **By the end of the negotiation**: ITC, p. 46, & North American Free Trade Agreement, Volume I (hereafter called Nafta Text &) p. 3A2.

10. **The U.S. team also agreed**: Nafta Text I, pp. 3A4 to 3A21.

10. **Even worse, the United States**: ITC study, p. 43.

10. **The United States will immediately**: ITC Study, pp. 252 and 253.

10. **The remaining Mexican tariffs**: ITC Study, pp. 252 and 253.

11. **In the process, Florida's**: ITC Study, p. 254.

11. **NAFTA also exempts Mexico**: Nafta text, p. 39 & 710.

11. **At the same time**: ITC Study, footnote 3, p. 272.

Chapter 2 A Secret Deal

13. **Salinas also accelerated**: "Mexico's President Salinas Courts European Investors," Journal of Commerce, July 21, 1992.

14. **It gave President George Bush**: ITC Study, p. E2.

15. **But there was a catch**: ITC Study, p. E2.

17. **These insiders**: The Trading Game,Inside Lobbying for the North American Free Trade Agreement, (hereafter called The Trading Game), The Center for Public Integrity, Washington, D.C., May 1993.

17. **One participant reports**: "The North American Free Trade Agreement/Area (NAFTA): How Trade Agreements Affect the Domestic Regulatory Process," (hereafter called Colloquium), Interagency Regulatory Colloquium, Washington, D.C., January 27, 1993.

18. **The Bush White House**: "Preliminary Report: Labor Advisory Committee on the North American Free Trade Agreement," (hereafter called LAC), Labor Advisory Committee for Trade Negotiations and Trade Policy, Washington, D.C., September 16, 1992. p.i.

19. **Of the 45 members**: "Membership of Advisory Committee on Trade Policy and Negotiations," Office of the U.S. Trade Representative, Washington, D.C. 1991.

19. **To get Turkey to join**: Paul Craig Roberts, "Textile jobs discarded in pursuit of Gulf goals," syndicated column, 1991.

19. **In the 1970s U.S. negotiators**: Alfred E. Eckes, "Trading American Interests," Foreign Affairs, Council on Foreign Affairs, New York, Fall 1992.

NOTES

20. **After the trade pact**: Colloquium.

21. **Early in the NAFTA negotiations**: William Libman, Testimony before the Committee on Small Business, U.S. House of Representatives, Washington, D.C., December 15, 1993.

22. **When President Bush announced**: "Description Of The Proposed North American Free Trade Agreement," Prepared by the Governments of Canada, The United Mexican States, and The United States of America, August 12, 1992.

Chapter 3   American Jobs Matter

25. **In April 1993**: Scarlett Bachman, "Deportation of Jobs to Mexico," (hereafter called Bachman)Testimony before the Subcommittee on Oversight of Government Management, Committee on Governmental Affairs, United States Senate, April 1, 1993.

27. **In 1992 Modine**: "Notice of Annual Meeting of Shareholders," July 21, 1993, Modine, Files at the Securities and Exchange Commission, Washington, D.C.

28. **It also matters**: Dean Baker and Thea Lee, "Employer Multipliers in the U.S. Economy," (hereafter called Baker & Lee) Economic Policy Institute, Washington, D.C., table 1, p. 7.

28. **The Economic Policy Institute**: Baker & Lee, Tables 26, pp. 914.

28. **By contrast, 100 retail**: Baker & Lee, Appendix Table 1, p. 19.

29. **More people in the United States**: "Annual Survey of Manufactures," U.S. Department of Commerce, March 1993 reports that U.S. manufacturing employed 18,061,900 workers in 1991. The U.S. Bureau of Labor Statistics, "Monthly Labor Review," November 1991 (reprinted in Statistical Abstract of the United States, 1992, table 633) reports that government employed 18,322,000 workers in 1991.

31. **A decade ago**: North American Free Trade Agreement: U.S Mexican Trade and Investment Data, (hereafter called GAONAFTA) General Accounting Office, Washington, D.C., September 25, 1993, pp.413.

31. **Mexican auto workers**: Calculated from "Hourly Compensation Costs for Production Workers in National Currency," (hereafter called BLS), U.S. Bureau of Labor Statistics, March 1993.

31. **500,000 Vehicles**: ITC Study, footnote 68, p. 48, Mexico produced 989,373 vehicles in 1991, of which 642,981 were sold in Mexico.

31. **Within seven years**: Jay and Maggie Jessup, Doing Business in Mexico, Prima Publishing, Rocklin, California, 1993, p. 90.

32. **Today, one hundred twenty-nine**: Calculated from "U.S. Companies in Mexico," an unpublished report by the Manufacturing Policy Project, Washington, D.C., August 1993.

32. **Mexican workers are paid**: Information for Mexican apparel workers is from BLS, p.8. Information for U.S. apparel workers is from U.S. Industrial Outlook, 1993, (hereafter called Industrial Outlook), U.S. Department of Commerce, p. 321.

33. **If NAFTA is enacted**: Industrial Outlook, p. 91.

33. **The International Brotherhood**: Robert Wood, Testimony before Committee on Small Business, U.S. House of Representatives, Washington, D.C., December 15, 1992, p. 18.

34. **According to the U.S. Commerce Department**.: Charles W. McMillion, "The Status of American Manufacturing and Jobs," (hereafter called McMillion report), MBG Washington, Washington, D.C., September, 1992.

34. **The University of Illinois**: David C. Ranney, "Transnational Investment and Job Loss: The Case of Chicago, Center for Urban Economic Development, University of Illinois at Chicago, October 1992, pp., i and 24.

35. **For instance, the University of South Carolina**: Douglas P. Woodward, "Composition Counts," The University of South Carolina, December 1992.

36. **Half of all the manufacturing**: David C. Ranney and William Cecil, "Transnational Investment and Job Loss in Chicago: Impacts on Women, African Americans and Latinos," (hereafter called Impacts), Center for Urban Economic Development, University of Illinois at Chicago, January 1993, p. 3.

36. **In 1980, for instance, 18 percent**: Ross Perot, Not for Sale at Any Price, Hyperion Press, New York, 1993.

36. **But by 1990**: Not For Sale at Any Price.

36. **The Texas Department of**: "Texas Consortium Report on Free Trade: Final Report" Texas Department of Commerce, Austin, Texas, October 16, 1991.

36. **The New York metropolitan**: McMillion report.

37. **In study after study**: "A Budgetary and Economic Analysis of the North American Free Trade Agreement," (hereafter called CBO Study), Chapter Five, Congressional Budget Office, Washington, D.C., pp. 8395.

39. **Again, the Illinois study**: Impacts, p. 3.

Chapter 4   A Giant Sucking Sound

41. **For more than a year**: "Yes You Can Yucatan," Government of the State of Yucatan, World Trade (magazine), monthly editions, 1992 & January & April 1993.

42. **The United States Department of Labor**: "Mexico's Labor Costs are 15% of U.S. Level, Germany's 160 %, BLS Reports," The Bureau of National Affairs, Inc., Washington D.C, Table 2, May 26, 1993.

42. **The New York Times**: Louis Uchitelle, "America's Newest Industrial Belt: Northern Mexico becomes a big draw for high tech plants and U.S. jobs," (hereafter called Uchitelle), New York Times, March 21, 1993.

42. **The experiences of U.S.**: Harley Shaiken, "Myths About Mexican Workers," (hereafter called Shaiken), Democratic Study Center, Washington, D.C., June 1993.

42. **He found that**: Shaiken, p. 4.

44. **When benefits are included**: BLS.

45. **The CEO of Zenith**: Uchitelle.

45. **The catch is this**: Andrew Reding, Testimony before the Committee on Small Business, U.S. House of Representatives, February 25, 1993.

45. **In the summer of 1992**: Shaiken.

46. **In a bitter two month strike**: Richard Rothstein, "Continental Drift, NAFTA and Its Aftershocks," The American Prospect, Winter 1993, p. 69.

46. **To sweeten the deal**: Sandy Hendry, "Chinese Textile Firms Seek Plants in Mexico," The Journal of Commerce, August 3, 1992.

47. **The U.S. General Accounting Office**: "Assessment of Mexico's Environmental Controls for New Companies," United States General Accounting Office, Washington, D.C, August 1992.

47. **While the U.S. government**: Harry Browne and Beth Sims, "Runaway America," InterHemispheric Education Resource Center, Albuquerque, New Mexico, May 1993.

48. **Many of these U.S. and**: GAONAFTA, pp. 8-9.

50. **Multinational corp**: Robert A. Blecker and William E. Spriggs, "Manufacturing Employment in North America: Where the Jobs Have Gone," Economic Policy Institute, Washington, D.C., October 1992.

50. **In 1992, almost a third**: Calculated from unpublished trade data provided by the U.S. Department of Commerce, June 1993.

52. **One facilitator**: Kirstin Downey Grimsley, "Dark Clouds, Silver Linings Over the Trail to Mexico," Washington Post, July 1, 1993.

53. **These results are similar**: Wall Street Journal, September 24, 1992.

53. **An illustration of this strategy**: Prospectus AmeriMex Maquiladora Fund L.P., New York, February 1993.

Chapter 5   "Selling" NAFTA – Myth vs. Reality

59. **In June 1990, the United Nations**: "Latin American and Caribbean Lobbying for International Trade in Washington, D.C.," United Nations, Economic Commission for Latin America and the Caribbean ECLAC, 29 June 1990.

60. **Two months later**: The Trading Game.

63. **Since Mexico began its campaign**: Bob Davis, "Mexico Mounts a Massive Lobbying Campaign To Sell North American Trade Accord in U.S.," The Wall Street Journal, May 20, 1993.

64. **The Mexican lobbying campaign**: Lobbying registration report to the Clerk of the House of Representatives, USA*NAFTA, March 1993.

66. **In July 1993, the Congressional**: CBO Study, p. xv.

66. **As absurd as these assumptions**: ITC Study, pp. G 1 to G5.

73. **How did the Administration**: Thea M. Lee, "The North American Free Trade Agreement, A Misguided Economic Development Strategy for North America," Testimony delivered to Committee on Government Operations, U.S. House of Representatives, Washington, D.C., May 27, 1993.

74. **One U.S. Senator has written**: Phil Graham, "Leaving Mexico at the Altar," The Washington Post, June 1, 1993.

74. **A former Secretary of State**: Lawrence S. Eagleburger, "NAFTA: Good for America," The Washington Post, July 4, 1993.

Chapter 6 What's in NAFTA

75. **As the battle over the**: Ann Devroy, "Hallelujah! for Economic Change, New White House 'Message Team' Aims to Sell Clinton Budget Plan," The Washington Post, July 17, 1993.

77. **Part One - General Matters**: Unless noted otherwise, the references are drawn directly from the designated portion of text in the North American Free Trade Agreement, Volume I, Government Printing Office, Washington D.C., 1993.

78. **In the late 1980s**: Patti Goldman, "The Legal Effect of Trade Agreements on Domestic Health and Environmental Regulation," Journal of Environmental Law and Litigation, University of Oregon School of Law, Volume 7, 1992, p. 13.

80. **The State of California**: Frank Radoslovich and Philip Romero, "The North American Free Trade Agreement, Implications for California," Governor's Office of Planning and Research, Sacramento, California, May 1993, p. 61.

81. **According to the General Accounting**: "U.S. Mexico Trade, Concerns About the Adequacy of Border Infrastructure," United States General Accounting Office, Washington, D.C., May 1991.

82. **The leader of the U.S.**: Tom Hilliard, "Trade Advisory Committees," (hereafter called Hilliard) Public Citizen's Congress Watch, Washington, December 1991.

83. **A comparison**: Tim Lang, "Food fit for the world?" The Public Health Alliance, Birmingham, UK, March 29, 1992, p. 23.

87. **Today, more than 15 million**: LAC, p. 12.

88. **Mexico will have to allow**: ITC Study, p. 42-3.

89. **Today, only 20 percent**: ITC Study, footnote 5, p. 43-2.

Chapter 7 How To Make NAFTA Work

94. **One basic requirement**: Richard Rothstein, "Setting the Standard," Economic Policy Institute, Washington, D.C., March 1993.

Appendix A

Former U.S. Government Officials Working for NAFTA's Passage, 1989 – Present*
As Reported to the Department of Justice

Registrant	Current Firm	Frmr Gov't Position (Yrs Served)
Toney Anaya	Independent Lobbyist	• Gov. of New Mexico, 1983-87 • Attorney General of New Mexico, 1975-79 • Admin. Asst. to New Mexico Governor Bruce King, 1971-72 • Leg. Counsel for Sen. Joseph Montoya, 1966-69 • Exec. Asst. to the Asst. Sec. of State, 1966
Timothy Bennett	SJS Advanced Strategies	• Deputy Asst., U.S. Trade Rep. for Mexico, 1985-88 • U.S. Trade Attache to the E.E.C, U.S. Trade Rep., 1981-85 • Exec. Dir., U.S. Generalized System of Preferences, U.S.T.R, 1980-81
John Bode	Olsson, Frank, and Weeda	• Asst. Sec. for Food and Consumer Services, U.S. Dept. of Agriculture, 1985-89
William Brock	The Brock Group	• Secretary of Labor, 1985-87 • U.S. Trade Rep., 1981-85 • Chairman, Republican Nat'l Comm., 1977-81 • Sen., 1970-76 • Member, U.S. House of Reps., 1962-70

119

SAVE YOUR JOB, SAVE OUR COUNTRY

Registrant	Current Firm	Frmr Gov't Position (Yrs Served)
Doral Cooper	Crowell & Moring International	• Asst. U.S. Trade Rep., Office of Bilateral and Multilateral Affairs, 1981-85 • Deputy Asst. Special Trade Rep. for Japan and Developing Countries, 1978-81 • Economist and Exec. Dir. of the Generalized System of Preferences, U.S.T.R., 1977-78 • Economist for Int'l Finance and Trade Matters, Council of Econ. Advisers, 1975-77
Peter Ehrenhaft	Bryan Cave	• Deputy Asst. Sec. and Special Counsel (Tariff Affairs), Dept. of the Treasury, 1977-79
James Free	Walker/Free Associates	• Cong. Liaison to the White House (Carter Admin.)
James Frierson	The Brock Group	• Coord., U.S. government's policy on the functioning of the GATT system in the Uruguay Round, 1987-89 • Chief of Staff, Off. of the U.S. Trade Rep., 1985-89 • Special Asst. to Amb. William Brock, U.S. Trade Rep., 1981-85
Lee Fuller	Walker/Free Associates	• Majority Staff Dir. under Sen. Lloyd Bentsen, Sen. Comm. on Environment and Public Works, 1985-87 • Minority Staff Dir., Sen. Comm. on Environ. and Pub. Works, 1978-85
Peter Glavas	Gold and Liebengood	• Special Asst. to Sen. David Boren, 1987-88 • Tax Counsel, Sen. Boren, 1984-88 • Chief of Staff, Sen. Boren, 1984-86 • Campaign Mgr. and Field Rep., Oklahomans for Boren, 1980-84
Martin Gold	Gold and Liebengood	• Legal Counsel for Sen. Howard Baker, 1981-82 • Counsel for Floor Operators to Baker, 1979-80

APPENDIX A - FORMER U.S. OFFICIALS FOR NAFTA

Registrant	Current Firm	Frmr Gov't Position (Yrs Served)
Martin Gold (cont.)	Gold and Liebengood	• Min. Staff Dir. and Counsel, Sen. Comm. on Rules & Administration, 1977-79 • Staff, Sen. Intell. Comm., 1976 • Legal Asst. to Sen. Mark Hatfield, 1973-76
Gabriel Guerra-Mondragon	Guerra & Associates TKC International	• Adviser on Nat. Security issues, Clinton transition team, 1992-93 • Special Asst. to the U.S. Amb. to Mexico, 1980-83
Robert Herzstein	Shearman & Sterling	• Under Sec. for Int'l Trade, Dept. of Commerce, 1980-81
Edward Hidalgo	Independent Lobbyist	• Sec. of the Navy, 1979-81 • Asst. Sec. of the Navy, 1977-79 • General Counsel and Cong. Liaison, U.S. Information Agency, 1973-76 • Special Asst. to Director of the U.S. Information Agency, 1972 • Special Asst. to the Sec. of the Navy, 1945-46, 1965-66
William Hildenbrand	Gold and Lienbengood	• Sec. of the Senate, 1980-84 • Sec. for the Min., U.S. Senate, 1974-80 • Chief of Staff, Sen. Hugh Scott, 1969-74 • Leg. Asst. to Sen. Caleb Boggs, 1961-68 • Asst. Cong. Liaison, Dept. of Health, Education & Welfare, 1959-60 • Aide to Rep. H.G. Haskell, 1957-58
Patricia Jarvis	Gold and Liebengood	• Special Asst., Off. of Leg., Dept. of Health and Human Services, 1986-87
Ruth Kurtz	Independent Lobbyist	• Aide to Sen. William Roth, mid-1980s (left in 1989) • Trade Adviser, Int'l Trade Comm., 1980-83 • Int'l Economist and U.S. Trade Neg., Dept. of Comm., 1970-80

Registrant	Current Firm	Frmr Gov't Position (Yrs Served)
Stephen Lande	Manchester Trade	• Assistant U.S. Trade Rep. for Bilateral Affairs (left 1982) • Office of the Special Trade Rep., including Deputy Asst. U.S.T.R., 1973-82 • State Dept., Chief of Econ. and Info. Services, U.S. Embassy, Luxenbourg, 1970-73 • State Dept., Consular Off., Athens, Greece, 1966-68
Howard Liebengood	Gold and Liebengood	• Sergeant-at-Arms, U.S. Senate, 1981-84 • Leg. Counsel to Sen. Min. Leader, 1977-81 • Min. Staff Dir., Sen. Select Comm. on Intell., 1976-77 • Consultant to Sen. Howard Baker, 1975-76 • Asst. Min. Counsel, Watergate, 1973-74
George Mannina	O'Connor & Hannan	• Chief Min. Counsel, House Merchant Marine and Fisheries Comm., 1983-85 • Min. Counsel, House Subcomm. on Fisheries, Wildlife, Conservation and the Environment, 1975-83 • Leg. Asst. to Rep. Edwin B. Forsythe, 1972-75 • Admin. Aide to Rep. Gilbert Gude, 1971-72
Mary Lou McCormick	formerly of Gold and Liebengood	• Press Asst., Deputy Press Sec., and Press Sec. to Sen. Bob Packwood, 1981-87
Joseph O'Neill	Public Strategies	• Admin. Asst. to Sen. Lloyd Bentsen, 1980-84 • Exec. Asst. to Sen. Bentsen's Texas office, 1972-79
Phil Potter	Walker/Free Associates	• Aide to Sen. Peter Dominick, 1969-70 • Senior positions, Dept. of Treasury, 1970-71
William Ratchford	Gold and Liebengood	• Member, House of Reps., 1979-85

APPENDIX A - FORMER U.S. OFFICIALS FOR NAFTA

Registrant	Current Firm	Frmr Gov't Position (Yrs Served)
Otto Reich	The Brock Group	• Amb. to Venezuela, 1986-89
		• Special Adviser to the Sec. of State, Interagency Office of Pub. Diplomacy for Latin America and the Caribbean, 1983-86
		• Asst. Admin., U.S. Agency for Int'l Devel. Progs. on Latin America and the Caribbean, 1981-83
		• Staff Assistant, House of Representatives, 1970-71
Mark Robertson	Gold and Liebengood	• Legal Director for Rep. Stan Parris, 1980's
John Scruggs	Gold and Liebengood	• Asst. Sec. for Legislation, Dept. of Health and Human Services, 1983-84
		• Special Asst. to the Pres. for Legal Affairs, 1981-82
		• Floor Asst. to House Republican Whip Trent Lott, 1980-81
		• Staff Member of the House Rules Comm., late 1970s
Peter Slone	Gold and Liebengood	• Deputy, Nat'l Campaign Mgr., Mondale for President, 1984
		• U.S. House Approps. Comm. Assoc. Staff, and Cong. Liaison to the House Educ. and Labor Comm. and Select Comm. on Aging, office of Rep. William Ratchford, 1978-83
James Smith	Walker/Free Associates	• U.S. Compt. of the Currency, 1973-76
		• Dep. Under Sec., Treasury Dept., and Dir., Off. of Cong. Relations, Treasury Dept., 1969-73
		• Min. Counsel to the Sen. Subcomm. on Intergovt'l Rel., 1960-62
		• Leg. Asst., Sen. Karl Mundt, 1957-60
Michael Smith	SJS Advanced Strategies	• Deputy U.S. Trade Rep., 1980-88
		• U.S. Amb. to GATT, Geneva, 1979-83

SAVE YOUR JOB, SAVE OUR COUNTRY

Registrant	Current Firm	Frmr Gov't Position (Yrs Served)
Michael Smith (cont.)	SJS Advanced Strategies	• Chief, U.S. Textile Negotiator, 1975-79
		• Deputy Chief, then Chief, Fibers and Textile Div., U.S. State Dept., 1973-74
		• Chief of Pres. Corres. for the White House, 1970-73
		• Foreign Service, various positions, including Foreign Service Off., 1958-70
David Tarullo	Shearman & Sterling	• Nominated to be Asst. Sec. for Econ. and Bus. Aff., State Dept., 3/19/93; not confirmed as of press time
		• Chief Employ. Counsel of the Sen. Comm. on Labor and Human Resources , 1987-89
		• Exec. Asst. to the Under Sec., Dept. of Commerce (Int'l Counsel), 1980-81
Abelardo Valdez	Independent Lobbyist	• Amb., Chief of Protocol, State Dept., 1979-81
		• Asst. Admin. for Latin America & the Caribbean, U.S. Agency for Int'l Devel., 1977-79
Charls Walker	Walker/Free Associates	• Deputy Sec. of the Treas., 1972-73
		• Under Sec. of the Treas., 1969-72
		• Asst. to the Sec. of the Treasury, 1959-61

* Chart reflects those who have lobbied or done other pro-NAFTA or trade-related work.

Source: Center for Public Integrity, <u>The Trading Game</u>, Washington, D.C., 1993, Appendix C, pp. 70-73.

Appendix B

Telephone and Fax Numbers of United States Senators and Representatives

	State Office	Washington Off	Fax
Senators			
ALASKA			
Frank H Murkowski (R)	907-271-3735	202-224-6665	202-224-5301
Ted Stevens (R)	907-271-5915	202-224-3004	202-224-2354
ALABAMA			
Richard C. Shelby (D)	205-759-5047	202-224-5744	202-224-3416
Howell Heflin (D)	205-381-7060	202-224-4124	202-224-3149
ARKANSAS			
David Pryor (D)	501-324-6336	202-224-2353	202-224-8261
Dale Bumpers (D)	501-324-6286	202-224-4843	202-224-6435
ARIZONA			
Dennis DeConcini (D)	602-670-6831	202-224-4521	202-224-2302
John McCain (R)	602-640-2567	202-224-2235	202-228-2862
CALIFORNIA			
Dianne Feinstein (D)	415-249-4777	202-224-3841	202-224-0656
Barbara Boxer (D)	415-403-0100	202-224-3553	202-224-6252
COLORADO			
Ben Nighthorse Campbell (D)	303-866-1900	202-224-5852	202-224-3714
Hank Brown (R)	303-844-2600	202-224-5941	202-224-6471
CONNECTICUT			
Joseph I. Lieberman (D)	203-240-3566	202-224-4041	202-224-9750
Christopher J. Dodd (D)	203-240-3470	202-224-2823	202-224-5431
DELAWARE			
Joseph R. Biden, Jr. (D)	302-573-6345	202-224-5042	202-224-0139
William V. Roth, Jr. (R)	302-573-6291	202-224-2441	202-224-2805
FLORIDA			
Graham, Bob (D)	904-422-6100	202-224-3041	202-224-2237
Connie Mack (R)	813-275-6252	202-224-5274	202-224-9365
GEORGIA			
Sam Nunn (D)	404-331-4811	202-224-3521	202-224-0072
Paul Coverdell (R)	404-264-1998	202-224-3643	202-224-8227

SAVE YOUR JOB, SAVE OUR COUNTRY

	State Office	Washington Off	Fax
HAWAII			
Daniel K. Akaka (D)	808-541-2534	202-224-6361	202-224-2126
Daniel Inouye (D)	808-541-2542	202-224-3934	202-224-6747
IOWA			
Tom Harkin (D)	515-284-4574	202-224-3254	202-224-9369
Charles E. Grassley (R)	515-284-4890	202-224-3744	202-224-6020
IDAHO			
Larry E. Craig (R)	208-3427985	202-224-2752	202-224-2573
Dirk Kempthome (R)	208-334-1776	202-224-6142	202-224-5893
ILLINOIS			
Paul Simon (D)	312-353-4952	202-224-2152	202-224-0868
Carol Mosley-Braun (D)	312-353-5420	202-224-2854	202-224-2854
INDIANA			
Dan Coats (R)	317-226-5555	202-224-5623	202-224-1966
Richard G. Lugar (R)	317-226-5555	202-224-4814	202-224-7877
KANSAS			
Robert Dole (R)	913-295-2745	202-224-6521	202-224-8952
Nancy Kassebaum (R)	913-648-3103	202-224-4774	202-224-3514
KENTUCKY			
Wendell H. Ford (D)	606-233-2484	202-224-4343	202-224-1144
Mitch McConnell (R)	502-582-6304	202-224-2541	202-224-2499
LOUISIANA			
John B. Breaux (D)	504-589-2531	202-224-4623	202-224-2435
J. Bennett Johnston (D)	504-389-0395	202-224-5824	202-224-2952
MASSACHUSETTS			
Edward M. Kennedy (D)	617-565-3170	202-224-4543	202-224-2417
John F. Kerry (D)	617-565-8519	202-224-2742	202-224-8525
MARYLAND			
Barbara A. Mikulski (D)	410-962-4510	202-224-4654	202-224-8858
Paul S. Sarbanes (D)	410-962-4436	202-24-4524	202-224-1651
MAINE			
George J. Mitchell (D)	207-874-0883	202-224-5344	202-224-6853
William S. Cohen (R)	207-780-3575	202-224-2523	202-224-2693
MICHIGAN			
Carl Levin (D)	313-226-6020	202-224-6221	202-224-5908
Donald W. Riegle, Jr. (D)	517-377-1713	202-224-4822	202-224-8834
MINNESOTA			
Paul Wellstone (D)	612-645-0323	202-224-5641	202-224-8438
Dave Durenberger (R)	612-370-3382	202-224-3244	202-224-9931
MISSOURI			
John C. Danforth (R)	314-725-4484	202-224-6154	202-224-7615
Christopher S. Bond (R)	314-634-2488	202-224-5721	202-224-7491
MISSISSIPPI			
Thad Cochran (R)	601-965-4459	202-224-5054	202-224-3576
Trent Lott (R)	601-965-4644	202-224-6253	202-224-2262

APPENDIX B - TELEPHONE AND FAX NUMBERS

	State Office	Washington Off	Fax
MONTANA			
Max Baucus (D)	406-657-6790	202-224-2651	
Conrad Burns (R)	406-252-0550	202-224-2644	202-224-8594
NORTH CAROLINA			
Lauch Faircloth (R)	919-856-4401	202-224-3154	202-224-7406
Jesse Helms (R)	919-856-4630	202-224-6342	202-224-7588
NORTH DAKOTA			
Byron L. Dorgan (D)	701-250-4618	202-224-2551	202-224-1193
Kent Conrad (D)	701-232-8030	202-224-2043	202-224-7776
NEBRASKA			
J. James Exon (D)	402-437-5591	202-224-4224	202-224-5213
Robert J. Kerrey (D)	402-391-3411	202-224-6551	202-224-7645
NEW HAMPSHIRE			
Judd Gregg (R)	603-225-7115	202-224-3324	202-224-4952
Robert C. Smith (R)	603-634-5000	202-224-2841	202-224-1353
NEW JERSEY			
Frank R. Lautenberg (D)	201-645-3030	202-224-4744	202-224-9707
Bill Bradley (D)	908-688-0960	202-224-3224	202-224-8567
NEW MEXICO			
Jeff Bingaman (D)	505-766-3636	202-224-5521	202-224-1810
Pete V. Domenici (R)	505-766-3481	202-224-6621	202-224-7371
NEVADA			
Richard H. Bryan (D)	702-784-5007	202-224-6244	202-224-1867
Harry Reid (D)	702-388-6545	202-224-3542	202-224-7327
NEW YORK			
Daniel P. Moynihan (D)	212-661-5150	202-224-4451	202-224-9293
Alfonse M. D'Amato (R)	212-947-7390	202-224-6542	202-224-5871
OHIO			
John Glenn (D)	614-469-6697	202-224-3353	202-224-7983
Howard Metzenbaum (D)	216-522-7272	202-224-2315	202-224-6519
OKLAHOMA			
David L. Boren (D)	405-231-4381	202-224-4721	
Don Nickles (R)	405-767-1270	202-224-5754	202-224-6008
OREGON			
Bob Packwood (R)	503-326-3370	202-224-5244	202-228-3576
Mark O. Hatfield (R)	503-588-9510	202-224-3753	202-224-0276
PENNSYLVANIA			
Harris Wofford (D)	215-597-9914	202-224-6324	202-224-4161
Arlen Specter (R)	215-597-7200	202-224-4254	202-224-1893
RHODE ISLAND			
Claiborne Pell (D)	401-528-5456	202-224-4642	202-224-4680
John H. Chafee (R)	401-528-5294	202-224-2921	202-224-7472
SOUTH CAROLINA			
Ernest F. Hollings (D)	803-765-5731	202-224-6121	202-224-3573
Strom Thurmond (R)	803-765-5496	202-224-5972	202-224-1300

SAVE YOUR JOB, SAVE OUR COUNTRY

	State Office	Washington Off	Fax
SOUTH DAKOTA			
Thomas A. Daschle (D)	605-334-9596	202-224-2321	202-224-2047
Larry Pressler (R)	605-335-1990	202-224-5842	202-224-1630
TENNESSEE			
Jim Sasser (D)	615-736-7353	202-224-3344	202-224-8062
Harlan Mathews (D)	615-736-5129	202-224-1036	202-228-3679
TEXAS			
Kay Bailey Hutchison (D)	512-482-5839	202-224-5922	202-224-0776
Phil Gramm (R)	214-767-3000	202-224-2934	202-228-2856
UTAH			
Robert Bennett (R)	801-524-5933	202-224-5444	202-224-6717
Orrin G. Hatch (R)	801-524-4380	202-224-5251	202-224-6331
VIRGINIA			
Charles S. Robb (D)	804-771-2221	202-224-4024	202-224-8689
John W. Warner (R)	804-771-2579	202-224-2023	202-224-6295
VERMONT			
Patrick J. Leahy (D)	802-863-2525	202-224-4242	202-224-3595
Jim M. Jeffords (R)	802-223-5273	202-224-5141	202-224-8330
WASHINGTON			
Patty Murray (D)	206-553-5545	202-224-2621	202-224-0238
Slade Gorton (R)	206-553-0350	202-224-3441	202-224-9393
WISCONSIN			
Russ Feingold (D)	608-828-1200	202-224-5323	202-224-2725
Herbert H. Kohl (D)	414-297-4451	202-224-5653	202-224-9787
WEST VIRGINIA			
Jay Rockefeller (D)	304-347-5372	202-224-6472	202-224-7665
Robert C. Byrd (D)	304-342-5855	202-224-3954	202-224-4025
WYOMING			
Alan K. Simpson (R)	307-527-7121	202-224-3424	202-224-1315
Malcolm Wallop (R)	307-634-0626	202-224-6441	202-224-3230

Representatives

	State Office	Washington Off	Fax
ALASKA			
Don Young (R)	907-271-5978	202-225-5765	202-225-0425
ALABAMA			
Sonny Callahan (R-1)	205-690-2811	202-225-4931	202-225-0562
Terry Everett (R-2)	205-277-9113	202-225-2901	
Glen Browder (D-3)	205-236-5655	202-225-3261	202-225-9020
Tom Bevill (D-4)	205-221-2310	202-225-4876	202-225-1604
Robert E. Cramer, Jr. (D-5)	205-551-0190	202-225-4801	202-225-4392
Spencer Bachus (R-6)	205-969-2296	202-225-4921	202-225-2082
Earl Hilliard (D-7)	205-752-3578	202-225-2665	202-226-0772
AMERICAN SAMOA			
Eni F.H. Faleomavaega (D)	684-633-1372	202-225-8577	202-225-8757
ARKANSAS			
Blanche Lambert (D-1)	501-972-4600	202-225-4076	202-225-4654
Ray Thornton (D-2)	501-324-5941	202-225-2506	202-225-9273

APPENDIX B - TELEPHONE AND FAX NUMBERS

	State Office	Washington Off	Fax
Tim Hutchinson (R-3)	501-442-5258	202-225-4301	202-225-7492
Jay Dickey (R-4)	501-536-3376	202-225-3772	202-225-1314
ARIZONA			
Sam Coppersmith (D-1)	602-921-5500	202-225-2635	202-225-2607
Ed Pastor (D-2)	602-256-0551	202-225-4065	202-225-1655
Stump, Bob (R-3)	602-379-6923	202-225-4576	202-225-6328
Jon L. Kyl (R-4)	602-840-1891	202-225-3361	202-225-1143
Jim Kolbe (R-5)	602-881-3588	202-225-2542	202-225-0378
Karan English (D-6)	602-774-1314	202-225-2190	202-225-8819
CALIFORNIA			
Dan Hamburg (D1)	707-462-1716	202-225-3311	202-225-7710
Wally Herger (R-2)	916-893-8363	202-225-3076	202-225-1609
Vic Fazio (D-3)	916-666-5521	202-225-5716	202-225-0354
Jon Doolittle (R-4)	916-786-5560	202-225-2511	202-225-5444
Robert T. Matsui (D-5)	916-551-2846	202-225-7163	202-225-0566
Lynn Woolsey (D-6)	707-795-1462	202-225-5161	202-225-5163
George Miller (D-7)	510-602-1880	202-225-2095	202-225-5609
Nancy Pelosi (D-8)	415-556-4862	202-225-4965	202-225-8259
Ronald V. Dellums (D-9)	510-763-0370	202-225-2661	202-225-9817
Bill Baker (R-10)	510-932-8899	202-225-1880	202-225-2150
Richard Pombo (R-11)	209-951-3091	202-225-1947	202-226-0861
Tom Lantos (D-12)	415-342-0300	202-225-3531	202-225-3127
Fortney (Pete)Stark (D-13)	510-635-1092	202-225-5065	
Anna Eshoo (D-14)	415-323-2984	202-225-8104	202-225-8890
Norman Y. Mineta (D-15)	408-984-6045	202-225-2631	
Don Edwards (D-16)	408-345-1711	202-225-3072	202-225-9460
Sam Farr (17)		408-649-3555	202-225-2861
Gary Condit (D-18)	209-527-1914	202-225-6131	202-225-0819
Richard H. Lehman (D-19)	209-248-0800	202-225-4540	202-225-5274
Calvin Dooley (D-20)	202-733-8348	202-225-3341	202-225-9308
William M. Thomas (R-21)	805-327-361	202-225-2915	202-225-8798
Michael Huffington (R-22)	805-682-6600	202-225-3601	202-226-1015
Elton Gallegly (R-23)	805-485-2300	202-225-5811	202-225-0713
Anthony C. Beilenson (D-24)	818-999-1990	202-225-5911	
Howard (Buck) McKeon (R-25)	805-254-2111	202-225-1956	202-226-0683
Howard L. Berman (D-26)	818-891-0543	202-225-4695	202-225-5279
Carlos J. Moorhead (R-27)	818-247-8445	202-225-4176	202-226-1279
David Dreier (R-28)	818-339-9078	202-225-2305	202-225-4745
Henry A. Waxman (D-29)	213-651-1040	202-225-3976	202-225-4099
Xavier Becerra (D-30)	213-550-8962	202-225-6235	202-225-2202
Matthew G. Martinez (D-31)	818-458-4524	202-225-5464	202-225-5467
Julian C. Dixon (D-32)	213-678-5424	202-225-7084	202-225-4091
Lucille RoybalAllard (D-33)	213-628-9230	202-225-1766	202-226-0350
Esteban Edward Torres (D-34)	310-695-0702	202-225-5256	202-225-9711
Maxine Waters (D-35)	213-757-8900	202-225-2201	202-225-7854
Jane Harman (D-36)	310-348-8220	202-225-8220	202-226-0684
Walter Tucker (D-37)	310-763-5850	202-225-7924	202-225-7926
Steve Horn (R-38)	310-425-1336	202-225-6676	202-226-1012
Edward Royce (R-39)	714-992-8081	202-225-4111	202-225-0335
Jerry Lewis (R-40)	714-862-6030	202-225-5861	202-225-6498
Jay Kim (R-41)	908-988-1055	202-225-3201	202-226-1485
George E. Brown, Jr. (D-42)	714-825-2472	202-225-6161	202-225-8671
Ken Calvert (R-43)	909-784-4300	202-225-1986	
Al A. McCandless (R-44)	909-6561444	202-225-5330	202-226-1040

SAVE YOUR JOB, SAVE OUR COUNTRY

	State Office	Washington Off	Fax
Dana Rohrabacher (R-45)	714-847-2433	202-225-2415	202-225-0145
Robert K. Dornan (R-46)	714-971-9292	202-225-2965	202-225-3694
C. Christopher Cox (R-47)	714-756-2244	202-225-5611	202-225-9177
Ron Packard (R-48)	619-619-1364	202-225-3906	202-225-0134
Lynn Schenk (D-49)	619-291-1430	202-225-2040	202-225-2042
Bob Filner (D-50)	619-422-5963	202-225-8045	202-225-9073
Randy Cunningham (R-51)	619-737-8438	202-225-5452	202-225-2558
Duncan Hunter (R-52)	619-579-3001	202-225-5672	202-225-0235
COLORADO			
Patricia Schroeder (D-1)	303-866-1230	202-225-4431	202-225-5842
David E Skaggs (D-2)	303-650-7886	202-225-2161	202-225-9127
Scott McInnis (R-3)	719-543-8200	202-225-4761	202-226-0622
Wayne Allard (R-4)	303-493-9132	202-225-4676	202-225-8630
Joel Hefley (R-5)	719-520-0055	202-225-4422	202-225-1942
Dan Schaefer (R-6)	303-762-8890	202-225-7882	202-225-7885
CONNECTICUT			
Barbara B. Kennelly (D-1)	203-278-8888	202-225-2265	202-225-1031
Sam Gejdenson (D-2)	203-886-0139	202-225-2076	202-225-4977
Rosa DeLauro (D-3)	203-562-3718	202-225-3661	202-225-4890
Christopher Shays (R-4)	203-579-5870	202-225-5541	202-225-9629
Gary Franks (R-5)	203-573-1418	202-225-3822	202-225-5085
Nancy L. Johnson (R-6)	203-233-8412	202-225-4476	202-225-4488
DISTRICT OF COLUMBIA			
Eleanor Holmes Norton (D)	202-783-5065	202-225-8050	202-225-3002
DELAWARE			
Michael Castle (R)	302-573-6181	202-225-4165	202-225-2291
FLORIDA			
Earl Hutto (D-1)	904-478-1123	202-225-4136	202-225-5785
Pete Peterson (D-2)	904-561-3979	202-225-5235	202-225-1586
Corrine Brown (D-3)	904-398-8567	202-225-0123	202-225-2256
Tillie Fowler (R-4)	904-739-6600	202-225-2501	202-226-9318
Karen Thurman (D-5)	904-344-3044	202-225-1002	202-226-0329
Cliff Stearns (R-6)	904-351-8777	202-225-5744	202-225-3973
John Mica (R-7)	407-339-8080	202-225-4035	202-226-0821
Bill McCollum (R-8)	407-645-3100	202-225-2176	202-225-0999
Michael Bilirakis (R-9)	813-441-3721	202-225-5755	202-225-4085
C.W. Bill Young (R-10)	813-893-3191	202-225-5961	202-225-9764
Sam Gibbons (D-11)	813-870-2101	202-225-3376	
Charles Canady (R-12)	813-688-2651	202-225-1252	202-225-2279
Dan Miller (R-13)	813-951-6643	202-225-5015	202-226-0828
Porter J. Goss (R-14)	813-332-4677	202-225-2536	202-225-6820
Jim Bacchus (D-15)	407-632-1776	202-225-3671	202-225-9039
Tom Lewis (R-16)	407-627-6192	202-225-5792	202-225-1860
Carrie Meek (D-17)	305-381-9541	202-225-4506	202-226-0777
Ileana RosLehtinen (R-18)	305-262-1800	202-225-3931	202-225-5620
Harry Johnston II (D-19)	407-732-4000	202-225-3001	202-225-8791
Peter Deutsch (D-20)	305-437-3936	202-225-7931	202-225-8456
Lincoln Diaz-Balart (R-21)	305-470-8555	202-225-4211	202-225-8576
E. Clay Shaw, Jr. (R-22)	305-522-1800	202-225-3026	202-225-8398
Alcee Hastings (D-23)	305-733-2800	202-225-1313	202-226-0690
GEORGIA			
Jack Kingston (R-1)	912-352-0101	202-225-5831	202-226-2269

APPENDIX B - TELEPHONE AND FAX NUMBERS

	State Office	Washington Off	Fax
Sanford Bishop (D-2)	912-439-8067	202-225-3631	202-225-2203
Michael (Mac)Collins (R-3)	404-603-3395	202-225-5901	202-225-2515
John Linder (R-4)	404-936-9400	202-225-4272	202-225-4696
John Lewis (D-5)	404-659-0116	202-225-3801	202-225-0351
Newt Gingrich (R-6)	404-565-6398	202-225-4501	202-225-4656
George (Buddy)Darden (D-7)	404-422-4480	202-225-2931	202-225-0473
J. Roy Rowland (D-8)	912-743-0150	202-225-6531	202-225-7719
Nathan Deal (D-9)	404-535-2592	202-225-5211	202-225-8272
Don Johnson (D-10)	706-353-6444	202-225-4101	202-226-1466
Cynthia McKinney (D-11)	404-244-9902	202-225-1605	202-226-0691

GUAM

	State Office	Washington Off	Fax
Robert Underwood (D)	671-477-2587	202-225-1188	202-226-0341

HAWAII

	State Office	Washington Off	Fax
Neil Abercrombie (D-1)	808-541-2570	202-225-2726	202-225-4580
Patsy Mink (D-2)	808-541-1986	202-225-4906	202-225-4987

IOWA

	State Office	Washington Off	Fax
Jim Leach (R-1)	319-326-1841	202-225-6576	202-226-1278
Jim Nussle (R-2)	319-235-1109	202-225-2911	202-225-9129
Jim Lightfoot (R-3)	712-246-1984	202-225-3806	202-225-6973
Neal Smith (D-4)	515-284-4634	202-225-4426	
Fred Grandy (R-5)	712-276-5800	202-225-5476	202-225-5796

IDAHO

	State Office	Washington Off	Fax
Larry LaRocco (D-1)	208-343-4211	202-225-6611	202-226-1213
Michael Crapo (R-2)	208-334-1953	202-225-5531	202-225-8216

ILLINOIS

	State Office	Washington Off	Fax
Bobby Rush (D-1)	708-422-4055	202-225-4372	202-226-0333
Mel Reynolds (D-2)	312-568-7900	202-225-0773	202-225-0774
William O. Lipinski (D-3)	312-886-0481	202-225-5701	202-225-1012
Luis Gutierrez (D-4)	312-509-0999	202-225-8203	202-225-7810
Dan Rostenkowski (D-5)	312-481-0095	202-225-4061	202-225-4064
Henry J. Hyde (R-6)	708-832-5950	202-225-4561	202-226-1240
Cardiss Collins (D-7)	312-353-5754	202-225-5006	202-225-8396
Phillip M. Crane (R-8)	708-394-0790	202-225-3711	202-225-7830
Sidney R. Yates (D-9)	312-353-4596	202-225-2111	202-225-3493
John Edward Porter (R-10)	708-940-0202	202-225-4835	202-225-0157
George E. Sangmeister (D-11)	815-740-2028	202-225-3635	202-225-4447
Jerry F. Costello (D-12)	618-233-8026	202-225-5661	202-225-0285
Harris W. Fawell (R-13)	708-655-2052	202-225-3515	202-225-9420
J. Dennis Hastert (R-14)	708-406-1114	202-225-2976	202-225-0697
Thomas Ewing (R-15)	815-844-7660	202-225-2371	202-225-8071
Donald Manzullo (R-16)	815-394-1231	202-225-5676	202-225-5284
Lane Evans (D-17)	309-793-5760	202-225-5905	202-225-5396
Robert H. Michel (R-18)	309-671-7027	202-225-6201	202-225-9249
Glenn Poshard (D-19)	618-993-8532	202-225-5201	202-225-1541
Richard J. Durbin (D-20)	217-492-4062	202-225-5271	202-225-0170

INDIANA

	State Office	Washington Off	Fax
Peter J. Visclosky (D-1)	219-884-1177	202-225-2461	202-225-2493
Philip R. Sharp (D-2)	317-747-5566	202-225-3021	202-225-8140
Tim J. Roemer (D-3)	219-288-3301	202-225-3915	202-225-6798
Jill L. Long (D-4)	219-424-3041	202-225-4436	202-225-8810
Steve Buyer (R-5)	317-454-7551	202-225-5037	
Dan Burton (R-6)	317-848-0201	202-225-2276	202-225-0016
John T. Myers (R-7)	812-238-1619	202-225-5805	202-225-1649

131

SAVE YOUR JOB, SAVE OUR COUNTRY

	State Office	Washington Off	Fax
Frank McCloskey (D-8)	812-465-6484	202-225-4636	202-225-4688
Lee H. Hamiliton (D-9)	812-288-3999	202-225-5315	202-225-1101
Andrew Jacobs, Jr. (D-10)	317-226-7331	202-225-4011	202-226-4093
KANSAS			
Pat Roberts (R-1)	316-227-2244	202-225-2715	202-225-5375
Jim Slattery (D-2)	913-233-2503	202-225-6601	202-225-1445
Jan Meyers (R-3)	913-621-0832	202-225-2865	202-225-0554
Dan Glickman (D-4)	316-262-8396	202-225-6216	202-225-5398
KENTUCKY			
Tom Barlow (D-1)	502-444-7216	202-225-3115	202-225-2169
William H. Natcher (D-2)	502-842-7376	202-225-3501	
Romano Mazzoli (D-3)	502-582-5129	202-225-5401	
Jim Bunning (R-4)	606-341-2602	202-225-3465	202-225-0003
Harold Rogers (R-5)	606-679-8346	202-225-4601	202-225-0940
Scotty Baesler (D-6)	606-253-1124	202-225-4706	202-225-2122
LOUISIANA			
Bob Livingston (R-1)	504-589-2753	202-225-3015	202-225-0739
William J. Jefferson (D-2)	504-589-2274	202-225-6636	202-225-1988
W.J. (Billy)Tauzin (D-3)	504-876-3033	202-225-4031	202-225-0563
Cleo Fields (D-4)	504-343-9773	202-225-8490	202-225-8959
Jim McCrery (R-5)	318-226-5080	202-225-2777	202-225-8039
Richard H. Baker (R-6)	504-929-7711	202-225-3901	202-225-7313
James A. Hayes (D-7)	318-233-4773	202-225-2031	202-225-1175
MASSACHUSETTS			
John W. Olver (D-1)	413-532-7010	202-225-5335	202-226-1224
Richard E. Neal (D-2)	413-785-0325	202-225-5601	202-225-8112
Peter Blute (R-3)	508-752-6789	202-225-6101	202-225-2217
Barney Frank (D-4)	617-332-3920	202-225-5931	202-225-0182
Marty Meehan (D-5)	508-459-0101	202-225-3411	202-225-0771
Peter Torkildsen (R-6)	508-745-5800	202-225-8020	202-225-8037
Edward J. Markey (D-7)	617-396-2900	202-225-2836	202-225-8689
Joseph P. Kennedy (D-8)	617-242-0200	202-225-5111	202-225-9322
Joe Moakley (D-9)	617-565-2920	202-225-8273	202-225-3984
Gerry E. Studds (D-10)	508-771-0666	202-225-3111	202-225-2212
MARYLAND			
Wayne Gilchrest (R-1)	410-778-9407	202-225-5311	202-225-0254
Helen Delich Bentley (R-2)	410-337-7222	202-225-3061	202-225-4251
Benjamin L Cardin (D-3)	410-433-8886	202-225-4016	202-225-9219
Albert Wynn (D-4)	301-350-5055	202-225-8699	202-225-8714
Steny H. Hoyer (D-5)	301-464-6440	202-225-4131	202-225-4300
Roscoe Bartlett (R-6)	301-662-8622	202-225-2721	202-225-2193
Kweisi Mfume, (D-7)	410-367-1900	202-225-4741	202-225-3178
Constance A. Morella (R-8)	301-424-3501	202-225-5341	202-225-1389
MAINE			
Thomas H. Andrews (D-1)	207-772-8240	202-225-6116	202-225-9065
Olympia J. Snowe (R-2)	207-786-2451	202-225-6306	202-225-8297
MICHIGAN			
Bart Stupak (D-1)	616-929-4711	202-225-4735	202-225-4744
Peter Hoekstra (R-2)	616-395-0030	202-225-4401	202-226-0779
Vacant (R-3)			
Dave Camp (R-4)	517-631-2552	202-225-3561	202-225-9679

APPENDIX B - TELEPHONE AND FAX NUMBERS

	State Office	Washington Off	Fax
James Barcia (D-5)	517-754-6075	202-225-8171	202-225-2168
Fredrick S. Upton (R-6)	616-982-1986	202-225-3761	202-225-4986
Nick Smith (R-7)	517-783-4486	202-225-6276	202-225-6281
Bob Carr (D-8)	517-351-7203	202-225-4872	202-225-1260
Dale E. Kildee (D-9)	313-239-1437	202-225-3611	202-225-6393
David E. Bonior (D-10)	313-469-3232	202-225-2106	202-226-1169
Joseph Knollenberg (R-11)	313-851-1366	202-225-5802	202-226-2356
Sander M. Levin (D-12)	313-559-4444	202-225-4961	202-226-1033
William D. Ford (D-13)	313-722-1411	202-225-6261	202-225-0489
John Conyers, Jr. (D-14)	313-961-5670	202-225-5126	202-225-0072
Barbara-Rose Collins (D-15)	313-567-2233	202-225-2261	202-225-6645
John D. Dingell (D-16)	313-846-1276	202-225-4071	202-225-7426

MINNESOTA

	State Office	Washington Off	Fax
Timothy J. Penny (D-1)	507-455-9151	202-225-2472	202-225-0051
David Minge (D-2)	612-269-9311	202-225-2331	202-226-0836
Jim Ramstad (R-3)	612-881-4600	202-225-2871	202-225-6351
Bruce F. Vento (D-4)	612-224-4503	202-225-6631	202-225-1968
Martin Olav Sabo (D-5)	612-348-1649	202-225-4755	202-225-4886
Rod Grams (R-6)	612-427-5921	202-225-2271	202-225-9802
Collin Peterson (D-7)	218-847-5056	202-225-2165	202-225-1593
James L. Oberstar (D-8)	218-727-7474	202-225-6211	202-225-0699

MISSOURI

	State Office	Washington Off	Fax
William (Bill)Clay (D-1)	314-725-5770	202-225-2406	202-225-1725
James Talent (R-2)	314-872-9561	202-225-2561	202-225-2563
Richard A. Gephardt (D-3)	314-631-9959	202-225-2671	202-225-7414
Ike Skelton (D-4)	816-228-4242	202-225-2876	202-225-2695
Alan Wheat (D-5)	816-842-4545	202-225-4535	202-225-5990
Pat Danner (D-6)	816-455-2256	202-225-7041	202-225-8221
Melton D. Hancock (R-7)	417-862-4317	202-225-6536	202-225-7700
Bill Emerson (R-8)	314-335-0101	202-225-4404	202-225-9621
Harold L. Volkmer (D-9)	314-221-1200	202-225-2956	202-225-7834

MISSISSIPPI

	State Office	Washington Off	Fax
Jamie L. Whitten (D-1)	601-647-2413	202-225-4306	202-225-4328
BennyThompson (2)	601-866-9003	202-225-5876	202-225-5898
G.V. Montgomery (D-3)	601-693-6681	202-225-5031	202-225-3375
Mike Parker (D-4)	601-965-4085	202-225-5865	202-225-5886
Gene Taylor (D-5)	601-864-7670	202-225-5772	202-225-7074

MONTANA

	State Office	Washington Off	Fax
Pat Williams (D)	406-443-7878	202-225-3211	202-226-0244

NORTH CAROLINA

	State Office	Washington Off	Fax
Eva Clayton (D-1)	919-257-4800	202-225-3101	202-225-3354
Tim Valentine (D-2)	919-383-9404	202-225-4531	202-225-1539
H. Martin Lancaster (D-3)	919-736-1844	202-225-3415	202-225-0666
David E. Price (D-4)	919-856-4611	202-225-1784	202-225-6314
Stephen L. Neal (D-5)	919-631-5125	202-225-2071	202-225-4060
Howard Coble (R-6)	919-333-5005	202-225-3065	202-225-8611
Charlie Rose III (D-7)	919-323-0260	202-225-2731	202-225-2470
W.G. (Bill)Hefner (D-8)	704-786-1612	202-225-3715	202-225-4036
J. Alex McMillan (R-9)	704-372-1976	202-225-1976	202-225-8995
Cass Ballenger (R-10)	704-327-6100	202-225-2576	202-225-0316
Charles H. Taylor (R-11)	704-251-1988	202-225-6401	202-225-0519
Melvin Watt (D-12)	704-344-9950	202-225-1510	202-225-1512

SAVE YOUR JOB, SAVE OUR COUNTRY

	State Office	Washington Off	Fax
NORTH DAKOTA			
Earl Pomeroy (D)	701-224-0355	202-225-2611	202-226-0893
NEBRASKA			
Doug Bereuter (R-1)	402-438-1598	202-225-4806	202-226-1148
Peter Hoagland (D-2)	402-344-8701	202-225-4155	202-225-4684
Bill Barrett (R-3)	308-381-5555	202-225-6435	202-225-0207
NEW HAMPSHIRE			
Bill H. Zeliff, Jr. (R-1)	603-669-6330	202-225-5456	202-225-4370
Dick Swett (D-2)	603-224-6621	202-225-5206	202-225-0046
NEW JERSEY			
Robert E. Andrews (D-1)	609-627-9000	202-225-6501	202-225-6583
William J. Hughes (D-2)	609-927-9063	202-225-6572	202-225-8530
Jim Saxton (R-3)	609-261-5800	202-225-4765	202-225-0778
Christopher H. Smith (R-4)	609-890-2800	202-225-3765	202-225-7768
Marge Roukema (R-5)	201-447-3900	202-225-4465	202-225-9048
Frank Pallone, Jr. (D-6)	908-571-1140	202-225-4671	202-225-9665
Bob Franks (R-7)	908-686-5576	202-225-5361	202-225-9460
Herbert Klein (D-8)	201-523-5152	202-225-5751	202-226-2273
Robert G. Torricelli (D-9)	201-646-1111	202-225-5061	202-225-0843
Donald M. Payne (D-10)	201-645-3213	202-225-3436	202-225-4160
Dean A. Gallo (R-11)	201-984-0711	202-225-5034	202-225-0658
Richard A.Zimmer (R-12)	609-895-1559	202-225-5801	202-226-0792
Robert Menendez (D-13)	201-222-2828	202-225-7919	202-226-0792
NEW MEXICO			
Steven Schiff (R-1)	505-766-2538	202-225-6316	202-225-4975
Joe Skeen (R-2)	505-622-0055	202-225-2365	202-225-9599
Bill Richardson (D-3)	505-988-7230	202-225-6190	202-225-1950
NEVADA			
James H. Bilbray (D-1)	702-792-2424	202-225-5965	202-225-8808
Barbara F. Vucanovich (R-2)	702-784-5003	202-225-6155	202-225-2319
NEW YORK			
George Hochbrueckner (D-1)	516-689-6767	202-225-3826	202-225-0776
Rick Lazio (R-2)	516-893-9010	202-225-3335	202-225-4669
Peter King (R-3)	516-541-4202-225	202-225-7896	202-226-2279
David Levy (R-4)	516-872-9550	202-225-5516	202-225-4672
Gary L. Ackerman (D-5)	718-423-2154	202-225-2601	202-225-1589
Floyd H. Flake (D-6)	718-949-5600	202-225-3461	202-225-4169
Thomas J. Manton (D-7)	718-706-1400	202-225-3965	202-225-1909
Jerrold Nadler (D-8)	212-489-3530	202-225-5635	202-225-6923
Charles E. Schumer (D-9)	718-965-5400	202-225-6616	202-225-4183
Edolphus Towns (D-10)	718-387-8696	202-225-5936	202-225-1018
Major Robert Owens (D-11)	718-773-3100	202-225-6231	202-226-0112
Nydia Velazquez (D-12)	718-599-3658	202-225-2361	202-226-0327
Susan V. Molinari (R-13)	718-987-8400	202-225-3371	202-226-1272
Carolyn Maloney (D-14)	212-832-6531	202-225-7944	202-225-4709
Charles B. Rangel (D-15)	212-663-3900	202-225-4365	202-225-0816
Jose Serrano (D-16)	212-538-5400	202-225-4361	202-225-6001
Eliot L. Engel (D-17)	718-796-9700	202-225-2464	202-225-5513
Nita M. Lowey (D-18)	914-428-1707	202-225-6506	202-225-0546
Hamilton Fish, Jr. (R-19)	914-297-5711	202-225-5441	202-225-0962
Benjamin A. Gilman (R-20)	914-343-6666	202-225-3776	202-225-2541
Michael R. McNulty (D-21)	518-465-0700	202-225-5076	202-225-5077

APPENDIX B - TELEPHONE AND FAX NUMBERS

	State Office	Washington Off	Fax
Gerald B.H. Solomon (R-22)	518-587-9800	202-225-5614	202-225-6234
Sherwood L. Boehlert (R-23)	315-793-8146	202-225-3665	202-225-1891
John McHugh (R-24)	315-782-3150	202-225-4611	202-226-0621
James T. Walsh (R-25)	315-423-5657	202-225-3701	202-225-4042
Maurice Hinchey (D-26)	607-773-2768	202-225-6335	202-226-0774
Bill Paxon (D-27)	716-634-2324	202-225-5265	202-225-5910
Louise M. Slaughter (D-28)	716-232-4850	202-225-3615	202-225-7822
John J. LaFalce (D-29)	716-284-9976	202-225-3231	202-225-8693
Jack Quinn, (R-30)	716-845-5257	202-225-3306	202-226-0347
Amo Houghton (R-31)	607-937-3333	202-225-3161	202-225-5574

OHIO

	State Office	Washington Off	Fax
David Mann (D-1)	513-684-2723	202-225-2216	202-225-4732
Rob Portman (2)	513-791-0381	202-225-3164	202-225-1992
Tony P. Hall (D-3)	513-225-2843	202-225-6465	202-225-6766
Michael Oxley (R-4)	419-423-3210	202-225-2676	202-226-1160
Paul E. Gillmor (R-5)	419-734-1999	202-225-6405	202-225-1985
Ted Strickland (D-6)	614-353-5171	202-225-5705	202-226-0331
David Hobson (R-7)	513-325-0474	202-225-4324	202-225-1984
John A. Boehner (R-8)	513-894-6003	202-225-6205	202-225-0704
Marcy Kaptur (D-9)	419-259-7500	202-225-4146	202-225-7711
Martin Hoke (R-10)	216-356-2010	202-225-5871	202-226-0994
Louis Stokes (D-11)	216-522-4900	202-225-7032	202-225-1339
John R. Kasich (R-12)	614-469-7318	202-225-5355	
Sherrod Brown (D-13)	216-282-5100	202-225-3401	202-225-2266
Thomas C. Sawyer (D-14)	216-375-5710	202-225-5231	202-225-5278
Deborah Pryce (R-15)	614-469-5614	202-225-2015	202-226-0986
Ralph Regula (R-16)	216-489-4414	202-225-3876	202-225-3059
James Traficant, Jr. (D-17)	216-788-2414	202-225-5261	202-225-3719
Douglas Applegate (D-18)	614-283-3716	202-225-6265	202-225-3087
Eric Fingerhut (D-19)	216-943-1919	202-225-5731	202-225-9114

OKLAHOMA

	State Office	Washington Off	Fax
James M. Inhofe (R-1)	918-581-7111	202-225-2211	202-225-9187
Mike Synar (D-2)	918-687-2533	202-225-2701	202-225-2796
Bill Brewster (D-3)	405-436-1980	202-225-4565	202-225-9029
Dave McCurdy (D-4)	405-329-6500	202-225-6165	202-225-9746
Ernest Jim Istook (R-5)	405-942-3636	202-225-2132	202-226-1463
Glenn English (D-6)	405-231-5511	202-225-5565	202-225-8698

OREGON

	State Office	Washington Off	Fax
Elizabeth Furse (D-1)	503-326-2901	202-225-0855	202-225-9497
Bob F. Smith (R-2)	503-776-4646	202-225-6730	202-225-3129
Ron Wyden (D-3)	503-231-2300	202-225-4811	202-225-8941
Peter A. DeFazio (D-4)	503-465-6732	202-225-6416	202-225-0694
Michael J. Kopetski (D-5)	503-588-9100	202-225-5711	202-225-9477

PENNSYLVANIA

	State Office	Washington Off	Fax
Thomas M. Foglietta (D-1)	215-925-6840	202-225-4731	202-225-0088
Lucien Blackwell (D-2)	215-387-2543	202-225-4001	202-225-7362
Robert A. Borski (D-3)	215-335-3355	202-225-8251	202-225-4628
Ron Klink (D-4)	412-864-8681	202-225-2565	202-226-2274
Bill F. Clinger, Jr. (R-5)	814-238-1776	202-225-5121	202-225-4681
Tim Holden (D-6)	215-371-9931	202-225-5546	202-226-0996
Curt Weldon (R-7)	215-259-0700	202-225-2011	202-225-8137
James Greenwood (R-8)	215-348-7511	202-225-4276	202-225-9511
Bud Shuster (R-9)	814-946-1653	202-225-2431	202-225-2486

SAVE YOUR JOB, SAVE OUR COUNTRY

	State Office	Washington Off	Fax
Joseph M. McDade (R-10)	717-346-3834	202-225-3731	202-225-9594
Paul E. Kanjorski (D-11)	717-825-2200	202-225-6511	202-225-9024
John P. Murtha (D-12)	814-535-2642	202-225-2065	202-225-5709
M. Margolies-Mezvinsky (D-13)	215-667-3666	202-225-6111	202-226-0798
William J. Coyne (D-14)	412-644-2870	202-225-2301	202-225-1844
Paul McHale (D-15)	215-866-0916	202-225-6411	202-225-5320
Robert S. Walker (R-16)	717-393-0666	202-225-2411	202-225-2484
George W. Gekas (R-17)	717-232-5123	202-225-4315	202-225-8440
Rick Santorum (R-18)	412-882-3205	202-225-2135	202-225-7747
William F. Goodling (R-19)	717-843-8887	202-225-5836	202-226-1000
Austin J. Murphy (D-20)	412-489-4217	202-225-4665	202-225-4772
Thomas J. Ridge (R-21)	814-456-2038	202-225-5406	202-225-1081

PUERTO RICO

Carlos RomeroBarcelo (D)	809-723-6333	202-225-2615	202-225-2154

RHODE ISLAND

Ronald K. Machtley (R-1)	401-725-9400	202-225-4911	202-225-4417
Jack Reed (D-2)	401-943-3100	202-225-2735	202-225-9580

SOUTH CAROLINA

Arthur Ravenel, Jr. (R-1)	803-727-4175	202-225-3176	202-225-4340
Floyd Spence (R-2)	803-254-5120	202-225-2452	202-225-2455
Butler Derrick (D-3)	803-224-7401	202-225-5301	202-225-5383
Bob Inglis (R-4)	803-232-1141	202-225-6030	202-226-1177
John M. Spratt, Jr. (D-5)	803-327-1114	202-225-5501	202-225-0464
James Clyburn (D-6)	803-799-1100	202-225-3315	202-225-2313

SOUTH DAKOTA

Tim Johnson (D)	605-332-8896	202-225-2801	202-225-2427

TENNESSEE

Jim H. Quillen (R-1)	615-247-8161	202-225-6356	202-225-7812
John J. Duncan, Jr. (R-2)	615-523-3772	202-225-5435	202-225-6440
Marilyn Lloyd (D-3)	615-267-9108	202-225-3271	202-225-6974
Jim Cooper (D-4)	615-684-1114	202-225-6831	202-225-4520
Bob Clement (D-5)	615-736-5295	202-225-4311	202-226-1035
Bart Gordon (D-6)	615-896-1986	202-225-4231	202-225-6887
Don Sundquist (R-7)	901-382-5811	202-225-2811	202-225-2814
John S. Tanner (D-8)	901-885-7070	202-225-4714	202-225-1765
Harold E. Ford (D-9)	901-544-4131	202-225-3265	202-225-9215

TEXAS

Jim Chapman (D-1)	903-885-8682	202-225-3035	202-225-7265
Charles Wilson (D-2)	409-637-1770	202-225-2401	202-225-1764
Sam Johnson (R-3)	214-739-0182	202-225-4201	202-225-1485
Ralph M. Hall (D-4)	214-771-9118	202-225-6673	202-225-3332
John Bryant (D-5)	214-767-6554	202-225-2231	202-225-9721
Joe Barton (D-6)	214-875-8488	202-225-2002	202-225-3052
Bill Archer (R-7)	713-467-7493	202-225-2571	202-225-4381
Jack Fields (R-8)	713-540-8000	202-225-4901	202-225-2772
Jack Brooks (D-9)	409-839-2508	202-225-6565	202-225-1584
J.J. Pickle (D-10)	512-482-5921	202-225-4865	202-225-3018
Chet Edwards (D-11)	817-752-9600	202-225-6105	202-225-0350
Pete Geren (D-12)	817-338-0909	202-225-5071	202-225-2786
Bill Sarpalius (D-13)	817-767-0541	202-225-3706	202-225-6142
Greg Laughlin (D-14)	512-576-1231	202-225-2831	202-225-1108
E. (Kika)De La Garza (D-15)	210-682-5545	202-225-2531	202-225-2534
Ronald D. Coleman (D-16)	915-534-6200	202-225-4831	202-225-4831

	State Office	Washington Off	Fax
Charles W. Stenholm (D-17)	915-773-3623	202-225-6605	202-225-2234
Craig A. Washington (D-18)	713-739-7339	202-225-3816	202-225-6186
Larry Combest (R-19)	806-763-1611	202-225-4005	202-225-9615
Henry B. Gonzalez (D-20)	512-229-6195	202-225-3236	202-225-1915
Lamar S. Smith (R-21)	512-229-5880	202-225-4236	202-225-8628
Tom DeLay (R-22)	713-240-3700	202-225-5951	202-225-5241
Henry Bonilla (R-23)	210-697-9055	202-225-4511	202-225-2237
Martin Frost (D-24)	817-293-9231	202-225-3605	202-225-4951
Michael A. Andrews (D-25)	713-229-2244	202-225-7508	202-225-4210
Richard K. Armey (R-26)	214-556-2500	202-225-7772	202-225-7614
Solomon P. Ortiz (R-27)	512-883-5868	202-225-7742	202-226-1134
Frank Tejeda (D-28)	210-924-7383	202-225-1640	202-225-1641
Gene Green (D-29)	713-923-9961	202-225-1688	202-225-9903
Eddie Bernice Johnson (D-30)	214-922-8885	202-225-8885	202-226-1477
UTAH			
James V. Hansen (R-1)	801-625-5677	202-225-0453	202-225-5857
Karen Shepherd (D-2)	801-524-4394	202-225-3011	202-226-0354
Bill H. Orton (D-3)	801-379-2500	202-225-7751	202-226-1223
VIRGINIA			
Herbert H. Bateman (R-1)	804-873-1132	202-225-4261	202-225-4382
Owen B. Pickett (D-2)	804-486-3710	202-225-4215	202-225-4218
Robert C. Scott (D-3)	804-380-1000	202-225-8351	202-225-8354
Norman Sisisky (D-4)	804-393-2068	202-225-6365	202-226-1170
Lewis F. Payne, Jr. (D-5)	804-792-1280	202-225-4711	202-226-1147
Bob Goodlatte (R-6)	703-342-1470	202-225-5431	202-225-9681
Thomas J. Bliley, Jr. (R-7)	804-771-2809	202-225-2815	202-225-0011
James P. Moran (D-8)	703-971-4700	202-225-4376	202-225-0017
Rick Boucher (D-9)	703-628-1145	202-225-3861	202-225-0442
Frank R. Wolf (R-10)	703-734-1500	202-225-5136	202-225-0437
Leslie Byrne (D-11)	703-750-1992	202-225-1492	202-225-2274
VIRGIN ISLANDS			
Ron De Lugo (D)	809-778-5900	202-225-1790	202-225-9392
VERMONT			
Bernard Sanders (I)	802-862-0697	202-225-4115	202-225-6790
WASHINGTON			
Maria Cantwell (D-1)	206-640-0233	202-225-6311	202-225-2286
Al Swift (D-2)	206-252-3188	202-225-2605	202-225-2608
Jolene Unsoeld (D-3)	206-696-7942	202-225-3536	202-225-9095
Jay Inslee (D-4)	509-452-3243	202-225-5816	202-226-1137
Thomas S. Foley (D-5)	509-353-2155	202-225-2006	202-225-7181
Norman D. Dicks (D-6)	206-593-6536	202-225-5916	202-226-1176
Jim McDermott (D-7)	206-553-7170	202-225-3106	202-225-9212
Jennifer Dunn (R-8)	206-450-0161	202-225-7761	202-225-8673
Mike Kreidler (D-9)	206-840-5688	202-225-8901	202-226-2361
WISCONSIN			
Peter W. Barca (1)	414-632-4446	202-225-3031	202-225-9820
Scott Klug (R-2)	608-257-9200	202-225-2906	202-225-6942
Steve Gunderson (R-3)	715-284-7431	202-225-5506	202-225-6195
Gerald D. Kleczka (D-4)	414-297-1140	202-225-4572	202-225-0719
Thomas Barrett (D-5)	414-297-1331	202-225-3571	202-225-2185
Thomas E. Petri (R-6)	414-922-1180	202-225-2476	202-225-2356
David R. Obey (D-7)	715-842-5606	202-225-3365	202-225-0561

SAVE YOUR JOB, SAVE OUR COUNTRY

	State Office	Washington Off	Fax
Toby Roth (R-8)	414-739-4167	202-225-5665	202-225-0087
F. James Sensenbrenner (R-9)	414-784-1111	202-225-5101	202-225-3190
WEST VIRGINIA			
Alan B. Mollohan (D-1)	304-292-3019	202-225-4172	202-225-7564
Robert E. Wise, Jr. (D-2)	304-342-7170	202-225-2711	202-225-7856
Nick Joe Rahall II (D-3)	304-252-5000	202-225-3452	202-225-9061
WYOMING			
Craig Thomas (R)	307-261-5413	202-225-2311	202-225-0726

Index

INDEX

Let Your Senators and Representative Know How You Feel About NAFTA

The only way your elected servants will know how you feel about NAFTA is for you to tell them. The following page contains forms which you can fill out, detach, and send to your elected servants to let them know that you are informed and you want your voice heard.

To mail your ballot to your Member of the House of Representatives, simply fill in his or her name and mail one ballot form in an envelope to the following address:

Representative _____
Washington, D.C. 20510

To mail your ballot to each of your Senators, use the following address:

Senator _____
Washington, D.C. 20515

If you prefer to fax your opinion to your Members of Congress,
see Appendix B for a listing of fax numbers.

Together our voices will be heard.

The New York Times
on
Mexico's NAFTA Lobbying Campaign in the United States

*The Salinas administration
and its many lobbyists in Washington
have fashioned what appears likely to be
one of the most elaborate efforts at
political persuasion ever conducted
in America by a foreign country.*

The New York Times, August 12, 1993

☐ I Support NAFTA
☐ I Oppose NAFTA

☐ I Support NAFTA
☐ I Oppose NAFTA

☐ I Support NAFTA
☐ I Oppose NAFTA

Your Name

Address

Telephone

Your Name

Address

Telephone

Your Name

Address

Telephone

UNITED WE STAND AMERICA

A nonpartisan effort involving citizens in their local, state, and federal government.

A nationwide educational movement that will keep you informed on important issues facing our country.

A nonprofit organization dedicated to bringing about the necessary reforms in our nation's economy, government and election laws.

You Can Make A Difference!

United We Stand America gives you the opportunity to have an impact on the critical issues facing our country. We are focused on:

Reforming Government

Political reform must begin with implementing the line item veto, limiting the role of the lobbyists, and eliminating special privileges for elected servants paid for with taxpayer dollars.

Balancing the Budget

The interest on the national debt is now the third largest expenditure of the federal government. Since 1981, the national debt has increased an average of $1 trillion every four years.

UNITED WE STAND AMERICA Members Receive:

- A personalized membership card.
- A quarterly newsletter focusing on the issues such as the national debt, government reform, and UNITED WE STAND AMERICA organizational news.
- Special mailings from UNITED WE STAND AMERICA about local meetings and events.
- An opportunity to express your opinions on critical issues.

For information about your state or college UWSA chapter, call the UWSA Information Center at 214-960-9100.

Individual Membership

For only $15, you will receive an
annual membership in UWSA. As an
individual member, you will receive a
personalized membership card.

Family Membership

A family may join UWSA for the same
price as an individual membership. Your
membership card will be personalized
with your family name. Each individual
listed on the reverse side of the
enrollment form will receive a
membership number. All correspondence
will be sent to the adress listed on the
enrollment form.

Gift Membership

You may also give an annual
membership as a gift. Complete the
form for the individual or family and
include a check or credit card number.
Also include your name and address. A
membership card will be sent to
the gift recipient.

Founding Membership
ENROLLMENT FORM

☐ YES, Ross! I want to be a Founding Member of
UNITED WE STAND AMERICA.

Name _____
        First   M.I.   Last

Please enroll family members on reverse side.

Address _____ Apt. # _____
City _____ State ____ Zip _____
Day Phone   (___) _____
Evening Phone   (___) _____

☐ Enclosed is my $15 annual fee. $ _____

☐ In addition to my $15 membership
fee, I would like to make the
following contribution to UWSA.
    ☐ $50   ☐ $30   ☐ $15   ☐   Other $ _____

☐ I am already a UWSA member, but I would like to make a contribution.
    ☐ $50   ☐ $30   ☐ $15   ☐   Other $ _____

                                   TOTAL $ _____

☐ Enclosed is a check for the total made payable to:
UNITED WE STAND AMERICA

☐ Please charge the total to the credit card I have indicated below:
    ☐ Visa   ☐ MasterCard   ☐ Discover   ☐ American Express
Credit Card #   Exp. Date

| | | | | | | | | | | | | | | | | | | |

Signature _____

Mail to: United We Stand America, P.O. Box 6, Dallas, TX 75221-0006.
If you would like to join by phone, call 214-960-9100.

Contributions and membership fees are not tax deductible, nor will they be used to
defray any expenses of the Perot '92 Campaign.

Please List Additional Family Members
to be Included on Your Family Membership

Name _____
First   M.I.   Last

Name _____
First   M.I.   Last

Name _____
First   M.I.   Last

Name _____
First   M.I.   Last

Name _____
First   M.I.   Last

Name _____
First   M.I.   Last

Name _____
First   M.I.   Last

Name _____
First   M.I.   Last

Name _____
First   M.I.   Last

Name _____
First   M.I.   Last